Vanished

BOOKS THREE & FOUR

PREVIOUSLY PUBLISHED AS 1-800-WHERE-R-YOU

Includes
Safe House
Sanctuary

MEG CABOT

WRITING AS JENNY CARROLL

Simon Pulse

NEW YORK LONDON TORONTO SYDNEY

SIMON PULSE

An imprint of Simon & Schuster Children's Publishing Division
1230 Avenue of the Americas, New York, NY 10020
This Simon Pulse paperback edition January 2011
1-800-Where-R-You: *Safe House* copyright © 2002 by Meggin Cabot
1-800-Where-R-You: *Sanctuary* copyright © 2002 by Meggin Cabot
All rights reserved, including the right of reproduction in
whole or in part in any form.
SIMON PULSE and colophon are registered trademarks of Simon & Schuster, Inc.
For information about special discounts for bulk purchases, please contact
Simon & Schuster Special Sales at 1-866-506-1949
or business@simonandschuster.com.
The Simon & Schuster Speakers Bureau can bring authors to your live event. For more
information or to book an event contact the Simon & Schuster Speakers Bureau
at 1-866-248-3049 or visit our website at www.simonspeakers.com.
Designed by Mike Rosamilia
The text of this book was set in Berling.
Manufactured in the United States of America
4 6 8 10 9 7 5
Library of Congress Control Number 2010931372
ISBN 978-1-4424-0631-5
These titles were previously published individually.

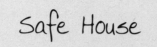

Safe House

With many thanks to Jen Brown,
John Henry Dreyfuss, David Walton,
and especially Benjamin Egnatz.

CHAPTER 1

I didn't know about the dead girl until the first day of school.

It wasn't my fault. I swear it wasn't. I mean, how was I supposed to have known? It wasn't like I'd been home. If I'd been home, of course I would have seen it in the paper, or on the news, or whatever. I would have heard people talking about it.

But I hadn't been home. I'd been stuck four hours north of home, at the Michigan dunes, in my best friend Ruth Abramowitz's summerhouse. The Abramowitzes go to the dunes for the last two weeks of August every summer, and this year, they invited me to go along.

I wasn't going to go at first. I mean, who'd want to spend two weeks trapped in a summerhouse with Ruth's twin brother Skip? Um, not me. Skip still chews with his mouth open even though he is sixteen and should know better. Plus he is like Grand Dragon Master of our town's Dungeons & Dragons population, in spite of the Trans Am he bought with his bar mitzvah money.

On top of which, Mr. Abramowitz has this thing about cable, and the only telephone he'll allow in his vacation house is his cell, which is reserved for emergency use only, like if one of his clients gets thrown in the clink or whatever. (He's a lawyer.)

So you can see, of course, why I was like, "Thanks, but no thanks," to Ruth's invitation.

But then my parents said that they were spending the last two weeks of August driving my brother Mike and all his stuff up to Harvard, where he was going to be starting his freshman year, and that Great-aunt Rose would be coming to stay with me and my other brother, Douglas, while they were gone.

Never mind that I am sixteen and Douglas is twenty and that we do not need parental supervision, particularly in the form of a seventy-five-year-old lady who is obsessed with solitaire and my sex life (not that I have one). Great-aunt Rose was coming to stay, and I was informed that I could like it or lump it.

I chose neither. Instead of coming home after my stint as a camp counselor at the Lake Wawasee Camp for Gifted Child Musicians, which was how I got to spend my summer vacation, I went with the Abramowitzes to the dunes.

Hey. Even watching Skip eat grilled peanut-butter-and-banana sandwiches morning, noon, and night for two weeks beat spending five minutes with Great-aunt Rose, who likes to talk about how in her day, only cheap girls wore dungarees.

Seriously. Dungarees. That's what she calls them.

You can see why I chose the dunes instead.

And truthfully, the two weeks didn't go so badly.

Oh, don't get me wrong. I didn't have a good time or anything. How could I? Because while we'd been slaving away at Camp Wawasee, Ruth had been working very hard on her teen social development, and she'd managed to acquire a boyfriend.

That's right. An actual boyfriend, whose parents—wouldn't you know it—also had a house on the dunes, like ten minutes away from Ruth's.

I tried to be supportive, because Scott was Ruth's first real boyfriend—you know, the first guy she'd liked who actually liked her back, and who didn't seem to mind being seen holding her hand in public, and all of that.

But let's face it, when someone invites you to stay with them for two weeks, and then spends those two weeks basically hanging out with somebody else, it can be a little disappointing.

I spent the majority of my daylight hours lying on the beach, reading used paperbacks, and most of my nights trying to beat Skip at Crash Bandicoot on his Sony PlayStation.

Oh, yeah. It was a real thrill, my summer vacation.

The good part, Ruth kept pointing out to me, was that by being at the dunes, I was not at my house waiting for my boyfriend—or whatever he is—to call. This, Ruth informed me, was an important part of the courtship ritual . . . you know, the not-being-there-when-he-calls part. Because then, Ruth explained, he'll wonder where you are, and start making up these scenarios in his head about where you could be. Maybe he'll even think you're with another guy!

Somehow, this is supposed to make him like you more.

Which is all good, I guess, but is sort of contingent on one thing:

The guy actually has to call.

See, if he doesn't call, he can't discover that you aren't home. My boyfriend—or should I say, the guy I like, since he is not technically my boyfriend, as we have never been out on an actual date—never calls. This is because he is of the opinion that I am what is commonly referred to in the great state of Indiana as jailbait.

And he's already on probation.

Don't ask me what for. Rob won't tell me.

That's his name. Rob Wilkins. Or the Jerk, as Ruth refers to him.

But I don't think it's fair to call him the Jerk, because it isn't as if he ever led me on. I mean, he made it pretty much clear from the moment he found out I was sixteen that there could never be anything between us. At least, not for a couple more years.

And really, you know, I am fine with that. I mean, there are lots of fish in the sea.

And okay, maybe they don't all have eyes the color of fog as it rolls in over the lake just before sunrise, or a set of washboard abs, or a completely cherried-out Indian motorcycle they've rebuilt from scratch in their barn.

But, you know, they're male. Ostensibly.

Whatever. The point is, I was gone for two weeks: no phone, no TV, no radio, no media resources whatsoever. It was a vacation, all right? A real vacation. Well, except for the having fun part.

So how was I supposed to know that while I was gone, a girl in my class had croaked? No one mentioned a word about it to me.

Not until homeroom, anyway.

That's the problem, really, with living in such a small town. I've been in the same homeroom with the same people since middle school. Oh, sure, occasionally somebody will move out of town, or a new kid will show up. But for the most part, it's the same old faces, year after year.

Which was why, the first day of my junior year at Ernest

Pyle High School, I slid into the second seat from the door in homeroom. I always ended up in the second seat from the door in homeroom. That's because, in homeroom, we sit alphabetically, and my last name—Mastriani—puts me second in the *Ms* for my class, behind Amber Mackey. Amber Mackey always sits in front of me in homeroom. Always.

Except that day. That day, she didn't show up.

Hey, I didn't know why. How was I supposed to know? Amber had never not shown up for the first day of school before. She was no more of an intellectual dynamo than I am, but you never actually *do* anything the first day of school, so why not show up? Besides, unlike me, Amber had always liked school. She was a cheerleader. She was always all, "We've got spirit, yes, we do, we've got spirit, how 'bout *you?*"

You know the type.

A type like that, I don't know, you'd expect she'd show up the first day of school, just in order to show off her tan.

So I left the first chair in the row of seats by the door empty. Everyone filed in, looking carefully nonchalant, even though you knew most of them—the girls, anyway—had spent hours putting together exactly the right outfit to show off how much weight they'd lost over their summer . . . or their new highlights . . . or their chemically whitened teeth.

Everyone sat down where they were supposed to—we'd done this enough times to know by the eleventh grade who sat behind whom in homeroom—and people were all, "Hey, how was your summer?" or "Oh, my God, you're so tan," or "That skirt is so *cute!*"

And then the bell rang, and Mr. Cheaver came in with the roster and told us all to settle down, even though at eight fifteen in the morning, nobody was exactly boisterous.

Then he looked down at the roster, hesitated, and said, "Mastriani."

I raised my hand, even though Mr. Cheaver was standing practically in front of me, and had had me last year for World Civ, so it wasn't as if he didn't recognize me. Granted, Ruth and I had spent a considerable amount of our Wawasee paychecks at the clothing outlet stores outside Michigan City, and I was wearing, at Ruth's insistence, an actual skirt to school, something that might have thrown Mr. C off a little, since I had never before shown up to school in anything besides jeans and a T-shirt.

Still, as Ruth pointed out, I was never going to get Rob to realize how much he had erred in not going out with me unless I got someone else to take me out (and was seen by Rob in this other person's company), so, according to Ruth, I had to "make an effort" this year. I was in Esprit from head to toe, but it wasn't as much that I was hoping to attract potential suitors as it was that, having gotten back as late as I had the night before (Ruth absolutely refuses to exceed the speed limit when she drives, even when there is not a culvert in sight in which a highway patrolman could be hiding), I had no other clean clothes.

Maybe, I thought, Mr. Cheaver doesn't recognize me in my miniskirt and cotton sweater set. So I went, "Here, Mr. C," to show him I was present.

"I can see you, Mastriani," Mr. C said, in his usual lazy drawl. "Move up one."

I looked at the empty seat in front of me.

"Oh, no, Mr. C," I said. "That's Amber's seat. She must be late or something. But she'll be here."

There was a strange silence. Really. I mean, not all silences are the same, even though you would think by definition— the absence of sound—they would be.

This one, however, was *more* silent than most silences. Like everyone, all at once, had suddenly decided to hold their breath.

Mr. Cheaver—who was also holding his breath—narrowed his eyes at me. There weren't many teachers at Ernie Pyle High whom I could stand, but Mr. C was one of them. That's because he didn't play favorites. He hated every single one of us just about equally. He maybe hated me a little less than some of my peers, because last year, I had actually done the homework he'd assigned, as I'd found World Civ quite interesting, especially the parts about the wholesale slaughter of entire populations.

"Where have you been, Mastriani?" Mr. Cheaver wanted

to know. "Amber Mackey's not coming back this year."

Seriously, how was I to have known?

"Oh, really?" I said. "Did her parents move or something?"

Mr. C just looked at me in a very displeased manner, while the rest of the class suddenly exhaled, all at once, and started buzzing instead. I had no idea what they were talking about, but from the scandalized looks on their faces, I could tell I had really put my foot in it this time. Tisha Murray and Heather Montrose looked particularly contemptuous of me. I thought about getting up and cracking their heads together, but I've tried that before, and it doesn't actually work.

But another thing I was trying to "make an effort" to do my junior year—besides cause some innocent young man to fall completely in love with me so I could stroll, ever so casually, hand-in-hand with him in front of the garage where Rob had been working since he graduated last year—was not get into fistfights. Seriously. I had spent enough weeks in detention back in tenth grade thanks to my inability to control my rage impulse. I was not going to make the same mistake this year.

That was one of the other reasons—besides my total lack of clean Levis—that I'd gone for the miniskirt. It wasn't so easy to knee somebody in the groin while clad in a Lycra/rayon blend.

Maybe, I thought, as I observed the expressions of the people around me, Amber had gotten herself knocked up, and

13

everyone knew it but me. Hey, in spite of Coach Albright's Health class, mandatory for all sophomores, in which we were warned of the perils of unsafe sex, it happens. Even to cheerleaders.

But apparently not to Amber Mackey, since Mr. C looked down at me and went, tonelessly, "Mastriani. She's dead."

"Dead?" I echoed. "Amber Mackey?" Then, like an idiot: "Are you sure?"

I don't know why I asked him that. I mean, if a teacher says somebody is dead, you can pretty much count on the fact that he's telling the truth. I'd just been so surprised. It probably sounds like a cliché, but Amber Mackey had always been . . . well, full of life. She hadn't been one of those cheerleaders you could hate. She'd never been purposefully mean to anyone, and she'd always had to try really hard to keep up with the other girls on the squad, both socially as well as athletically. Academically, she'd been no National Merit Scholar, either, if you get my drift.

But she'd tried. She'd always really tried.

Mr. C wasn't the one who answered me. Heather Montrose was.

"Yeah, she's dead," she said, her carefully glossed upper lip raised in disgust. "Where have you been, anyway?"

"Really," Tisha Murray said. "I'd have thought *Lightning Girl* would have had a clue, at least."

"What's the matter?" Heather asked me. "Your psychic radar on the fritz or something?"

I am not precisely what you would call popular, but since I do not make a habit of going around being a total bitch to people, like Heather and Tisha, there are folk who actually will come to my defense against them. One of them, Todd Mintz—linebacker on the varsity football team who was sitting behind me—went, "Jesus, would you two cool it? She doesn't do the psychic thing anymore. Remember?"

"Yeah," Heather said, with a flick of her long, blond mane. "I heard."

"And I heard," Tisha said, "that just two weeks ago, she found some kid who'd been lost in a cave or something."

This was patently untrue. It had been a month ago. But I wasn't about to admit as much to the likes of Tisha.

Fortunately, I was spared from having to make any reply whatsoever by the tactful intervention of Mr. Cheaver.

"Excuse me," Mr. C said. "But while this may come as a surprise to some of you, I have a class to conduct here. Would you mind saving the personal chat until after the bell rings? Mastriani. Move up one."

I moved up one seat, as did the rest of our row. As we did so, I whispered to Todd, "So what happened to her, anyway?" thinking Amber had gotten leukemia or something, and that the cheerleaders would probably start having car washes all the time in order to raise money to help fight cancer. The Amber Fund, they'd probably call it.

But Amber's death had not been from natural causes, apparently. Not if what Todd whispered back was the truth.

"They found her yesterday," he said. "Facedown in one of the quarries. Strangled to death."

Oh.

CHAPTER 2

Now, who would do that?

Seriously. I want to know.

Who would strangle a cheerleader, and dump her body at the bottom of a limestone quarry?

I can certainly understand *wanting* to strangle a cheerleader. Our school harbors some of the meanest cheerleaders in North America. Seriously. It's like you have to pass a test proving you have no human compassion whatsoever just to get on the squad. The cheerleaders at Ernest Pyle High would sooner pluck out their own eyelashes than deign to speak to a kid who wasn't of their social caliber.

But actually to go through with it? You know, off one of them? It hardly seemed worth the effort.

And anyway, Amber hadn't been like the others. I had actually seen Amber smile at a Grit—the derogatory name for the kids who were bused in from the rural routes to Ernie Pyle, the only high school in the county; kids who did not live on a rural route are referred to, imaginatively, as Townies.

Amber had been a Townie, like Ruth and me. But I had never observed her lording this fact over anyone, as I often had Heather and Tisha and their ilk. Amber, when selected as a team captain in PE, had never chosen all Townies first, then moved on to Grits. Amber, when walking down the hall with her books and pompons, had never sneered at the Grits' Wranglers and Lee jeans, the only "dungarees" they could afford. I had never seen Amber administer a "Grit test": holding up a pen and asking an unsuspecting victim what she had in her hand. (If the reply was "A pen," you were safe. If, however, you said, "A pin," you were labeled a Grit and laughed at for your Southern drawl.)

Is it any wonder that I have anger-management issues? I mean, seriously. Wouldn't you, if you had to put up with this crap on a daily basis?

Anyway, it just seemed to me a shame that, out of all the cheerleaders, Amber had been the one who'd had to die. I mean, I had actually liked her.

And I wasn't the only one, as I soon found out.

"Good job," somebody hissed as they passed me in the hallway while I walked to my locker.

"Way to go," somebody else said as I was coming out of Bio.

And that wasn't all. I got a sarcastic "Thanks a lot, *Lightning Girl*," by the drinking fountains and was called a "skank" as I went by a pack of Pompettes, the freshmen cheerleaders.

"I don't get it," I said to Ruth in fourth period Orchestra as we were unpacking our instruments. "It's like people are blaming me or something for what happened to Amber. Like I had something to do with it."

Ruth, applying rosin to her cello bow, shook her head.

"That's not it," she said. She had gotten the scoop, apparently, in Honors English. "I guess when Amber didn't come home Friday night, her parents called the cops and stuff, but they didn't have any luck finding her. So I guess a bunch of people called your house, you know, thinking you might be able to track her down. You know. Psychically. But you weren't home, of course, and your aunt wouldn't give any of them my dad's emergency cell number, and there's no other way to reach us up at our summer place, so . . ."

So? So it *was* my fault. Or at the very least, Great-aunt Rose's fault. Now I had yet another reason to resent her.

Never mind that I have taken great pains to impress upon everyone the fact that I no longer have the psychic ability to find missing people. That thing last spring, when I'd been struck by lightning and could suddenly tell, just by looking at a photo of someone, where that someone was, had been a total fluke. I'd told that to the press, too. I'd told it to the cops, and to the FBI. Lightning Girl—which was how I'd been referred to by the media for a while there—no longer existed. My ESP had faded as mysteriously as it had arrived.

Except of course it hadn't really. I'd been lying to get the press—and the cops—off my back. And, apparently, everyone at Ernest Pyle High School knew it.

"Look," Ruth said as she practiced a few chords. "It's not your fault. If anything, it's your whacked-out aunt's fault. She should have known it was an emergency and given them my dad's cell number. But even so, you know Amber. She wasn't the shiniest rock in the garden. She'd have gone out with Freddy Krueger if he'd asked her. It really isn't any wonder she ended up facedown in Pike's Quarry."

If this was meant to comfort me, it did not. I slunk back to the flute section, but I could not concentrate on what Mr. Vine, our Orchestra teacher, was saying to us. All I could think about was how at last year's talent show, Amber and her longtime boyfriend—Mark Leskowski, the Ernie Pyle High Cougars quarterback—had done this very lame rendition of *Anything You Can Do I Can Do Better*, and how serious Amber had been about it, and how certain she'd been that she and Mark were going to win.

They didn't, of course—first prize went to a guy whose

Chihuahua howled every time it heard the theme song to *CSI*—but Amber had been thrilled by winning second place.

Thrilled, I couldn't help thinking, to death.

"All right," Mr. Vine said just before the bell rang. "For the rest of the week, we'll hold chair auditions. Horns tomorrow, strings on Wednesday, winds on Thursday, and percussion on Friday. So do me a favor and practice for a change, will you?"

The bell for lunch rang. Instead of tearing out of there, though, most people reached beneath their seats and pulled out sandwiches and cans of warm soda. That's because the vast majority of kids in Symphonic Orchestra are geeks, afraid of venturing into the caf, where they might be ridiculed by their more athletically endowed peers. Instead, they spend their lunch hour in the music wing, munching soggy tuna fish sandwiches and arguing about who makes a better starship captain, Kirk or Picard.

Not Ruth and me, though. In the first place, I have never been able to stand the thought of eating in a room in which the words "spit valve" are mentioned so often. In the second place, Ruth had already explained that what with our new wardrobes—and her recent weight loss—we were not going to hide in the bowels of the music wing. No, we were going to see and be seen. Though Ruth's heart still belonged to Scott, the fact was, he lived three hundred miles away. We had only ten more months to secure a prom date, and Ruth insisted we start immediately.

Before we got out of the orchestra room, however, we were accosted by one of my least favorite people, fellow flutist Karen Sue Hankey, who made haste to inform me that I could give up all hope of hanging onto third chair this year, as she had been practicing for four hours a day and taking private lessons from a music professor at a nearby college.

"Great," I said, as Ruth and I tried to slip past her.

"Oh, and by the way," Karen Sue added, "that was real nice, how you were there for Amber and all."

But if I thought that'd be the worst I'd hear on the subject, I was sadly mistaken. It was ten times worse in the cafeteria. All I wanted to do was get my Tater Tots and go, but do you think they'd let me? Oh, no.

Because the minute we got in line, Heather Montrose and her evil clone Tisha slunk up behind us and started making remarks.

I don't get it. I really don't. I mean, the way I'd left things last spring, when school let out, was that I didn't have my psychic powers anymore. So how was everyone so sure I'd lied? I mean, the only person who knew any differently was Ruth, and she'd never tell.

But somebody had been doing some talking, that was for sure.

"So, what's it like?" Heather wanted to know as she sidled up behind us in the grill line. "I mean, knowing that somebody died because of you."

"Amber didn't die because of anything I did, Heather," I said, keeping my eyes on the tray I was sliding along past the bowls of sickly looking lime Jell-O and suspiciously lumpy tapioca pudding. "Amber died because somebody killed her. Somebody who was not me."

"Yeah," Tisha agreed. "But, according to the coroner, she was held against her will for a while before she was killed. They were lickator marks on her."

"Ligature," Ruth corrected her.

"Whatever," Tisha said. "That means if you'd been around, you could have found her."

"Well, I wasn't around," I said. "Okay? Excuse me for going on vacation."

"Really, Tish," Heather said in a chiding voice. "She's got to go on vacation sometime. I mean, she probably needs it, living with that retard and all."

"Oh, God," I heard Ruth moan. Then she carefully lifted her tray out of the line of fire.

That's because, of course, Ruth knew. There aren't many things that will make me forget all the anger-management counseling I've received from Mr. Goodhart, upstairs in the guidance office. But even after nearly two years of being instructed to count to ten before giving in to my anger—and nearly two years of detention for having failed miserably in my efforts to do so—any derogatory mention of my brother Douglas still sets me off.

About a second after Heather made her ill-advised remark, she was pinned up against the cinder block wall behind her.

And my hand was what was holding her there. By her neck.

"Didn't anyone ever tell you," I hissed at her, my face about two inches from hers, "that it is rude to make fun of people who are less fortunate than you?"

Heather didn't reply. She couldn't, because I had hold of her larynx. "Hey." A deep voice behind me sounded startled. "Hey. What's going on here?"

I recognized the voice, of course.

"Mind your own business, Jeff," I said. Jeff Day, football tackle and all-around idiot, has also never been one of my favorite people.

"Let her go," Jeff said, and I felt one of his meaty paws land on my shoulder.

An elbow, thrust with precision, soon put an end to his intervention. As Jeff gasped for air behind me, I loosened my hold on Heather a little.

"Now," I said to her. "Are you going to apologize?"

But I had underestimated the amount of time it would take Jeff to recover from my blow. His sausage-like fingers again landed on my shoulder, and this time, he managed to spin me around to face him.

"You let her alone!" he bellowed, his face beet red from the neck up.

I think he would have hit me. I really do. And at the time, I sort of relished the idea. Jeff would take a swing at me, I would duck, and then I'd go for his nose. I'd been longing to break Jeff Day's nose for some time. Ever since, in fact, the day he'd told Ruth she was so fat they were going to have to bury her in a piano case, like Elvis.

Only I didn't get a chance to break Jeff's nose that day. I didn't get a chance because someone strode up behind him just as he was drawing back his fist, caught it midswing, and wrapped his arm around his back.

"That how you guards get your kicks?" Todd Mintz demanded. "Beating up girls?"

"All right." A third and final voice, equally recognizable to me, broke the little party up. Mr. Goodhart, holding a tossed salad and a container of yogurt, nodded toward the cafeteria doors. "All of you. In my office. Now."

Jeff and Todd and I followed him resentfully. It wasn't until we were nearly at the door that Mr. Goodhart turned and called, with some exasperation, "You, too, Heather," that Heather came slinking along after us.

In Mr. Goodhart's office, we were informed that we were not "Starting the Year Off Right," and that we really ought to be "Setting a Better Example for the Younger Students," seeing as how we were all juniors now. It would "Behoove Us to Come Together and Try to Get Along," especially in the wake of the tragedy that had occurred over the weekend.

"I know Amber's death has shaken us all up," Mr. Goodhart said, sincerity oozing out of his every pore. "But let's try to remember that she would have wanted us to comfort one another in our grief, not get torn apart by petty bickering."

Out of all of us, Heather was the only one who'd never before been dragged into a counselor's office for fighting. So, of course, instead of keeping her mouth shut so we could all get out of there, she pointed a silk-wrapped fingernail at me and went, "She started it."

Todd and Jeff and I rolled our eyes. We knew what was coming next.

Mr. Goodhart launched into his "I Don't Care Who Started It, Fighting Is Wrong" speech. It lasted four and a half minutes, twenty seconds longer than last year's version. Then Mr. Goodhart went, "You're all good kids. You have unlimited potential, each of you. Don't throw it all away through violence against one another."

Then he said everyone could go.

Everyone except me, of course.

"It wasn't my fault," I said as soon as the others were gone. "Heather called Douglas a retard."

Mr. Goodhart shoveled a spoonful of yogurt into his mouth.

"Jess," he said, with his mouth full. "Is this how it's going to be again? You, in my office every day for fighting?"

"No," I said. I tugged on the hem of my miniskirt. Though I knew I looked good in it, I did feel just a tad naked. Also, it hadn't worked.

I'd gotten into a fight anyway. "I'm trying to do what you said. You know, the whole counting to ten thing. But it's just . . . everyone is going around, *blaming* me."

Mr. Goodhart looked puzzled. "Blaming you for what?"

"For what happened to Amber." I explained to him what everyone was saying.

"That's ridiculous," Mr. Goodhart said. "You couldn't have stopped what happened to Amber, even if you did still have your powers. Which you don't." He looked at me. "Do you?"

"Of course not," I said.

"So where are they getting the idea that you do?" Mr. Goodhart wondered.

"I don't know." I looked at the salad he was eating. "What happened to you?" I asked. "Where's the Quarter Pounder with cheese?" Ever since I'd met him, Mr. Goodhart's lunches had always consisted of a burger with a side of fries, usually super-sized.

He made a face. "I'm on a diet," he said. "Blood pressure

and cholesterol are off the scale, according to my GP."

"Wow," I said. I knew how much he loved his fries. "Sorry."

"I'll live," he said with a shrug. "The question is, what are we going to do about you?"

What we decided to do about me was "Give Me Another Chance." "One More Strike," though, and "I Was Out."

Which meant detention. With a capital D.

We were chatting amiably about Mr. Goodhart's son, Russell, who'd just started crawling, when the secretary came in, looking worried.

"Paul," she said. "There are some men here from the sheriff's office. They want to pull Mark Leskowski out for questioning. You know, about the Mackey girl."

Mr. Goodhart looked concerned. "Oh, God," he said. "All right. Get Mark's parents on the phone, will you? And let Principal Feeney know."

I watched, fascinated, as the administrative staff of Ernie Pyle High went on red alert. The sudden burst of activity drove me from Mr. Goodhart's office, but I sank down onto a vinyl couch in the waiting room outside it, where I could observe uninterrupted. It was interesting to see what happened when somebody else, other than me, was in trouble for a change. Somebody was dispatched to find Mark, someone else alerted his parents, and yet another person argued with the two sheriff's deputies. Apparently, as Mark was only seventeen, there was some problem with letting the cops remove him from school grounds without his parents' permission.

After a while, Mark showed up, looking bewildered. He was a tall, good-looking guy, with dark hair and even darker eyes. Even though he played football, he didn't have a football player's thick neck or waist or anything. He was the team quarterback, which was why.

"What's up?" he said to the secretary, who darted a nervous look at Mr. Goodhart. He was still yelling at the sheriff's deputies, in his office.

"Um," the secretary said. "They aren't quite ready for you. Have a seat."

Mark took a seat on the orange vinyl couch across from mine. I studied him over the top of the Army brochure I was pretending to read. Most murder victims, I remembered seeing somewhere, know their killers. Had Mark strangled his girlfriend and dumped her body in Pike's Quarry? And if so, why? Was he some kind of sick pervert? Did he suffer from that killing rage they were always talking about on *America's Most Wanted*?

"Hey," Mark said to the secretary. "You got a water cooler in here?"

The secretary nervously admitted that they had, and pointed to its location, a little bit down the corridor. Mark got up to get a cup of water. I could not help noticing, from behind my brochure, that his 505s fit him very nicely.

On his way back from the water cooler, Mark noticed me and went, politely, "Oh, hey, sorry. Did you want one?"

I looked up from the brochure as if I were noticing him for the first time. "Who, me?" I asked. "Oh, no, thank you."

"Oh." Mark sat down again. "Okay." He finished all the water in his cup, crumpled it, looked around for a wastebasket, and, not seeing one, left the cup on the magazine-strewn table in front of us.

"So, what are you in for?" he asked me.

"I tried to choke Heather Montrose," I said.

"Really?" He grinned. "I've felt like doing that myself, coupla times."

I wanted to point out to him that this was something he'd be wise to keep from the sheriff, but didn't think I could do so in front of the secretary, who was busy pretending not to listen to our conversation.

"I mean, that Heather," Mark said. "She can be a real . . ." He politely refrained from swearing. A real Boy Scout, Mark Leskowski. "Well, you know."

"I *do* know," I said. "Listen. I'm sorry about Amber. She was your girlfriend, right?"

"Yeah." Mark's gaze strayed from my face to the center of the table between us. "Thanks."

The door to Mr. Goodhart's office opened, and he came out and spoke with forced joviality.

"Mark," he said. "Good to see you. Come in here a minute,

will you? There are some folks here who want to have a word with you."

Mark nodded and stood up. As he did so, he wiped his hands nervously on the denim covering his thighs. When he took his hands away again, I saw damp spots where they'd been.

He was sweating, even though, with the air conditioning on full blast, I was a little chilly, in spite of my sweater set.

Mark Leskowski was nervous. Very nervous.

He looked down at me as he passed by my couch.

"Well," he said. "See you later."

"Sure," I said. "Later."

He went into Mr. Goodhart's office. Just before following Mark, Mr. Goodhart noticed I was still sitting there.

"Jessica," he said, jerking a thumb toward the door to the central hallway. "Out."

And so I left.

CHAPTER 3

"I figured it out," Ruth said as we drove home—with the top down—after school let out that day. I was too distracted to reply, however, as we'd just sailed past the turn-off to Pike's Creek Road.

"Dude," I said. "You missed it."

"Missed what?" Ruth demanded, taking a healthy sip from the Diet Coke she'd picked up from the drive-through. Then she made a face. "Oh, God. You have *got* to be kidding me."

"It's not *that* far out of the way," I pointed out to her.

"You," Ruth said, "are never going to learn. Are you?"

"What?" I shrugged innocently. "What is so wrong about driving past his place of work?"

"I'll tell you what's wrong with it," Ruth said. "It is a direct violation of The Rules."

I snorted.

"I'm serious," Ruth said. "Boys don't like to be chased, Jess. They like to do the chasing."

"I am not chasing him," I said. "I am merely suggesting that we drive past the garage where he works."

"That," Ruth said, "is chasing him. As is calling him and hanging up when he answers." Oops. Guilty. "As is haunting the places he normally hangs out in, memorizing his schedule, and pretending to bump into him by mistake."

Guilty. Guilty. Guilty

I snapped my seatbelt in irritation. "He'd never know we were swinging by just to see him," I said, "if you pretended like you needed an oil change or something."

"Would you," Ruth said, "get your mind off Rob Wilkins for five minutes and listen to me? I am trying to tell you, I think I figured out why everybody believes you still have psychic powers."

"Oh, yeah?" I was so not interested. It had been an exhausting day. It was bad enough a girl we knew had been murdered. The fact that people were going around blaming me for her death was even harder to take. "You know, Mark Leskowski actually offered me water today in the guidance office. If I were stranded in the desert, I would never have expected him to—"

"Karen Sue," Ruth said as we made the turn by Kroger's.

I looked around. "Where?"

"No. Karen Sue," Ruth said, "is the one going around telling everyone you're still psychic. Suzy Choi told me she overheard Karen Sue telling everyone at the Thirty-one Flavors last Saturday night that, over the summer, you found this kid who'd gone missing inside a cave."

I forgot all about Rob. "I'll kill her," I said.

"I know." Ruth shook her head so that her blond curls bounced. "And we thought we'd covered our tracks so well."

I couldn't believe it. Karen Sue and I had never exactly been friends, or anything, but that she'd out me so extremely . . . well, I was shocked.

I shouldn't have been *that* shocked, however. It *was* Karen Sue we were talking about, after all. The girl about whom my mother had, for years, asked, "Why can't you be more like her? Karen Sue never gets into fights, and she always wears whatever her mother tells her, and I've never heard that Karen Sue refused to go to church because she wanted to stay home to watch old *Battlestar Galactica* reruns."

Karen Sue Hankey. My mortal enemy.

"I'll kill her," I said, again.

"Well," Ruth said as she pulled into the driveway to my house, "I wouldn't suggest going to that extreme. But a firm lecture might be in order."

Right. I'd firm lecture her to death.

"Now," Ruth said. "What's this about Mark Leskowski?"

I told her about seeing Mark in the guidance office.

"That's awful," Ruth said when I was done. "Mark and Amber were always so cute together. He loved her so much. How can the police possibly suspect that he had anything to do with her death?"

"I don't know," I said, remembering his sweaty palms. I'd left that part out when I'd repeated the story to Ruth. "Maybe he was the last person to see her or something."

"Maybe," Ruth said. "Hey, maybe his parents will hire my dad to represent Mark. You know, if the cops do charge with him anything."

"Yeah," I said. Ruth's dad was the best lawyer in town. "Maybe. Well. I better go." We'd gotten home so late the night before, I'd barely had a chance to say a word to my family. Another reason, I might add, I hadn't heard about Amber. "See you later."

"Later," Ruth said as I started to get out of the car. "Hey, what was that with Todd Mintz in the caf today, coming to your defense against Jeff Day?"

I looked at her blankly. "I don't know," I said. I hadn't actually realized that's what Todd had been doing, but now that I thought about it . . .

"I guess he hates Jeff as much as we do," I said, with a shrug.

Ruth laughed as she backed out of my driveway. "Yeah,"

she said. "That's probably why. And that miniskirt had nothing to do with it. I told you a makeover would do wonders for your social life."

She honked as she drove away, but she wasn't going far. The Abramowitzes lived right next door.

Which was how, as I was going up the steps to the front door of my own house, I was able to hear Ruth's twin brother Skip call from his own front porch, "Hey, Mastriani. Want to come over later and let me beat you at Bandicoot?"

I leaned over and peered at Skip through the tall hedge that separated our two houses. Good God. It was bad enough I'd had to spend two weeks of my summer practically incarcerated with him. If he thought I was going to willingly extend my sentence, he had to be nuts.

"Uh," I called. "Can I take a rain check on that?"

"No problem," Skip hollered back.

Shuddering, I went inside.

And was greeted by someone even more frightening than Skip.

"Jessica," Great-aunt Rose said, intercepting me in the foyer before I had a chance to make a break for the stairs up to my room. "There you are. I was beginning to think I wouldn't get a chance to see you this trip." I had managed to elude her last night by getting home so late, and then again that morning, before school, by darting out of the house before breakfast. I had thought she'd be gone by the time I got home from school.

"Your father's driving me back to the airport," Great-aunt Rose went on, "in half an hour, you know."

Half an hour! If Ruth had just driven by the garage where Rob worked, like I asked, I might have been able to avoid Great-aunt Rose altogether this trip!

"Hi, Auntie," I said, bending down to give her a kiss on the cheek. Great-aunt Rose is the only member of my family I can honestly say I tower over. But that's only because osteoporosis has shrunk her down to about four foot eleven, an inch shorter than me.

"Well, let me look at you," Great-aunt Rose said, pushing me away. Her watery brown-eyed gaze ran over me critically from head to toe.

"Hmph," she said. "Nice to see you in a skirt for once. But don't you think it's a little short? They let girls go to school in skirts that short these days? Why, in my day, if I'd shown up in a skirt like that, I'd have been sent home to change!"

Poor Douglas. For two weeks he'd been sentenced to undiluted Great-aunt Rose. No wonder he'd feigned sleep the night before when I'd gotten home. I wouldn't have wanted to talk to a traitor like me, either.

"Toni!" Rose called, to my mother. "Come out here and look at what your daughter has got on. Is that how you're letting her dress these days?"

My mom, still looking sunburned and happy from her trip out east, from which she and my dad had only returned the day before, came into the foyer.

"Why, I think she looks fine," Mom said, taking in my ensemble with approval. "Far better than she used to dress last year, when I couldn't peel her out of jeans and a T-shirt."

"Um," I said, uncomfortably. I'd gotten as far as the landing, but didn't see how I was going to be able to sneak any farther upstairs without them noticing. "It was great to see you, Aunt Rose. Sorry you have to leave so soon. But I have a lot of homework—"

"Homework?" my mother said. "On the first day of school? Oh, I don't think so."

She'd seen through me, of course. My mom knew good and well how I felt about Great-aunt Rose. She just didn't want to be stuck with the old biddy herself. And she'd left Douglas alone with her for two weeks! Two weeks!

Talk about cruel and unusual punishment.

Then again, if she'd been counting on Great-aunt Rose keeping an eagle eye on him, she couldn't have found anyone better. Nothing got past Great-aunt Rose.

"Is that lipstick you're wearing, Jessica?" Great-aunt Rose demanded when we got out of the darkness of the foyer and into the brightly lit kitchen.

"Um," I said. "No. Cherry ChapStick."

"Lipstick!" Great-aunt Rose cried in disgust. "Lipstick and miniskirts! No wonder all of those boys kept calling while you were away. They probably think you're easy."

I raised my eyebrows at this. "Really? Boys called me?" I'd known, of course, that girls had called—Heather Montrose, among others. But I hadn't known any boys had phoned. "Were any of them named Rob?"

"I didn't ask their names," Great-aunt Rose said. "I told them never to call here again. I explained that you weren't that kind of girl."

I said an expletive that caused my mother to throw me a warning look. Fortunately, Great-aunt Rose didn't hear it, as she was still too busy talking.

"An emergency, they kept calling it," she said. "Had to get in touch with you right away, because of some emergency. Ridiculous. You know what kind of emergencies teenagers have, of course. They'd probably run out of Cherry Coke down at the local soda shop."

I looked at Great-aunt Rose very hard as I said, "Actually, a girl from my class got kidnapped. One of the cheerleaders. They found her yesterday, floating in one of the quarries. She'd been strangled."

My mother looked startled. "Oh, my God," she said. "That girl? The one I read about in the paper this morning? You knew her?"

Parents. I swear.

"I've only sat behind her," I said, "in homeroom every year since the sixth grade."

"Oh, no." My mom had her hands on her face. "Her poor parents. They must be devastated. We'd better send over a platter."

Restauranteurs. That's how they think. Any crisis, and it's always, "Let's send over a platter." Last spring, when half our town's police force had been camped out in our front yard, holding off the hordes of reporters who wanted to score an interview with Lightning Girl, all my mom had been able to think about was making sure we had enough biscotti to go around.

Great-aunt Rose wasn't nearly as upset as my mom. She went, "Cheerleader? Serves her right. Prancing around in those little short skirts. You better watch out, Jessica, or you'll be next."

"Aunt Rose!" my mom cried.

"Well," Great-aunt Rose said, with a sniff. "It could happen. Particularly if you let her continue to wear outfits like that." She nodded at my ensemble.

I decided I had had enough visiting. I got up and said, "It's been swell seeing you again, Auntie, but I think I'll go up and say hi to Douglas. He was asleep when I got home last night, so—"

"Douglas," Great-aunt Rose said with a roll of her rheumy eyes. "When *isn't* he asleep?"

Which gave me a clue as to how Douglas had borne Great-aunt Rose's company for the two weeks he'd been alone with her. Feigning sleep.

He was still at it when I burst into his room a minute later.

"Douglas," I said, looking down at him from the side of his bed. "Give it up. I know you're not really asleep."

He opened one eye. "Is she gone?" he asked.

"Almost," I said. "Dad's coming to pick her up and take her to the airport in a few minutes. Mom wants you to come down and say good-bye."

Douglas moaned and pulled a pillow over his head.

"Just kidding," I said, sinking down onto the bed beside him. "I think Mom's getting a dose of what you must have had to put up with this whole time. I don't believe Great-aunt Rose will be invited back any time soon."

"The horror," Douglas said from beneath the pillow. "The horror."

"Yeah," I said. "But hey, it's over now. How are you doing?"

Douglas said, his voice still muffled by the pillow, "Well, I didn't slash my wrists this time, did I? So I must be doing okay."

I digested this. The reason Douglas, at twenty years of age, could not be trusted to stay in the house alone for two weeks is because of his tendency to hear voices inside his head. The voices are held pretty much at bay with the help of medication, but occasionally Douglas still has episodes. That's what his doctors call it when he listens to the voices, and then does what they tell him to do, which is generally something bad, like, oh, I don't know, kill himself.

Episodes.

"I'll tell you what," he said from beneath the pillow. "I almost episoded Great-aunt Rose, is what I almost did."

"Really?" Too bad he hadn't. I might have gotten the message about Amber being missing in time to have saved her. "What about the Feds? Any sign of them?"

The Federal Bureau of Investigation, like my classmates, refuses to believe I am no longer psychic. They were mightily taken with me last spring, when word got out about my "special ability." They were so taken with me, in fact, that they decided to enlist my aid in locating some unsavory individuals on their most wanted list. They forgot one slight detail, however: to *ask* me if I wanted to work for them.

Which of course I did not. It took all sorts of unpleasantness— including lying that I no longer have any psychic powers—to extricate myself from their clutches. Since then, they had taken to following me around, waiting for me to slip up, at which point I suppose they will point their finger and yell, "Liar, liar, pants on fire."

At least, that's all I hope they'll do.

Douglas pushed the pillow away and sat up. "No white vans mysteriously parked across the street since you took off for camp," he said. "Except for Rose, it's been downright restful around here. I mean, with both you and Mike gone."

We were quiet for a minute, thinking about Mike. Across the hall, his bedroom door stood open, and I could see that his computer, all of his books, and his telescope were gone. They were sitting in some dorm room at Harvard now. Mike would be torturing his new roommate, instead of Douglas and me, with his obsession over Claire Lippman, the cute redhead into whose bedroom window Mike had spent so many hours peering.

"It's going to be weird with him gone," Douglas said.

"Yeah," I said. But actually, I wasn't thinking about Mike. I was thinking about Amber. Claire Lippman, the girl Mike had loved from afar for a few years now, spent almost all of her free time in the summer tanning herself at the quarries. Had she, I wondered, seen Amber there, before the crime that had taken her life?

"What," Douglas asked a second later, "are you so dressed up for, anyway?"

I looked down at myself in surprise. "Oh," I said. "School."

"School?" Douglas seemed shocked. "Since when have you ever bothered dressing up for school?"

"I'm turning over a new leaf," I informed him. "No more jeans, no more T-shirts, no more fighting, no more detention."

"Interesting corollary," Douglas said. "Equating jeans with fighting and detention. But I'll bite. Did it work?"

"Not exactly," I said, and told him about my day, leaving out the part about what Heather had said concerning him.

When I was through, Doug whistled, low and long.

"So they're blaming you," he said. "Even though you couldn't possibly have known anything about it?"

"Hey," I said with a shrug. "Amber was in with the popular crowd, and popular kids are not popular for their ability to objectively reason. Just for their looks, mainly. Or maybe their ability to suck up."

"Jeez," Douglas said. "What are you going to do?"

"What *can* I do?" I asked with a shrug. "I mean, she's dead."

"Couldn't you—I don't know. Couldn't you summon up a picture of her killer? Like in your mind's eye? Like if you really concentrated?"

"Sorry," I said in a flat voice. "It doesn't work like that."

Unfortunately. My psychic ability does not extend itself toward anything other than addresses. Seriously. Show me a picture of anyone, and that night, I'll dream up the person's most current location. But precognitive indications of the lottery numbers? No. Visions of plane crashes, or impending national doom? Nothing. All I can do is locate missing people. And I can only do that in my sleep.

Well, most of the time, anyway. There'd been a strange incident over the summer when I'd managed to summon up someone's location just by hugging his pillow. . . .

But that, I remained convinced, had been a fluke.

"Oh," Douglas said suddenly, leaning over to pull something out from beneath his bed. "By the way, I was in charge of collecting the Abramowitzes' mail while they were away, and I took the liberty of relieving them of this." He presented me with a large brown envelope that had been addressed to Ruth. "From your friend at 1-800-WHERE-R-YOU, I believe?"

I took the envelope and opened it. Inside—as there was every week, mailed to Ruth, since I suspected the Feds were going through my mail, just waiting for something like this to prove I'd been lying to them when I'd said I was no longer psychic—was a note from my operative at the missing children's organization—Rosemary—and a photo of a kid she had determined was really and truly missing . . . not a runaway, who might be missing by choice, or a kid who'd been stolen by his noncustodial parent, who might be better off where he was. But an actual, genuinely missing kid.

I looked at the picture—of a little Asian girl, with buckteeth and butterfly hair clips—and sighed. Amber Mackey, who'd sat in front of me in homeroom every day for six years, might be dead. But for the rest of us, life goes on.

Yeah. Try telling that to Amber's parents.

CHAPTER 4

When I woke up the next morning, I knew two things: One, that Courtney Hwang was living on Baker Street in San Francisco. And two, that I was going to take the bus to school that day.

Don't ask me what one had to do with the other. My guess would be a big fat nothing.

But if I took the bus to school, I'd have an opportunity that I wouldn't if I let Ruth drive me to school in her Cabriolet: I'd be able to talk to Claire Lippman, and find out what she knew about the activities at the quarry just before Amber went missing.

I called Ruth first. My call to Rosemary would have to

wait until I found a phone that no one could connect me to, if 1-800-WHERE-R-YOU happened to trace the call. Which they did every call they got, actually.

"You want to take the bus," Ruth repeated, incredulously.

"It's nothing against the Cabriolet," I assured her. "It's just that I want to have a word with Claire."

"You want to take the bus," Ruth said again.

"Seriously, Ruth," I said. "It's just a one-time thing. I just want to ask Claire a few questions about what was up at the quarry the night Amber disappeared."

"Fine," Ruth said. "Take the bus. See if I care. What have you got on?"

"What?"

"On your body. What are you wearing on your body?"

I looked down at myself. "Olive khaki mini, beige crocheted tank with matching three-quarter-sleeve cardigan, and beige espadrilles."

"The platforms?"

"Yes."

"Good," Ruth said, and hung up.

Fashion is *hard*. I don't know how those popular girls do it. At least my hair, being extremely short and sort of spiky, didn't have to be blow-dried and styled. That would just about kill me, I think.

Claire was sitting on the stoop of the house where the bus picked up the kids in our neighborhood. I live in the kind of neighborhood where people don't mind if you do this. Sit on their stoop, I mean, while waiting for the bus.

Claire was eating an apple and reading what looked to be a script. Claire, a senior, was the reigning leading lady of Ernie Pyle High's drama club. In the bright morning sunlight, her red bob shined. She had definitely blow-dried and styled just minutes before.

Ignoring all the freshmen geeks and car-less rejects that were gathered on the sidewalk, I said, "Hi, Claire."

She looked up, squinting in the sun. Then she swallowed what she'd been chewing and said, "Oh, hi there, Jess. What are you doing here?"

"Oh, nothing," I said, sitting down on the step beneath the one she'd appropriated. "Ruth had to leave early, is all." I prayed Ruth wouldn't drive by as I said this, and that if she did, she wouldn't tootle the horn, as she was prone to when we passed what we've always considered the rejects at the bus stop.

"Huh," Claire said. She glanced admiringly down at my bare leg. "You've got a great tan. How'd you get it?"

Claire Lippman has always been obsessed with tanning. It was because of this obsession, actually, that my brother Mike had become obsessed with her. She spent almost every waking hour of the summer months on the roof of her house, sunbathing . . . except when she could get someone to drive her to the quarries. Swimming in the quarries was, of course, against the law, which was why everyone did it, Claire Lippman more than anyone. Though, as a redhead, her hobby must have been a particularly frustrating one for her, since it took almost a whole summer of exposure to turn her skin even the slightest shade darker. Sitting beside her, I felt a little like Pocahontas. Pocahontas hanging out with The Little Mermaid.

"I worked as a camp counselor," I explained to her. "And then Ruth and I spent two weeks at the dunes, up at Lake Michigan."

"You're lucky," Claire said wistfully. "I've just been stuck at the stupid quarries all summer."

Pleased by this smooth entré into the subject I'd been longing to discuss with her, I started to say, "Hey, yeah, that's right. You must have been there, then, the day Amber Mackey went missing—"

That's what I started to say, anyway. I didn't get a chance to finish, however. That was because, to my utter disbelief, a red Trans Am pulled up to the bus stop, and Ruth's twin brother Skip leaned out of the T-top to call, "Jess! Hey, Jess! What are you doing here? D'ju and Ruth have another fight?"

All the geeks—the backpack patrol, Ruth and I called them, because of their enormous, well, backpacks—turned to look at me. There is nothing, let me tell you, more humiliating than being stared at by a bunch of fourteen-year-old boys.

I had no choice but to call back to Skip, "No, Ruth and I

did not get into a fight. I just felt like riding the bus today."

Really, in the history of the bus stop, had anyone ever uttered anything as lame as that?

"Don't be an idiot," Skip said. "Get in the car. I'll drive you."

All the nerds, who'd been staring at Skip while he spoke, turned their heads to look expectantly at me.

"Um," I said, feeling my cheeks heating up and thankful my tan hid my blush. "No, thanks, Skip. Claire and I are talking."

"Claire can come, too." Skip ducked back inside the car, leaned over, and threw open the passenger door. "Come on."

Claire was already gathering up her books.

"Great!" she squealed. "Thanks!"

I followed more reluctantly. This was so not what I'd had in mind.

"Come on, Claire," Skip was saying as I approached the car. "You can get in back—"

I saw Claire, who was a willowy five-foot-nine if she was an inch, hesitate while looking into the cramped recesses of Skip's backseat. With a sigh, I said, "I'll get in back."

When I was wedged into the dark confines of the Trans Am's rear seat, Claire threw the passenger seat back and climbed in.

"This is so sweet of you, Skip," she said, checking out her reflection in his rearview mirror. "Thanks a lot. The bus is okay, and all, but, you know. This is much better."

"Oh," Skip said, fastening his seatbelt. "I know. You all right back there?" he asked me.

"Fine," I said. I had, I knew, to turn the conversation back to the subject of the quarries. But how?

"Great." Skip threw the car into gear and we were off, leaving the geeks in our dust. Actually, that part I sort of enjoyed.

"So," Skip said, "how are you ladies this morning?"

See? This is the problem with Skip. He says things like "So, how are you ladies this morning?" How are you supposed to take a guy who says things like that seriously? Skip's not ugly, or anything—he looks a lot like Ruth, actually: a chubby blond in glasses. Only, of course, Skip doesn't have breasts.

Still, Skip just isn't dream date material, despite the Trans Am.

Too bad he hasn't seemed to figure that out yet.

"I'm fine," Claire said. "How about you, Jess?"

"I'm fine," I said, from the manger-sized backseat. Then I took the plunge. "What were you saying, Claire? About being at the quarry the day Amber disappeared?"

"Oh," Claire said. The wind through the T-top was unstyling her bob, but Claire didn't appear to care. She ran her fingers through it delightedly. You don't get that kind of fresh air on the bus.

"My God, what a nightmare *that* was. We'd all just been hanging out, you know, all day. No big deal. Some of those guys from the football team, they brought a grill, and they were barbecuing, and everyone was, you know, pretty drunk, even though I warned them they'd get dehydrated, drinking beer in the sun—" For someone whose primary goal was to bake her skin to a crisp, Claire had always been surprisingly health-conscious. One of the reasons it took her so long to achieve the tan she wanted each summer was that she insisted on slathering herself with SPF 15.

"And then the sun went down, and some people started packing up their stuff to, you know, go home. And that's when Mark—Leskowski, you know? He and Amber were going out for, like, ever. Anyway, he was all, 'Has anybody seen Amber?' And we all started looking for her, through the woods, you know, and then, thinking maybe she'd tripped or something, in the water. I mean, we thought maybe she'd fallen in, or something. The drop's pretty steep. When we couldn't find her, we figured, well, she must have gone home with somebody else, or whatever. We didn't say that to *Mark*, of course, but that's what we were all thinking."

Claire turned to look at me, her pretty blue eyes troubled. "But then she never came home. And the next day, as soon as it was light, we all went back to the quarry, you know, to look for her."

"But you didn't," I said, "find anything."

"Not that day. Her body didn't show up until Sunday morning." Claire went on, " A bunch of people tried to call you, you know. Hoping you could help find her. This one girl, Karen Sue Hankey, she says you found some kid over the summer who'd been lost in a cave, so we thought maybe you still had, you know, that whole psychic thing going—"

That psychic thing. That was one way of putting it, anyway.

I was seriously going to kill Karen Sue Hankey.

"I wasn't exactly reachable last weekend," I said. "I was up at—" I broke off, noticing we were approaching the turnoff to Pike's Creek Road. "Hey, Skip, turn here."

Skip obediently took the turn. "And I'm turning here because?"

"I want, um, a cruller," I said, since there was a Dunkin' Donuts near the garage where Rob worked.

"Ooh," Claire said. "Crullers. Yum. You don't get crullers on the bus."

When we buzzed past Rob's uncle's garage, I sank down real low in the seat, so in case Rob was outside, he wouldn't see me.

Rob was outside, and he didn't see me. He was bent inside the hood of an Audi, his soft dark hair falling forward over his square-jawed face, his jeans looking properly snug and faded in all the right places. It was warm out, even though it wasn't quite eight in the morning yet, and Rob had on a short-sleeved shirt, revealing his nicely pronounced triceps.

It had been nearly three weeks since I'd last seen him. He'd shown up at the Wawasee All-Camp recital, where I'd had a solo. I'd been surprised . . . I hadn't expected him to come four hours, one way, just to hear me play.

And then, since I had to go out with my parents afterwards— and let's face it, my parents would not approve of Rob, a guy with a criminal record who comes, as they say in books, from the wrong side of the tracks—he just had to get back on his bike afterward and drive four hours home. That's a long way to go, just to hear some girl you aren't even going out with play a nocturne on her flute.

It got me thinking. You know, since he'd driven so far to hear me play. Maybe he liked me after all, in spite of the whole jailbait thing.

Except, of course, that I'd been back two days already, and he still hadn't called.

Anyway, that brief glimpse of Rob, checking that Audi's oil, was all I was probably going to see of him for a while, so I watched until we pulled into the parking lot of the Dunkin' Donuts and I couldn't see him anymore.

Hey, I know it was uncool to be scoping on boys at the same time as I was trying to solve a murder. But Nancy Drew still had time to date Ned Nickerson, didn't she, in between solving all those mysteries?

Except of course, Ned wasn't on probation, and I don't

think any of those mysteries Nancy solved involved a dead cheerleader.

While Skip and Claire went to the counter to get crullers, I said I had to make a call. Then I went to the untraceable payphone by the door to the rest-room and dialed 1-800-WHERE-R-YOU.

Rosemary was glad to hear from me, even though of course we had to keep the call brief. Rosemary is totally risking her job, doing what she does for me. You know, sending me those photos and reports on missing kids. Those files aren't supposed to leave the office.

But I guess Rosemary thinks it is worth it, if even one kid gets found. And since we've started working together, we've found a lot of kids, between the two of us. We kind of have to cool it, of course, so no one gets too suspicious. We average about a kid a week, which, let me tell you, is way better than 1-800-WHERE-R-YOU was doing before I came along.

The good thing about working with Rosemary, as opposed to like the FBI or the police or something, is that Rosemary is totally discreet and would never, say, call the *National Enquirer* and have them come to my house to interview me. Having too many reporters around has a tendency to send Douglas into an episode. That is why I lied last spring, and told everyone I didn't have my psychic powers anymore.

And up until recently, everyone believed it.

Everyone except Karen Sue Hankey, apparently.

Anyway, after Rosemary and I were through chatting, I hung up, and walked out to find Skip telling Claire about the time in third grade when he and I shot his GI Joe into space using a lead pipe and gunpowder extracted from about three hundred Blackcats. I noticed that he left out the part about putting a Roman candle inside my Barbie's head, an act about which I had not been consulted and which had not been part of our space shuttle program as I'd understood it. Also the part where we nearly blew ourselves up.

"Wow," Claire said as she licked sugar off her fingertips. "I always saw you two hanging out together, but I never knew you did cool stuff like that."

"Oh, yeah," I overheard Skip say. "Jess and I go way back. *Way* back."

Hello. What was *this* all about? Just because I'd spent two weeks hanging out with the guy at his parents' lakehouse did not mean I wanted to renew a relationship that had been formed due to a mutual love of explosives and which had disintegrated as soon as our parents discovered our illicit hobby and took away all our firecrackers. Skip and I had nothing in common. Nothing except our past.

"Ready to go?" Skip asked brightly as I came up to their table. "We better get a move on, or we'll be late for homeroom."

Homeroom. I forgot all about my annoyance with Skip.

"Hey, Claire," I asked her as we headed back toward the car.

"That Friday Amber disappeared. Did she and Mark Leskowski hang out with the rest of you the whole day, or did they ever go off by themselves?"

"Are you kidding?" Claire tossed her copper-colored curls, which, in spite of having become windblown, still looked fresh and pretty. Claire was that kind of girl. "Those two were inseparable. I mean, Mark sits in front of me first period, and let me tell you, it was like he had to pry himself out of that girl's arms. . . ."

I raised my eyebrows. No wonder Amber had never made it into her seat before the first bell. "What about the day she disappeared?" I asked. "Were they still . . . inseparable."

Claire nodded. "Oh, yeah. They were all over each other. We were joking about how they were going to come down with some serious poison ivy, what with the number of trips they took into the woods with each other in order to 'be alone.'"

I climbed into the backseat. "And that last time they went off together, to be alone—was that how Mark came back?"

Claire plopped down into the passenger seat. "What do you mean?"

"I mean, did he come back alone?"

Claire tilted her head to one side as she thought about it. Beside her, Skip started up the car. I wondered what Rob, back at the garage, would think if he'd known I'd driven right by him and hadn't even said hi.

"You know," Claire said, "I can't imagine that he did. Come back alone, I mean. I wasn't paying that close attention—those guys aren't really my crowd, you know? I mean, that whole cheerleading, football thing. That is so not my scene. I mean, if they gave just half the amount of money to support the drama department as they do the athletics department, we could put on a *lot* better shows. We could have rented costumes, instead of making them ourselves, and we could get mikes so we don't have to scream to be heard in the back row—"

I could see that Claire was slipping off track. To steer her back to the subject at hand, I said, "You're right. It isn't fair. Somebody should do something. So you didn't see Mark come back alone from any of his and Amber's trips into the woods together?"

"No," Claire said. "I don't think so. I mean, somebody would have said something if Mark had come back alone. Don't you think? Don't you think somebody would have said 'Hey, Mark, where's Amber?'"

"You'd think so," Skip said.

"Yes," I said, thoughtfully. "Wouldn't you?"

CHAPTER 5

They held Amber Mackey's memorial service later that day. Instead of having it in a church or a funeral home or whatever, they had it in the gym.

That's right. The gym of Ernest Pyle High School.

And they had it during seventh period. Attendance was mandatory. The only person who was not there, actually, was Amber. I guess Principal Feeney drew the line at letting Amber's parents drag her coffin out in front of all two thousand of their daughter's peers.

The band played a slowed-down rendition of the school song, I guess so it would sound sad. Then Principal Feeney got up and talked about what a great person Amber had been. I doubt he had ever even met her, but whatever. He looked good in the dark gray suit he'd donned for the occasion.

When the principal was done talking, Coach Albright came out and said a few words. Coach Albright is not known for his eloquence as a speaker, so fortunately he didn't say much. He just announced that his players would be wearing black armbands on their uniforms for the season in honor of Amber. Never having been to a sporting event at my school, I had no idea what he was talking about until Ruth explained it to me.

Then Mrs. Tidd, the cheerleading coach, got up and said a bunch of stuff about how much they were going to miss Amber, especially when it came to her ability to do standing back tucks. Then she said that, in honor of Amber, both the varsity and junior varsity cheerleading squads had put together an interpretive dance.

Then—and I kid you not—the cheerleaders and Pompettes did this dance, in the middle of the gym floor, to Celine Dion's "My Heart Will Go On," from *Titanic*.

And people *cried* during it. I swear. I looked around, and people were totally crying.

It was a good dance and all. You could tell they'd worked totally hard on it. And they'd only had like two days or something to memorize it.

Still, it didn't make me feel like crying. Seriously. And I don't think I'm like a hardened person or anything. I just hope that when I die, nobody does an interpretive dance at my memorial service. I can't stand that kind of thing.

I can tell you what did make me feel like crying, though. The fact that, as the dance was going on, some people walked into the gym. I was sitting midway up the bleachers—Ruth wanted to make sure we could see everything, and she hadn't even known, at the time, that there was going to be an interpretive dance—but I could still make out their features. Well enough to know they weren't high-school students.

They weren't high-school teachers, either.

What they were was Feds.

Seriously. And not just any Feds, either, but my old friends Special Agents Johnson and Smith.

You would think that, by now, they'd have given up. I mean, they've been following me around since May, and they still don't have anything solid to pin on me. Not like what I'm doing is even wrong. I mean, okay, yeah, I help reunite missing kids with their families. Oooh, lock me up. I'm a dangerous criminal.

Except of course they don't want to lock me up. They want me to work for them.

But I have a real problem with working for an institution that routinely railroads people who might conceivably be innocent of the crimes with which they've been accused, just like The Fugitive. . . .

And apparently it wasn't enough, my telling them I no

longer had the power to find missing people. Oh, no. They have to tap my phone, and read my mail, and follow me all the way to Lake Wawasee.

And now they have the nerve to show up at a memorial service for one of my dead friends. . . .

And yeah, okay, Amber wasn't really my friend, but I sat behind her for like half an hour every single weekday for six years. That has to count for something, right?

"I'm outta here," I said to Ruth as I started gathering up my things.

"What do you mean, you're outta here?" Ruth demanded, looking alarmed. "You can't leave. It's an assembly."

"Watch me," I said.

"They've got student council members posted at all the exits," Ruth whispered.

"That's not all they got posted by the exits," I said, and pointed at Special Agents Johnson and Smith, who were talking to Principal Feeney off to one side of the gym.

"Oh, God," Ruth breathed, when she saw them. "Not again."

"Oh, yes," I said. "And if you think I'm sticking around here to get the third degree about Courtney Hwang, which is for sure why they're here, you got another think coming, sister. See you around."

Without another word, I inched my way over to the far end of the bleacher—past a number of people who gave me dirty looks as I went by, though because I'd stepped on their toes, not because they were mad at me about Amber—until I'd reached the gap between the bleachers and the wall. This I slithered through without any major difficulty—although my landing, in my platform espadrilles, was no ten-pointer, let me tell you. After that, it was an easy stroll beneath the bleachers to the nearest door, where I planned to fake an illness and be given leave to make my way to the nurse's office. . . .

Except of course when I emerged from beneath the bleachers and saw the student council member guarding that particular exit, I knew I wouldn't have to fake an illness.

No, I felt pretty genuinely sick.

"Jessica," Karen Sue Hankey said, clutching the pile of *Remember Amber* booklets she'd handed out to each of us as we filed in. The booklet, four pages long, had color copies of photos of Amber in various cheerleader poses, interposed with the printed lyrics to "My Heart Will Go On." Most people, I'd noticed as I'd made my way beneath the bleachers, had dropped theirs.

"What are you doing?" Karen Sue hissed. "Get back to your seat. It's not over yet."

I clutched my stomach. Not enough to draw attention to myself. The last thing I wanted was for Special Agents Johnson and Smith to notice me. But enough to get the point across.

"Karen Sue," I hiccuped. "I think I'm going to—"

I stumbled past her and dove through the doors. They let out into the music wing. Free. I was free! Now all I had to do was make my way to the student parking lot, and wait for Ruth to get to her car when they let everybody out. I might even get a chance to stretch out on her hood and work on my tan.

Except that Karen Sue followed me into the hallway, throwing a definite crimp in my plans.

"You are not sick, Jessica Mastriani," she said firmly. "You are faking it. You do the exact same thing in PE every time Mrs. Tidd announces the Presidential Fitness tests."

I couldn't believe this. It's not enough she has to go around outing me as a psychic to everyone. No, Karen Sue has to bar my escape from the Feds who are after me, too.

But I was not about to let my anger get the best of me. No way. I'd turned over a new leaf. It was already day two of the new school year, and guess what? I did not have detention.

And I was not going to ruin this excellent record by letting Karen Sue Hankey get under my skin.

"Karen Sue," I said, straightening up. "You're right. I'm not sick. But there are some people out there I don't want to see, if it's all the same to you. So could you please be a human being"—I barely restrained myself from adding, *for once in your life*—"and let me go?"

"Who do you not want to see?" Karen Sue wanted to know.

"Some Feds, if you must know. You see, I've had a lot of problems with people thinking I still have psychic powers, when in fact"—I added this last part with all the emphasis I could muster—"*I do not.*"

"You are such a liar, Jess," Karen Sue said, shaking her head so that her honey-blond hair, the ends of which curled into perfect flips just above her shoulders, swung. "You know you found that Shane kid at camp this summer, when he got lost inside that cave."

"Yeah, I found him," I said. "But not because I'd had a psychic vision he was there or anything. Just because I had a hunch he'd been in there. That's all."

"Is that so?" Karen Sue looked prim. "Well, what you call a hunch, I call ESP. You have a gift from God, Jessica Mastriani, and that makes it a sin for you to try to deny it."

The problem, of course, is that Karen Sue goes to my church. She's been in my Sunday school class since forever.

The other problem is that Karen Sue is a goody-two-shoes suck-up we used to lock in the janitor's closet whenever the Sunday school teacher didn't show up on time. Which happened quite often, actually.

"Look, Karen Sue," I said. It was getting harder to repress my urge to knock those booklets out of her arms and grind her face into them. "I appreciate everything you've tried to do for me, in the name of the Lord and all, but could you just once try that whole turning-the-other-cheek thing—turn it toward the wall so you don't see me while I get the hell out of here? That way, if anyone asks, you won't be lying when you say you didn't see where I went."

Karen Sue looked at me sadly. "No," she said, and started for the door, clearly to seek the aid of someone larger than she was in detaining me.

I grabbed her wrist. But I wasn't going to hurt her. I swear I wasn't. I'd turned over a new leaf. I was in a brand new crocheted sweater set and espadrilles. I had on cherry ChapStick. Girls dressed like me do not get into fights. Girls dressed like me reason with one another, in a friendly manner.

"Karen Sue," I said. "The thing is, the whole thing with the psychic power and all, it really upsets my brother Douglas, you know? I mean, the reporters coming around the house and calling and all of that. So you can see why I want to kind of keep it a secret, right? I mean, because of my brother."

Karen Sue's gaze never left mine as she wrenched her wrist from my hand.

"Your brother Douglas," she said, "is sick. His sickness is obviously a judgment from God. If Douglas went to church more often, and prayed harder, he would get better. And your denying your God-given gifts isn't helping. In fact, you are probably making him worse."

Well. What could I say to that?

Nothing, really. I mean, something like that, there's no appropriate response.

No appropriate *verbal* response, that is.

Karen Sue's screams brought Principal Feeney, Coach Albright, Mrs. Tidd, most of the student council, and Special Agents Johnson and Smith running. When she saw Karen Sue, Special Agent Smith got on her cell phone and called an ambulance.

But I guarantee her nose isn't even broken. She probably only burst a blood vessel or two.

As Principal Feeney and Special Agent Johnson led me away, I called out, "Hey, Karen Sue, maybe if you pray hard enough, God'll make the bleeding stop."

Taken out of context, I could see how this might sound callous. But none of them had heard what Karen Sue had said to me. And no amount of me going, "But she said—" seemed to impress upon them the fact that I was completely justified in my behavior.

"And I thought you'd been making some real progress," Mr. Goodhart said sadly when I was dragged into the guidance office.

"I *was* making progress." I threw myself onto one of the orange couches. "I'd like to see how long you could put up with Karen Sue's *stuff* before hauling off and slugging her."

Only I didn't say *"stuff."*

"I'll tell you one thing," Mr. Goodhart said. "I wouldn't let a girl like that push my buttons."

"She said it's my fault Douglas is sick," I said. "She said his sickness is a punishment from God for me not using my gift!"

Special Agent Johnson, who'd been sequestered away with Principal Feeney—consulting about me, I was sure—chose this moment to emerge from the principal's office.

"Really, Jessica," he said, sounding surprised. "I wouldn't have thought you'd be susceptible to that sort of nonsense."

"Well, if I am," I said, "it's because you're making me. Following me around all the time. Showing up at school. Badgering me. Well, I had nothing to do with finding that girl in San Francisco. Nothing!"

Special Agent Johnson raised his eyebrows. "I wasn't aware a girl in San Francisco had been found," he said mildly. "But thank you for letting me know."

I eyed him. "You . . . you aren't here about Courtney Hwang?"

"Contrary to what you apparently believe, Jessica," Special Agent Johnson said, "the world, much less my job, does not revolve around you. Jill and I are here for something quite unrelated to you."

The door to the guidance office opened, and Special Agent Smith came in.

"Well," she said. "That was exciting. The next time, Jessica, you feel the need to plunge your fist into a girl's face, please do it when I'm not around."

I looked from her to Special Agent Johnson and then back again.

"Wait a minute," I said. "If you two aren't here because of me, what are you here for?"

The door to the guidance office opened yet again, and this time, Mark Leskowski walked in, looking bewildered and strangely vulnerable for a guy who, at six feet tall, probably tips the scales at one eighty.

"You wanted to see me again, Mr. Goodhart?" Mark asked.

Mr. Goodhart glanced at Special Agents Johnson and Smith.

"Uh," he said. "Yes, Mark, I did. Actually, these, um, officers here wanted a word with you. But before you meet with him, um, officers, can I just have a word with you?"

Special Agent Johnson smiled. "Certainly," he said, and he and Special Agent Smith disappeared into Mr. Goodhart's office, and closed the door behind them.

Incredible. More than incredible. Indescribable. I punch Karen Sue Hankey in the face and get summoned to the guidance office for disciplinary action, *only to be forgotten about*?

What's more, my two archenemies, Special Agents Johnson and Smith, show up at Ernest Pyle High School, not to give *me* a hard time, but *someone else*?

Amber Mackey's murder had done a lot more than rob us of Amber. It had turned the universe as I had once known it upside down and backward.

This became even more apparent when Mark Leskowski—quarterback, senior class vice-president, and all-around hottie—

smiled down at me—*me*, Jessica Mastriani, who's spent almost more time in detention than she has in class—and said, "Well. We meet again, I guess."

Oh, yeah. Call the Pentagon. Someone's gone and created a new world order.

CHAPTER 6

"So," Mark Leskowski said to me. "What are you in for this time?"

I looked at him. He was so beautiful. Not as beautiful as Rob Wilkins, of course, but then what guy was?

Still, Mark Leskowski was a close second in the dreamy department.

"I punched Karen Sue Hankey in the face," I said.

"Whoa." He actually looked impressed. "Good for you."

"You think so?" I asked. I can't tell you how good it felt, having the approval of a guy who looked that good in a pair of 505s. Seriously. Most of what I did on a regular basis, it seemed, Rob didn't approve of. Primarily because he was afraid it was going to get me killed, but still. He didn't have to be so bossy about it.

"Heck, yeah," Mark said. "That girl's such a wannabe, it hurts."

My God! My feelings about Karen Sue exactly! And yet somehow, when expressed through a set of such masculine lips, they seemed to have more validity than ever.

"Yeah," I said. "Yeah, she is, isn't she?"

"Is she! I'll tell you what. Amber used to call her the Klingon. You know, because she was always clinging onto the rest of us, trying to get in with the in crowd."

His mention of Amber snapped me back into reality. What was I doing? What was I doing, sitting on an orange vinyl couch in the guidance office, lusting after Mark Leskowski? He was being pulled in for questioning by the FBI. The FBI! That was some serious stuff.

"So," I said, my gaze darting toward the glass window in Mr. Goodhart's office door. Through it, I could see Special Agent Johnson speaking rapidly. Mr. Goodhart was Mark Leskowski's guidance counselor, as well as mine. Mr. Goodhart had all the *L*s through *P*s.

Mark noticed the direction of my gaze and nodded. "I guess I'm in some trouble now, huh?"

I said carefully, "Well, you know. If they're bringing in the FBI . . ."

"They always do," he said. "In cases of kidnapping. Or at

least, that's what Mr. Goodhart says. Those two in there are the regional operatives."

Special Agents Johnson and Smith, regional operatives? Really? It had never occurred to me that Allan and Jill might actually have homes. I had always pictured them living out of skanky motel rooms. But of course it made sense that they lived in the area. I heaved a shudder at the idea that I might one day bump into one of them at the grocery store.

"They are classifying what happened to Amber as a kidnapping/murder," Mark went on, "because Amber was . . . alive for a while before she got killed."

"Oh," I said. "Shouldn't you . . . I don't know. Have a lawyer, or something?"

"I have one," he said, looking down at his hands resting between his thighs. "He's on his way. My parents, too. I thought I had explained it all to the sheriff, but I guess . . . I don't know. I'm going to have to do it again. With those guys."

I followed his gaze. Now Mr. Goodhart was speaking to Special Agent Johnson. I couldn't see Special Agent Smith. She was probably sitting in my chair, the one by the window. I wondered if she was looking out at the car wash, the way I always did when I sat there.

"I just don't get it," Mark said, staring at a spot in the center of the coffee table between us, at a brochure that had I'M AN ARMY OF ONE written on it. "I mean, I loved Amber. I would never hurt her."

I glanced at the secretary. She was totally listening, but she was pretending not to, seeming to be very absorbed in a game of Minesweeper. She would click a button on her keyboard if Principal Feeney wandered this way, and the computer game would disappear, to be replaced by a spreadsheet.

I should know. I had spent enough time in this office.

"Of course you wouldn't," I said to Mark.

"The thing is," he said, raising his gaze from the Army brochure and looking at me with soulful brown eyes. "I mean, it isn't like we weren't having problems. Every couple has problems. But we were working them out. We were totally working them out."

I'll say. At least if what Claire Lippman had told me was any indication. He and Amber had been the Make-out King and Queen of that little barbecue, anyway.

"And then, for this to happen . . ." He let his gaze drift away from me, toward the clock on the wall behind me. "Especially when everything else was going so great. You know, we have a real shot at the state championship this year. I just . . ."

I swear, as I was sitting there, looking at him, I noticed an unnatural glimmer in his eyes. At first I thought it was just a trick of the flourescent lights overhead. And then it hit me.

Mark Leskowski was crying. Crying. Mark Leskowski. A football player. Crying because he missed his dead girlfriend.

"And there are going to be scouts, you know, from all

the major universities," he said, with a barely suppressed sob. "Checking me out. Checking *me* out. I have a solid chance at getting out of this Podunk town, of going all the way."

Or maybe it was because his football scholarship was going down the drain. Whatever the reason, Mark was *crying*.

I flung a startled glance in the secretary's direction, because I did not know what to do. I mean, I have never dealt with crying football players before. Suicidal brothers, sure. Homicidal maniacs who wanted to kill me, easy. But crying football players?

The secretary was no longer pretending to be absorbed in her game of Minesweeper. She, too, had noticed Mark's tears. And she, too, looked as if she did not know what to do. Her startled gaze met mine, and she shrugged in bewilderment. Then, as if she'd had an idea, she jumped and waved a box of Kleenex at me.

Oh, great. Some help.

Still, there didn't seem to be anything else I could do. I got up and took the Kleenex box from her, then went and sat down beside Mark, and offered it to him.

"Here," I said, laying one hand on his shoulder. "It's okay."

Mark took a handful of Kleenex and pressed them to his eyes. He was swearing softly beneath his breath.

"It's *not* okay," he said vehemently, into the Kleenex. "This is unacceptable. All of this is *unacceptable*."

"I know," I said, patting his shoulder. It felt strong and

muscular beneath my fingers. "But really, it will all work out. Everything is going to be okay."

It was at that moment that the door to Mr. Goodhart's office swung open, and Special Agents Johnson and Smith came out. They looked down at Mark and me curiously, then seemed to realize what was happening. When they did, both their faces grew hard.

"Mark," Special Agent Smith said, in a voice that I did not think was very friendly, as she took a step toward us. "Would you please come with me?"

When she reached the couch, she bent down and slipped a hand beneath Mark's arm. He rose without protest, keeping the Kleenex to his eyes. Then he let her lead him away, toward one of the conference rooms down the hall.

Special Agent Johnson stood looking down at me, his arms folded across his chest.

"Jessica," he said. "Don't even think about going there."

"What?" I spread my hands out in the universal gesture for innocence. "I didn't say anything."

"But you were about to. Jessica, I'm telling you now, leave this one alone. Unless you know something—"

"Which I don't," I said.

"Then stay out of it. A young woman is dead. I don't want you to be next."

Whoa. Okay, Officer Friendly.

As if realizing how unctuous he'd sounded, Special Agent

Johnson changed the subject. "I'm still anxious to hear"—he unfolded his arms—"about this girl in San Francisco."

"There is no girl in San Francisco," I protested. "Really. I swear."

Special Agent Johnson nodded. "Right. Okay. If that's the way you want it. Read my lips then, Jess. Stay out of this one. Way out."

Then he turned around and followed his partner and Mark.

I looked at the secretary. She looked back at me. Our looks said it all. No way was Mark Leskowski, a boy unafraid to cry in public about his dead girlfriend, a murderer.

"Jessica." Mr. Goodhart came out of his office and looked surprised to see me still sitting there, waiting for him. "Go home."

Go home? Was he nuts? I had just sunk my fist into another student's face. And he was just letting me go home?

"But . . ."

"Go." Mr. Goodhart turned to the secretary. "Get Sheriff Hawkins on the line for me, will you, Helen?"

Go? That was it? Just *go*? I thought I had one more strike, and then "I Was Out"? Where was the anger-management lecture? Where were the sighs, the "Oh, Jess, I just don't know what I'm going to do with you"s? Where was my week-long detention? That was it? I could just . . . go?

Helen, noticing that I was still sitting there, put her hand over the phone receiver so whoever she was calling wouldn't hear her when she hissed to me, "Jess. What are you waiting for? Go, before he remembers."

I didn't waste any more time after that. I went.

I was sitting on the hood of Ruth's Cabriolet when she came out of the assembly, looking vaguely harassed.

"Oh, hey," she said in surprise when she saw me. "What are you doing here? I thought Mulder and Scully were on your case again."

"It wasn't me they were after this time," I said. I still couldn't keep the wonder out of my voice. The whole thing had just been so bizarre.

"Really?" Ruth unlocked the door to the driver's side and climbed into her car. "What did they want, then?"

"Mark," I said.

"Leskowski?" Ruth looked shocked as she leaned over to unlock the door to my side. "Oh, my God. They must really think he did it."

"Yeah, only he didn't." I opened the door and slid in. "Ruth, you should have seen him. Mark, I mean. I was sitting next to him, you know, outside of Mr. Goodhart's office, and he . . . he was crying."

"Crying?" Ruth turned away from her examination of her lips in the rearview mirror. "He was not."

I assured her that he had been. "It was so sweet," I went

on. "I mean, you could tell. He really, really loved her. He feels so bad."

Ruth still looked shocked. "Mark Leskowski. Crying. Who would have thought it?"

"I know. So how did the rest of the memorial service go?"

Ruth described it as she drove us home. Apparently, after the interpretive dance, there'd been a long lecture from a grief counselor the school had hired to help us through this trying time, followed by a moment of silent reflection in which we were all to remember what we had loved about Amber. Then the cheerleaders announced that, directly after school, they were heading back up to Pike's Quarry, to throw flowers into the water as a tribute to Amber. Anyone whose heart had ever been touched by Amber was invited to come along to watch.

"Yeah," Ruth said. "Anyone whose heart was ever touched by Amber was invited. You know what that means."

"Right," I said. "In Crowd Only. You're not going, right?"

"Are you kidding me? Perhaps I didn't make it clear. This particular soiree is being hosted by the Ernie Pyle High School varsity cheerleading squad. In other words, 'fat girls, stay home.'"

I blinked at her, a little taken aback at the vehemence in her tone.

"Ruth," I said. "You're not—"

"Once a fat girl," Ruth said, "always a fat girl. In their eyes, anyway."

"But how you look is not important," I said. "It's what's inside that—"

"Spare me," Ruth said. "Besides, I have chair auditions tomorrow. I have to practice."

I eyed her. Ruth was hard to figure out sometimes. She was so supremely confident about some things—academic stuff, and not chasing boys—but so insecure about others. She really was one of those enigmas wrapped in a mystery people are always talking about. Especially since the same way Ruth claimed cheerleaders felt about fat girls, she felt about Grits.

"I mean, I'm sorry she's dead and all," Ruth went on, "but I highly doubt they'd ever hold an all-school memorial service for you or me, you know, if either of us happened to croak."

"Well," I said. "She did die kind of tragically."

Ruth said a bad word as she turned down Lumley Lane. "Please. She was a cheerleader, all right? Doesn't that about say it all? They don't hold all-school assemblies in the memory of dead cellists or flutists. Just cheerleaders. Hey." Pulling into my driveway, Ruth gaped at me. "Wait a minute. We drove right by Pike's Creek Road, and you didn't say a word. What gives? Don't tell me Mark Leskowski's big baby-blues have replaced the memory of the Jerk's."

"Mark's eyes," I said, with some annoyance, "happen to be

brown. And Rob is not a jerk. And I happen to think you're right. Chasing Rob is not the way to get him."

"Uh-huh." Ruth shook her head. "Skip mentioned he gave you and Claire a lift from the bus stop this morning. You talked him into stopping for crullers, didn't you?"

"I didn't talk him into doing anything," I said indignantly. "He stopped of his own volition."

"Oh, please." Ruth rolled her eyes. "Well? Did you see him?"

"Did I see who?" I asked, stalling for time.

"You know who. The Jerk."

I sighed. "I saw him."

"And?"

"And what? I saw him. He didn't see me. End of story."

"God." Ruth laughed. "You are a piece of work. Hey. What's that?"

I looked down at myself, since that's where she was pointing. "What's what?"

"That. That red spot on your shoe."

I lifted my foot, examining a minuscule drop of red on my beige espadrille.

"Oh," I said. "That's just some of Karen Sue Hankey's blood."

"Her blood?" Ruth looked flabbergasted. "Oh, my God. What did you do to her?"

"Punched her in the face," I said, still feeling a little smug at the memory. "You should have seen it, Ruth. It was beautiful."

"Beautiful?" Ruth banged her head against the steering wheel a few times. "Oh, God. And you were doing so well."

I couldn't understand her dismay.

"Ruth," I said. "She fully deserved it."

"That's no excuse," Ruth said, raising her head. "There's only one justification for hitting someone, Jess, and that's if they try to hit you first, and you swing back in self-defense. You can't just go around *hitting* people all the time, just because you don't like what they say to you. You're going to get into serious trouble."

"I am not," I said. "Not this time. I totally got caught, and Mr. Goodhart didn't even say anything. He just told me to go home."

"Yeah," Ruth said. "Because there was a suspected murderer in his office! He was probably just a little distracted."

"Mark Leskowski," I said, "is not a murderer. What's more, he thoroughly supported my breaking Karen Sue's face. He says she's a wannabe."

"Oh, God," Ruth said. "Why was I cursed with such a screwed-up best friend?"

Since I had just been thinking the same nice thing about her, I did not take offense.

"Let's practice together," I said, "at nine. Okay?" Since we live next door to one another, we frequently open our living room windows and play at the same time, giving the neighborhood a free concert, while also getting in some valuable practice time.

"Okay," Ruth said. "But if you think you can just pop Karen Sue Hankey in the face and never hear about it again, you're the one with another think coming, girlfriend."

I laughed as I hurried up the steps to my house. As if! Karen Sue would probably be so afraid of me from now on, I'd never have to put up with her noxious taunting again. As an added bonus, she probably wasn't going to play so well during her chair audition on Thursday, on account of her swollen nose.

It was with these delicious thoughts that I slipped into the house. I had set only one foot on the stairs leading up to my room when my mother's voice, not sounding too pleased, reached me from the kitchen.

Meekly, I made my way to the back of the house.

"Hi, Mom," I said when I saw her at the kitchen table. To my surprise, my dad was there, too.

But my dad never got home before six on a Tuesday.

"Hey, Dad," I said, noting that neither one of them looked particularly happy. Then my heart started to thump uncomfortably.

"What's the matter?" I asked quickly. "Is Douglas—"

"Douglas," my mother said, her voice so hard it was like ice, "is fine."

"Oh." I looked at the two of them. "It isn't—"

"Michael," my mother said, in that same hard voice, "is also fine."

Relief coursed through me. Well, if it wasn't Douglas, and it wasn't Mike, it couldn't be too bad. Maybe it was even something good. You know, something my parents would think was bad, but I might think was good. Like Great-aunt Rose having dropped dead from a heart attack, for instance.

"So," I said, preparing to look sad. "What's up?"

"We got a call a little while ago," my father said, looking grim.

"You'll never guess who it was," said my mother.

"I give up," I said, thinking, Wow, Great-aunt Rose really *is* dead. "Who was it?"

"Mrs. Hankey," my mother said. "Karen Sue's mother."

Oops.

CHAPTER 7

Busted.

I was so busted.

But you know, I really don't think they had any right to be so mad, seeing as how I was defending the family honor and all.

And what a whiny baby, that Karen Sue, ratting me out to her mother. Of course, in Karen Sue's version of the events leading up to my punching her in the face, she hadn't said any of the things we both know she'd really said. In Karen Sue's version of how it all happened, I was trying to sneak out of assembly, and she tried to stop me—for my own good, of course, and because my leaving early was besmirching

Amber Mackey's memory—and I hit her for her efforts.

The whole part about how my denying my psychic powers was what was making Douglas sick? Yeah, Karen Sue left that part out.

Oh, and the part about how Douglas doesn't attend church or pray often enough? Yeah, left that part out, too.

My mom didn't believe me when I told her about that part. See, Karen Sue has my mom snowed, just like she's got her own mother snowed. All my mom sees when she looks at Karen Sue is the daughter she always wished she had. You know, the sweet compliant daughter who enters her homemade cookies in the county fair bake-off every year, and puts her hair in curlers at night so the ends will flip just the right way in the morning. My mom never counted on having a daughter like me, who is saving up for a Harley and has her hair cut as short as she possibly can so she won't have to mess with it.

And oh, yeah, who gets into fights all the time, and is in love with a guy who is on probation.

My poor mom.

My dad believed me. The part about what Karen Sue said and all. My mom, like I said before, didn't.

I heard them arguing about it after I was banished to my room, to "Think About What I Had Done." I was also supposed to think about how I was going to pay back Karen Sue's medical bill (two hundred and forty nine dollars for a trip to the emergency room. She didn't even have to get stitches). Mrs. Hankey was also threatening to sue me for the mental anguish I'd inflicted on her daughter. Karen Sue's mental anguish, according to her mother, was worth about five thousand dollars. I didn't have five thousand dollars. I only had about a thousand dollars left in my bank account, after my Michigan City outlet store shopping spree.

I was supposed to sit in my room and think about how I was going to raise another four thousand, two hundred and forty-nine dollars.

Instead, I went into Douglas's room to see what he was doing.

"Hey, loser," I started to say as I barged in, as is my tradition where Douglas is concerned. "Guess what happened to me to—"

Only I didn't finish, because Douglas wasn't there.

Yeah, that's right. He wasn't in his room. About eight million comic books were lying around his bed, but no Douglas.

Which was kind of weird. Because Douglas, ever since he got sent home from State College for trying to kill himself, never went anywhere. Seriously. He just sat in his room, reading.

Oh, sure, sometimes Dad forced him to go to one of the restaurants and bus tables or whatever, but except for that and when he was at his shrink's office, Douglas was always in his room.

Always.

Maybe, I decided, he'd run out of comic books and gone downtown to get more. That made sense. Because the few times he had strayed from his room in the past six months, that's where he'd gone.

It was no fun sitting in my room, thinking about what I'd done. For one thing, I didn't think what I'd done was so bad. For another, it was August, so it was still pretty nice out, for late afternoon. I sat in the dormer window and gazed down at the street. My room is on the third floor of our house—in the attic, actually, which is the former servants' quarters. Our house is the oldest one on Lumley Lane, built around the turn of the century. The *twentieth* century. The city even came and put a plaque on it (the house, I mean), saying it was a historic landmark.

From the third floor dormer windows—my bedroom windows—you could see all up and down Lumley Lane. For once there was no white van parked across the street, monitoring my activities. That's because Special Agents Johnson and Smith were back at the school with Mark Leskowski.

Poor Mark. I had no way of knowing how he must be feeling—I mean, if Rob ever turned up dead, God only knew what I'd do, and we'd never even gone out. Well, for more than like five minutes, anyway. And if I got blamed for having done it—you know, killing him—I'd flip out for true.

Still, it looked as if Mark was everyone's lead suspect. His parents had, as Ruth had predicted, hired Mr. Abramowitz as their son's attorney—not that he'd been officially charged with the murder, but it certainly looked as if he would be.

The way I found this out was, my parents yelled up the stairs to me that they were going next door to consult with Ruth's dad about Karen Sue's case against me. Mr. Abramowitz had apparently just got home from a consult he'd been doing over at Ernie Pyle. What else could he have been consulting about over there? The new mascot uniform?

"There's some leftover ziti in the fridge," my mom hollered up the stairs to me. "Heat it up if you get hungry. Did you hear that, Douglas?"

Which was when I realized my mom didn't know Douglas was gone.

"I'll tell him," I called to her. Which wasn't a lie. I *would* tell him. When he got home.

You wouldn't think it was a big deal, a twenty-year-old guy going out for a while. But really, for Douglas, it was. A big deal, I mean. Mom was totally spastic about him, thinking he was like this delicate flower that would wilt at the slightest exposure to the elements.

Which was such a joke, really, because Douglas was no flower. He was just, you know, figuring things out. Like the rest of us.

Only he was being a little more cautious than the rest of us.

"And don't you," my mother yelled up the stairs, "even think about going anywhere, Jessica. When your father and I get home, the three of us are going to sit down for a nice long *chat.*"

Well. That certainly didn't sound like Dad had convinced her I'd been telling the truth about what Karen Sue had said. Yet, anyway.

From my dormer window, I watched them leave. They crossed our front lawn, then cut through the hedge that separated our property from the Abramowitzes', even though they were always telling me to take the long way, or the hedge would suffer permanent root damage. Whatever. I got up from the window and went downstairs to see what was up with the ziti.

I had just opened the fridge when someone turned the crank to our doorbell. Because our house is so old, it has this antique doorbell with a handle you have to turn, not a button you push.

"Coming," I called, wondering who it could be. Ruth would never ring the doorbell. She'd just walk right in. And everyone else we knew would call first before coming over.

When I got into the foyer, I saw what definitely appeared to be a masculine shape behind the lace curtain that covered the window in the front door. It looked to be about the right size and shape for Rob.

My heart, ridiculously, skipped a beat, even though I

knew perfectly well Rob would never just walk up to my front door and ring the bell. Not since I told him how much it would freak out my mom if she ever found out I liked a guy who a) wasn't college-bound and b) had spent time in the Big House.

Maybe, I thought, for one panic-stricken moment, Rob *did* see me in the back of Skip's Trans Am, and he was coming over to ask me if I was completely out of my mind, going around, spying on him like that.

But when I flung open the door, I saw that it wasn't Rob at all. My heart didn't stop its crazy gymnastics, though.

Because instead of Rob Wilkins standing on my front porch, it was Mark Leskowski.

"Hey," he said when he saw me. His smile was nervous and shy and wonderful, all at the same time. "Whew. I'm glad it was you. You know. Who answered the door. All of a sudden I was like, 'Whoa, what if her dad answers.' But it's you."

I just stood there and stared. You would have, too, if you'd opened up your front door and found your school's star quarterback standing there, smiling shyly.

"Um," Mark said, when I didn't say anything right away. "Can I, um, talk to you? Just for a few minutes?"

I looked behind me. There was no one in the house, of course. Looking behind me had been pure reflex.

The thing was, even though I'd never had a boy come over to my house to visit me before, I was pretty sure my parents wouldn't like it if I invited him in when they weren't home.

Mark must have realized what I was thinking, since he said, "Oh, I don't have to come in. We could sit out here, if you want."

I shook my head. I was still feeling a little dazed. It is not every day you open up your door and see a guy like Mark Leskowski standing on your porch.

I guess it was on account of this dazed feeling that I opened up my mouth and blurted, "Why aren't you at the memorial service?"

Mark didn't seem offended by my bluntness, however. He looked down at his feet and murmured, "I couldn't. I mean, the one today at school was bad enough. But to go back there, where it happened . . . I just couldn't."

Oh, God. My heart lurched for him. The guy was clearly hurting.

"The only time since all of this started that I've felt even semi-human was when I was talking to you," Mark said, lifting his gaze to meet mine. "I was hoping we could . . . you know. Talk some more. If you haven't eaten, I was thinking maybe we could go grab something. To eat, I mean. Nothing fancy or anything. Maybe just pizza."

Pizza. Mark Leskowski wanted to take me out for pizza.

I said, "Sure," and closed the front door behind me. "Pizza's fine."

Yeah, I know, okay? I know my mother said not to leave the house. I know I was being punished for trying to deviate Karen Sue Hankey's septum.

But look, Mark needed me, all right? You could *see* the need right there in his face.

And seriously, who else was he going to turn to? Who else but me had ever been in anything like the kind of trouble he was in? I mean, I knew what it was like to be hunted, like an animal, by the so-called authorities. I knew what it was like to have everyone, everyone in the whole world against you.

And yeah, okay, no one had ever suspected me of committing murder. But hadn't everyone at school been going around blaming me for Amber's death? Wasn't that almost the same thing?

So I went with him. I got into his car—a black BMW. It so totally figured—and we drove downtown, and no, I never once thought, *Gee, I hope he doesn't drive out into the woods and try to kill me.*

This is because, for one thing, I didn't believe Mark Leskowski was capable of killing anyone, on account of his being so sensitive and all. And for another thing, it was broad daylight. No one tries to kill someone else in broad daylight.

Furthermore, even though I am only five foot tall, I have bested bigger guys than Mark Leskowski. As Douglas is fond of pointing out, I feel no compunction whatsoever against fighting dirty if I have to.

Can I just tell you that the world looks different from the inside of a BMW? Or maybe it is just that it looks different from the inside of Mark Leskowski's BMW. His BMW has tinted windows, so everything looks kind of . . . *better* from inside his car.

Except for Mark, of course. He, I was discovering, always looks good.

Especially when, like now, he was worried. His dark eyebrows kind of furrowed together in this adorably vulnerable way . . . kind of like a golden retriever puppy that wasn't sure where it had put its ball.

"It's just that they all think I did it," he said as we started down Lumley Lane. "And I . . . I just can't believe it. I mean, that they'd think that. I loved Amber."

I murmured something encouraging. All I could think was, *Heather Montrose, please be downtown when we get there. Please see me getting out of Mark Leskowski's BMW. Please see me eating pizza with him. Please.*

It was wrong of me—so wrong—to want to be seen in the BMW of a boy whose girlfriend had, just days before, died tragically.

On the other hand, it was wrong of Heather—so wrong—to have been so mean to me about something that was in no way my fault.

"But these Feds . . . ," Mark went on. "Well, you know them. Right? I mean, they seem to know you. They're just so . . . secretive. It's like they know something. Like they have some kind of proof I did it."

"Oh," I said as we turned onto Second Street. "I'm sure they don't."

"Of course they don't," Mark said. "Because I didn't do it."

"Right," I said. Too bad I didn't have a cell phone. Because then I could make up some excuse about how I had to call Ruth, and then I could tell her I was with Mark. Mark *Leskowski.* That I was with *Mark Leskowski* in his *BMW.*

Why does every sixteen-year-old girl in the entire world have a cell phone but me?

"That's right," Mark said. "They don't. Because if they did, they'd have arrested me already. Right?"

I looked at him. Beautiful. So beautiful. No Rob Wilkins, of course. But a hottie, just the same.

"Right," I said.

"And they'd have told you. Wouldn't they? I mean, wouldn't they have told you? If they had something on me?"

"Of course they wouldn't have told me," I said. "Why would they have told me? What do you think I am, some kind of narc?"

"Of course not," Mark said. "It's just that you seem to be, you know, real friendly with one another. . . ."

I let out a bark of laughter at that.

"Sorry to disappoint you, Mark," I said. "But Special Agents Johnson and Smith and I are not exactly friends.

Basically, I have something they want, and that's about it."

Mark glanced at me curiously. We were stopped at an intersection, so it was okay that he was looking at me and not at the road, but I'd noticed that Mark also had a tendency to stare at me when he should have been paying attention to where we were going. This, in addition to his seeming to think that stop signs were mere suggestions, and that it wasn't in the least bit necessary to maintain a distance of at least two car lengths from the vehicle in front of him, led me to believe Mark wasn't the world's best driver.

"What," he asked me, "do you have that they want?"

I looked back at him, but my look wasn't curious. I was amazed. How could he not know? How could he not have heard? It had been all over the local papers for weeks, and most of the national papers for about the same amount of time. It had been on the news, and there'd even been some talk about making a movie out of the whole thing, except of course I wasn't too enthused about seeing my personal life transferred to the big screen.

"Hello," I said. "Lightning Girl. Remember?"

"Oh," he said. "That whole psychic thing. Yeah. Right."

But that wasn't the only thing Mark had forgotten about. I figured that out when he swung his car into the parking lot for Mastriani's. Mastriani's is one of my family's restaurants. It is the fanciest of the three, though it does indeed serve pizza. I thought it was a little weird that Mark was taking me to my own family's restaurant, but I figured, well, it *is* the best pizza in town, so why complain?

It wasn't until we'd walked through the door—Heather Montrose had not, unfortunately, been downtown to see me get out of Mark Leskowski's BMW—and the waitress who had been assigned to show us to our table went, "Why, Jessica. Hello," that I realized what a huge, colossal mistake I had just made.

Because of course Mark wasn't the only one forgetting things. I'd forgotten that the new waitress my dad had just hired for Mastriani's was none other than Rob's mom.

CHAPTER 8

Yeah. That's right. Rob's mom.

Not that my dad knew she was Rob's mom, of course. I mean, he might have known she had a kid and all, but he didn't know that I was sort of seeing that kid.

Well, all right, that I was madly in love with that kid.

No, my dad had hired Mrs. Wilkins because she'd been out of work after losing her job when the local plastics factory closed down, and I'd told him about her, saying she was a real nice lady and all. I never said how I knew her, though. I never went, Hey, Dad, you should hire the mother of the guy I am madly in love with, even though he won't go out with me because he considers me jailbait and he's eighteen and on probation.

Yeah. I didn't say that.

But of course up until the moment I saw Mrs. Wilkins standing there with a couple of menus in her hand, I totally forgot she worked at Mastriani's . . . that she had been working there most of the summer while I'd been away at camp, and had been doing, from what I'd heard, a real good job.

And now she was going to get to wait on me—the girl who might, if she played her cards right, one day be her daughter-in-law—while I ate pizza with the Ernie Pyle High quarterback who, by the way, appeared to be a suspect in his girlfriend's murder.

Great. Just great. I tell you, with that, in addition to Skip's apparent crush on me, everyone thinking I was responsible for Amber turning up dead, and Karen Sue Hankey's lawsuit against me, my school year was shaping up nicely, thank you.

"Hi, Mrs. Wilkins," I said, with a smile so forced, I thought my cheeks would break. "How are you?"

"Well, I'm just fine, thanks," Mrs. Wilkins said. She was a pretty lady with a lot of red hair piled up on her head with a tortoiseshell clip. "It's great to see you. I heard you were away at music camp."

"Um, yes, ma'am," I said. "Working as a counselor. I got back a couple of days ago."

And your son still hasn't called me. Three days, three days I've been back in town, and has he so much as even driven past my house on his Indian?

No. Nothing. Nada. Zilch.

"That must have been fun," Mrs. Wilkins said.

It was right then that I saw, with horror, that she was leading us to Table Seven, the "makeout" table in the darkest corner of the dining room.

No! I wanted to scream. Not the make-out table, Mrs. Wilkins! This isn't a date, I swear it! This . . . is . . . not . . . a . . . date!

"Here you go," Mrs. Wilkins said, putting the menus down on top of Table Seven. "Now you all have a seat and I'll be right with you with some ice waters. Unless you'd prefer Cokes?"

"Coke sounds good to me," Mark said.

"I'll . . . I'll just have water," I managed to choke. The make-out table! Oh, God, not the make-out table!

"Coke and a water it is, then," Mrs. Wilkins said, and then she bustled away.

Great. Just great. I knew what was going to happen now, of course. Mrs. Wilkins was going to tell Rob that she'd seen me, on a date, with Mark Leskowski. She might even tell him about the make-out table.

Then Rob was going to think I'd finally accepted his mandate that we not see each other romantically. And what was going to happen after that? I'll tell you: He was going to start thinking it'd be okay for him to go out with one of those floozies from Chick's Biker Bar, where he hangs out sometimes. How am I supposed to compete with a twenty-seven-year-old named Darla with tattoos and her own hog? I can't, I tell you. Not with an eleven o'clock curfew.

My life was over. So over.

"Hey," Mark said, lowering his menu. In the candlelight—yes, there was candlelight. Come on. It was the make-out table—he looked more handsome than ever. But what did it matter? What did it matter, how handsome Mark was? Mark wasn't the one I wanted.

"I forgot," Mark said. "You own this place, or something, don't you?"

"Something like that," I said, not even attempting to hide my misery.

"Whoa," Mark said. "I'm sorry. I mean, I don't want you to think I picked this place so I wouldn't have to pay or anything. I just really like Mastriani pizza." He put the menu down. "But we can totally go somewhere else, if you want to—"

"Oh, yeah? Where, exactly?" I asked.

"Well," he said. "There's Joe's. . . ."

"We own Joe's, too," I said with a sigh.

"Oh." Mark winced. "That means you probably own Joe Junior's, too, then, huh?"

"Yeah," I said. I lifted my chin. Okay. It was the make-out table. But that didn't mean I had to make out with Mark Leskowski. Not that that would be such a sacrifice and all, but, under the circumstances, it would hardly be appropriate.

"Look, it's all right," I said, trying to rally my downtrodden spirits. "We can stay. You just have to tip really good, okay? Because I . . . know this waitress. Really well."

"No problem," Mark said, and then he started asking me what I liked on my pizza.

Look, despite all the evidence to the contrary, I'm not the world's biggest dope. I knew why Mark had asked me out, and it wasn't because since I'd started wearing miniskirts to school he'd suddenly realized what a great pair of legs I've got. It wasn't even because in the guidance office earlier that day we'd had that lovely little bonding moment, before the Feds so rudely busted in on us.

No, Mark had asked me out because he thought he could pump me for information . . . information I didn't have. Did Special Agents Johnson and Smith suspect him of murdering his girlfriend? Maybe.

Or maybe they'd just wanted to ask him some questions, so they could figure out who else might possibly have done it.

And hadn't I wanted to do the exact same thing? Pump him for information, I mean, about Amber's last moments on earth . . . or at least her last moments with Mark? Because however strenuously I tried to deny that Amber's death was my fault, there was still a part of me that felt like, if I'd only been around, it wouldn't have happened. I was convinced that if Heather and those guys had managed to reach me, I'd have been able to find Amber before she was killed. I knew it. I knew it the way I knew that when Kurt, the head chef at Mastriani's, found out I was sitting at Table Seven, he'd arrange the pepperonis on my pizza in the shape of a heart. Which he did, to my utter mortification.

Mark hardly even noticed. That's how strung out he was about the whole being-suspected-of-his-girlfriend's-murder thing. He just handed me a slice, and, as we ate, we talked about how it felt to be grilled by the FBI.

And the sad part was, that was about all we had in common. The both of us having been interrogated by the FBI, I mean. That, and our mutual dislike of Karen Sue Hankey. Mark's whole life, it appeared, was about football. He was being scouted, he explained, by the coaches at several Big Ten schools, and even a couple out east. He was going to take the best scholarship he could get, and play college ball until the NFL came knocking.

This seemed like a reasonable plan to me, except that even I, a football ignoramus, knew that the NFL did not come knocking on the door of every college player. What if, I asked, that plan fell through? What was his backup plan? Medical school? Law school? What?

Mark stared at me blankly over our pepperoni with extra

cheese. "Backup plan?" he echoed. "There's no backup plan."

I thought maybe I hadn't expressed my meaning with sufficient clarity. "No," I said. "Really. Like what if you don't make it to the pros? Then what?"

Mark shook his head, but more like he was flicking away something unpleasant that had landed on his head than actually disagreeing with me.

"Failure," he said, "is unacceptable."

There it was again. The whole unacceptable thing he'd mentioned back in the guidance office. These athletes, I couldn't help noting, really took their calling seriously.

"Unacceptable?" I coughed. "Yeah, okay. Failure is unacceptable, of course. But sometimes it happens. And then . . . well, you have to accept it."

Mark regarded me calmly from across the table.

"That's a common mistake," he said. "Many people actually believe that. But not me. That's what makes me different than everybody else, Jess. Because to me, failure is simply not an option."

Oh. Well. Okay.

It was kind of weird, I have to say, being out with Amber Mackey's boyfriend. Not just the fact that we were being waited on by the mother of the guy I really liked, either. No, it was the whole Amber-Was-Here thing. I couldn't help thinking, What had Amber seen in this guy? Yeah, he was totally buff, but he was also kind of . . . boring. I mean, he didn't know anything about music, or motorcycles, or anything fun like that. He'd seen most of the latest movies, but the ones I thought were good, he hadn't liked, and the one he'd liked, I'd thought were stupid beyond belief. And he didn't have time for anything else, like reading books or watching TV, because he was always at football practice.

Seriously. Not even comic books. Not even the WWE.

Not that Amber had been Ms. Intellectual herself. But she at least had had interests beyond cheerleading. I mean, she'd always been organizing bake sales for some charity or another. It seemed like every week she had a new cause, from collecting baby things for unwed mothers to holding food drives for starving people in African nations none of us had ever even heard of.

But maybe I was being too hard on Mark. I mean, at least he had a goal, right? A lot of guys don't. My brother Douglas, for instance. Well, I guess his goal is to get better. But what is he going to do when he's accomplished that?

Rob has a goal. He wants to have a motorcycle repair shop of his own. Until he's saved up enough money for it, he's going to work in his uncle's garage.

You know who doesn't have a goal? Yeah, that'd be me. No goal. I mean, beyond keeping the Federal Bureau of Investigation from finding out I'm still psychic. Oh, and getting a Harley when I turn eighteen. And one day being Mrs. Robert Wilkins.

But I have to have a career first. Before I can get married, I mean. And I don't even know what kind I want. You know, career-wise. I mean, you can't make a living finding missing kids. Well, you probably could, but I wouldn't want to. You can't take money for doing something any decent human being should do for free. I'd attended church often enough to know *that*, at least.

So I told myself to stop being so critical of Mark. The guy was going through a hard time.

And he did leave a really nice tip for Mrs. Wilkins, so that was all right.

As we were on our way out, she waved at us and said, "Y'all have fun now."

Y'all have fun now. My heart lurched. I did not want to have fun. Not with Mark Leskowski. The only person I wanted to have fun with was Rob Wilkins. Your son Rob, okay, Mrs. Wilkins? He's the only person I want to have fun with. So would you please do me a favor and DON'T tell him you saw me here tonight with Mark Leskowski? Please? Would you do that for me?

And for Pete's sake, whatever else you do, DON'T tell him about the make-out table. For the love of God, don't mention the make-out table.

Only of course I couldn't say that to her. I mean, how could I say that to her?

So instead all I did was wave back at her, feeling sick to my stomach, and say, "Thank you!"

Oh, God. I was so dead.

I tried not to think about it. I tried to be all bright and chipper, like Amber had always been. Seriously. No matter how early in the morning it was, or how foul the weather outside, Amber had always been cheerful in homeroom. Amber had really liked school. Amber had been one of those people who'd woken up every day and gone, Good morning, Sunshine, to herself in the mirror.

At least, she'd always seemed that way to me.

Of course, a fat lot of good it had done her, in the end.

I tried not to think about this as Mark walked me back to his car. I tried to keep my mind on happier subjects.

The only problem was, I couldn't think of any.

Happy things, I mean.

"I guess you probably have to be getting home," Mark said as he opened the passenger door for me.

"Yeah," I said. "I mean, I'm sort of in trouble. For the whole Karen Sue Hankey thing, I mean."

"Okay," Mark said. "But do you want to maybe stop at the Moose for a minute? For a shake or something?"

The Moose. The Chocolate Moose. That was the ice-cream stand across from the movie house on Main where all the popular kids hung out. Seriously. Ruth and I hadn't been to the Moose since we were little kids because as soon as we'd hit puberty, we'd realized only the beautiful people from school were allowed to go there. If you weren't a jock or a cheerleader and you showed up at the Moose, everybody there gave you dirty looks.

Which was actually okay, because the ice cream there wasn't as good as it was at the Thirty-one Flavors down the street. Still, the idea of going to the Moose with Mark Leskowski . . . well, it was strange and off-putting and thrilling, all at the same time.

"Sure," I said, casually as if boys asked me to go to the Moose with them every day of the week. "A shake'd be good, I guess."

There weren't many people hanging out at the Moose at first. Just Mark and me, and a couple of Wrestlerettes, who gave me the evil eye when I first walked up. But when they saw I was with Mark Leskowski, they relaxed, and even smiled. Todd Mintz was there with a couple of his friends. He grunted a hello to me and high-fived Mark.

I had a mint-chocolate-chip blizzard. Mark had something with Heath candy bar crunches sprinkled in. We sat on top of a picnic table that had a view all the way up Main Street, right up to the courthouse. The courthouse and, I couldn't help noticing, the jail. Behind the jail, the sun was setting in all these vibrant colors. It was beautiful and all—a true Indian summer sunset. But it was still, you know. The *jail*.

The jail where Mark might end up, admiring the sunset from behind bars.

I think he sort of realized that, too, because he turned away from the sunset and started asking me about my classes. That's desperation for you, when you start asking someone about their classes. I mean, if I hadn't realized before then that Mark and I had nothing in common, that would have been a real big clue.

Fortunately, a car pulled up about midway through my description of my U.S. Government class, and the people who piled out of it all started calling out Mark's name.

Only it wasn't, as I'd first thought, because they were so glad to see him. It was because they had something to tell him.

"Oh, my God." It was Tisha Murray, from my homeroom. She still had on her uniform from the memorial service—Tisha was on the varsity cheerleading squad—but she'd apparently left her pompons in the car.

"Oh, God, I'm so glad we found you," she gushed. "We were looking everywhere. Look, you've got to come quick. It's an emergency!"

Mark slid off the picnic table, his shake forgotten.

"What?" he asked, reaching out to take Tisha by either shoulder. "What's happened? What do you need me to do?"

"Not *you*," Tisha said, rudely. Except I don't think she meant to be rude. She was just too hysterical to remember social niceties. *"Her."*

She pointed. At me.

"You," Tisha said to me. "We need you."

"Me?" I nearly fell off the picnic table. Never before had a member of the Ernie Pyle varsity cheerleading squad expressed even the slightest interest in me. Well, except for the past two days, when they'd been berating me for letting Amber die. "What do you need *me* for?"

"Because it's happened again!" Tisha said. "Only this time it's Heather. He's got her. Whoever killed Amber has got Heather now! You've got to find her. Do you hear me? You've got to find her, before he strangles her, too!"

CHAPTER 9

It probably isn't politic to slap a cheerleader. That's exactly what I did, though.

Hey, she was hysterical, all right? Isn't that what you're supposed to do to people who can't get ahold of themselves?

Looking back, though, it probably wasn't the smartest thing to do. Because all it did was reduce Tisha to tears. Not just tears, either, but big baby sobs. Mark had to get the story out of Jeff Day, who didn't know nearly as many words as Tisha did.

"We were at the memorial thingie," he said as Tisha wept in the arms of Vicky Huff, a Pompette. "You know, up at the quarry. The girls threw a bunch of the wreaths and flowers and crap from the service into the water. It was all symbolic and shit."

Have I mentioned that Jeff Day is not exactly on the honor roll?

"And then it was time to go, and everyone went back to their cars . . . everyone except Heather. She was just . . . gone."

"What do you mean," Mark demanded, "by *gone?*"

Jeff shrugged his massive shoulders.

"You know, Mark," he said. "Just . . . just gone."

"That's unacceptable," Mark said.

I wasn't sure what Mark was referring to . . . the fact that Heather had disappeared, or Jeff's shrugging off that disappearance. When, however, Jeff stammered, "What I mean . . . what I mean is, we looked, but we couldn't find her," I realized Mark had meant Jeff's answer. Jeff's hurrying to correct himself reminded me that, as quarterback, Mark was in a position of some authority over these guys.

"People don't do that, Jeff," I said. "People just don't just disappear."

"I know," Jeff said, looking a little miserable. "But Heather did."

"It was just like in that movie," Tisha said, lifting her tear-stained face. "That *Blair Witch* movie, where those kids disappeared in the woods. It was just like that. One second, Heather was there, and the next, she was gone. We called and called for her, and looked everywhere, but it was like . . . like she had vanished. Like that witch had gotten her."

I regarded Tisha with raised eyebrows.

"I highly doubt," I said, "that Heather's disappearance is the result of witchcraft, Tisha."

"No," Tisha said, wiping her eyes with her twig-like fingers. The tiniest member of the varsity squad, Tisha was the one who always ended up on the top of the trophy pyramid, or came popping up into the air, to land in a cradle of arms on the gym floor beneath her. "I know it wasn't really a witch. But it was probably, you know, a Grit."

"A Grit," I said.

"Yeah. I saw this movie once about these Grits who lived in the mountains, and they totally kidnapped this woman. She was an Olympic biathlete, and they kidnapped her and tried to make her, like, tote their water and all. Until she, like, escaped."

I can't believe my life sometimes. I really can't.

"Maybe some freaky Grits like those ones in the movie, who live out in the woods by the quarry, got her. I've seen them out there, you know. They live in shacks, with no running water or electricity, and, like, an outhouse." Tisha started sobbing all over again. "They've probably stuffed her in the bottom of their outhouse!"

I had to give Tisha her propers for having such a colorful imagination. But still, this seemed a bit much to me.

"Let me see if I have this straight," I said. "You think a deranged hillbilly, who lives out by Pike's Quarry, has kidnapped Heather and stuffed her down his toilet."

"I've heard of that kinda thing happening," Jeff Day said.

But instead of supporting his fellow team member, Mark snapped, "That's the stupidest thing I ever heard."

Jeff Day was the kind of guy who, if anybody else had called him stupid, would have slammed his fist into the speaker's face. But not, evidently, if it happened to be Mark Leskowski. Mark, it appeared, was next to godlike in Jeff's book.

"Sorry, dude," he murmured, looking shamefaced.

Mark ignored his teammate.

"Have any of you," he wanted to know, "called the police?"

"Course we did," another player, Roy Hicks, said indignantly, not wanting to look bad, the way his teammate Jeff had, in front of the QB.

"A bunch of sheriff's deputies came up to the quarry," Tisha chimed in, "and they're helping everyone look for her. They even brought some of those sniffer dogs. We only left"—she turned mascara-smudged eyes toward me—"to look for *her.*" Tisha could not seem to remember my name. And why should she? I was so far out of her social sphere as to be invisible. . . .

Except when it came to rescuing her friends from psychotic hillbillies, apparently.

"You've got to find her," Tisha said, her damp eyes aglow

with the last rays of the setting sun. *"Please.* Before . . . it's too late."

This blew. I mean it. How was I supposed to convince the Federal Bureau of Investigation that I don't have psychic powers anymore, when I can't even convince my own peers of it?

"Look, Tisha," I said, aware that not just Tisha was gazing at me hopefully, but also Mark, Jeff Day, Todd Mintz, Roy Hicks, and a veritable Whitman's Sampler of cheerleaders. "I don't . . . I mean, I can't . . ."

"Please," Tisha whispered. "She's my best friend. How would *you* like it if your best friend got kidnapped?"

Damn.

Look, it wasn't like I harbored ill feelings toward Heather Montrose. I did, of course, but that wasn't the point. The point was, I was trying to keep a low profile with the whole psychic thing.

But if Tisha was right, then there was a serial killer loose. He might very well have Heather in his clutches, the same way that, a few days earlier, he'd had Amber in his clutches. Could I really sit around and let a girl—even a girl like Heather Montrose, who, after Karen Sue Hankey, was one of my least favorite people—die?

No. No, I could not.

"I don't have ESP anymore," I said, just so that later on, no one would be able to say I'd agreed to any of this. "But I'll give it a try."

Tisha exhaled gustily, as if she'd been holding her breath until I gave my answer.

"Oh, thank you," she cried. "Thank you!"

"Yeah," I said. "Whatever. But look, I need something of hers."

"Something of whose?" Tisha cocked her head, making her look a lot like a bird. A sparrow, maybe, eyeing a worm.

Yeah. That'd be me. I'd be the worm.

"Something of Heather's," I explained, slowly, so she'd be sure to understand. "Do you have a sweater of hers, or something?"

"I have her pompons," Tisha said, and she bounced back toward the car she'd arrived in.

Todd Mintz looked perplexed. "That's really how you find them?" he asked. "By touching something that belongs to the missing person?"

"Yeah," I said. "Well. Sort of."

It wasn't, of course. Because here's the thing: since that day last spring, when I was hit by lightning, I'd found a lot of people, all right. But I'd only found one of them while I'd been awake. Seriously. Everybody else, it had taken sleep to summon their location to, as Douglas had put it, my mind's eye. That's how my particular psychic ability worked. While I slept.

Which meant that, as a future career option, I was going to have to rule out fortune-telling. You were never going to catch me sitting in a tent with a crystal ball and a big old turban on my head. I could no sooner predict the future than I could fly. All I can do—all I've *ever* been able to do, since the day of that storm—is find missing people.

And I can only do that in my sleep.

Except once. One time, when one of the campers I'd been assigned to watch had run away, I'd hugged his pillow and gotten this weird flash. Really. It was just like a picture inside my head, of exactly where the kid was, and what he was doing.

Whether or not this would happen with the help of Heather's pompons, I had no way of knowing. But I knew that if the same person who'd killed Amber had gotten hold of Heather, we couldn't afford to wait until morning to find her.

"Here." Tisha rushed up to me and shoved two big balls of shimmery silver and white streamers into my hands. "Now find her, quick."

I looked down at the pompons. They were surprisingly heavy. No wonder all the girls on the squad had such cut arm muscles. I'd thought it was from all those cartwheels, but really, it was from hauling these things around.

"Uh, Tisha," I said, aware that every single patron of the Chocolate Moose was looking down at me. "I can't, um . . . I think maybe I need to go home and try it. How about if I come up with anything, I'll call you and let you know?"

Tisha didn't seem particularly enthused by this idea, but

what else could I say? I wasn't going to stand there and inhale the scent of Heather Montrose's pompons. (Which was how I'd found Shane. By smelling his pillow, though, not his pompons.)

Fortunately, Mark, at least, seemed to understand, and, taking me by the elbow, said, "I should be getting you home, anyway."

And so, under the watchful gazes of most of Ernie Pyle High's elite, Mark Leskowski escorted me back to his BMW, tucked me gently into the passenger seat, and then got behind the wheel and drove me slowly home.

Slowly not because he didn't want our evening together to end, but because he was so busy talking, I guess it was hard for him to accelerate at the same time.

"You get what this means, don't you?" he asked as we inched down Second Street. "If Heather really is missing—if the same person who killed Amber really has done the same thing to Heather—well, they can't keep on suspecting me, can they? Because I was with you the whole time. Right? I mean, right? Those FBI people can't say I had anything to do with it."

"Right," I said, looking down at Heather's pompons. Was this going to work? I wondered. I mean, would a lapful of pompons really lead me to a missing girl? It didn't seem very likely, but I closed my eyes, dug my fingers into the feathery strands, and tried to concentrate.

"And before I was with you," Mark was saying, "I was with

them. Seriously. I came straight to your house from my interview with them. The FBI guys, I mean. So I never had an opportunity to do anything to Heather. She was all the way out at the quarry, with everybody else. And that waitress. She saw me with you, too."

"Right." It was really hard to concentrate, what with Mark talking so much.

Oh, well, I thought. I'll just wait until I get home, and try it there, in the privacy of my own bedroom. I'll have plenty of opportunity, once I get home.

Only of course I didn't. Because my parents had gotten home before I had, and were waiting for me on the front porch, their expressions on the grim side.

Busted again!

Mark, as he pulled into our driveway, went, "Are those your parents?"

"Yes," I said, gulping. I was so dead.

"They look nice." Mark waved at them as he got out of his car and walked around it to open my door. One thing you had to say about Mark Leskowski: He was a gentleman and all.

"Hello, Mr. and Mrs. Mastriani," he called to them. "I hope you don't mind my taking your daughter out for a quick bite to eat. I tried to have her home promptly, as it's a school night."

Whoa. Didn't Mark realize he was laying it on a little thick? I mean, my parents aren't morons.

My mom and dad just sat there—my mom on the porch

swing, my dad on the porch steps—and stared as I emerged from Mark's BMW. I had never seen them looking so worried. That was it. I was dead meat.

"Well, it was very nice to meet you, Mr. and Mrs. Mastriani," Mark said. Exercising some of that charm that made him such an effective leader on the ball field, he added, "And may I say that I have enjoyed dining in your restaurants many times? They are particularly fine."

My dad, looking a little astonished, went, "Um, thank you, son."

To me, Mark said, picking up the hand that was not clutching Heather Montrose's pompons, "Thank you, Jessica, for being such a good listener. I really needed that tonight."

He didn't kiss me or anything. He just gave my hand a squeeze, winked, climbed back into his car, and drove away.

Leaving me to face the firing squad alone.

I turned around and squared my shoulders. Really, this was ridiculous. I mean, I am sixteen years old. A grown woman, practically. If I want to punch a girl in the face and then go have a nice dinner with the quarterback of the football team, well, that is my God-given prerogative. . . .

"Mom," I said. "Dad. Listen. I can explain—"

"Jessica," my mother said, getting up from the porch swing. "Where is your brother?"

I blinked at them. The sun had set, and it wasn't easy to see them in the gloom. Still, there wasn't anything wrong with my ears. My mom had just asked me where my brother was. Not where I had been. Where my brother was.

Was it possible that I was not in trouble for going out after all?

"You mean Douglas?" I asked stupidly, because I still could not quite believe my good fortune.

"No," my father said sarcastically. He wasn't worried enough, apparently, to have lost his sense of humor. "Your brother Michael. Of course we mean Douglas. When's the last time you saw him?"

"I don't know," I said. "This morning, I guess."

"Oh, God!" My mother started pacing the length of the porch floor. "I knew it. He's run away. Joe, I'm calling the police."

"He's twenty years old, Toni," my father said. "If he wants to go out, he can go out. There's no law against it."

"But his medicine!" my mom cried. "How do we know he took his medication before he left?"

My dad shrugged. "His doctor says he's been taking it regularly."

"But how do we know he took it *today*?" My mother pulled open the screen door. "That's it. I'm calling the—"

We all heard it at the same time. Whistling. Someone was coming down Lumley Lane, whistling.

I knew who it was at once, of course. Douglas had always been the best whistler in the family. It was he, in fact, who'd taught me to do it. I could still only manage a few folk songs, but Douglas could whistle whole symphony pieces, without even seeming to pause for breath.

When he emerged into the circle of light thrown by the porch lamp, which my mother had hastily turned on, he stopped, and blinked a few times. From one of his hands dangled a bag from the comic book store downtown.

"Hey," he said, looking at us. "What's this? Family meeting? And you started without me?"

My mother just stood there, sputtering. My dad heaved a sigh and got up.

"There," he said to my mother. "You see, Toni? I told you he was all right. Come on, let's go inside. I'm missing the ballgame."

My mother, without a word, turned and went into the house.

I looked at Douglas and shook my head.

"Ordinarily," I said, "I'd be truly pissed at you for going off like that and not telling them where you were going or when you'd be home. But since they were so worried about you, they forgot to be mad at me, I will forgive you, this time."

"Well," Douglas said. "That's gracious of you." We went up the porch steps together, and he looked down at the pompons in my hand. "Who do you think you are?" he wanted to know. "Marcia Brady?"

"No," I said with a sigh. "Madame Zenda."

CHAPTER 10

It didn't work, of course.

The pompons, I mean. All I got from them was a big fat nothing . . . and some of those streamery things up my nose, from when I tried sniffing them.

This isn't as weird as it sounds, since the vision I'd had about Shane seemed to have had an olfactory trigger. But what had worked with Shane's pillow most definitely did not work with Heather's pompons.

Maybe because I had actually liked Shane, and had felt responsible when he'd run away from the cabin we'd shared.

But Heather? Yeah, don't like her so much. And don't really feel responsible for her disappearing, either.

So why couldn't I fall asleep? I mean, if I felt so damned not responsible for what had happened to Heather, why was I lying there, staring at the ceiling?

Gee, I don't know. Maybe it was because of all the phone calls I'd gotten that evening, demanding to know why I hadn't found her already. Seriously, if I'd heard from every single member of the pep squad—with the exception of Heather and Amber, of course—I would not have been surprised. My mom, who was already in what could in no way be described as a good mood, on account of Mrs. Hankey's pending lawsuit against me and Douglas's sudden streak of wanderlust, threatened to disconnect the phone if it rang one more time.

Finally I was like, Go ahead, because I was sick of telling people I didn't know anything. It was bad enough the entire student population of Ernest Pyle High seemed to think I was still in full possession of my psychic powers. Now they apparently thought that I was refusing to use them for certain people, because I resented their popularity.

"Oh, no," Ruth said when I called her to tell her what was going on. "They did not say that to you."

"Yeah," I said. "They did. Tisha came right out with it. She was all, 'Jess, if you're holding back on us because of what Heather said to you in the caf the other day, may I just point out that she has been on the Homecoming court two years running, and that it would behoove you to get to work."

Ruth said, "Tisha Murray did not say the word 'behoove.'"

"Well," I said. "You know what I mean."

"So I guess this means Mark didn't kill Amber after all." I heard a scratching sound, which meant that Ruth was filing her nails as she talked, as was her custom. "I mean, if he was with you when Heather disappeared."

"I guess," I said.

"Which means, you know. He's Do-able."

"He's not just Do-able," I said. "He's a hottie. And I think he kind of likes me." I told Ruth about how Mark had squeezed my hand and winked before leaving me to my fate with my parents. I did not mention that he seemed to have no goals other than making it to the pros. This would not have impressed Ruth.

"Wow," Ruth said. "If you start going out with the Cougars' quarterback, do you have any idea what kind of parties and stuff you're going to get invited to? Jess, you could run for Homecoming Queen. And maybe even win. If you grew your hair out."

"One thing at a time," I said. "First I have to prove he didn't kill his last girlfriend, by finding the guy who did. And," I added, "besides. What about Rob?"

"What *about* Rob?" Ruth demanded. "Jess, Rob's totally dissed you, all right? It's been three whole days since you got back, and he hasn't even called. Forget the Jerk. Go out with the quarterback. He's never been arrested for anything."

"Yet," I said.

"Jess, he didn't do it. This thing with Heather proves it."

There was a click, and then Skip went, "Hello? Hello? Who's using this line?"

"Skip," Ruth said, with barely suppressed fury. "I am on the phone."

"Oh, yeah?" Skip said. "With who?"

"With whom," Ruth thundered. "And I'm talking to Jess, all right? Now hang up. I'll be off in a minute."

"Hi, Jess," Skip said, instead of hanging up like he was supposed to.

"Hi, Skip," I said. "Thanks again for the ride this morning."

"Jess," Ruth roared. "DO NOT ENCOURAGE HIM!"

"I better go, I guess," Skip said. "Bye, Jess."

"Bye, Skip," I said. There was a click, and Skip was gone.

"You," Ruth said, "had better do something about this."

"Aw, Ruth," I said. "Don't worry about it. Skip and I are cool."

"No, you are not cool. He has a crush on you. I told you not to play so many video games with him, back at the lakehouse."

I wanted to ask her what else I'd been supposed to do, since she had never been around, but restrained myself.

"So what are you going to do now?" Ruth wanted to know.

"I don't know. Go to bed, I guess. I mean, by morning I'll know. Where Heather is, I mean."

"You hope," Ruth said. "You know, you've never looked

for somebody you didn't like before. Maybe it only works with people you don't hold in complete contempt."

"God," I said before hanging up, "I hope that's not true."

But apparently it was, because when I did wake up, after seeming to have nodded off somewhere around midnight, I did not even remember I was supposed to be finding Heather. All I could think was, *Now what was* that?

This was because I'd wakened, not to the sound of my alarm, or the twittering of birds outside my bedroom window, but to a sharp, rattling noise.

Seriously. I opened my eyes, and instead of morning light pouring into my room, there was nothing but shadow. When I turned my head to look at my alarm clock, I saw why. It was only two in the morning.

Why, I wondered, had I woken up at two? I never wake up in the middle of the night for no reason. I am a sound sleeper. Mike always joked that a twister could rip through town, and I wouldn't so much as roll over.

Then I heard it again, what sounded like hailstones against my window.

Only they weren't hailstones, I realized this time. They were actual stones. Someone was throwing *rocks* at my window.

I threw back the blankets, wondering who on earth it could be. Heather's friends were the only people I knew who might be anxious enough to see me to pull a stunt like this.

But none of them had any way of knowing that my bedroom was the only one in the house that faced the street, or that it was the one with the dormer windows.

Staggering to one of those windows, I peered through the screen. Somebody, I saw, was standing in my front yard. There was hardly any moon, but from what little light it shed, I could see that the figure was tall and distinctly male—the distance across the shoulders was too wide for it to be a girl.

What guy did I know, I wondered, who would throw a bunch of rocks at my windows in the middle of the night? What guy did I know who even knew where my bedroom windows were?

Then it hit me.

"Skip," I hissed down at the figure in my yard. "What the hell do you think you're doing? Go home!"

The figure tipped his face up toward me and hissed back, "Who's Skip?"

I jumped back from the window with a start. That wasn't Skip. That wasn't Skip at all.

My heart slamming in my chest, I stood in the center of my bedroom, uncertain what to do. This had never happened to me before, of course. I was not the kind of girl who had guys tossing pebbles at her window every night. Claire Lippman, maybe, was used to that sort of thing, but I was not. I didn't know what to do.

"Mastriani," I heard him call in a loud stage whisper.

There was no chance, of course, of him waking my parents, whose room was all the way at the opposite end of the house. But he might wake Douglas, whose windows looked out toward the Abramowitzes', and who was a light sleeper besides. I didn't want Douglas waking up and finding out that his little sister had a nocturnal caller. Who knew if that kind of thing might cause an episode.

I darted forward and, leaning over the sill, with my face pressed up against the screen, called softly, "Stay there. I'll be right down."

Then I spun around and reached for the first articles of clothing I could find—my jeans and a T-shirt. Slipping into some sneakers, I hopped down the hall to the bathroom, where I rinsed my mouth with some water and toothpaste— hey, a lady does not greet her midnight callers with morning breath. That much I *do* know about these things.

Then I crept down the stairs, carefully avoiding the notoriously creaky step just before the second landing, until I reached the front door and quietly unlocked it.

Then I stepped into the cool night air and Rob's warm embrace.

Look, I know, okay? Three days. *Three days* I'd been home, and he hadn't called. I should have been mad. I should have been livid. At the very least, I should have greeted him with cold civility, maybe a sneer and a "Hey, how you doing," instead of how I did greet him, which was by throwing my arms around him.

But I just couldn't help myself. He just looked so adorable standing there in the moonlight, all big and tall and manly and everything. You could tell he'd just taken a shower, because the dark hair on the back of his head was still wet, and he smelled of soap and shampoo and Goop, that stuff mechanics use on their hands to get the grease and motor oil out from beneath their nails. How could I not jump into his arms? You'd have done the exact same thing.

Except that Rob must have been supremely unaware of how stunningly hot he was, since he seemed kind of surprised to find me clinging to him the way those howler monkeys on the Discovery Channel cling to their mothers.

"Well," he said. He didn't exactly seem displeased. Just a little taken aback. "Hey. Nice to see you, too."

Well. Hey. Nice to see you, too. Not exactly what a girl expects to hear from the guy who has just woken her in the middle of the night by throwing pebbles at her bedroom window. A "Jess, I love you madly, run away with me" might have been nice. Heck, I'd have settled for an "I missed you."

But what did I get? Oh, no. That'd be a big "Well. Hey. Nice to see you, too."

I am telling you, my life *sucks*.

I let go of him and, since I was hanging about a foot in the air, Rob being that much taller than me, slithered back to the ground. Which I then stared at, in abject mortification. I had just, I could not help feeling, made a great big fool out of myself in front of him.

Again.

"Did I wake you up?" Rob wanted to know as we stood there on my front porch, awkward as two strangers, thanks to my underdeveloped social skills.

"Um," I muttered. "Yeah." What did he think? It was *two in the morning.* A perfect time, in my opinion, for a little romance.

But not, apparently, to Rob.

"Sorry," he said. He had shoved his hands into the pockets of his jeans, but not because he had to in order to keep himself from snatching me up and raining kisses down upon my face, like the heroes in the books I sometimes catch my mom reading, but rather because he didn't know what else to do with them. "I just found out you were back in town. My mom said you came into the restaurant tonight. Or last night, I guess."

Oh, God! His mother had told! Mrs. Wilkins had told him about waiting on me and Mark Leskowski at Table Seven. The make-out table! I sincerely hoped she'd mentioned that Mark and I had not, in point of fact, been making out.

"Yeah," I said. "I got back Sunday night. I had to. You know. School. It started on Monday."

What I did not add, though I wanted to, was, "You moron."

And I was glad I hadn't, when he said, "I know. I mean, I figured it out tonight, that of course school must have started again. Last week of August and all. It's just that when you aren't going anymore, it's kind of hard to keep track."

Of course! Of course he hadn't known I was back! He wasn't in school anymore. How would he know it had started on Monday? And, being at work all day, it wasn't as if he'd have seen the buses, or anything.

So that's why he hadn't called or stopped by. Well, that and the fact that I'd asked him not to, on account of my parents not knowing about him, and all.

I gazed up at him, feelings of warmth and happiness coursing through me. Until Rob asked, "So, who's the guy?"

Oops.

The feelings of warmth and happiness vanished.

"Guy?" I echoed, stalling for time. A part of me was going, *Why, he's jealous! Ruth's stupid Rules thing actually works,* while another part went, *Hey, he's the one who insists on the two of you not dating, and now he's got a problem because you're seeing someone else? Tell him to deal with it,* while a third part of me felt sorry for hurting him, if indeed he was hurt, which was impossible to tell from his voice or expression, both of which were neutral.

Way neutral.

"Yeah," Rob said. "The one my mom saw you with."

"Oh, *that* guy," I said. "That's just, um, Mark."

"Mark?" Rob took his hand out of his pocket and ran his fingers through his still-damp hair. Which didn't, I decided, mean anything, really. "Yeah? You like him? This Mark guy?"

Oh, my God. I could not believe I was having this conversation. I mean, I was not the one with the problem with his arrest record and his age and all of that. *He* was the one who seemed to think he'd be robbing the cradle if he went out with me, even though he was only two years older and I am, I think, exceptionally mature for my age. And now he was upset because I'd gone out with somebody else—somebody else who, by the way, was his exact age, just minus the conviction?

So far, anyway.

I almost wished Ruth had been around to witness this. It was truly classic.

On the other hand, of course, I was wracked with guilt. Because if I'd had a choice between going out for pizza with Mark Leskowski and going to the dump to scrounge for used car parts with Rob Wilkins, I'd have chosen the dump any day of the week.

Which was why, a second later, I realized I could take it no longer. That's right, I broke the Rules. I ruined all that hard work, all that not calling, all that not chasing him, all that making him think I liked someone else, by saying, "Look, it's not what you think. Mark's girlfriend is the one who turned up dead on Sunday. I just went out with him to, you know, talk. The Feds are after him, now, see, so we have a lot in common."

Both of Rob's hands shot out of his pockets and landed, to my great surprise, on my shoulders. The next thing I knew, he was shaking me, rather hard.

"Mark Leskowski?" he wanted to know. "You went out with Mark Leskowski? Are you nuts? Are you trying to get yourself killed?"

"No," I said, between shakes. "He didn't do it."

"Bullshit!" Rob stopped shaking me. "Everyone knows he did it. Everyone except you, apparently."

I shushed him. "Do you want to wake my parents up?" I hissed. "That's the last thing I need, them finding me out on the front porch in the middle of the night with—"

"Hey," Rob said. "At least I'm not a murderer!"

"Neither is Mark," I said.

"Says you."

"No, says everyone. I know he didn't kill Amber, Rob, because while we were out together, another girl disappeared, Heather—"

I broke off with a gasp, as if somebody had pinched me. Pinched me? It felt more as if somebody had punched me.

"What is it?" Rob asked, grabbing my arm and looking down at me worriedly, all of his anger forgotten. "What's wrong, Jess? Are you all right?"

"I am," I said, when I had caught my breath. "But Heather Montrose isn't."

A fact I knew for certain, because the moment I'd uttered

her name, I remembered the dream I'd been having, just as Rob's pebbles had woken me up.

Dream? What am I talking about? It had been a nightmare.

Except, of course, that it wasn't. A nightmare, I mean.

Because that was the thing. It had been real.

All too real.

CHAPTER 11

"Come on," I said to Rob as I darted down the porch steps into the yard. "We've got to get to her, before it's too late."

"Get to whom?" Rob followed me, looking confused. On him, of course, even confusion looked way sexy.

"Heather," I said, pausing by the dogwood tree at the end of the driveway. "Heather Montrose. She's the girl who disappeared this afternoon. I think I know where she is. We've got to go to her, now, before—"

"Before what?" Rob wanted to know.

I swallowed. "Before he comes back."

"Before who comes back? Jess, what, exactly, did you see?"

I shivered, even though it couldn't have been much under seventy outside.

But it wasn't the temperature that was giving me goose-bumps. It was the memory of my dream about Heather.

Rob's question was a good one. Just what *had* I seen? Not much. Blackness, mostly.

It was what I had felt that had scared me most. And what I'd felt was surely what Heather was feeling.

Cold. That was one thing. Really, really cold.

And wet. And cramped. And in pain. A lot of pain, actually.

And fear. Fear that he was coming. Not just fear, either, but terror. Stark white terror, unlike anything I had ever known. That Heather had ever known, I mean.

No. That *we* had ever known.

"We've got to go," I said with a moan, my fingers sinking into his arm. Good thing I keep my nails short, or Rob would have been the one in some pain. "We've got to go *now*."

"Okay," Rob said, prying my hand from his arm and taking it, instead, in his warm fingers. "Okay, whatever you say. You want to go find her? We'll go find her. Come on. My bike's over here."

Rob had parked his bike a little ways down the street. When we got to it, he opened up the compartment in the back and handed me his spare helmet and an extremely beat-up leather jacket he kept in there for emergencies, along with some other weird stuff, like a flashlight, tools, bottled water and, for reasons I'd never been able to fathom, a box of strawberry Nutri-Grain bars. I think this was just because he liked them.

"Okay," he said, as I swung onto the seat behind him. "All set?"

I nodded, not trusting myself to speak. I was afraid if I did, I might start screaming. In my dream, that's what Heather had wanted to do. Scream.

Only she couldn't. Because there was something in her mouth.

"Uh, Mastriani?" Rob said.

I took a deep breath. All right. It was all right. It was happening to Heather, not to me.

"Yeah?" I asked, unsteadily. The sleeves of the leather jacket were way too long for me, and dangled past the hands I'd locked around his waist. I could feel Rob's heart beating through the back of his jean jacket. I tried to concentrate on that, rather than on the dripping sound that was the only thing Heather could hear.

"Where are we going?"

"Oh," I said. "P-Pike's Quarry."

Rob nodded, and a second later, the Indian roared to life, and we were off.

Ordinarily, of course, taking a moonlit motorcycle ride with Rob Wilkins would have been my idea of heaven on earth. I mean, let's face it: I am warm for the guy's form, and have been ever since that day in detention last year when he'd first asked me out, not knowing, of course, that I was only a sophomore and had never been out with a guy before in my life. By the time he'd figured it out, it was way too late. I was already smitten.

I like to think that the same could be said of him. And you know, the way he'd reacted when he'd heard I'd been out with another guy was kind of indicative that maybe he did like me as more than just a friend.

But I could no sooner rejoice over this realization than I could enjoy our ride. That, of course, was because of what I knew lay at the end of it. The road, I mean.

We did not encounter a single other vehicle along the way. Not until we reached the turnoff for the quarry, and saw a lone squad car sitting there with its interior light on as the officer within studied something attached to a clipboard. Rob slowed automatically as we approached—a speeding ticket he did not need—but didn't stop. His distrust of law enforcement agents is almost as finely honed as mine, only with better reason, since he'd actually been on the inside.

When we'd gotten far enough past the sheriff's deputy that we could pull over without him seeing us, Rob did say, keeping the motor running as he asked, "You want to ask him to join us?"

"Not yet," I said. "I'd rather . . . I want to make sure first."

Even though I was sure. Unfortunately, I was really sure.

"All right," Rob said. "Where to now?"

I pointed into the thick woods off to the side of the road. The thick, dark, seemingly impenetrable woods to the side of the wood.

"Great," Rob said without enthusiasm. Then he put down his helmet's visor again and said, "Hang on."

It was slow going. The floor of the woods was soft with decaying leaves and pine needles, and the trees, only a few feet apart, made a challenging obstacle course. We could only see what was directly in front of the beam from the Indian's headlamp, and basically, all that was was trees, and more trees. I pulled back the sleeve of Rob's leather jacket and pointed whenever we needed to change directions.

Don't ask me, either, how I knew where we going, me—who can't read a map to save my life and who's managed to flunk my driving test twice. God knew I had never been in these woods before. I was not allowed, like Claire Lippman, to swim in the quarries, and had never been to them before. There was a reason swimming here was illegal, and that was because the dark, inviting water was filled with hidden hazards, like abandoned farm equipment with sharp spikes sticking up, and car batteries slowly leaking acid into the county's groundwater.

Sounds like paradise, huh? Well, to a bunch of teenagers who weren't allowed to drink beside their parents' pools, it was.

So even though I had never been here before, it was like . . . well, it was like I had. In my mind's eye, as Douglas would say, I had been here, and I knew where we going. I knew exactly.

Still, when we hit the road again, I was surprised. It wasn't even a road, exactly, just a strip of land that, decades before, had become flattened by the heavy limestone-removing equipment that had passed over it, day after day. Now it was really just a grass-strewn pair of ruts. Ruts that led up to a dirty, abandoned-looking house, all of the windowpanes of which were dark—and busted out—and which had a DANGER—KEEP OUT sign attached to the front door.

I signaled for Rob to stop, and he did. Then we both sat and stared at the house in the beam from his headlight.

"You have got," Rob said, switching off the engine, "to be kidding me."

"No," I said. I took off my helmet. "She's in there. Somewhere."

Rob pulled his own helmet from his head and sat for a minute, staring at the house. No sound came from it—or from anywhere, actually—except the chirping of crickets and the occasional hoo-hoo of an owl.

"Is she dead?" Rob asked. "Or alive?"

"Alive," I said. Then I swallowed. "I think."

"Is anybody in there with her?"

"I don't . . . I don't know."

Rob looked at the house for a minute more. Then he said,

"Okay," and swung off the bike. He went to the back storage compartment and dug around in it. In the glow of the bike's head lamp and the dim light afforded from the tiny sliver of moon, I saw him pull out the flashlight, and something else.

A lug wrench.

He noticed the direction of my gaze.

"It never hurts," he said, "to be prepared."

I nodded, even though I doubted he could see this small gesture in the minimal moonlight.

"Okay," he said, closing the lid to the storage compartment and turning around to face me. "Here's how it's going to go down. I'm going to go in there and look around. If you don't hear from me in five minutes—oh, here, take my watch—you get on this bike and you go for that cop car we saw. Understand?"

I took his watch, but shook my head as I slipped it into the pocket of his leather jacket.

"No," I said. "I'm coming with you."

Rob's expression—what I could see of it, anyway—was eloquent with disapproval.

"Mastriani," he said. "Wait here. I'll be all right."

"I don't want to wait here." I couldn't, I knew very well, send him in to do what by rights should only have been done by me. I'd had the vision. I should be the one to go into the creepy house to see if the vision was real. "I want to come with you."

"Jess," Rob said. "Don't do this."

"I'm coming with you," I said. To my surprise, my voice broke. Really. Just like Tisha's had, when she'd gone into hysterics outside the Chocolate Moose. Was I, I wondered, going into hysterics?

If Rob heard the break in my voice, he gave no sign. "Jess," he said, "you're staying here with the bike, and that's final."

"And what if," I asked, the break having turned into a throb, "they come back—if they aren't in there now—and find me out here all alone?"

I did not, of course, even remotely believe that this might happen, or that, in the unlikely event that it did, I would not be able to get away on the Indian, which went from zero to sixty in mere seconds, thanks to Rob's dedicated tinkering.

My question did, however, have the desired effect on Rob, in that he sighed and, hooking the lug wrench through one of the belt loops of his jeans, reached out and took my hand.

"Come on," he said, though he didn't look too happy about it.

The steps to the house's tiny front porch were nearly rotted through. We had to step carefully as we climbed them. I wondered who had lived here, if anyone. It might, I thought, have served as the management office during the time the limestone had been carved out of the quarry down the road. Certainly no one had lived in it for years. . . . Though someone had certainly been inside recently, because the door, which had been nailed shut, swung easily under Rob's palm. In the bright beam from the Indian's headlamp, I could see the shiny points of the nails gleaming where they'd been pried from the wood, while their heads were nearly rusted through with weather and age.

Rob, shining his flashlight into the dank blackness past the door, muttered, "I have a really bad feeling about this."

I didn't blame him. I had a pretty creepy feeling about it myself. All I could hear were the crickets outside and the drumming of my own heart. And one other sound, much fainter than the other two. But, unfortunately, familiar. A dripping sound. Like water from a faucet that had not been properly shut off.

The drip, drip, drip from my dream.

I mean, my nightmare. Heather's reality.

Rob took a firmer grip on my hand, and we stepped inside.

We were not the first ones to have done so recently. Not by a long shot. In the first place, animals had clearly been making use of the space, leaving scattered droppings and nests of leaves and sticks all over the rotting wooden floor.

But raccoons and opossums weren't the dilapidated building's most recent tenants. Not if the many beer bottles and crumpled bags of chips on the floor were any indication. Someone had been doing some major partying. I could even smell, faintly, the intoxicating scent of human vomit.

"Nice," Rob said as we picked our way across the floor

toward the only door, which hung crazily on its hinges. He paused and, letting go of my hand for a second, stooped to pick up a beer bottle.

"Imported," he said, reading the label by flashlight. Then he put the bottle down again. "Townies," he said, taking my hand again. "It figures."

The next room had apparently been a kitchen, but all of the fixtures were gone, except for a few rusted-out cabinets and a gas oven that looked beyond repair. There were less animal droppings in the kitchen, but more beer bottles, and, interestingly, a pair of pants. They were too big—and unstylish—to have belonged to Heather, so we continued our tour.

The kitchen led to the third and what I thought was the final room. This one had a fireplace, in which rested an empty keg.

"Someone," Rob said, "didn't care whether or not he got his deposit back."

That's when I noticed the stairs and tightened my grip on Rob's hand. He followed the direction of my gaze, and sighed.

"Of course," he said. "Let's go."

The stairs were in only a little better condition than the porch steps. We climbed them slowly, taking care where we put each foot. One wrong step, and we'd have fallen through. As we climbed, the dripping sound grew steadily louder. Please, I prayed. Don't let that be blood.

The second floor consisted of three rooms. The first, to the left, had obviously been a bedroom at one time. There was still a mattress on the floor, though a mattress covered with so many stains and discolorations that I'd have only touched it with latex gloves on. A crunching noise beneath our feet revealed that my fears had not been ill-founded. There were condom wrappers everywhere.

"Well," Rob remarked, "at least they're practicing safe sex."

The second room was even worse. Here there was no mattress, just a couple of old blankets . . . but just as many condom wrappers.

I really thought I might be sick, and hoped the pizza Mark and I had consumed earlier had had time to digest.

Then there was just one last door, and I really, really didn't want Rob to open it, because I knew what we were going to find behind it. The dripping sound was coming from behind its closed door.

"Must be the bathroom," Rob said, and he let go of my hand to reach for the knob. "No," I said, stepping forward. "No. Let me do it."

I couldn't see Rob's face in the darkness, but I could hear the concern in his voice as he said, "Sure . . . if you want to."

I gripped the doorknob. It felt cold beneath my palm.

Then the door flew open, and it was all exactly the way it had been in my vision. The dank, stained walls. The dark, windowless cell. The stained and ancient toilet, drip-drip-dripping.

And the figure curled up in the bathtub, her mouth stretched into a hideous grin by the dirty strip of material holding the gag in place, her hair unkempt, her arms and legs twisted at painful angles by matching strips of material around her wrists and ankles.

It was only because of the purple and white uniform that I knew who she was at all. Well, that, of course, and my dream.

"Oh, Heather," I said, in a voice that didn't sound at all like my own. "I'm so sorry."

CHAPTER 12

"Jesus," Rob said, holding the flashlight so that it shined on Heather's tear-stained face . . . which wasn't actually much help, since I was trying to loosen a knot at the back of her head, the one holding her gag in place, and I could barely see what I was doing.

"Rob," I said. I had crawled into the bathtub with Heather. "Hold the light over here, will you?"

He did as I asked, but it was like he was in a trance or something. I couldn't blame him, really. I mean, I'd had a pretty good feeling what kind of shape Heather would be in when we found her. He'd had no warning. No warning at all.

And it was bad. It was really bad. Worse even than I'd seen in my vision, because of course what I had seen, I had seen through Heather's eyes. I had not been able to see *her*, because in my dream, I'd *been* her.

Which was how I'd known she'd been in pain. Only now was I able to see why. "Heather," I said when I'd gotten the gag out of her mouth. "Are you all right?"

It was a lame question, of course. She wasn't all right. The way she looked, I was willing to bet she'd never be all right again.

But what else was I supposed to say?

Heather didn't say anything. Her head lolled. She wasn't unconscious, but she was as close to it as a person could be.

"Here," Rob said, when he saw the trouble I was having with the knots at her wrists. He dug into his pocket and came up with a Swiss Army knife. It only took a second for the bright blade to sever the thin strip of material holding her hands behind her back.

It was only when one of those arms dangled limply after it was freed that I realized it was broken.

Not that Heather seemed to care, or notice, even. She'd balled up into a fetal position, and though Rob took his denim jacket off and draped it over her, she was shivering as if it were winter.

"I think she's in shock," Rob said.

"Yeah," I said. I'd heard things about shock. Like how

shock alone could kill someone after an accident, even someone who was not all that seriously injured.

And Heather, if you asked me, was very seriously injured.

"Heather?" I peered into her face. It was hard to tell whether or not she could hear me. "Heather, can you hear me? Listen, it's all right. Everything is going to be all right."

Rob gave it a try.

"Heather," he said. "You're safe now. Look, can you tell us who did this? Can you tell us who did this to you, Heather?"

That was when she finally opened her mouth. But what came out was not the name of her attacker.

"Go away," Heather wailed, pushing ineffectually at me with her one unbroken arm. "Go away before they come back . . . and find you here. . . ."

Rob and I exchanged glances. In my concern over Heather, I had forgotten that there was a very strong possibility this could happen. You know, that they might actually come back and find us, I mean. I hoped Rob still had that wrench handy.

"It's all right, Heather," I said, trying to calm her. "Even if they do come back, they can't take on all three of us."

"Yes, they can," Heather insisted. "Yes, they can, yes, they can, yes, they can, yes . . ."

Okay, this was getting creepier by the minute. I had thought, you know, we'd find her, and that would be it.

But clearly, that was *not* it. There was a lot more to it. Like, for instance, how the hell we were going to get her out of there.

No way was she going to be able to stay on the bike in her condition. I wasn't sure she could even sit up.

"Listen," I said to Rob. "You've got to go get that cop. The one by the turnoff? Tell him to call an ambulance."

Rob looked down at me like I was nuts. "Are you crazy?" he wanted to know. "You're the one who's going for the cop."

"Rob," I said, trying to keep my tone even and pleasant, so as not to alarm Heather, who seemed to have enough on her mind at the moment. "I am staying here with Heather. You are going for the cop."

"So you can get your arm broken like hers when they—whoever *they* are—come back?" Rob's tone was not even or pleasant. It was determined and grim-sounding. "Nuh-uh. I'm staying. You're going."

"Rob," I said. "No offense, but I think she'd be better off with someone she—"

But Rob didn't let me finish.

"And you'll be better off when you're miles away from here." Rob stood up and took me by the arm, half-lifting, half-dragging me out of the bathtub. "Come on."

I didn't want to go. Well, all right, I *did* want to go, but I didn't think I should go. I didn't want to leave Heather. I wasn't sure what, exactly, had happened to her, but whatever it had been, it had traumatized her to the point where I wasn't sure she even remembered her own name. How could I leave her alone with a guy she didn't know, especially since it was a fair guess that what had been done to her had been done by just that? Some random strange guy, I mean.

Or guys, I should say, since she'd said "they."

On the other hand, I didn't exactly want to stay with Heather alone while Rob went for help, either.

Fortunately, Rob made the decision for me. Bossy boy-friends do come in handy sometimes.

"You follow our tracks," he said when he'd pulled me down the stairs, through the party rooms, and out into the night air. "The tracks we made through the pine needles. See them? Follow those back to the road, then make a left. Got it? And do not stop. Do not stop for anything. When you find the guy, tell him to take the old pit road. Okay? The pit road. If he's local, he'll know what you're talking about."

He had shoved his helmet over my head, making speech difficult. Still, as I straddled the seat of the Indian, my feet barely reaching the boot rests, I tried to express my great unease with this plan.

Rob wasn't listening, however. He was busy starting the engine.

"Don't stop," he shouted again, when he'd successfully maneuvered the kickstart. "Do not stop for anyone not in uniform, understand?"

"But Rob," I said over the noise from the engine, which wasn't all that loud, actually, since Rob kept his bike in good repair. "I've never ridden on a motorcycle alone before. I'm not sure I know how."

"You'll be fine," he said.

"Um. I hesitate to mention this, but I think you should know, I don't exactly have a driver's license yet—"

"Don't worry about it. Just go."

He'd been holding on to the brake. Now he let go of it, and the bike jolted forward. My heart lurched as I grabbed for the handles. I was so short, I had to stretch out practically flat against the body of the bike to reach them . . . but reach them I did. I'd be all right, I realized . . . until I had to stop, anyway. No way were my short legs going to be able to reach the ground while still keeping the bike, which had to weigh eight hundred pounds, upright.

Rob had been right about one thing, anyway. I absolutely could not stop, and not because some of Heather's attackers might still be lurking around, but because once I stopped, I'd never be able to get the stupid thing up again.

And then I was careening back through the woods, trying to follow the ruts the Indian's wheels had made through the bracken on our way in from the road. It wasn't hard, exactly, to see where I was going—the headlight was bright enough that I could see a dozen or so feet ahead of me at all times. It was just that it was much harder to steer than I'd thought. My arms were straining with the effort of navigating the bike around all the trees that kept looming up in front of it.

This is what you always wanted, I told myself, as I drove. A bike of your own, to feel the wind on your face, to go as fast as you've always wanted, but no one would ever let you. . . .

Only when you are driving through the woods in the middle of the night looking for a cop, on your boyfriend's motorcycle that is, without a doubt, more bike than you can handle, you can't actually go very fast at all. Not if you don't want your wheels to spin out from beneath you.

My biggest fear was not that one of Heather's attackers might suddenly leap out at me from behind a tree, grab the handlebars of Rob's bike, and knock me to the ground. No, my biggest fear was that the engine was going to stall, because I was going so slowly.

I tried to kick up the speed a notch, and found that, by going another couple miles an hour faster, I could actually maneuver the bike much more easily. I tried not to concentrate so much on the trees, and instead concentrated on the open spaces around them. It sounds weird, but it actually helped. I figured it was like using the Force or something. *Trust your feelings, Jess*, I said to myself, in an Obi-Wan Kenobi voice. Know *the woods*. Feel *the woods*. Be *the woods*. . . .

I really hate the woods.

It was right after this that I burst out of the trees and skidded up the embankment to the road. There was a moment of panic when I thought I was going to tip over. . . .

But I threw out a foot and stopped myself at the last minute. I don't know how, but I managed to get the bike upright again and was off. The whole thing took barely a second, but in my mind, it seemed like an hour. My heart was thundering louder in my ears than the bike's engine.

Please be there, I was praying as I raced toward the place where we'd passed the squad car. *Please be there, please be there, please be there*. . . . Now that I was on the open road, I could really let loose, speedwise, and so I did, watching the speedometer go from ten, to twenty, to thirty, to forty. . . .

And then the squad car was looming up ahead of me, the overhead light still on, the cop inside, sipping a cup of coffee. The tinny sounds of the radio drifted out from the open window on the driver's side.

It was against the driver's side that I braced myself as I pulled up, to keep the bike from falling over.

"Officer," I said. I didn't have to say much to get his attention, because of course when someone on a motorcycle pulls up next to your car and leans on it, you notice right away.

"Yes?" The guy was young, probably only twenty-two or -three. He still had acne. "What is it?"

"Heather Montrose," I said. "We found her back there, inside a house off that road, the old pit road, the one they don't use anymore. You better call an ambulance, she's really hurt."

The guy looked at me a minute, as if trying to figure out whether or not I was putting him on. I had Rob's helmet over my head, of course, so I don't know how much of my face he could make out. But what little he could see of me, he must have decided looked sincere, since he got on the radio and said he needed backup, along with an ambulance and para- medics. Then he looked at me and said, "Let's go."

It turned out the cops already knew about the house. They'd searched it, Deputy Mullins—that was his name— said, twice already, once right after Heather had been reported missing, and then again after nightfall. But they hadn't found anything suspicious inside . . . unless one counted a plethora of empty beer bottles and used condoms.

In any case, Deputy Mullins led me toward a clearly little-used dirt track just off the road. It was better, I found, than the way we'd originally taken through the woods, since I didn't have to dodge any trees. I wondered why my psychic radar hadn't led me this way before. Maybe because it ended up taking longer. It took us almost fifteen minutes of slow going over weedy, bumpy terrain to reach the house. It had only taken me ten minutes to get to the road through the woods. I knew from Rob's watch.

Deputy Mullins, when the house appeared in his head- lights, pulled up beside it, then got on the radio again to describe his location. Then, leaving the headlights on, but his engine off, he got out of the car, while I leaned Rob's bike carefully against it, turned the engine off, and climbed down.

"She's in there," I said, pointing. "On the second floor."

Deputy Mullins nodded, but he looked nervous. Really nervous.

"Some people got her," I said. "She's afraid they might come back. She—"

Rob, having heard our approach, came out onto the porch. Deputy Mullins was even more nervous than I'd thought— either that, or the house was creeping him out as much as it had creeped me out—since he immediately went for his sidearm, sank down onto one knee, and, pointing the gun at Rob, yelled, "Freeze!"

Rob put both hands in the air and stood there, looking slightly bored, in the glare of the headlights.

May I just say that Rob Wilkins is the only person I know who would find having a gun drawn on him boring?

"Dude," I said to Deputy Mullins, in a voice high with suppressed emotion, "that's my boyfriend! He's—he's one of the good guys!"

Deputy Mullins lowered his gun. "Oh," he said, looking sheepish. "Sorry about that."

"It's cool," Rob said, putting his hands down. "Look, have you got a blanket and a first-aid kit in your car? She's not doing so hot."

Deputy Mullins nodded and raced around to the back of the squad car. I pulled my helmet off and hurried up to Rob.

"Did she say anything?" I asked him. "Like about who did it, or anything?"

"Not a word," Rob said. "All she'll talk about is how they—whoever they are—will be back soon, and how we're all going to be sorry when that happens."

"Yeah?" I said, running a hand through my sweaty hair. (It was hot inside that helmet.) "Well, I'm already sorry."

I was even more sorry when I led Deputy Mullins up the rickety stairs, and found out that, insofar as any sort of first aid knowledge was concerned, he was about as useless as Rob and me. All we could do was try to make her as warm and as comfortable as possible, then wait for the professionals.

It didn't take them long. It seemed as if no sooner had I crawled back into that bathtub than the wails from a half dozen sirens filled the night air. Seconds later, red lights were swirling across the inside walls of the house, like a lava lamp at a party, and voices could be heard outside. Deputy Mullins excused himself and went outside to show the EMT guys the way.

"Hear that, Heather?" I asked her, holding the hand on her unbroken arm. "That's the cops. Things are going to be okay now."

Heather only moaned. She obviously didn't believe me. It was almost as if she thought things were never going to be okay again.

Maybe she was right. At least, that's what I started to think as Rob and I, banished by the EMTs, who needed all the room to work on Heather that they could get in that cramped space, came down the stairs and onto the front porch. No, things weren't going to be okay. Not for a good long while, anyway.

Because Special Agents Johnson and Smith were coming toward us, their badges out and ready.

"Jessica," Special Agent Johnson said. "Mr. Wilkins. Will you two come with us, please?"

CHAPTER 13

"I told you," I said, for what had to have been the thirtieth time. "We were looking for a place to make out."

Special Agent Smith smiled at me. She was a very pretty lady, even when roused from her bed in the middle of the night. She had on pearl stud earrings, a crisply starched blue blouse, and black trousers. With her blond bob and turned-up little nose, she looked perky enough to be a stewardess, or even a real-estate agent.

Except, of course, for the Glock 9 mm strapped to her side. That sort of detracted from the overall image of perkiness.

"Jess," she said, "Rob already told us that isn't true."

"Yeah," I said. "Well, of course he would say that, being a gentleman and all. But believe me, that's how it happened. We went in there to make out, and we found Heather. And that's it."

"I see." Special Agent Smith looked down at the steaming cup of coffee she was holding between her hands. They'd offered me a cup, too, but I had declined. I didn't need my growth stunted anymore than it already had been thanks to my DNA.

"And do you and Rob," she went on, "always drive fifteen miles out of town just to make out?"

"Oh, yeah," I said. "It's more exciting that way"

"I see," Special Agent Smith said, again. "And the fact that Rob has the keys to his uncle's garage, where he works, and the two of you could have gone there, a place that is significantly closer and quite a bit cleaner than that house on the pit road . . . you still expect me to believe you?"

"Yes," I said, with some indignation. "We can't go to his uncle's garage to make out. Somebody might find out, and then Rob'd get fired."

Special Agent Smith propped her elbow up onto the table where we sat in the police station, then dropped her forehead into her hand.

"Jessica," she said, sounding tired. "You declined an invitation to your own best friend's lakehouse because you heard it didn't have cable television. Do you honestly expect me to believe that you would so much as enter a house like the one on the pit road if you didn't absolutely have to?"

I narrowed my eyes at her. "Hey," I said. "How'd you know about the cable thing?"

"We are the Federal Bureau of Investigation, Jess. We know everything."

This was distressing. I wondered if they knew about Mrs. Hankey's lawsuit. I figured they probably did.

"Well," I said. "Okay. I admit it's a little gross in there. But—"

"A little gross?" Special Agent Smith sat up straight. "I'm sorry, Jessica, but I think I'm well enough acquainted with you to know that if any boy—but especially, I suspect, Rob Wilkins—took you into a house like that to be intimate, we'd have a homicide on our hands. Namely, his."

I tried to take umbrage at this assessment of my personality, but the fact was, Jill was right. I could not understand how any girl would let a boy take her to such a place. Better to get down and dirty in his *car* than in that disgusting frat house.

Frat house? *Rat* house was more like it.

I am certainly not saying that if a girl is going to lose her virginity, it has to be on satin sheets or something. I am not *that* big of a prude. But there should at least *be* sheets. Clean ones. And no refuse from trysts past lying around on the floor. And a person should at least take his empty beer bottles to the recycling plant before even thinking of entertaining. . . .

Oh, what was the point? She had me, and she knew it.

"So can we please," Special Agent Smith said, "drop this ridiculous story that you and Mr. Wilkins went to that house in order to get hot and heavy? We know better, Jessica. Why won't you just admit it? You knew Heather was in that house, and that's why you and Rob went there."

"I swear—"

"Admit it, Jessica," Jill said. "You had a vision you'd find her there, didn't you?"

"I did not," I said. "You can ask Rob. We went to—"

"We did ask Rob," Special Agent Smith said. "He said that the two of you went to the quarry to look for Heather and just happened to stumble across the house."

"And that's exactly how it did happen," I said, proud that Rob had thought up such a good story. It was far better, I realized, than my make-out story. Though I certainly *wished* my make-out story was true.

"Jessica, I sincerely hope, for your sake, that that isn't true. The whole idea of you two just stumbling over a kidnapping victim *accidentally* strikes us as . . . well, as a little suspicious, to say the least."

I narrowed my eyes at her. I still had Rob's watch with me—it wasn't like we were under arrest or anything, and they'd taken all of our valuables to hold for safekeeping. Oh, no. We were just being held for *questioning.*

Which was what Special Agents Johnson and Smith had

been doing for the past two hours. *Questioning* us.

And now it was close to dawn, and you know what? I was really, really tired of being *questioned*.

But not so tired that I missed the implication in her words.

"What do you mean, it sounds 'suspicious'?" I demanded. "What are you suggesting?"

Special Agent Smith only regarded me thoughtfully with her pretty blue eyes.

I let out a laugh, even though I didn't really see anything all that funny about it.

"Oh, I get it," I said. "You think Rob and I did it? You think Rob and I kidnapped Heather and beat her up and left her for dead in that bathtub? Is that what you think?"

"No," Special Agent Smith said. "Mr. Wilkins was working in his uncle's garage at the time Heather first disappeared. We have a half dozen witnesses who will attest to that. And you, of course, were with Mr. Leskowski. Again, we have quite a number of people who saw you two together."

My jaw sagged. "Oh, my God," I said. "You checked on my alibi? You didn't wake Mrs. Wilkins up, did you? Tell me you didn't call Rob's mom and wake her up. Jill, how could you? Talk about embarrassing!"

"Frankly, Jessica," Special Agent Smith said, "your embarrassment doesn't concern me at all. All I am interested in is finding out the truth. How did you know Heather Montrose was in that house? The police searched there twice after learning another girl had disappeared. They didn't find any-thing. So how did you know to look there?"

I glared at her. Really, it was one thing to have the Feds following you around and reading your mail and tapping your phone and all. It was quite another to have them going around, waking up your future mother-in-law in the middle of the night to ask questions about your dinner with another boy, who wasn't even her son.

"Okay, that's it," I said, folding my arms across my chest. "I want a lawyer."

It was at this point that the door to the little interrogation room—a conference room, Special Agent Smith had called it, but I knew better—opened, and her partner came in.

"Hello, again, Jessica," he said, dropping into a chair beside me. "What do you want a lawyer for? You haven't done any-thing wrong, have you?"

"I'm a minor," I said. "You guys are required to question me in the presence of a parent or guardian."

Special Agent Johnson sighed and dropped a file onto the tabletop. "We've already called your parents. They're waiting for you downstairs."

I nearly beat my head against something. I couldn't believe it. "You told my *parents*?"

"As you pointed out," Special Agent Johnson said, "we are required to question you in the presence—"

"I was just giving you a hard time," I cried. "I can't believe you actually called them. Do you have any idea how much trouble I'm going to be in? I mean, I completely snuck out of the house in the middle of the night."

"Right," Special Agent Johnson said. "Let's talk about that for a minute, shall we? Just why *did* you sneak out? It wasn't, by any chance, because you'd had another one of your psychic visions, was it?"

I couldn't believe this. I really couldn't. Here Rob and I had done this fabulous thing—we'd saved this girl's life, according to the EMTs, who said that Heather, though she was only suffering from a broken arm and rib and some severe bruising, would have been dead by morning due to shock if we hadn't come along and found her—and all anybody could do was harp on how we'd known where she was. It wasn't fair. They should have been throwing a *parade* for us, not interrogating us like a couple of miscreants.

"I told you," I said. "I don't have ESP anymore, okay?"

"Really?" Special Agent Johnson flipped open the file he'd put on the table. "So it wasn't you who put in the call to 1-800-WHERE-R-YOU yesterday morning, telling them where they could find Courtney Hwang?"

"Never heard of her," I said.

"Right. They found her in San Francisco. It appears she was kidnapped from her home in Brooklyn four years ago. Her parents had just about given up hope of ever seeing her again."

"Can I go home now?" I demanded.

"A call was placed to 1-800-WHERE-R-YOU at approximately eight in the morning yesterday from the Dunkin' Donuts down the street from the garage where Mr. Wilkins works. But you wouldn't know anything about that, of course."

"I lost my psychic abilities," I said. "Remember? It was on the news."

"Yes, Jessica," Special Agent Johnson said. "We are aware that you told reporters that. We are also aware that, at the time, your brother Douglas was experiencing some, shall we say, troublesome symptoms of his schizophrenia, that were perhaps exacerbated by the stress of your being so persistently pursued by the press. . . ."

"Not just the press," I said, with some heat. "You guys had a little something to do with it, too, remember?"

"Regrettably," Special Agent Johnson said, "I do. Jessica, let me ask you something. Do you know what a profile is?"

"Of course I do," I said. "It's when law enforcement officers go around arresting people who fit a certain stereotype."

"Well," Special Agent Johnson said, "yes, but that's not exactly what I meant. I meant a formal summary or analysis of data, representing distinctive characteristics or features."

"Isn't that what I just said?" I asked.

"No."

Special Agent Johnson didn't have much of a sense of humor. His partner was much more fun . . . though that wasn't saying much. Allan Johnson, it had often occurred to me, just might be the most boring person on the entire planet. Everything about him was boring. His mouse-colored hair, thinning slightly on top and parted on the right, was boring. His glasses, plain old steel frames, were boring. His suits, invariably charcoal gray, were boring. Even his ties, usually in pale blues or yellows, without a pattern, were boring. He was married, too, which was the most boring thing about him of all.

"A profile," Special Agent Johnson said, "of the type of person who might commit a crime like the ones we've experienced this week—the strangulation of Amber Mackey, for instance, and the kidnapping of Heather Montrose—might sound something like this: He is most likely a white heterosexual male, in his late teens or early twenties. He is intelligent, perhaps highly so, and yet suffers from an inability to feel empathy for his victims, or anyone, for that matter, save himself. While he might seem, to his friends and family, to be a normal, even high-functioning member of society, he is, in fact, wracked with inner misgivings, perhaps even paranoia. In some cases, we have found that killers like this one act the way they do because inner voices, or visions, direct them to—"

That's when it hit me. I'd be listening to his little speech, going, Hmmm, white heterosexual male, late teens, sounds like Mark Leskowski, highly intelligent, inability to feel empathy, yeah, that could be him. He's a football player, after all, but a quarterback, which takes some smarts, anyway. Then there's that whole "unacceptable" thing.

Only it can't be him, because he was with me when Heather was kidnapped. And according to the EMTs, those wounds she'd sustained were a good six hours old, which meant whoever had done it—and Heather still wasn't talking—had attacked her at around eight in the evening. And Mark had been with me at eight. . . .

But when Allan got to the part about inner voices, I sat up a little straighter.

"Hey," I said. "Wait just a minute here. . . ."

"Yes?" Special Agent Johnson broke off and looked at me expectantly. "Something bothering you, Jessica?"

"You've got to be kidding me," I said. "You can't seriously be trying to pin this thing on my brother."

Jill looked thoughtful. "Why on earth would you think we were trying to do that, Jess?"

My jaw dropped. "What do you think I am, stupid or something? He just said—"

"I don't see what would make you jump to the conclusion," Special Agent Johnson said, "that we suspect Douglas, Jessica. Unless you know something we don't know."

"Yes," Special Agent Smith said. "Did Douglas tell you where you could find Heather, Jessica? Is that how you knew to look in the house on the pit road?"

"Oh!" I stood up so fast, my chair tipped over backwards. "That's it. That is so it. End of interview. I am out of here."

"Why are you so angry, Jessica?" Special Agent Johnson, not moving from his chair, asked me. "Could it be perhaps because you think we might be right?"

"In your dreams," I said. "You are *not* pinning this one on Douglas. *No way.* Ask Heather. Go ahead. She'll tell you it wasn't Douglas."

"Heather Montrose did not see her attackers," Special Agent Johnson said lightly. "Something heavy was thrown over her head, she says, and then she was locked in a small enclosed space—presumably a car trunk—until some time after nightfall. When she was released, it was by several individuals in ski masks, from whom she attempted to escape—but who dissuaded her most emphatically. She can only say that their voices sounded vaguely familiar. She recalls very little, other than that."

I swallowed. Poor Heather.

Still, as a sister, I had a job to do.

"It wasn't Douglas," I said vehemently. "He doesn't have any friends. And he certainly has never owned a ski mask."

"Well, it shouldn't be hard to prove he had nothing to do with it," Special Agent Smith said. "I suppose he was in his room the whole time, as usual. Right, Jessica?"

I stared at them. They knew. I don't know how, but they

knew. They knew Douglas hadn't been in the house when Heather had disappeared.

And they also knew I hadn't the slightest idea where he'd been, either.

"If you guys," I said, feeling so mad it was a wonder smoke wasn't coming out of my nostrils, "even *think* about dragging Douglas into this, you can kiss good-bye any hope you might have of me ever coming to work for you."

"What are you saying, Jessica?" Special Agent Johnson asked. "That you do, indeed, still have extrasensory perception?"

"How did you know where to find Heather Montrose, Jessica?" Jill asked in a sharp voice.

I went to the door. When I got to it, I turned around to face them.

"You stay away from Douglas," I said. "I mean it. If you go near him—if you so much as *look* at him—I'll move to Cuba, and I'll tell the government everything they ever wanted to know about your undercover operatives over there."

Then I flung the door open and stalked out into the hallway.

Well, they couldn't stop me. I wasn't under arrest, after all.

I couldn't believe it. I really couldn't. I mean, I knew the United States government was eager to have me on its payroll, but to stoop to suggesting that if I did not come to their aid, they would frame my own brother for a crime he most certainly did not commit . . . well, that was low. George Washington, I knew, would have hung his head in shame if he'd heard about it.

When I got to the waiting area, I was still so mad I almost went stalking right through it, right out the door and on down the street. I couldn't see properly, I was so mad.

Or maybe it was because I'd just gone for so long without sleep. Whatever the reason, I stalked right past Rob and my parents, who were waiting for me—on different sides of the room—in front of the duty desk.

"Jessica!"

My mother's cry roused me from my fury. Well, that and the fact that she flung her arms around me.

"Jess, are you all right?"

Caught up in the stranglehold that served as my mother's excuse for a hug, I blinked a few times and observed Rob getting up slowly from the bench he'd been stretched out across.

"What happened?" my mom wanted to know. "Why did they keep you in there for so long? They said something about you finding a girl—another cheerleader. What's this all about? And what on earth were you doing out so late?"

Rob, across the room, smiled at the eye-roll I gave him behind my mother's back. Then he mouthed, "Call me."

Then he—very tactfully, I thought—left.

But not tactfully enough, since my dad went, "Who was that boy over there? The one who just left?"

"No one, Dad," I said. "Just a guy. Let's go home, okay? I'm really tired."

"What do you mean, just a guy? That wasn't even the same boy you were with earlier. How many boys are you seeing, anyway, Jessica? And what, exactly, were you doing out with him in the middle of the night?"

"Dad," I said, taking him by the arm and trying to physically propel him and my mother from the station house. "I'll explain when we get to the car. Now just come on."

"What about the rule?" my father demanded.

"What rule?"

"The rule that states you are not to see any boy socially whom your mother and I have not met."

"That's not a rule," I said. "At least, nobody ever told me about it before."

"Well, that's just because this is the first time anyone's asked you out," my dad said. "But you can bet there are going to be some rules now. Especially if these guys think it's all right for you to sneak out at night to meet with them—"

"Joe," my mother whispered, looking around the empty waiting room nervously. "Not so loud."

"I'll talk as loud as I want," my dad said. "I'm a taxpayer, aren't I? I paid for this building. Now I want to know, Toni. I want to know who this boy is our daughter is sneaking out of the house to meet. . . ."

"God," I said. "It's Rob Wilkins." I was more glad than I

could say that Rob wasn't around to hear this. "Mrs. Wilkins's son. Okay? Now can we go?"

"Mrs. Wilkins?" My dad looked perplexed. "You mean Mary, the new waitress at Mastriani's?"

"Yes," I said. "Now let's—"

"But he's much too old for you," my mother said. "He's graduated already. Hasn't he graduated already, Joe?"

"I think so," my dad said. You could tell he was totally uninterested in the subject now that he knew he employed Rob's mother. "Works over at the import garage, right, on Pike's Creek Road?"

"A garage?" my mother practically shrieked. "Oh, my God—"

It was, I knew, going to be a long drive home.

"This," my father said, "had better have been one of those ESP things, young lady, or you—"

And an even longer day.

CHAPTER 14

I didn't get to school until fourth period.

That's because my parents, after I'd explained about rescuing Heather, let me sleep in. Not that they were happy about it. Good God, no. They were still excessively displeased, particularly my mother, who did NOT want me hanging out anymore with a guy who had no intention, now or ever, of going to college.

My dad, though . . . he was cool. He was just like, "Forget it, Toni. He's a nice kid."

My mom was all, "How would you know? You've never even met him."

"Yeah, but I know Mary," he said. "Now go get some sleep, Jessica."

Except that I couldn't. Sleep, that is. In spite of the fact that I lay in my bed from five, when I finally crawled back into it, until about ten thirty. All I could think about was Heather and that house. That awful, awful house.

Oh, and what Special Agent Johnson had said, too. About Douglas, I mean.

All Douglas's voices ever do is tell him to kill himself, not other people.

So it didn't make sense, what Special Agent Johnson was suggesting. Not for a minute.

Besides, Douglas didn't even drive. I mean, he had a license and a car and all.

But since that day they'd called us—last Christmas, when Douglas had had the first of his episodes, up where he was going to college—and we went to get him, and Mike drove his car back, it had sat, cold and dead, under the carport. Even Mike—who'd have given just about anything for a car of his own, having stupidly asked for a computer for graduation instead of a car, with which he might have enticed Claire Lippman, his lady love, on a date to the quarries—wouldn't touch Douglas's car. It was Douglas's car. And Douglas would drive it again one day.

Only he hadn't. I knew he hadn't because when I went outside, after Mom offered to give me a lift to school, I checked his tires. If he'd been driving around out by that pit house, there'd have been gravel in them.

But there wasn't. Douglas's wheels were clean as a whistle.

Not that I'd believed Special Agent Johnson. He'd just been saying that about Douglas to see if I maybe knew who the real killer was and just wasn't telling, for some bizarre reason. As if anybody who knew the identity of a murderer would go around keeping it a secret.

I am so sure.

I got to Orchestra in the middle of the strings' chair auditions. Ruth was playing as I walked in with my late pass in hand. She didn't notice me, she was so absorbed in what she was playing, which was a sonata we'd learned at music camp that summer. She would, I knew, get first chair. Ruth always gets first chair.

When she was done, Mr. Vine said, "Excellent, Ruth," and called the next cellist. There were only three cellists in Symphonic Orchestra, so it wasn't like the competition was particularly rough. But we all had to sit there and listen while people auditioned for their chairs, and let me tell you, it was way boring. Especially when we got to the violins. There were about fifteen violinists, and they all played the same thing.

"Hey," I whispered, as I pretended to be rooting around in my backpack for something.

"Hey," Ruth whispered back. She was putting her cello

away. "Where were you? What's going on? Everyone is saying you saved Heather Montrose from certain death."

"Yeah," I said modestly. "I did."

"Jeez," Ruth said. "Why am I always the last to know everything? So where was she?"

"In this disgusting old house," I whispered back, "on the pit road. You know, that old road no one ever uses anymore, off Pike's Quarry."

"What was she doing there?" Ruth wanted to know.

"She wasn't exactly there by choice." I explained how Rob and I had found Heather.

"Jeez," Ruth said again, when I was through. "Is she going to be all right?"

"I don't know," I said. "Nobody will say. But—"

"Excuse me. Would you two please keep it down? You are ruining this for the rest of us."

We both looked over and saw Karen Sue Hankey shooting us an annoyed look.

Only she was shooting it at us over a wide, white gauze bandage, which stretched across her nose and was stuck in place on either cheekbone with surgical tape.

I burst out laughing. Well, you would have, too.

"Laugh all you want, Jess," Karen Sue said. "We'll see who's laughing last in court."

"Karen Sue," I choked, between chortles. "*What* have you got that thing on for? You look completely ridiculous."

"I am suffering," Karen Sue said, primly, "from a contused proboscis. You can see the medical report."

"Contused pro—" Ruth, who'd gotten a perfect score on the verbal section of her PSATs, went, "For God's sake. All that means is that your nose is bruised."

"The chance of infection," Karen Sue said, "is dangerously high."

That one killed me. I nearly convulsed, I was laughing so hard. Mr. Vine finally noticed and said, "*Girls,*" in a warning voice.

Karen Sue's eyes glittered dangerously over the edge of her bandage, but she didn't say anything more.

Then.

When the bell for lunch finally rang, Ruth and I booked out of there as fast as we could. Not, of course, because we were so eager to sample the lunch fare being offered in the caf, but because we wanted to talk about Heather.

"So she said '*they,*'" Ruth said as we bent over our tacos, the entree of the day. Well, I bent over my taco. Ruth had crumbled hers all up with a bunch of lettuce and poured fat-free dressing all over it, making a taco salad. And a mess, in my opinion. "You're sure about that? She said, '*They're* coming back'?"

I nodded. I was starving, for some reason. I was on my third taco. "Definitely," I said, swilling down some Coke. "*They.*"

"Which makes it seem likely," Ruth said, "that more than one person was involved in Amber's attack, as well. I mean, if the two attacks are related. Which, face it, they must be."

"Right," I said. "What I want to know is, who's been using that house as their party headquarters? Somebody's been letting loose there, and pretty regularly, from the looks of it."

Ruth shuddered delicately. I had, of course, described the house on the pit road in all its lurid detail . . . including the condom wrappers.

"While I suppose we should be grateful, at least, that they—whoever *they* are—are practicing safe sex," Ruth said with a sigh, "it hardly seems like the kind of place one might refer to as a love shack."

"No kidding," I said. "The question is who have they—whoever *they* are—been taking there? Girl-wise, I mean. Unless, you know, they're having sex with each other."

Ruth shook her head. "Gay guys would have fixed the place up. You know, throw pillows and all of that. And they would have recycled their empties."

"True," I said. "So what kind of girl would put up with those kind of conditions?"

We looked around the caf. Ernest Pyle High was, I suppose, a pretty typical example of a mid-western American high school. There was one Hispanic student, a couple of Asian-Americans, and no African-Americans at all. Everyone else was white. The only difference between the white students, besides religion—Ruth and Skip, being Jewish, were in the minority—was how much their parents earned.

And that, as usual, turned out to be the crux of the matter.

"Grits," Ruth said simply, as her gaze fell upon a long table of girls whose perms were clearly of the at-home variety, and whose nails were press-on, not salon silk-wrapped. "It has to be."

"No," I said.

Ruth shook her head. "Jess, why not? It makes sense. I mean, the house is way out in the country, after all."

"Yeah," I said. "But the beer bottles on the floor. They were imports."

"So?"

"So Rob and his friends"—I swallowed a mouthful of taco—"they only drink American beer. At least, that's what he said. He saw the bottles and went, 'Townies.'"

Ruth eyed me. "Has it ever occurred to you that the Jerk might be covering up for his bohunk friends?"

"Rob," I said, putting my taco down, "is not a jerk. And his friends aren't bohunks. If you will recall, they saved me from becoming the U.S. Army's number one secret weapon last spring. . . ."

"I am not trying to be offensive," Ruth said. "Honest, Jess. But I think you might be too besotted with this guy to see the writing on the wall—"

"The only writing I'm looking at," I said, "is the writing that says Rob didn't do it."

"I am not suggesting that he did. I am merely saying that some of his peers might—"

Suddenly an enormous backpack plonked down onto the bench beside mine. I looked up and had to restrain a groan.

"Hi, girls," Skip said. "Mind if I join you?"

"Actually," Ruth said, her upper lip curling. "We were just leaving."

"Ruth," Skip said, "you're lying. I have never seen you leave a taco salad unfinished."

"There's a first time for everything," Ruth said.

"Actually," Skip said, "what I have to say will only take a minute. I know how you girls value your precious dining moments together. There's a midnight screening of a Japanese anime film at the Downtown Cinema this weekend, and I wanted to know if you'd be interested in going."

Ruth looked at her brother as if he'd lost his mind. *"Me?"* she said. "You want to know if I'd go to the movies with you?"

"Well," Skip said, looking, for the first time since I'd known him—and that was a long, long time—embarrassed. "Not you, actually. I meant Jess."

I choked on a piece of taco shell.

"Hey," Skip said, banging me on the back a few times. "You all right?"

"Yeah," I said, when I'd recovered. "Um. Listen. Can I get back to you on that? The movie thing, I mean? I've kind of got a lot going on right now. . . ."

"Sure," Skip said. "You know the number." He picked up his backpack and left.

"Oh . . . my . . . God," Ruth said as soon as he was out of earshot. I told her to shut up. Only she didn't.

"He loves you," Ruth said. "Skip is in love with you. I can't believe it."

"Shut up, Ruth," I said, getting up and lifting my tray.

"Jessica and Skip, sittin' in a tree." Ruth could not stop laughing.

I walked over to the conveyor belt that carries our lunch trays into the kitchen and dumped it. As I was dumping it, I saw Tisha Murray and a few of the other cheerleaders and jocks—and Karen Sue, who followed the popular crowd wherever they went, thus making her deserving of Mark's nickname for her, the Wannabe—leaving the caf. They were going outside to lounge by the flagpole, which was where all the beautiful people in our school sat on nice days, working on their tans until the bell rang.

"Skip's never been out on a date before," Ruth said, coming up behind me to dump her own tray. "I wonder if he'll know not to bring his backpack along."

Ignoring Ruth, I followed Tisha and the others outside.

It was another gorgeous day—the kind that made sitting inside a classroom really hard. Summer was over, but somebody had forgotten to tell the weatherman. The sun beat down on the long, outstretched legs of the cheerleaders in the grass beneath the flagpole, and on the backs of the jocks who stood above them. I could not see Mark anywhere, but Tisha was sitting on the grass with one hand shading her eyes, talking to Jeff Day.

"Tisha," I said, going up to her.

She swung her face toward me, then gaped.

"Ohmigod," Tisha cried, scrambling to her feet. "There she is! The girl who saved Heather! Ohmigod! You are, like, a total and complete hero. You know that, don't you?"

I stood there awkwardly as everyone congratulated me for being such a hero. I don't think I'd ever been spoken to by so many popular kids all at once in my life. It was like, suddenly, I was one of them.

And gee, all I'd had to do was have a psychic vision about one of their friends, and then gone and saved her life.

See? Anyone can be popular. It's not hard at all.

"Tisha," I said, trying to be heard over the cacophony of excited voices around me. "Can I talk to you a minute?"

Tisha broke free from the others and came up to me, her tiny bird-head tilted questioningly. "Uh-huh, Ms. Hero," she said. "What is it?"

"Look, Tisha." I took her by the arm and started steering her, slowly, away from the crowd and toward the parking lot. "About that house. Where I found Heather. Did you know about that place?"

Tisha pushed some of her hair out of her eyes. "The house

on the pit road? Sure. Everyone knows about that house."

I was about to ask her if she knew who'd scattered their beer bottles throughout the house, and what was up with that skanky old mattress, when I was distracted by a familiar sound. It was a sound that, for a long time now, my ears had become totally attuned to, separating it out from all other sounds.

Because it was the sound of Rob's engine.

Well, his motorcycle's engine, to be exact.

I turned around, and there he was, coming around the corner and into the student lot, looking, I have to say, even better in daylight than he had the night before in moonlight. When he pulled up beside me, cut the engine, and took off his helmet, I thought my heart would burst at how handsome he looked in his jeans, motorcycle boots, and T-shirt, with his longish dark hair and bright gray eyes.

"Hey," he said. "Just the person I wanted to see. How are you doing?"

Conscious that the curious gazes of the entire student population of Ernest Pyle High School—well, at least the people who were enjoying the last minutes of their lunch break out of doors, anyway—were upon us, I said, casually, "Hi. I'm fine. How about you?"

Rob got off his bike and ran a hand through his hair.

"I'm okay, I guess," he said. "You're the one who got the third degree, not me. First from the Feds and then from your parents. Or am I wrong about that?"

"Oh, no," I said. "You're right. They weren't too happy. None of them. Allan and Jill *and* Joe and Toni."

"That's what I thought," Rob said. "So I figured I'd come over on my lunch break and, you know, see if you were all right. But you seem fine." His gray-eyed gaze skittered over me. "More than fine, actually. You dressed up for any particular reason?"

I had on another one of my new outfits from the outlet stores. It consisted of a black V-neck cropped shirt, a pink miniskirt, and black platform sandals. I looked *très chic*, as they'd say in French class.

"Oh," I said, glancing down at myself. "Just, you know. Making an effort this year. Trying to stay out of trouble."

Rob, to my delight, scowled at the skirt. "I don't see that happening real soon, Mastriani," he said. Then his gaze strayed toward my wrist. "Hey. Is that my watch?"

Busted. So busted. I'd found his watch, a heavy black one, covered with buttons that did weird things like tell the time in Nicaragua and stuff, in the pocket of his leather jacket—a jacket that was now hanging in a place of honor off one of my bedposts.

Of course I'd worn it to school. What girl wouldn't?

"Oh, yeah," I said, with elaborate nonchalance. "You loaned it to me last night. Remember?"

"Now I do," Rob said. "I was looking everywhere for that. Hand it over."

Bumming excessively, I unstrapped it. I know it was ridiculous, me wanting to hang onto the guy's watch, of all things, but I couldn't help it. It was like my trophy. My boyfriend trophy.

Except, of course, that Rob wasn't really my boyfriend.

"Here you go," I said, handing it to him. He took it and put in on, looking down at me like I was demented or something. Which I probably am.

"Do you like this watch or something?" he wanted to know. "Do you want one like it?"

"No," I said. "Not really." I couldn't tell him the truth, of course. How could I?

"Because I could get you one," he said. "If you want. But I would think you'd want, you know, one of those ladies' watches. This one looks kind of stupid on you."

"I don't want a watch," I said. Just your watch.

"Well," he said. "Okay. If you're sure."

"I'm sure."

He looked down at me. "You're kind of weird," he said. "You know that, don't you?"

Oh, well, this was just great. My boyfriend rides all the way over on his lunch break to tell me he thinks I'm weird. How romantic.

Thank God Tisha and the rest of those guys were too far away to hear what he was saying.

"Well, look, I have to get back," he said. "You stay out of

trouble. Leave the police work to the professionals, under-stand? And call me, okay?"

"Sure," I said.

He squinted at me in the sunlight. "Are you sure you're okay?"

"Yeah," I said. But of course I wasn't. Well, I mean, I was, and I wasn't. What I really wanted was for him to kiss me. I know. Retarded, right? I mean, me wanting him to kiss me, just because Tisha and a whole bunch of people were watching.

But it was kind of like the reason I'd wanted to hang onto his watch. I just wanted everyone to know I belonged to somebody.

And that that somebody was not Skip Abramowitz.

Now, I am not saying that Rob read my mind or anything. I mean, I'm the psychic, not him.

And I am not even saying that maybe I somehow put the suggestion in his head, either. My psychic powers extend toward one thing, and one thing only, and that's finding missing people, not putting suggestions into boys' heads that they should kiss me.

But be that as it may, Rob rolled his eyes, said, "Aw, screw it," wrapped a hand around the back of my neck, pulled me forward, and kissed me roughly on the top of my head.

And then he got on his bike and rode away.

CHAPTER 15

Two things happened right after that.

The first was that the bell rang. The second was that Karen Sue Hankey, who had seen the whole thing, went, in her shrill voice, "Oh, my God, Jess. Let a Grit kiss you, why don't you?"

Fortunately for Karen Sue—and for me, I guess—Todd Mintz was standing nearby. So when I dove at her—which I did immediately, of course—with the intention of gouging her eyes out with my thumbs, Todd caught me in midair, swung me around, and said, "Whoa there, tiger."

"Let go of me," I said, red-hot anger replacing the joy that had, just moments before, been coursing through me, causing me to suspect that my heart might explode. "Seriously, Todd, let me go."

"Yeah, let her go, Todd," Karen Sue called. She had dashed up the steps to the main building, and knew she was a safe enough distance away that even if Todd did let go of me—which he didn't seem to have any intention of doing—I'd never catch up to her before she'd ducked into the safety of the building. "I could use another five thousand bucks."

"I bet you could!" I roared. "You could take it and go buy yourself a freaking clue!"

Only I didn't say freaking.

"Oh, very nice," Karen Sue called down from the top of the steps. "Exactly the kind of language I'd expect from a girl whose brother is a murder suspect."

I froze, conscious of the fact that everyone around us was ducking for cover. Or maybe they were just going off to class. It was hard to tell.

"What," I asked, as Todd, sensing from my paralysis that I was no longer a threat to anyone, put me down again, "is she talking about?"

Todd, a big guy in a crew cut who looked as if he wished he were just about anywhere than where, in fact, he was, shrugged.

"I don't know, Jess," he said uncomfortably. "There's just this rumor going around—"

"What rumor?" I demanded.

Todd shifted his weight. "I, um, gotta get to class. I'm gonna be late."

"You tell me what freaking rumor," I snapped, "or I guarantee, you'll be crawling to class on your hands and knees."

Only again, I didn't say freaking. Todd didn't look scared, though. He just looked tired.

"Look, Jess," he said. "It's just a rumor, okay? Jenna Gibbon's older sister is married to a deputy sheriff with the county, and she said he told her that it looked like they might bring your brother in for questioning, because he fits some kind of profile, and because he doesn't have an alibi for either of the times the attacks occurred. Okay?"

I couldn't believe it. I really couldn't believe it.

Because they'd done it again. Special Agents Johnson and Smith, I mean. They'd said they were going to, and, by God, they had.

Well, and why not? They were with the FBI. They could do anything, right? I mean, who was going to stop them?

One person. Me.

I just couldn't figure out how. I fumed about it for the rest of the day, causing more than one teacher to ask me if perhaps I wouldn't be happier sitting in the guidance office for the rest of the day.

I told them I would—at least there, I figured, I would be free of annoying questions like what's the square root of sixteen hundred and five, what's the pluperfect for *avoir*—

but unfortunately, none of them followed through with their threat. When the bell rang at three, I was still free as a bird. Free enough to go stalking past Mark Leskowski, on my way to Ruth's car, without so much as a second glance.

"Jess," he called after me. "Hey, Jess!"

I turned at the sound of my name, and was mildly surprised to see Mark leave his car, which he'd been unlocking, and hurry up to me.

"Hey," he said. He had on a pair of Ray Bans, which he lifted as he looked down at me. "How are you? I was hoping I'd run into you. I hope I didn't get you into trouble last night."

I just blinked up at him. All I could think about was how, at any minute, the Feds might be hauling Douglas in for questioning about a couple of crimes he in no way could have committed.

If, that is, I didn't come clean about the ESP thing, and promise to help them find their stupid criminals.

"You know," Mark said, I guess judging from my blank expression that I didn't know what he was talking about. "When I dropped you off. Your parents looked kind of . . . mad."

"They weren't mad," I said. "They were concerned." And about Douglas, not me. Because Douglas hadn't been home. He had been off somewhere, alone. . . .

"Oh," Mark said. "Well, anyway. I just wanted to make

sure you were, you know, all right. That was pretty terrific, how you found Heather and all."

"Yeah," I said, noticing Ruth coming toward us. "Well, you know. Just doing my job, and all. Listen, I gotta—"

"I was thinking," Mark said, "that maybe if you aren't doing anything this weekend, you and I could, uh, I don't know, hang out."

"Yeah, whatever," I said, though truthfully, the thought of going to see Japanese anime with Skip was a lot more appealing than "uh, I don't know, hanging out" with Mark. "Why don't you give me a call?"

"I'll do that," Mark said. He waved at Ruth as she went by, studying us so intently she nearly barked her shins on her own car's bumper. "Hey," he said to her. "How you doing there?"

"Fine," Ruth said, unlocking the driver's door to her car. "Thanks."

Mark opened his own driver's side door, reached inside his car, and pulled out a duffel bag. Then he closed the door again and locked it. At our glances, which I suppose he perceived as curious—though in my case, it was merely glazed— he went, "Football practice," then shouldered the bag, and headed off in the direction of the gym.

"Jess," Ruth said when he was out of earshot. "Did I hear that correctly? Did Mark Leskowski just ask you out?"

"Yeah," I said.

"So that's how many people who've asked you out today? Two?"

"Yeah," I said, climbing into the passenger seat after she unlocked it from the inside.

"Jeez, Jess," she said. "That's like a record, or something. Why aren't you happier?"

"Because," I said, "one of the guys who asked me out today was, up until recently, a suspect in his own girlfriend's murder, and the other one is your brother."

Ruth went, "Yeah, but isn't Mark off the hook now, on account of what happened to Heather?"

"I guess so," I said. "But . . ."

"But what?" Ruth asked.

"But . . . Ruth, Tisha says they all knew about that house. Almost like . . . they're the ones who hang out there."

"Meaning?"

"Meaning it must have been one of them."

"One of who?"

"The in crowd," I said, gesturing toward the football field, where we could see the cheerleaders and some of the players already out there, practicing.

"Not necessarily," Ruth said. "I mean, Tisha knew about the house. She didn't say she'd ever been in there partying, did she?"

"Well," I said. "No. Not exactly. But—"

"I mean, come on. Don't you think those guys could find

a nicer place to party? Like Mark Leskowski's parents' rec room, for instance? I mean, I hear the Leskowskis have an indoor/outdoor pool."

"Maybe Mr. and Mrs. Leskowski disapprove of Mark's friends bringing their girlfriends over for a quickie in their rec room."

"Puh-lease," Ruth said as we cruised out of the parking lot and turned onto High School Road. "Why would any of them kill Amber? Or try to kill Heather? They're all friends, right?"

Right. Ruth was right. Ruth was always right. And I was always wrong. Well, almost always, anyway.

I guess I didn't really believe—in spite of what Tisha had told me, about all of them knowing about the house on the pit road—that they'd actually been involved in Amber's murder and Heather's attack. I mean, seriously: Mark Leskowski, wrapping his hands around his girlfriend's neck and strangling her? No way. He'd loved her. He'd cried in the guidance office in front of me, he'd loved her so much.

At least, I think that's why he'd been crying. He certainly hadn't been crying about his chances at winning a scholarship being endangered by his status as a murder suspect. I mean, that would have been just plain cold. Right?

And what about Heather? Did I suppose that Jeff Day or someone else on the team had tied Heather up and left her in that bathtub to die? Why? So she wouldn't narc on Mark?

No. It was ridiculous, Tisha's theory about the deranged

hillbillies made more sense. Maybe the cheerleaders and the football team partied in the house on the pit road, but they weren't the ones who'd left Heather there. No, that had been the work of someone else. Some sick, perverted individual.

But not—absolutely not—my brother.

I made sure of that, the second I got home. Not, of course, that I'd had any reason to doubt it. I just wanted to set the record straight. I stalked up the stairs—my mother wasn't home, thank God, so I didn't have to listen to any more lectures about how unsuitable it was of me to sneak out in the middle of the night with a boy who worked in a garage—and banged once on Douglas's bedroom door. Then I threw it open, because Douglas's bedroom door doesn't have a lock. My dad took the lock off, after he slit his wrists in there and we had to break the door down to get to him.

He's so used to me barging in, he doesn't even look up anymore.

"Get out," he said, without lifting his gaze from the copy of *Starship Troopers* he was perusing.

"Douglas," I said. "I have to know. Where were you last night from five o'clock until eight, when you came back to the house?"

He looked up at that. "Why do I have to tell you?" he wanted to know.

"Because," I said.

I wanted to tell him the truth, of course. I wanted to

say, Douglas, the Feds think you may have had something to do with Amber Mackey's murder, and Heather Montrose's attack. I need you to tell me you didn't do it. I need you to tell me that you have witnesses who can verify your whereabouts at the time these crimes occurred, and that your alibi is rock solid. Because unless you can tell me these things, I may have to take an after-school job working with some particularly nasty people.

In other words, the FBI.

But I wasn't sure I could say these things to Douglas. I wasn't sure I could say these things to Douglas because it was hard to tell anymore what might set off one of his episodes. Most of the time, he seemed normal to me. But every once in a while, something would upset him—something seemingly stupid, like that we were out of Cheerios—and suddenly the voices—Douglas's voices—were back.

On the other hand, this was something serious. It wasn't about Cheerios or reporters from *Good Housekeeping* magazine standing in our yard wanting to interview me. Not this time. This time, it was about people dying.

"Douglas," I said. "I mean it. I need to know where you were. There's this rumor going around—I don't believe it or anything—but there's this rumor going around that you killed Amber Mackey, and that last night you kidnapped Heather Montrose and left her to die."

"Whoa." Douglas, who was lying on his bed, put down his

comic book. "And how did I do this, supposedly? Using my superpowers?"

"No," I said. "I think the theory is that you snapped."

"I see," Douglas said. "And who is promoting this theory?"

"Well," I said, "Karen Sue Hankey in particular, but also most of the junior class of Ernie Pyle High, along with some of the seniors, and, um, oh, yeah, the Federal Bureau of Investigation."

"Hmmm." Douglas considered this. "I find that last part particularly troubling. Does the FBI have proof or something that I killed these girls?"

"It's just one girl that's dead," I said. "The other one just got beat up."

"Well, why can't they ask her who beat her up?" Douglas wanted to know. "I mean, she'll tell them it wasn't me."

"She doesn't know who did it," I said. "She said they wore masks. And I figure even if she did know, she's not going to say. I am assuming whoever did this to her told her he'd finish the job if she talked."

Douglas sat up. "You're serious," he said. "People really do suspect me of doing this?"

"Yeah," I said. "And the thing is, the Feds are saying that unless I, you know, become a junior G-man, they're going to pin this thing on you. So before I sign up for my pension plan, I need to know. Have you got any kind of alibi at all?"

Douglas blinked at me. His eyes, like mine, were brown.

"I thought," he said, "that you'd told them you lost your psychic abilities."

"I did," I said. "I think my finding Heather Montrose in the middle of nowhere last night kind of tipped them off that maybe I hadn't been completely up front with them on that particular subject."

"Oh." Douglas looked uncomfortable. "The thing is, what I was doing last night . . . and the night that other girl disappeared . . . well, I was sort of hoping nobody would find out."

I stared at him. My God! So he *had* been up to something! But not, surely, lying in wait at that house on the pit road for an innocent cheerleader to go strolling by. . . .

"Douglas," I said. "I don't care what you were doing, so long as it didn't involve anything illegal. I just need something—preferably the truth—to tell Allan and Jill, or my butt is going to have 'Property of the U.S. Government' on it for the foreseeable future. So long as they have something on you, they own me. So I have to know. Do they have something on you?"

"Well," Douglas said, slowly. "Sort of. . . ."

I could feel my world tilting, slowly . . . so slowly . . . right off its axis. My brother, Douglas. My big brother Douglas, whom all my life, it seemed, I'd been defending from others, people who called him retard, and spaz, and dorkus. People who wouldn't sit near him when we went to the movies as kids because sometimes he shouted things—that usually didn't make sense to everyone else—at the screen. People who wouldn't let their kids swim in the pool near him, because sometimes Douglas simply stopped swimming and just sank to the bottom, until a lifeguard noticed and fished him out. People who, every time a bike, or a dog, or a plaster yard gnome disappeared from the neighborhood, accused Douglas of having been the one who'd taken it, because Douglas . . . well, he wasn't all there, was he?

Only of course they were wrong. Douglas *was* all there. Just not in the way *they* considered normal.

But maybe, all this time . . . maybe they'd been right. Maybe this time Douglas really had done something wrong. Something so wrong, he didn't even want to tell me about it. *Me*, his kid sister, the one who'd learned how to swing a punch when she turned seven, just so that she could knock the blocks off the kids down the street who were calling him a freakazoid every time he passed by their house on the way to school.

"Douglas," I breathed, finding that my throat had suddenly, and inexplicably, closed. "What did you do?"

"Well," he said, unable to meet my gaze. "The truth is, Jess . . . the truth is . . ." He took a deep breath.

"I got a job."

CHAPTER 16

The first call came right after dinner.

It was a quiet affair, dinner that night. Quiet because every single person at the table was angry with somebody else.

My mother, of course, was angry at me for having snuck out the night before with Rob Wilkins, a boy of whom she did not approve because a) he was too old for me, b) he had no aspirations for attending college, c) he rode a motorcycle, d) his mother was a waitress, and e) we did not know who Mr. Wilkins was or what he did, if anything, or if there even *was* a Mr. Wilkins, which Mary Wilkins had never admitted either way, at least in the presence of my father.

And she didn't even know about the whole probation thing.

My father was mad at my mother for being what he called an elitist snob and for not being more grateful that Rob had insisted on accompanying me on another of what he referred to as my idiotic vision quests, and making sure I didn't get myself killed.

I was mad at my dad for calling my psychic visions idiotic, when they had, as a matter of fact, saved a lot of lives and reunited a lot of families. I was also mad at him for thinking that, without some guy to watch over me, I could not take care of myself. And of course I was mad at my mom for not liking Rob.

Meanwhile, Douglas was mad at me because I had told him he had to 'fess up to Mom and Dad about the job thing. I fully understood why he didn't want to—Mom was going to flip out at the idea of her baby boy soiling his fingers at any sort of menial labor. She seemed to be convinced that the slightest provocation—like him maybe lifting a sponge to wipe the milk he'd spilled on the kitchen counter—was going to set him off into another suicidal tailspin.

But Dad was the one who was really going to bust a gut when he found out, and I don't mean from laughing, either. In our family, if you worked, you worked at one of Dad's restaurants, or not at all. That whole thing where they'd let me spend the summer as a camp counselor? Yeah, that had only come about because of the intensive musical training I would be receiving while I was at Wawasee. Otherwise, you can bet I'd have been relegated to the steam table at Joe's.

So I wasn't too happy with Mom, Dad, or Douglas during that particular meal, and none of them were too happy with me, either. So when the phone rang, you can bet I ran for it, just as a way to avoid the uncomfortable silence that had hung over the table, interrupted only by the occasional scraping fork, or request for more parmesan.

"Hello?" I said, snatching up the receiver from the kitchen wall phone, which was the closest one to the dining room.

"Jess Mastriani?" a male voice asked.

"Yes," I said, with some surprise. I had expected it to be Ruth. She's about the only person who ever calls us. I mean, unless something is wrong at one of the restaurants. "This is she."

"I saw you talking to Tisha Murray today," the person on the other end of the phone said.

"Uh," I said. "Yeah." The voice sounded weird. Sort of muffled, like whoever it was was calling from inside a tunnel or something. "So?"

"So if you do it again," the voice said, "you're going to end up just like Amber Mackey."

I took the receiver away from my ear and looked down at it, just like they always do in horror movies when the psychopathic killer calls (generally from inside the house). I've always thought that was stupid, because it's not like you can see the person through the phone. But you know, it must be instinctive or something, because there I was, doing it.

I put the phone back up to my ear and went, "You're kidding me with this, right?"

"Stop asking questions about the house on the pit road," the voice said. "Or you'll be sorry, you stupid bitch."

"What are you going to do," I asked, "when I hang up and star-six-nine you, and five minutes later, the cops show up and haul your ass into jail, you freaking perv?"

The line went dead in my ear. I banged down the receiver and pushed the star button, then the number six, then the number nine. A phone rang, and then a woman's voice said, "The number you are trying to call cannot be reached by this method."

Damn! They'd called from an untraceable line. I should have known.

I hung up and went back into the dining room.

"I wish Ruth would stop calling us during dinner," my mother said. "She knows we eat at six thirty. It really isn't very thoughtful of her."

I didn't see any reason to disabuse her of the idea that it had been Ruth on the phone. I was pretty sure she wouldn't have liked hearing the truth. I plunked down into my seat and picked up my fork.

Only suddenly, I couldn't eat. I don't know what happened, but I had a piece of pasta halfway to my lips when suddenly my throat closed up and the table—and all of the food on it—went blurry.

Blurry because my eyes had filled up with tears. Tears! Just like Mark Leskowski, I was crying.

"Jess," my mother said, curiously. "Are you all right?"

I glanced at her, but I couldn't really see her. Nor could I speak. All I could think was, *Oh, my God. They are going to do to me what they did to Heather.*

And then I felt really, really cold, like someone had left the door to the walk-in freezer at Mastriani's wide open.

"Jessica?" my dad said. "What's wrong?"

But how could I tell them? How could I tell them about that phone call? It would just upset them. They would probably even call the police. That was all I needed, the police. Like I didn't have the FBI practically camped in my front yard.

But Heather . . . what had happened to Heather . . . I didn't want that to happen to me.

Suddenly Douglas shoved his salad plate to the floor. It shattered with a crash into a million pieces.

"Take that," he yelled at the bits of lettuce with ranch dressing littering the floor.

I blinked at him through my tears. What was going on? Was Douglas having an episode? I could tell by the expressions on my parents' faces that they thought so, anyway. They exchanged worried glances. . . .

And while their attention was focused on one another, Douglas glanced at me, and winked.

A second later, my mother was on her feet. "Dougie," she cried. "Dougie, what is it?"

My dad, as always, was more laconic about the whole thing. "Did you take all your medication today, Douglas?" he asked.

Then I knew. Douglas was faking an episode—to get them off my back about the crying thing. I felt a wave of love for Douglas wash over me. Had there ever, in the history of time, been such a cool big brother?

While my parents were distracted, I reached up and wiped the tears from my eyes with the backs of my wrists. What was happening to me? I never cried. This thing with Amber, and now with Heather, was getting way personal. I mean, now they were after me. Me!

Between the Feds thinking Douglas was the killer, and the real killers threatening that I was going to be their next victim, I guess I had a reason to cry. But it was still demoralizing, seeing as how it was such a Karen-Sue-Hankey thing to do.

While I was trying to get my emotions under control, and my parents were questioning Douglas about his mental health, the phone rang again. This time, I practically knocked my chair over, diving to get it.

"It's for me," I said quickly, lifting the receiver. "I'm sure."

No one so much as glanced in my direction. Douglas was still getting the third degree for his assault on his dinner salad.

"Jessica?" a voice I did not recognize asked in my ear.

"It's me," I said. And then, turning my back on the scene in the dining room, I said in a low rapid voice, "Listen, you loser, if you don't quit calling me, I swear I'm going to hunt you down and kill you like the dog that you are."

The voice went, sounding extremely taken aback, "But, Jess. This is the first time I've called you. Ever."

I sucked in my breath, finally realizing who it was. *"Skip?"*

"Yeah," Skip said. "It's me. Listen, I was just wondering if you'd thought about what we discussed today at lunch. You know. The movie. This weekend."

"Oh," I said. My mother came into the kitchen and went to the pantry, from which she removed a broom and dustpan. "Yeah," I said. "The movie. This weekend."

"Yeah," Skip said. "And I thought maybe, before the movie, we could go out. You know, for dinner or something."

"Uh," I said. My mother, holding the broom and dustpan, was standing there staring at me, the way lions on the Discovery Channel stare at the gazelles they are about to pounce on. All her concern for Douglas seemed to be forgotten. This was, after all, the first time I had ever been asked out within her earshot. My mother, who'd been a cheerleader herself—and Homecoming Queen, Prom Queen, County Fair Princess, and

Little Miss Corn Detassler—had been waiting sixteen years for me to start dating. She blamed the fact that I hadn't been out on a million dates already, like she had at my age, on my slovenly dress habits.

She didn't know anything about my right hook.

Well, actually, I think she did now, thanks to Mrs. Hankey's lawsuit.

"Yeah, about that, Skip," I said, turning my back on her. "I don't think I can go. I mean, my curfew is eleven. My mom would never let me stay out for a movie that didn't even start until midnight."

"Yes, I would," my mother said loudly, to my utter horror and disbelief. I brought the phone away from my ear and stared at her. "Mom," I said, flabbergasted.

"Don't look at me that way, Jessica," my mom said. "I mean, I am not completely inflexible. If you want to go to a midnight show with Skip, that's perfectly all right."

I couldn't believe it. After the grief she'd been giving me about Rob, I was pretty sure she was never letting me out of the house again, let alone with a boy.

But apparently it was just one particular boy I was banned from seeing socially.

And that boy was not Skip Abramowitz.

"I mean," my mother went on, "it's not like your father and I don't know Skip. He has grown into a very responsible young man. Of course you can go to the movies with him."

I gaped at her. "Ma," I said. "The movie doesn't even start until midnight."

"So long as Skip has you home right after it ends," my mother said.

"Oh," came a voice from the receiver, which I was holding limply in my hand. "I will, Mrs. Mastriani. Don't worry!"

And just like that, I had a date with Skip Abramowitz.

Well, it wasn't like I could get out of it after that. Not without completely humiliating him. Or myself, for that matter.

"Mom," I yelled when I had hung up. "I don't want to go out with Skip!

"Why not?" Mom wanted to know. "I think he's a very nice boy."

Translation: He doesn't own a motorcycle, has never worked in a garage, and did really well on his PSATs.

And, oh, yeah, his dad happens to be the highest-paid lawyer in town.

"I think you're being unfair, Jessica," my mother said. "True, Skip may not be the most exciting boy you know, but he's extremely sweet."

"Sweet! He blew up my favorite Barbie!"

"That was years ago," my mom said. "I think Skip's grown into a real gentleman. You two will have a wonderful time." She grew thoughtful. "You know, I just found a skirt pattern the other day that would be perfect for a casual night out at the movies. And there are a few yards of gingham left over from those curtains I made for the guest room. . . ."

See, this is the problem with having a stay-at-home mom. She thinks up little projects to do all the time, like making me a skirt from material left over from curtains. I swear sometimes I'm not sure who she's supposed to be, my mother or Maria von Trapp.

Before I could say anything like, "No, thanks, Mom. I just spent a fortune at Esprit, I think I can manage to find something to wear on my own," or even, "Mom, if you think I'm not planning on coming down with something Saturday night just before this date, you've got another think coming," Douglas came into the kitchen, holding his dinner plate, and said, "Yeah, Jess. Skip's really neat."

I shot him a warning look. "Watch it, Comic-Book Boy," I growled.

Douglas, looking alarmed, noticed Mom standing there with the broom. "Oh, hey," he said, putting his empty dinner plate down in the sink. "I'll clean it up, don't worry. It was my fault, anyway."

My mom snatched the broom out of his reach. "No, no," she said, hurrying back into the dining room. "I'll do it."

Which was kind of sad. Because of course she was only doing it because she didn't want Douglas messing with bits of broken glass. His suicide attempt last Christmas had convinced her that he wasn't to be trusted around sharp objects.

"See," Douglas said, as the swinging door closed behind her, "what I go through for you? Now she's going to be watching me like a hawk for the next few days."

I suppose I should have been grateful to him. But all I could think was that things would be a lot less stressful if Douglas would just come clean.

"Why don't you go tell them now?" I asked. All right, begged. "Before *Entertainment Tonight.* You know Mom never lets a fight last more than five minutes into *ET.*"

Douglas was rinsing his plate.

"No way," he said, not looking at me.

I nearly burst a capillary, I was so mad.

"Douglas," I hissed. "If you think I'm not telling the Feds, you're out of your mind. I can't let them go around thinking they have something on me. I'm telling them. And if they know, how long do you think it's going to be before Mom and Dad find out? It's better for *you* to tell them than the damned FBI, don't you think?"

Douglas turned the water off.

"It's just that you know what Dad's going to say," he said. "If I'm well enough to work behind the counter at the comic book store, I'm well enough to work in the kitchens at Mastriani's. But I can't stand food service. You know that."

"Who can?" I wanted to know. But when your dad owned

three of the most popular restaurants in town, you didn't have much of a choice.

"And Mom." Douglas shook his head. "You know how Mom's going to react. That out there? That was nothing."

"That's why I'd tell them now," I said, "before they find out from somebody else. I mean, for God's sake, Douglas. You've been working there for two weeks already. You think they aren't going to hear about it from somebody?"

"Look, Jess," Douglas said. "I'll tell them. I swear I will. Just let me do it my own way, in my own time. I mean, you know how Mom is—"

The swinging door to the dining room banged open, and my mother, carrying the now full dustpan, came into the kitchen.

"You know how Mom is what?" she asked, looking suspiciously from Douglas to me and then back again.

Fortunately, the phone rang.

Again.

I leapt for it, but I was too late. My dad had already picked up the extension in the den.

"Jess," he yelled. "Phone for you."

Great. My mother's eyes lit up. You could totally tell that she thought it was starting for me. You know, the popularity that she had had when she was my age, which had so far eluded me during my tenure at Ernie Pyle High. As a daughter I was, I knew, pretty disappointing to her, because I wasn't already going steady with a guy like Mark Leskowski. I guess at this point, even a date with Skip was preferable to no date at all.

Or Rob.

Too bad she didn't know that the kind of calls I'd been receiving all night were not exactly from members of the pep squad, wanting to discuss the next day's bake sale.

No, more like members of the death squad, wanting to discuss my imminent demise.

But when I picked up, I found that it wasn't my prank caller at all. It was Special Agent Johnson. "Well, Jessica," he said. "Have you given any thought to our conversation this morning?"

I looked at my mom and Douglas. "Uh, do you guys mind?" I asked. "This is kind of personal."

My mom's eyebrows furrowed. "It isn't that boy, is it?" she wanted to know. "That Wilkins person?"

That Wilkins person. It was almost as bad as the Jerk.

"No," I said. "It's another boy."

Which wasn't technically even a lie. And which made my mom smile as happily as she left the room as if I'd just been voted Most Likely to Marry a Doctor. Douglas left too, only he didn't look half so happy as Mom did.

"Which conversation?" I asked Special Agent Johnson, as soon as my mother was gone. "Oh, you mean the one where you suggested my brother might, in fact, be Amber Mackey's killer? And that if I didn't help you track down your little Ten Most Wanteds, you'd haul him in for questioning about it?"

"Well, I don't think I put it quite like that," Special Agent Johnson said. "But that, in essence, is why I'm calling."

"I hate to break it to you," I said, "but Douglas has got a rock solid alibi for the times both those girls disappeared. Just ask his new employers down at Comix Underground."

There was silence on the line. Then Special Agent Johnson chuckled.

"I was wondering," he said, "how long it would take for him to work up the courage to tell you."

I felt a jolt of rage. *You knew?* I was going to scream into the receiver.

But then it hit me. Of course he'd known. He and his partner had known all along. They'd just been using the fact that I didn't know to yank my chain.

Well, that's what they get paid for. Covert operations.

"If you're done having your little fun with me," I said— with more irritation than was perhaps necessary, but I felt tears threatening again—"you might actually want to do some work for a change. I mean, I know it's more fun for you all to try to get me to do your job for you, but in this particular case, I think you've got the expertise."

I told him about my mysterious caller. Special Agent Johnson was, I must say, mightily interested.

"And you say you didn't recognize the voice?" he asked.

"Well," I said. "It sounded kind of muffled."

"He probably put something over the mouthpiece of the phone he was using," Special Agent Johnson said, "for fear you might recognize him. Let me ask you something. Was the voice distinctive in any way? Any accents, or anything?"

For some reason, I found myself remembering the Grit Test. You know, the pen versus pin thing.

"No," I said, with some surprise at myself for not having realized it before. "No accent at all."

"Good," Special Agent Johnson said. "Good girl. All right, we'll work on seeing if we can come up with the number this person called from."

"Well, I would think you should be able to come up with that pretty easily," I said. "Seeing as how you've had my phone tapped since like, forever."

"That's very funny, Jessica," Special Agent Johnson said, dryly. "You are aware, of course, that the Bureau would never do anything to violate a U.S. citizen's rights during an investigation."

"Haw," I said. Somehow, knowing Special Agent Johnson was on the case made me feel better. Crazy, huh, considering how much having the Feds following me around all the time used to bug me? "Haw, haw."

"And don't worry, Jessica," Special Agent Johnson said.

"You and your family are in no danger. We'll post plenty of operatives outside your home tonight."

Too bad that isn't what they chose to destroy in order to assure me of how serious they were about their threats. Our home, I mean.

Instead, they burned down Mastriani's.

CHAPTER 17

You'd have thought I'd be able to catch a break, wouldn't you? I mean, it wasn't like I'd gotten any sleep the night before. No, they had to make sure I didn't get any the next night, either.

Well, okay, I got *some.* The call didn't come until after three.

Three in the morning, I mean.

But when it did come, there was no sleep for anyone in the Mastriani household. Not for a long, long time.

I, of course, thought it was for me.

And why not? It wasn't like the phone had rung—not even once that night—for anybody else in the house. No, all of my mother's dreams for me were finally coming true: I was Miss Popularity, all right.

Too bad the only dates I was getting were dates with, um, death.

Well, and Skip Abramowitz.

When the phone started ringing its head off at three A.M., I shot out of bed before I was even fully awake and dove for the extension in my room, as if somehow, by catching it on the second ring, I was going to keep the rest of the house from waking up.

Yeah, nice try.

The voice on the other end of the line was familiar, but it wasn't one of my new friends. You know, the ones who'd promised to kill me if I talked to Tisha Murray anymore about the house on the pit road.

It was, instead, a woman's voice. It took me a minute to realize it was Special Agent Smith.

"Jessica," she said when I answered. And then, when my dad got on the line in his bedroom, and went, blearily, "Hullo?" she added, "Mr. Mastriani."

My dad and I didn't say anything. He, I think, was still trying to wake up. I, of course, was tensing for what I knew was going to follow . . . or thought I knew, anyway. Someone else was missing. Tisha Murray, maybe.

Or Heather Montrose. Despite the guard they'd put on her room in the hospital, someone had managed to sneak in, and finish the job they'd started. Heather was dead.

Either that, or they'd found someone. They'd found someone trying to sneak into my house to kill me.

But of course it wasn't that at all. It wasn't any of those things.

"I'm sorry to wake you, sir," Jill said, sounding as if she meant it. "But I think you should know that your restaurant, Mastriani's, is on fire. Could you please—"

But Jill never got to finish, because my dad had dropped the phone and was, if I knew him, already reaching for his pants.

"We'll be right there," I said.

"No, Jessica, not you. You should—"

But I never found out what I have should have done, because I'd hung up.

When I met him at the front door a few seconds later, I saw that I'd been right. My dad was fully dressed—well, he had on pants and shoes. He was still wearing his pajama top as a shirt. When he saw me, he said, "Stay here with your mother and brother."

I, however, had gotten dressed, too.

"No way," I said.

He looked annoyed but grateful at the same time, which was quite a feat, if you think about it.

As soon as we stepped outside, we could see it. An orange glow reflected against the low hanging clouds in the night sky. And not a small glow, either, but something that looked like that burning-of-Atlanta scene out of *Gone With the Wind*.

"Christ almighty," my dad said when he saw it.

I, of course, was busy consulting with my friends across the street. The ones in the white van.

"Hey," I said, tapping on the rolled up window on the driver's side. "I gotta go downtown with my dad. Stay here and keep an eye on the place while I'm gone, okay?"

There was no response, but I hadn't expected any. People who are supposed to be covertly following you don't like it when you come up and start talking to them, even if their boss knows that you know they're there.

Well, you know what I mean.

The drive downtown took no time at all. At least, it didn't usually. And yet it seemed to take ages that night. Our house is only a few blocks from downtown . . . a fifteen-minute stroll, at most, a four-minute drive. The streets, at three in the morning, were empty. That wasn't the problem. It was that orange glow hanging in the sky above our heads that we couldn't take our eyes off of. A couple of times, my dad nearly drove off the side of the road, he was so transfixed by it. It was a good thing, actually, that I was there, since I'd taken the wheel and gone, "Dad."

"Don't worry," I said to him, a minute later. "That isn't it. That orange light? That's probably, you know, heat lightning."

"Staying in one place?" my dad asked.

"Sure," I said. "I read about it. In Bio."

God, I am such a liar.

And then we turned the corner onto Main. And there it was.

And it wasn't heat lightning. Oh, no.

Once, a long time ago, the people who lived across the street from us had a log roll out of their fireplace and set the living room curtains on fire. That was how I'd expected the fire at Mastriani's to be. You know, flames in the windows, and maybe some smoke billowing out of the open front door. The fire department would be there, of course, and they'd put the flames out, and that would be the end of it. That's what had happened with our neighbors. Their curtains were lost, and the carpet had to be replaced, along with a couch that had gotten completely soaked by the fire hoses.

But you know that night—the night the curtains caught fire—the people who lived across the street slept in their own—somewhat smoky-smelling—beds. They hadn't needed to go stay with relatives or in a shelter or a hotel or anything, because of course their house was still standing.

The fire at Mastriani's was not that kind of fire. It was not that kind of fire at all. The fire at Mastriani's was a writhing, breathing, living thing. It was, to put it mildly, awesome in its destructive power. Flames were shooting thirty, forty feet in the air from the roof. The entire building was a glowing ball of fire. We couldn't get closer than two hundred feet away from it, there were so many fire engines parked along the street. Dozens of firefighters, wielding hoses spitting streams of water, weaved a dreamy, dancelike pattern in front of the building, trying to douse the flames.

But it was a losing battle. You did not need to be a fire marshall to tell that. The place was engulfed, consumed in flames. It was not even recognizable anymore. The green and gold awning above the door, that shielded customers from the rain? Gone. The matching green sign, with MASTRIANI'S spelled out across it in gold script? Gone. The window boxes on the second floor administrative offices? Gone. The new industrial freezers? Gone. The make-out table where Mark Leskowski and I had sat? Gone. Everything, gone.

Just like that.

Well, not just like that, actually. Because as my dad and I got out of the car and picked our way toward the place, carefully stepping over the hoses that, pulsing like live snakes, crisscrossed the road, we could see that a lot of people were working very hard to save what appeared to me, anyway, to be a lost cause. Firefighters shouted above the hiss of water and the roar of the flame, coughing in the thick, black smoke that instantly clogged the throat and lungs.

One of them noticed us and said to stand back. My dad yelled, "I own the place," and the firefighter directed us to a group of people who were standing across the street, their faces bathed in orange light.

"Joe," one of them yelled, and I recognized him as the mayor of our town, which is small. If there were going to be a catastrophic fire threatening not only one prominent downtown business, but the businesses around it as well, you would expect the mayor to be there.

"Jesus, Joe," the mayor said. "I'm sorry."

"Was anybody hurt?" my dad asked, coming to stand between the mayor and a man I knew from his periodic inspections to be the fire chief. "Nobody's been hurt, have they?"

"Naw," the mayor said. "Coupla Richie's guys, trying to be heroes, went in to make sure nobody was still inside, and got a chestful of smoke for their efforts."

"They'll be okay," Richard Parks, the fire chief, said. "Nobody was in there, Joe. Don't worry about that."

My dad looked relieved, but only moderately so. "What are the chances of it spreading?" Mastriani's was a freestanding structure, a Victorian-type house flanked on either side by a New Age bookstore and a bank branch, with a shared parking lot behind it. "The bank? Harmony Books?"

"We're watering them down," the fire chief said. "So far, so good. Coupla sparks landed on the roof of the bookstore and went out right away. We got here in time, Joe, don't worry. Well, in time to save the neighboring structures, anyway."

His voice was sorrowful. And why not? He'd eaten at Mastriani's a lot. Just like every single man there, pointing a hose at it.

"What happened?" my dad asked in a stunned voice. "I mean, how did it start? Does anybody know?"

"Couldn't say," Captain Parks told us. "Folks over at the jailhouse heard an explosion, looked out, saw the place was on fire. Couldn'ta been more than eight, nine minutes ago. Place went up like a cinder."

"Which suggests," a woman's voice said, "an accelerant to me."

We all looked around. And there stood Special Agents Smith and Johnson, looking concerned and maybe a little worse for wear. To be roused from a dead sleep two nights in a row was a little rough, even for them.

"My thinking exactly," the fire chief said.

"Wait a minute." My dad, his face scratchy-looking with a half-night's growth of beard bristle, stared at the FBI agents. "What are you saying? You're saying somebody purposefully started this fire?"

"No way it coulda spread that fast, Joe," the fire chief said, "or burned so hot. Not without some kind of accelerant. From the smell, I'm guessing gasoline, but we won't know until the fire's out and the place has cooled down enough for us to—"

"Gasoline?" My dad looked as if he was about to have a heart attack. Seriously. All these veins I had never noticed before were standing out in his forehead, and his neck looked kind of skinny, like it could barely support the weight of his head.

Or maybe it was just that, in the bright light from the fire, I was getting my first really good look at him in a while.

"Why in God's name would anybody do this?" my dad demanded. "Why would anybody deliberately burn the place down?"

The sheriff, whom I hadn't noticed before, cleared his throat and went, "Disgruntled employee, maybe."

"I haven't fired anybody," my dad said. "Not in months."

That was true. My dad didn't like firing people, so he only hired people he was pretty sure were going to work out. And mostly, his instincts were right on.

"Well," the sheriff said, gazing almost admiringly at the blaze across the street. "There'll be an investigation. That's for sure. Case of arson? You can bet your insurance company'll be all over it. We'll get to the bottom of it. Eventually."

Eventually. Sure. Or they could, I supposed, just have asked me. I'd have been able to tell them who started it. I knew good and well.

Well, actually, what I knew was the why. Not the who. But the why was clear enough.

It was a warning. A warning about what would happen to me if I didn't quit asking questions about the house on the pit road.

Which was so unfair. My dad. My poor dad. He'd done nothing to deserve this, nothing at all.

Looking at him, at his face as he tried to joke with the

mayor and the sheriff and the fire chief, my heart swelled with pity. He was joking, but inside, I knew, his heart was breaking. My dad had loved Mastriani's, which he'd opened shortly after he and my mom had married. It had been his first restaurant, his first baby . . . just like Douglas was Mom's first baby. And now that baby was going up in a puff of smoke.

Well, not really a puff, actually. More like a wall. A great big wall of smoke that would soon be floating across the county like a storm cloud.

"Don't even think about it, Jess," Special Agent Johnson said, not without some affability.

I turned to blink at him. "Think about what?"

"Finding out who did this," Allan said, "and going after them yourself. We're talking about some dangerous—and fairly sick—criminals here. You leave the investigating to us, understand?"

For once, I was perfectly willing to do so. I mean, I was mad and everything. Don't get me wrong. But a part of me was also scared. More scared even than I'd been when I'd seen Heather all tied up in that bathtub. More scared than I'd been on that motorcycle, careening through the darkness of those woods.

Because this—the fire—was more terrible, in a way, than either of those things. This was awful, more awful than Heather's broken arm, and way more awful than me tipping over beneath an eight-hundred-pound bike.

Because this . . . this was out of control. This was dangerous. This was deadly.

Like what had happened to Amber.

"Don't worry," I said, gulping. "I will."

"Yeah," Special Agent Johnson said, clearly not believing me. "Right."

And then I heard it. My mom's voice, calling out my dad's name.

She came toward us, picking her way through the fire hoses, with a trench coat thrown over her nightgown and Douglas holding onto her elbow to keep her from tripping in her high-heeled sandals. My dad, seeing her, started forward, meeting her just beside one of the biggest fire engines.

"Oh, Joe," my mom said, sighing as she watched the flames that still seemed to rise so high into the sky, they were practically licking it. "Oh, Joe."

"It's all right, Toni," my dad said, taking her hand. "I mean, don't worry. The insurance is all paid up. We're totally covered. We can rebuild."

"But all that work, Joe," my mom said. Her gaze never left the fire, as if it had transfixed her. And you know, even though it was this horrible thing, it was still beautiful, in a way. The firefighters had given up trying to put the flames out, and were instead concentrating on keeping them from spreading to the buildings next door. And so far, they were doing a good job.

"All your hard work. Twenty years of it." I saw my mom tilt her head until it was resting on my dad's shoulder. "I'm so sorry, Joe."

"It's okay," my dad said. He let go of her hand, and put his arm around her instead. "It's just a restaurant. That's all. Just a restaurant."

Just a restaurant. Just my dad's dream restaurant, that's all, the one he'd worked hardest and longest on. Joe's, my dad's less-expensive restaurant, brought in barely half the income of Mastriani's, and Joe Junior's, the take-out pizza place, even less than that. We were, I knew, going to be hurting financially for a while, insurance or no insurance.

But my dad didn't seem to care. He gave my mom a squeeze and said, with only somewhat forced jocularity, "Hey, if something had to go, I'm glad it's this and not the house."

They didn't say anything else after that. They just stood there with their arms around each other and their heads together, watching a big part of their livelihood go up in smoke.

Douglas came up to me. I didn't tell him what I was thinking, which was that the last time I'd seen our parents standing like that, it had been outside the emergency room, when he'd slashed his wrists last Christmas Eve.

"I guess," Douglas said, "now probably wouldn't be a good time to tell them, right?"

I looked at him. "Tell them what?"

"About my new job."

I couldn't help smiling a little at that.

"Uh, no," I said. "Now would definitely not be a good time to tell them about your new job."

And so the four of us stood and watched Mastriani's burn down.

CHAPTER 18

By the time I got to school the next day, it was noon, and everyone—everyone in the entire town—had heard what had happened. When I walked through the doors of the caf—it was my lunch period when Mom dropped me off—all these people came rushing up to me to express their condolences. Really, just like somebody had died.

And, in a way, I guess, somebody *had* died. I mean, Mastriani's was an institution in our town. It was where people went when they wanted to splurge, like on a birthday, or before prom or something.

But I guess not anymore.

I think I've mentioned how extremely not popular I am

at Ernest Pyle High. I mean, I don't have what you would call school spirit. I could really care less if the Cougars win State, or even if they win, period. And I don't think I've ever been invited to a party. You know the ones, where somebody's parents aren't home, so everybody comes over with a keg and trashes the place, like in the movies?

Yeah, I've never been invited to one of those.

So I guess you could say I was pretty surprised by the outpouring of sympathy for my situation from a certain segment of the student population at Ernie Pyle High. Because it wasn't just Ruth and Skip and people from the orchestra who came up to say they were sorry to hear about what had happened.

No, Todd Mintz came up, and a bunch of the Pompettes, and Tisha Murray and Jeff Day, and even the king of the popular crowd himself, Mark Leskowski.

It was almost enough to take a girl's mind off the fact that there was someone out there who wanted her dead—and who'd see that she got that way, if she came too close to the truth.

"I can't believe it," Mark said, plopping his truly magnificent rear end down on the bench beside me and regarding me with those deep brown eyes. "I mean, we were just *there*, you and I."

"Yeah," I said, uncomfortably aware of the number of envious glances coming my way. After all, with Amber gone,

Mark was fair game. I saw more than one cheerleader nudge the girl next to her and point to the two of us, sitting there with our heads so close together at the otherwise empty table.

Of course, they had no way of knowing that my heart belonged—and always would—to another.

"At least nobody was hurt," Mark said. "I mean, could you imagine if it had happened during the dinner rush or something?"

"It would have been hard," I said to him, "for whoever poured gasoline all over the place, to have done so without anybody noticing during the dinner rush."

Mark's dark eyebrows lifted. "You mean somebody did it on *purpose*? But *why*? And *who*?"

"My guess would be whoever killed Amber and then beat up Heather. And they did it as a warning," I said. "To me. To back off."

Mark looked stunned. "God," he said. "That *sucks*."

It was more or less an adequate representation of my feelings on the matter, and so I nodded.

"Yeah," I said. "Doesn't it?"

It was right after that that the bell rang. Mark said, "Hey, listen. Maybe we could get together or something this weekend. I mean, if you're up for it. I'll give you a call."

Okay, I'll admit it. It was kind of cool to have the best-looking guy in school—vice-president of the senior class, quarterback, and all around hottie—say things to me like "I'll give you a call." I mean, don't get me wrong: he was no Rob Wilkins or anything. There was that whole "unacceptable" thing, which was a little, I don't know, militaristic for me.

But hey. He'd asked me out. Twice now. All of a sudden, I had a clue as to how my mom must have felt, when she was in school. You know, Little Miss Corn Detassler and all of that. I could see why she'd been so excited for me when Skip had called. Being popular—well, it's pretty fun.

Or at least it was, up until Karen Sue Hankey came up to me on my way to my locker and went, in her snotty Karen-Sue-Hankey voice, "Missed you at chair auditions this morning."

I froze, one hand on my combination lock. The auditions for chair placement in Orchestra. I had completely forgotten. After all, I had been dealing with some pretty heavy stuff lately . . . threats to my life, and the destruction of a large portion of my family's business. It wasn't any wonder I hadn't been able to keep my schedule straight.

But wait a minute . . . the winds had been scheduled for Thursday.

Which was today.

"I suppose, since you missed them," Karen Sue said, "you'll have to be last chair until next semester's try outs. Too bad. Mr. Vine is posting the placements after school and I'm betting I'll be—Hey!"

The reason Karen Sue yelled "Hey" is because I pushed

her. Not hard or anything. I just had to get somewhere, and fast, and she was in my way.

And that somewhere was the teachers' lounge, where I knew Mr. Vine spent fifth period, decompressing after freshman Orchestra.

I tore down the hall, bumping into people rushing off to class, and not even saying excuse me. It wasn't fair. It totally wasn't fair. A person with an excused absence like mine—and my absence *was* excused—should be allowed to audition like everybody else, not relegated to last chair just because some psycho had burned her parents' restaurant down.

The thing was, I had totally learned to sight read over the summer. I had had this big plan of blowing Mr. Vine away with my awesome new musical abilities. I didn't want to be first chair or anything, but I definitely deserved third, maybe even second. No way was I going to take last chair. Not lying down, anyway.

I skidded to a halt in front of the door to the teachers' lounge. I was going to be late for Bio, but I didn't care. I banged on the door.

As I was doing so, somebody touched my shoulder. I turned around, and was surprised to see Claire Lippman, who hardly ever spoke to me in the hallways. Not because she was snotty or anything, just because, usually, she had her head buried in a script.

"Jess," she said. Claire did not look good. Which was also

unusual, because Claire is one of those, you know, raving beauties. The kind you maybe don't notice right off, but the more you look at her, the more you realize that she is perfect.

She didn't look so perfect just then, though. She'd chewed all the lipstick off her lower lip, and the pink sweater she'd flung around her shoulders—she was wearing a white sleeveless top—was in grave danger of slipping off and landing on the floor.

"Jess, I . . ." Claire looked up and down the hallway. It was clearing out, as people darted into class. "I really need to talk to you."

I could tell something was wrong. Really wrong.

"What's wrong, Claire?" I asked, putting my hand on her arm. "Are you—"

All right. Are you all right. That's what I'd been going to ask her.

Only I never got the chance, because of two things that happened at almost the same time.

The first was that the door to the teachers' lounge opened, and Mr. Lewis, the chemistry teacher, stood there, looking down at me like I was crazy, because of course people aren't supposed to bother teachers when they are in the lounge.

The second thing that happened was that Mark Leskowski emerged from the guidance office, which was across the hall from the teachers' lounge, holding a stack of college applications they'd evidently been keeping there for him.

"What may I do for you, Miss Mastriani?" Mr. Lewis asked. I had never had Chemistry, but he apparently knew my name from last spring, when I'd been in the paper so much.

"Hey," Mark said, to Claire and me. "How you two doing?"

Which was when Claire did an extraordinary thing. She spun around and took off down the hallway, so fast that she didn't even notice her sweater slip off her shoulders and fall to the carpet.

Mr. Lewis, looking after her, shook his head.

"Drama club," he muttered.

Mark and I—staring after Claire, who disappeared around the corner, heading in the direction of the drama wing, where the auditorium and stuff were—glanced at one another. Mark rolled his eyes and shrugged, as if to say, "Dames. What can you do?"

"See ya," he said, and started off in the opposite direction, toward the gym.

Not knowing what else to do, I bent down and picked up Claire's sweater. It was really soft, and when I glanced at the tag, I saw why. One hundred percent cashmere. She was going to miss this. I'd hang onto it, I decided, until I saw her again.

"Well, Miss Mastriani?" Mr. Lewis said, startling me.

I asked to see Mr. Vine. Mr. Lewis sighed, then went and got him.

Mr. Vine, when he came to the door, seemed to find my

concern that I would be relegated to last chair in the flute section very amusing.

"Do you really think," he said, his eyes twinkling, "that I'd do that to you, Jess? We all know why you weren't there. Don't worry about it. Meet me right after last period today and we'll hold your audition. All right?"

I felt relief wash over me. "All right," I said. "Thanks a lot, Mr. Vine."

Shaking his head, Mr. Vine went back into the lounge. When the door closed, I heard him laughing.

But I didn't care. I had my audition. That's all that mattered.

Or at least, that's all that mattered to me, then. But as the day wore on, something else began to nag me.

And it wasn't the same thing that had been nagging me all week, either. I mean, the fact that somebody was going around, attacking cheerleaders, making threatening phone calls to the local psychic, and burning down her parents' restaurant.

No, it was something more than that. It was something I couldn't quite put my finger on. It wasn't until the middle of seventh period that I realized what it was.

I was scared.

Seriously. I was walking around the hallways of Ernest Pyle High School, feeling frightened out of my mind.

Oh, not like I was a quivering mess, or anything. I wasn't

going around, grabbing people and weeping into their shirt-fronts.

But I was scared. I was scared about what was happening at home, at my house on Lumley Lane. The Feds were still watching it—heck, they were probably watching me, though I hadn't noticed any tails as I flitted through the hallways.

But that wasn't all. It wasn't just that I was scared. It was that I knew something was wrong. Something more than just Mastriani's exploding and Amber being dead and Heather hospitalized.

Look, I'm not saying it was a psychic thing. Not at all. Not then.

But there was definitely something not right going on, and it wasn't just that all these things had been happening, and the Feds, so far as I knew, didn't even have a suspect, let alone an arrest. It was more than that. It was . . .

Creepy.

Like the idea of being out a date with Skip. Only much, much worse.

Which was why, midway through seventh period, I couldn't take it anymore. I don't know. I guess I snapped. My hand shot up into the air before I knew what was happening.

And when Mademoiselle MacKenzie, not particularly thrilled to have me interrupt in the middle of our in-depth look at the never-ending battle of wills between Alix and Michel (*Alix mes du sel dans la boule de Michel*), asked, "Qu'est-ce que *vous voulez, Jessica?"* and I went, in English, "I need the hall pass," she made no effort whatsoever to hide her annoyance.

"Can't you wait," she wanted to know, "for the bell?"

It was a logical question, of course. It was two-thirty. Only a half hour of school left.

But the answer was no. No, I couldn't wait. I couldn't even say why, but one thing I definitely knew I could not do was wait.

Disgusted, Mademoiselle MacKenzie handed me the wooden bathroom pass, and I beat it out of there before she could say *"Au revoir."*

But I didn't head for the bathroom. Instead, I went downstairs—the language labs are on the third floor—to the guidance office. I wasn't even sure why I was heading in that direction until I saw them. The doors to the guidance office, and across from it, the teachers' lounge.

That's when I knew. Claire. Claire, touching my shoulder, just before fifth period. She had wanted to tell me something, but she hadn't gotten the chance. Her eyes—those pretty blue eyes—had widened as she'd looked down at me, and filled—I knew it now, though at the time, I think I had been too worried about myself, and my stupid chair position, to notice—with fear.

Fear. *Fear.*

I burst into the guidance office and startled Helen, the secretary, half out of her wits.

"I need to know what class Claire Lippman's in," I said, throwing my books down onto her desk. "And I need to know *now.*"

Helen stared up at me, her expression friendly but quizzical. "Jess," she said. "You know I can't just give you confidential student—"

"I need to know *now*!" I yelled.

The door to Mr. Goodhart's office opened. To my surprise, not just Mr. Goodhart, but also Special Agent Johnson, stepped out into the waiting area.

"Jessica?" Mr. Goodhart looked perplexed. "What are you doing here? What's wrong?"

Helen had hit the button on her computer keyboard that made Minesweeper, which she'd been playing, disappear. Now she was bringing up the student schedules. Mr. Goodhart noticed and went, "Helen, what are you doing?"

"She needs to know where Claire Lippman is," Helen said. "I'm just looking it up for her."

Mr. Goodhart looked more perplexed than ever. "You know you can't tell her that, Helen," he said. "That's confidential."

"Why do you need to know where this girl is, Jessica?" Special Agent Johnson asked. "Has something happened to her?"

"I don't know," I said. Which was the truth. I didn't know. Except . . . Except that I did.

"I just need to know," I said. "Okay? She said she had something to tell me, but then she didn't get a chance to, because—"

"Claire Lippman," Helen said, "has PE seventh period."

"Helen!" Mr. Goodhart was genuinely shocked. "What's the matter with you?"

"Thanks," I said, gathering up my books and giving the secretary a grateful smile. "Thanks a lot."

I was almost out the door when Helen called, "Except that she isn't there, Jess. . . ."

I froze.

And then slowly spun around.

"What do you mean, she isn't there?" I asked carefully.

Helen was studying her computer screen with a concerned expression. "I mean she isn't there," she said. "According to this afternoon's attendance rosters, Claire hasn't been in class since . . . fourth period."

"But that's impossible," I said. Suddenly I felt funny all over. Really. Like someone had shot me full of Novocain. My lips were numb. So were my arms, holding onto my books. "I saw her just before fifth."

"No," Helen said, reaching for some printouts. "It's right here. Claire Lippman has skipped fifth through seventh."

"Claire Lippman has never skipped a class in her life," Mr. Goodhart—who would know, being her guidance counselor—declared.

"Well," Helen said, "she has today."

I must have looked like I was going to pass out or something, because suddenly, Special Agent Johnson was at my side, holding onto my elbow, going, "Jess? Jessica? Are you all right?"

"No, I'm not all right," I said. "And neither is Claire Lippman."

CHAPTER 19

It was my fault, of course.

What had happened to Claire, I mean.

I should have listened. I should have taken her by the arm and dragged her someplace quiet and listened to what she had to tell me.

Because whatever it had been, I was convinced, was directly linked to the fact that she was missing now.

"It's a beautiful day out," Mr. Goodhart said. "Maybe she just took off. I mean, you know how she likes to sunbathe, and with this Indian summer we've been having, attendance, especially in the afternoon, has been sliding. . . ."

I was sitting on one of the orange vinyl couches, my books

in my lap, my arms limp at my side. I looked up at Mr. Good-hart and said, my voice sounding as tired as I felt, "Claire didn't skip class. They got her."

Special Agent Johnson had called Jill, and now the two of them were sitting across from me, staring, like I was some new breed of criminal they had only read about in text books at FBI training school or something.

"Who got her, Jessica?" Special Agent Smith asked, gently.

"They did." I couldn't believe she didn't know. How could she not know? "The same ones who got Amber. And Heather. And the restaurant."

"And who *are* they, Jessica?" Special Agent Smith leaned forward. She was looking like her old self again, her bob curling just right, her suit neatly pressed. Today she had on the diamond studs. "Do you know, Jess? Do you know who they are?"

I looked at them. I was so tired. Really. And not just from hardly having gotten any sleep the past couple days. I was tired *inside*, bone-tired. Tired of being afraid. Tired of not knowing. Just tired.

"No, of course I don't know who *they are*," I said. "Do you? Do you have any idea at all?"

Special Agent Smith and Special Agent Johnson exchanged glances. I saw him shake his head, just a little. But then Jill said, "Allan. We have to tell her."

I was too tired to ask what she meant. I didn't care. I

truly didn't. Claire Lippman, I was convinced, was lying dead somewhere, and it was all my fault. What was my brother Mike going to say when he found out? He'd been in love with Claire for as long as I could remember. Granted, he'd never uttered a word to her in his life, that I knew of, but he loved her just the same. That year she'd starred in *Hello, Dolly!* he'd gone to every single performance, even the kiddie matinee. He'd gone around humming the title song for weeks afterward.

And I hadn't even been able to protect her for him. The love of my brother's life.

"Jessica," Special Agent Smith said. "Listen to me a minute. Amber. Amber Mackey, you know, the dead girl?"

I looked at her. There was enough energy left in me—not a lot, but enough—to go, very sarcastically, "I know who Amber Mackey is, Jill. She only sat in front of me every day for *six years.*"

"Agent Smith," Special Agent Johnson said in a sharp voice. "That information is confidential and not for—"

"She was pregnant," Special Agent Smith said. She said it fast and she said it to me. "Amber Mackey was seven weeks pregnant when she was killed, Jess. The coroner just completed his autopsy, and I thought—"

I blinked at her, once. Then twice. Then I said, *"Pregnant?"*

Mr. Goodhart, who'd been leaning against Helen's desk, watching us, went, *"Pregnant?"*

Even Helen went, *"Pregnant? Amber Mackey?"*

"Please," Special Agent Johnson said. You could tell he was way annoyed. "This is not something we want spread around. The victim's family hasn't even been told. I would ask that you keep this information to yourself for the time being. It will, of course, get out, as these things invariably do. But until then—"

But I wasn't listening to him anymore. All I could think was: *Amber. Pregnant. Amber. Pregnant. Amber. Pregnant.*

Which meant only one thing, of course. That Mark Leskowski was the father. The father of Amber's baby. He had to be. Amber would never have slept with anybody else. I mean, I was surprised she'd slept with *him*. She just hadn't been that type of girl, you know.

But I guess I'd been wrong. I guess she *had* been that type of girl.

But I'll tell you what type of girl she wasn't: The type to get rid of an unwanted pregnancy. Not Amber. How many bake sales had she organized to raise funds for the single moms of the county? How many car washes had she held to help out the March of Dimes? How many times had she passed me a Unicef carton and asked for my spare change?

Suddenly, I wasn't feeling tired anymore. It was like energy was pouring through me . . . almost like I was filled with electricity again, like I'd been that day I'd been struck by lightning.

Okay, well, not quite like that. But I was no longer exhausted. And I'll tell you something else: I wasn't scared.

Not anymore.

Because I had remembered one more thing. And that was that the fear I'd seen in Claire Lippman's eyes? Yeah, that hadn't been there when she'd first started speaking to me. No, the fear hadn't shown up until later. Not until Mark Leskowski—*Mark Leskowski*—had strolled out of the guidance office and said hello to us.

Mark Leskowski. The father of Amber's baby.

Mark Leskowski, who'd sat at Table Seven—the make-out table—at Mastriani's and told me, when I'd asked him what he was going to do if his plans of making it to the NFL didn't work out, *"Failure is not an option."*

And your sixteen-year-old girlfriend giving birth to your baby, out of wedlock, the same year you were being scouted by colleges? That, to Mark, would certainly fall under the category of "unacceptable."

I stood up. My books fell to the floor. But I was still holding onto Claire's sweater. It had never left my fingers, all afternoon. "Jessica?" Jill climbed to her feet as well. "What is it? What's wrong?"

When I didn't answer her, Special Agent Johnson said, in a commanding voice, "Jessica. Jessica, do you hear me? Answer Special Agent Smith, please. She asked you a question. Do you want me to call your parents, young lady?"

But it didn't matter. What they were saying, I mean. It didn't matter that Helen, the secretary, was looking up my home number, or that Mr. Goodhart was waving his hand in front of my face, yelling my name.

Oh, don't get me wrong. It was *annoying*. I mean, I was trying to concentrate, and all these people were hopping around me like Mexican jumping beans or whatever.

But it didn't matter. It didn't really matter what they said or did, because I had Claire Lippman's sweater. Her pink cashmere sweater that her mother, I now knew—though there was no rational way I *could* know this—had given to her for her sixteenth birthday. The sweater smelled like *Happy*, the perfume Claire always wears. Her grandmother gave her a new bottle every Christmas. People complimented her on her perfume all the time. They didn't know it was just *Happy*, from Clinique. They thought it was something exotic, something super expensive. Even Mark Leskowski, who sat in front of Claire in homeroom every day—Leskowski, Lippman—had said something about it once. Asked her what it was called. He'd wanted to buy a bottle, he'd said, for his girlfriend.

His girlfriend Amber. Whom he'd killed.

Just like he was going to kill Claire.

Suddenly, I couldn't breathe. I couldn't breathe because it was so hot. It was hot, and something was covering my mouth and nose. I was suffocating. I couldn't get out. Let me out. Let me out. *Let me out.*

Something hard hit me in the face. I started, and then found myself blinking into Mr. Goodhart's face. Special Agents Johnson and Smith had him by both arms.

"I told you," Allan was yelling, "not to hit her!"

"What was I supposed to do?" Mr. Goodhart demanded. "She was having a fit!"

"It wasn't a fit." Jill looked really mad. "It was a vision. Jessica? Jessica, are you all right?"

I stared at the three of them. My cheek tingled where Mr. Goodhart had slapped it. He hadn't hit me very hard.

"I've got to go," I said to them, and, clutching Claire's sweater, I left the office.

They followed me, of course. It wasn't easy, though, because no sooner had I stalked out into the hallway than the bell rang. The last bell of the day. Kids poured out of the classrooms and into the corridors, slamming their locker doors, high-fiving one another, making plans to meet up at the quarries later. The halls were teeming with people, crowded with bodies, everyone streaming toward the exits.

And I let them take me. I let the tide sweep me away, through the doors and out toward the flagpole, where the buses were waiting to take people home. Everyone but the kids who'd come in their own cars or who had to stay after for ball practice or tutoring or detention.

Everyone but Claire. Claire wouldn't be making her bus today.

"Jessica," I heard someone yell behind me. Special Agent Johnson. Somebody was waiting by the flag pole. Somebody familiar. He was easy to make out in the hordes streaming toward the buses, because he was a head taller than most of them and was standing still, besides.

Rob. It was Rob.

A part of me was glad to see him. Another part of me didn't notice him at all.

"Jess," he said when he saw me. "Oh, my God. I heard what happened last night. Are you okay?"

"I'm fine," I said. I didn't slow down. I walked right past him.

Rob, falling into step beside me, went, "Mastriani, what's the matter with you? Where are you going?"

"There's something I have to do," I said. I was walking fast, so fast that I was pretty sure I had lost Special Agents Johnson and Smith somewhere back in the crowd in front of the buses.

"What do you have to do?" Rob wanted to know. "Mastriani, why are we *here*?"

Here was the football field, off to one side of the student parking lot. It was under the metal bleachers surrounding the field that Ruth and I had ducked, that day last spring when we'd been caught in the storm. The storm that had changed everything.

It didn't look much different, the football field, than it had that day, except that now it was in use. Coach Albright was standing in the middle of it with a whistle in his mouth, as his players streamed out from the locker room for practice.

Most of the cheerleaders were already there. They were holding auditions for Amber's position. It was sad and all, but what were they supposed to do? They couldn't do a pyramid with just nine girls. They needed a tenth. The bleachers were crowded with girls eager to take Amber's spot. When they saw Rob and me, they stopped chatting amongst themselves and stared. Maybe they thought I was there to try out. I don't know.

"Jess," Rob said. "What is the matter with you? You're acting really weird. Weirder than usual, even."

Coach Albright noticed us and blew his whistle. "Mastriani," he yelled. He knew me only too well from my many altercations with his more fractious players. "What are you doing here? Are you here for the tryouts?"

I didn't answer him. I was scanning the field, looking for one person and one person only.

"If you ain't here for the tryouts," Coach Albright yelled, "get off the field. I don't need you around, making my boys nervous."

I saw him, finally. He was just coming out from the gym, his shoulder pads making him look bigger than he actually was . . . though of course, he was pretty big without them. The bright sun shone down on his bare head as he hurried, helmet in hand, toward the rest of the team.

I headed toward him, meeting him halfway.

"Jess," he said, in some surprise, looking from me to Rob, who stood just behind me, then back again. "What's up?"

I held out my hand. The hand that wasn't clutching Claire's sweater. I held out my hand and said, "Give them to me."

Mark looked down at me, a half smile on his face. He was playing it cool.

"What are you talking about?" he asked.

"You know," I said. "You know good and well."

"What's going on here?" Coach Albright demanded, stomping over to us. He was followed by most of the rest of the team—Todd Mintz, Jeff Day—and more than a few of the cheerleaders. It wasn't every day a civilian walked out onto the field and interrupted practice.

Especially one who wasn't even part of their crowd.

"Mark, this girl giving you a hard time?" Coach Albright asked.

"No, Coach," Mark said. He was still smiling. "She's cool. Jess, what's going on?"

"You know what's going on," I said, in a voice that didn't sound like mine. It was harder than my voice had ever been. Harder and, in a way, sadder, at the same time. "You all know." I looked around at the other ball players. "Every last one of you knows."

Todd, blinking in the strong sunlight, went, "*I* don't know."

"Shut up, Mintz," Jeff Day said.

Coach Albright looked from me to Mark and then back again. Then he went, "Look, I don't know what this is about, but if you got a problem with one of my players, Mastriani, you bring it to me during office hours. You do not interrupt practice—"

I stepped forward and sank my fist into Mark Leskowski's gut.

"Now give me," I said, as he dropped to his knees with a gasp, "your car keys."

Everything happened at once after that. Mark, recovering with amazing quickness, lunged at me, only to find himself in a headlock, courtesy of Rob. I was yanked off my feet by Jeff Day, who planned, I think, on hurling me over the nearest goalpost. He was stopped by Todd Mintz, who grabbed him by the Adam's apple and squeezed.

And Coach Albright, in the middle of the fray, blew and blew on his whistle.

There was a jingle, and something bright fell from Mark's waistband into the grass. Rob snatched it up and said, "Mastriani." By that time, Jeff, unable to breathe with Todd crushing his larynx, had dropped me. I reached up and caught the keys on the fly, one-handed.

And then I turned around and started for the student parking lot.

"You can't do this," I heard Mark bleating behind me. "This is illegal. Illegal search and seizure. That's what this is."

"Consider yourself," Rob said, "under citizen's arrest."

They were following me. They were all following me, Rob and Mark and Todd and Jeff, Coach Albright, and the cheerleaders. Like the Pied Piper of Hamlin, leading the village children to their doom, I led the Ernest Pyle High School football team and pep squad to Mark Leskowski's BMW, which was parked, I saw when I got to it, just a little bit away from Ruth's Cabriolet and Skip's Trans Am.

"Oh, my God," Ruth said, when she saw me. "There you are. I've been looking all over for you. What's . . ."

Her voice trailed off as she got a look at what was behind me.

"This is *bullshit*," Mark bellowed.

"Mastriani," Coach Albright yelled. "You put those keys down. . . ."

Only I didn't listen to him, of course. I walked right up to Mark's car and put the key in the lock to the trunk.

Which was when Mark tried to make a break for it. Only Rob wouldn't let him. He reached out almost casually and grabbed hold of the back of Mark's shirt.

"Let me go," Mark screamed. "Lemme freaking go!"

Only he didn't say "freaking."

I turned the key, and the BMW's trunk popped open.

And that's how Special Agents Johnson and Smith found us, a minute or so later. With the entire in crowd of Ernest Pyle High School crowded around Mark Leskowski's

BMW, while Rob Wilkins hung onto Mark, and Todd Mintz hung onto Jeff Day (who'd also tried to get away at the last minute).

And me half-in, half-out of Mark Leskowski's trunk, trying to get Claire Lippman to start breathing again.

CHAPTER 20

"Well, that certainly sucked," Claire said, later that evening.

"Tell me about it," I said.

"No, I mean, really. Like, I was sure I was going to die."

"You *looked* dead," Ruth pointed out.

"Really?" Claire seemed very interested in this piece of information. "How, exactly, did I look?"

Ruth, sitting on the windowsill across from Claire Lippman's hospital bed, glanced at me, as if unsure whether or not to answer the question.

"No, really," Claire said. "I want to know. So in case I ever have to do a death scene, I'll know how to look."

"Well," Ruth said, hesitantly. "You were really pale, and your eyes were closed, and you weren't breathing. But that was on account of the tape over your mouth."

"And the heat," Skip pointed out. "Don't forget the heat."

"It was a hundred and ten inside that trunk," Claire said cheerfully. "That's what the EMTs said, anyway. I would have died of dehydration way before Mark got around to killing me."

"Uh," Ruth said. "Yeah. About that. That's the part I'm not real clear on. *Why* did Mark want to kill you, again?"

Claire rolled her pretty blue eyes. "Duh," she said. "Because he saw me talking to Jess."

Ruth looked over at me, where I was sitting between the dozens of huge floral arrangements people had been sending to Claire ever since she'd been admitted. She was due to be released in the morning, so long as the results of her CAT scan confirmed she had not, in fact, suffered a concussion. But still the flowers kept coming.

Claire Lippman was actually a lot more popular than I had ever realized.

"Explanation, please," Ruth said.

"It's really very simple," I said. "Amber Mackey got pregnant—"

"Pregnant!" Ruth cried.

"Pregnant!" her twin brother echoed.

"Pregnant," I said. "And she told Mark she wanted to keep

the baby. In fact, Amber wanted him to marry her, so they could raise their child together, be a little happy family. That's what they were talking about that day at the quarry, when Claire said she saw Amber and Mark keep going off together, alone. Amber's pregnancy."

"Right," Claire said. "Only a pregnant girlfriend was not part of Mark's plan for the future."

"Far from it," I said. "Getting married, or even paying child support, was going to totally mess up Mark's football career. It was, in his book, 'unacceptable.' So, near as we can figure it out—and he hasn't confessed, mind you—Mark beat Amber up, in the hopes that she'd change her mind, and left her somewhere—probably in his trunk. They're checking it for fibers now. When that didn't manage to convince Amber to see things his way, he killed her and tossed her body into the quarry."

"Okay," Ruth said. "I can see all that, I guess. But what about Heather? Wasn't Mark with you when Heather disappeared?"

"Yes," I said. "He was. That was the point of Heather's attack. Mark was starting to feel the heat, you know, with the Feds breathing down his neck, so he figured if another girl got attacked at a time during which he had a rock-solid alibi, he'd be in the clear."

"And what's more rock-solid," Skip said, "than the fact that he was with the FBI's friend, Lightning Girl."

"Right," I said. "Well, more or less. And you know, it worked. When Heather disappeared, no one suspected Mark."

"Except you," Claire pointed out.

"Well," I said, a little guiltily. "I didn't exactly suspect Mark." Quite the opposite, in fact. I'd been convinced no one as hot as he was could be a criminal. Stupid me. "But that house . . . I knew there was something up with that house. So when I started asking around about it, Mark got scared again and had Jeff Day—the same guy who'd kidnapped, and then later beat up, Heather—make some threatening phone calls. And then, when that didn't seem to be working, Mark and Jeff broke into Mastriani's, poured gasoline all over the place, then lit a match and burned the place down."

At least according to Jeff Day, who'd started crying like a baby the minute the cops arrived, then spilled his guts like a squashed caterpillar.

"Mark's biggest mistake," I went on, "was enlisting the help of someone like Jeff Day in getting him out of his little jam. I mean, on the one hand, it makes sense, since Jeff is used to taking direction from Mark, on account of Mark being the team quarterback and all. But Jeff needs a *lot* of direction. He was always coming up to Mark and asking him what to do . . . especially right before the first class of the day, homeroom."

"Where Mark sat in front of me," Claire said. She was taking her role as victim very seriously, and waved her arm, the one with the IV in it, as much as possible, to bring attention to her infirmity. "So of course this morning, when he and Jeff were whispering before the bell rang, something about the way they looked . . . so sneaky . . . triggered something. I just knew. I can't say how I knew. I just put two and two together. But you can't go to the police, you know, with a hunch. But I figured I could go to Jess—"

"But when she tried," I said, "Mark caught her. And she was so startled—"

"I ran," Claire said gravely. "Like a startled fawn."

I wasn't so sure about the fawn part. Claire was kind of tall for a fawn. A gazelle, maybe.

"But Mark went around the side of the building," I said, "and caught up with her, and—"

"—hit me right back here," Claire said, touching the back of her head, "with something heavy. And when I woke up again, I was in his trunk."

"My guess is he was going to take her to the house on the pit road," I said, "and do to her what he'd done to Amber. . . ."

"So what," Ruth asked, "is going to happen? To Mark, I mean?"

"Well," I said. "With the help of Jeff's testimony—which I'm sure he'll give in exchange for a reduced sentence for his part in the whole thing—Mark's going to prison. For a long time."

Which was really going to mess up his plan for getting drafted right out of college by the NFL.

Before anyone could say anything in reply to this, Claire's parents, Dr. and Mrs. Lippman, came back into the room.

"Oh, thanks, kids," Mrs. Lippman said, "for keeping our baby entertained while we were gone. Here, Claire, a mint-chocolate-chip shake, just like you asked."

Claire immediately lost all of the animation she'd had when talking to Ruth and Skip and me. Instead, she fell back against the pillows, and let her head loll a little.

She was really milking this for all she was worth. Well, she was in the drama club, after all.

"Thanks, Mom," she said weakly.

"Well, uh," I said. "We better go."

"Yeah," Ruth said, slipping off the windowsill. "Visiting hours are up anyway. Bye, Claire. Bye, Dr. and Mrs. Lippman."

"Bye, kids," Dr. Lippman said. But Mrs. Lippman couldn't let it go with a simple good-bye. No, she had to come over and give me a big hug and call me her little girl's savior and tell me that if there was anything—anything at all—she or her husband could do for me, I needed only to ask. The Lippmans—along with, surprise, surprise, Heather's parents—were starting a Restore Mastriani's Fund. I wished that instead they were starting a Pay Off Karen Sue Hankey's Medical Bills Fund, so that Mrs. Hankey would drop her suit against me.

But beggars can't be choosers, I guess, so all I said, as Mrs. Lippman attempted to squeeze the life out of me, was, "Uh, you're welcome."

Barely escaping with my ribs intact, I followed Ruth and Skip out into the hall.

"Whew," Ruth said. "Now I know where Claire gets her sense of the dramatic."

"Tell me about it," I said, scrubbing Mrs. Lippman's lipstick off my cheek, where she'd kissed me.

"Should we stop by and see Heather?" Skip asked as we made our way to the elevators.

"They released her already," I said. "Broken arm, couple of busted ribs, and a concussion, but otherwise, she's going to be all right."

"Physically," Ruth said, punching the button marked DOWN. "Mentally, though? After having been through what she went through?"

"Heather's pretty tough," I said. The elevator came, and we all got on it. "She'll be back out there, shaking her pompons, in no time."

"Yeah, but what is she going to shake those pompons for?" Ruth wanted to know. "I mean, without Mark and Jeff, the Cougars don't have much of a chance of making it to State. Or anywhere, for that matter."

"Well," I said. "There's always the basketball team. None of them, as far as I know, have murdered anyone lately."

"So, Jess," Skip said, as the doors opened to the hospital lobby. "How does it feel to be a hero? Again?"

"I don't know," I said. "Not so great, really. I mean, if I'd have been able to figure it out sooner, I might have saved Amber. Not to mention Mastriani's."

"How *did* you figure it out?" Ruth asked. "I mean, how'd you know Claire was locked inside Mark's trunk?"

It was a question I knew I'd get asked eventually, though I'd been hoping against hope to avoid it. How was I going to explain that for a moment, I'd *been* Claire, inside that trunk? And all because she'd dropped her sweater . . . a sweater I'd just returned to her, by the way.

"I don't know," I lied. "I just . . . I just knew is all."

Ruth looked at me sarcastically. "Yeah," she said. "Right. Just like this summer, with Shane and the pillow. I get it."

Ruth got it, all right. I just hoped nobody else did.

"What pillow?" Skip wanted to know.

"Never mind," I said. "Listen, you guys, I better get home. My mom's having a big enough cow as it is, what with the restaurant, and now Douglas and this job thing. Not to mention Karen Sue's lawsuit—"

"I can't believe she's really suing," Skip said, looking indignant. "I mean, after Jess pretty much single-handedly caught a murderer and all, in her own school."

"Well," I said, a little sheepishly. "I did almost break Karen Sue's nose. Not that she didn't deserve it."

Ruth tactfully changed the subject.

"So what's with that, anyway?" Ruth asked. "Douglas, I mean. Comix Underground is totally skeevy. Why would anyone want to work there? It's always packed with members of the turtle patrol."

"Hey," Skip said, sounding offended. Skip, I knew, often shopped at Comix Underground.

"I don't know," I said with a shrug. "He's Douglas. He's always marched to a different drummer."

"I'll say." Ruth shook her head. "God, I'm sure glad I'm not living in your house. It's going to be like World War—" She broke off, and, looking toward the sliding doors by the ambulance bay, said, "Well, I was going to say World War Three, but I think I'm going to have to amend that to World War Four."

I followed her gaze. "What? What are you talking about?"

Skip saw him before I did. "Whoa," he said. "Alert the Pentagon. The Mastriani household has just gone to Def Con One."

And then I saw him. And froze in my tracks. *"Mike!"* I couldn't believe it. "What are you doing here?"

Mike had obviously just come from the airport. He had an overnight bag with him and looked, to put it mildly, like crap. He hurried up to us and said, "How is she? Is she all right?"

"Why are you here?" I demanded. "Didn't Mom and Dad just drop you off at Harvard last *week*? What are you doing back?"

Michael glared down at me. "You think I could stay there, knowing what happened?"

"Mike," I said. "For God's sake. The insurance is going to pay to rebuild the place. It is not that big a deal. I mean, yeah, it's sad and all, but when I talked to Dad a little while ago, he was totally into the idea of redesigning. He is going to kill you when he finds out you—"

"I don't care about the stupid restaurant," Mike said, his voice filled with scorn. "I didn't come back for that. It's Claire I care about."

I blinked at him. "Claire?"

"Yes, Claire." Mike looked down at me worriedly. "Claire Lippman. How is she? Is she going to be all right?"

I could only stare up at him with, I am sorry to say, my mouth hanging open. *Claire?* He'd come all the way back from college—probably blown an entire semester's allowance buying an airline ticket at the last minute—because of *Claire*, a girl who'd never spoken to him before in her life? Were *both* my brothers insane?

It was Ruth who said, "Claire's going to be fine, Michael." I was proud of her for being so calm. Ruth had had her own little crush on Mike awhile back. Her summer romance with Scott had apparently cured her of it, however. "She's just, you know, being held overnight for observation."

"I want to see her," Mike said. "What room is she in?"

"Four-seventeen," Skip said, at the same time that I finally burst out with, "Are you crazy? You flew a thousand miles just to make sure a girl who doesn't even know you're alive is okay?"

Mike looked down at me and shook his head, completely

unimpressed by my outburst. "Tell Mom and Dad," he said, "that I'll be home in a little while."

Then he started for the hospital elevators with a little swagger in his step, as if he were Clint Eastwood or somebody.

"Visiting hours are over," I yelled after him.

But it didn't do any good. He was like a man possessed. He disappeared into an elevator, his shoulders thrown back and his head held high.

"That," Ruth said, gazing after him, "is the most romantic thing I have ever seen."

"Are you kidding?" I was appalled. "It's completely . . . well, it's . . . it's . . ."

"Romantic," Ruth finished for me.

"Sick," I corrected her.

"I don't know," Skip said. "Claire's kind of hot."

Ruth and I looked at him. Then we both looked away in disgust.

"Well," Skip said, "she is."

Ruth took me by the arm and started steering me from the hospital. "Come on," she said. "We'll stop at the Thirty-one Flavors on the way home, and you can pick up a pint of Rocky Road for your mom. That'll help, you know, when you break the news about Mikey."

We walked out into the mild evening air. The sun had only just set, and the sky to the west was all purple and red. It occurred to me that Mark was probably looking at the same

SAFE HOUSE

sky. Only he'd be looking at it from behind bars—from now on.

Talk about unacceptable.

"First thing we'll do tomorrow," Ruth was saying as we started for her car, "is reschedule your chair audition—"

I groaned. I had forgotten all about Mr. Vine and my after-school appointment with him.

"Then," Ruth said, "you're going to have to get Rosemary to send you some photos of kids who've got some reward money posted for their return. You're going to need some extra cash, what with the restaurant and Karen Sue's lawsuit and all."

I groaned louder.

"And then, I'm sorry, but we're going to have to do something about your hair. I've been thinking about this, and I really believe what you need are some highlights. Saturday nights they do free coloring at the beauty college—"

"Hey," Skip said. "Saturday night Jess and I are going to the movies."

"Oh, you are not," Ruth said grumpily. "I can't have my brother dating my best friend. It's too gross."

Skip looked taken aback. "But—"

"Shut up, Skip," Ruth said. "It's gross, and you know it. Besides, she doesn't like you. She likes that guy over there."

Curious what she meant, I looked where Ruth was pointing. . . .

And saw Rob, leaning against his bike, waiting for somebody.

And that somebody, I knew, was me.

He straightened up when he saw me and waved.

"Oh," I said. "Uh, I'll see you guys later, okay?"

"Whatever," Ruth said airily. "Come on, Skip."

"But—" Skip was looking at Rob with suspicion and, it must be admitted, a small amount of dismay.

"Sorry, Skip," I said, patting him on the arm as Ruth led him away. "But Ruth's right, you know. It'd never work. I can't stand all that hobbit stuff."

Then, giving Skip a big smile to show how sorry I was, I hurried over to where Rob was standing.

"Hey," I said, my smile turning shy.

"Hey," Rob said. His smile wasn't shy at all. "How are you doing?"

"Oh," I said with a shrug. "Okay, I guess."

"How about Claire?" His mentioning Claire reminded me of Mike. I couldn't help scowling a little as I said, "Oh, she's going to be fine."

Rob didn't seem to notice the scowl. "Thanks to you," he said.

"And you," I said. "I mean, you kept Mark from getting away."

"That was nothing," Rob said modestly. "Anyway, I stopped by to see if you wanted a ride home. Do you?"

"You bet," I said. "Hey, did your mom tell you about my dad's scheme to keep all the staff from Mastriani's on payroll while the new restaurant's being built? He's converting Joe Junior's from counter service to waitress-only service."

"She told me," Rob said with a grin. "Your dad's a good guy. Oh, hey, here, I almost forgot."

He turned from the side compartment, where he'd been fishing out his spare helmet for me, and dropped something heavy into my hand. I looked down and was shocked to see that I was holding his watch.

"But," I said, "this is your watch."

"Yeah," Rob said, "I know it's my watch. I thought you wanted it."

"But what are you going to use?" I wanted to know. Although I have to admit that, while I was asking this, I was already strapping the thing on.

"I don't know," Rob said. "I'll make do." When he turned to hand me the helmet and saw that his watch was already on my wrist, he shook his head. "You really *are* weird," he said. "Do you know that?"

"Yes," I said, and stood up on my tiptoes to kiss him. . . .

Only before I got a chance to, somebody nearby cleared his throat and said, "Uh, Miss Mastriani?"

I turned my head. And stared.

Because there, standing in front of a black four-door sedan—clearly an unmarked law-enforcement vehicle—stood a tall man I had never seen before. The man, who was wearing a hat and a trench coat even though it was like seventy degrees outside, said, "Miss Mastriani, I am Cyrus Krantz, director of Special Operations with the Federal Bureau of Investigation. I happen to be Special Agent Johnson and Smith's immediate supervisor."

I glanced at the car behind him. It had tinted windows, so I couldn't tell if anyone else was inside of it.

"Yeah," I said. "So?"

Which probably sounded pretty rude and all, but I had way better things to do than hang around outside the county hospital talking to the FBI.

"So," Cyrus Krantz said, seemingly unmoved by my rudeness, "I'd like a word with you."

"Everything I've got to say," I told him, pulling Rob's spare helmet over my head, "I already told Jill and Allan." I swung a leg over Rob's bike and settled in behind him. "Ask them about it. They'll tell you."

"I have asked *Special Agents* Johnson and Smith about it," Cyrus Krantz replied, enunciating their proper titles, which I had neglected to use, with care. "I found their answers to my questions unsatisfactory, which is why I've had them removed from your case, Miss Mastriani. You will now be dealing with me, and me alone. So—"

I lifted up the visor to my helmet and stared at him in shock. "You *what*?"

"I've removed them from your case," Cyrus Krantz repeated. "Their handling of you has, in my opinion, been amateurish and entirely unfocused. What is clearly needed in your case, Miss Mastriani, is not kid gloves, but an iron fist."

I could only stare. "You fired Allan and Jill?"

"I removed them from your case." Cyrus Krantz, director of Special Operations, turned around and opened the rear passenger door of the car behind him. "Now, get into this car, Miss Mastriani, so that you can be taken to our regional headquarters for questioning about your involvement in the Mark Leskowski case."

I tightened my grip around Rob's waist. My mouth had gone dry.

"Am I under arrest?" I managed to croak.

"No," Cyrus Krantz said. "But you are a material witness in possession of vital—"

"Good," I said, snapping my helmet's visor back into place. "Go, Rob."

Rob did as I asked. We left Cyrus Krantz in our dust.

The only problem, of course, is that I'm pretty sure he knows where I live.

Sanctuary

CHAPTER 1

This time when it started, I so totally wasn't expecting it.

You would think I'd have figured it out by now. I mean, after all this time. But apparently not. Apparently, in spite of everything, I am just as big an idiot as I ever was.

This time when it started, it wasn't with a phone call, or a letter in the mail. This time it was the doorbell. It rang right in the middle of Thanksgiving dinner.

This wasn't so unusual. I mean, lately, our doorbell? Yeah, it's been ringing a lot. That's because a couple of months ago, one of my parents' restaurants burned down, and our neighbors— we live in a pretty small town—wanted to show their sympathy for our loss by bringing over beef Stroganoff and the occasional persimmon pie.

Seriously. As if someone had died. People always bring over gifts of food when someone has died, because the grieving family isn't supposed to feel up to cooking, and would starve to death if friends and neighbors didn't come over all the time with lemon squares or whatever.

Like there was no such thing as Dominos.

Only in our case, it wasn't a person who had died. It was Mastriani's, an Establishment for Fine Dining—*the* choice for pre-prom dinner, or catering local weddings or bar mitzvahs—which got burned down thanks to some juvenile delinquents who'd wanted to show me just how much they didn't appreciate the way I was poking my nose into their business.

Yeah. It was my fault the family business got torched.

Never mind the fact that I'd been trying to stop a killer. Never mind that the folks this guy had been trying to kill weren't just, you know, strangers to me, but people I actually knew, who went to my school.

What was I supposed to do, just sit back and let him off my friends?

Whatever. The cops nailed the guy in the end. And it wasn't like Mastriani's wasn't insured, or that we don't own two other restaurants that didn't get incinerated.

I'm not saying it wasn't a terrible loss, or anything. Mastriani's was my dad's baby, not to mention the best restaurant in town. I'm just saying, you know, the persimmon pies weren't strictly necessary. We were bummed and all, but it wasn't like we didn't feel like cooking. Not in *my* family. I mean, you grow up around a bunch of restaurants, you learn how to cook— among other things, like how to drain a steam table or make sure the perch is fresh and that the fish guy isn't trying to rip you off again. There was never a shortage of food in my house.

That Thanksgiving, in fact, the table was groaning with it. Food, I mean. There was barely room for our plates, there were so many serving dishes stacked with turkey, sweet potatoes, cranberry relish, two kinds of dressing, string beans, salad, rolls, scalloped potatoes, garlic mashed potatoes, glazed carrots, turnip puree, and creamed spinach in front of us.

And it wasn't like we were expected to take, you know, just a little bit of everything. No way. Not with my mom and dad around. It was like, if you didn't pile your plate sky-high with stuff, you were insulting them.

Which was a very big problem, you see, because I had a second Thanksgiving dinner to attend—something I hadn't exactly mentioned to them, on account of how I knew they wouldn't exactly be too thrilled about it. I was just trying to save a little room, you know?

Only maybe I should have said something. Because certain people at the table observed my apparent lack of appetite and felt obligated to comment upon it.

"What's wrong with Jessica?" my great-aunt Rose, who was down from Chicago for the holiday, wanted to know. "How come she's not eating? She sick?"

"No, Aunt Rose," I said, from between gritted teeth. "I am not sick. I'm just not that hungry right now."

"Not that hungry?" Great-aunt Rose looked at my mother. "Who's not hungry at Thanksgiving? Your mother and father slaved all day making this delicious meal. Now you eat up."

My mother broke off her conversation with Mr. Abramowitz to say, "She's eating, Rose."

"I'm eating, Aunt Rose," I said, sticking some sweet potato in my mouth to prove it. "See?"

"You know what the problem with her is," Great-aunt Rose said conspiratorially to Claire Lippman's mother, but in a voice still loud enough for the guys working down at the Stop and Shop on First Street to hear. "She's got one of those eating disorders. You know. That anorexia."

"Jessica doesn't have anorexia, Rose," my mom said, looking annoyed. "Douglas, pass the string beans to Ruth, will you?"

Douglas, who in the best of circumstances does not like to have attention drawn to him, quickly passed the string beans to my best friend Ruth, as if he thought he could ward off Great-aunt Rose's evil death glare by doing so.

"You know what they call that?" Great-aunt Rose asked Mrs. Lippman, in a chummy sort of way.

"I'm sorry, Mrs. Mastriani," Mrs. Lippman said. I gathered

from her slightly harassed tone that, in accepting my mother's invitation to Thanksgiving dinner, Mr. and Mrs. Lippman had not known what they were getting themselves into. Clearly, no warning had been issued about Great-aunt Rose. "I don't know what you mean."

"Denial," Great-aunt Rose said, snapping her fingers triumphantly. "I saw that on *Oprah*. I suppose you're just going to let Jessica pick at that dressing, Antonia, and not make her eat it, just like you let her get away with everything. Those disgraceful dungarees she goes around in, and that hair . . . and don't even get me started on that whole business last spring. You know, nice girls don't have armed federal officers following them around—"

Thankfully, at that moment, the doorbell rang. I threw my napkin down and got up so fast, I nearly knocked over my chair.

"I'll get it!" I yelled, then tore for the foyer.

Well, you would have run out of there, too. I mean, who wanted to hear that whole thing—about how I'd been struck by lightning and consequently developed the psychic power to find missing people; how I'd been more or less kidnapped by a less-than-savory arm of the government, who'd wanted me to come work for them; and how some friends of mine sort of had to blow up a few things in order to get me safely back home—again? I mean, hello, that subject is way tired, can we change it, please?

"Now, who could that be?" my mother wondered, as I rushed for the door. "Everyone we know is right here at this table."

This was pretty much true. Besides Great-aunt Rose and me and my mom and dad, there were my two older brothers, Douglas and Michael, Michael's new girlfriend (it still felt weird to call her that, since for years Mikey had only dreamed that Claire Lippman might one day glance in his direction, and now, flying in the face of societal convention, they were going together—the Beauty and the Geek), and her family, as well as my best friend Ruth Abramowitz and her twin brother Skip and their parents. In all, there were thirteen people gathered around our dining room table. It sure didn't seem to me like anyone was missing.

But when I got to the door, I found out someone was. Oh, not from our dinner table. But from someone else's.

It was dark outside—it gets dark early in November in Indiana—but the porch light was on. As I approached the front door, which was partly glass, I saw a large, African-American man standing there, looking out onto the street while he waited for someone to answer the bell.

I knew who he was right away. Like I said, our town is pretty small, and up until a few weeks ago, there hadn't been a single African American living in it. That had changed when the old Hoadley place across the street from our house was finally bought by Dr. Thompkins, a physician who'd taken a job as chief surgeon at our county hospital, relocating his family, which included a wife, son, and daughter, from Chicago.

I opened the door and said, "Hey, Dr. Thompkins."

He turned around and smiled. "Hello, Jessica. Er, I mean, hey." In Indiana, hey is what you say instead of hello. Dr. Thompkins, you could tell, was still trying to adjust to the lingo.

"Come on in," I said, moving out of the way so he could get out of the cold. It hadn't started to snow yet, but on the Weather Channel they'd said it was going to. Not enough snow was expected, however, for them to cancel school on Monday, much to my chagrin.

"Thanks, Jessica," Dr. Thompkins said, looking past me through the foyer, to where he could see everybody gathered in the dining room. "Oh, I'm sorry. I didn't mean to interrupt your meal."

"No biggie," I said. "Want some turkey? We have plenty."

"Oh, no. No, thank you," Dr. Thompkins said. "I just stopped by because I was hoping . . . well, it's sort of embarrassing, but I wanted to see if . . ."

Dr. Thompkins seemed pretty nervous. I assumed he needed to borrow something. Whenever anybody in the neighborhood needs to borrow something, particularly something cooking related, we are almost always their first stop. Because my parents are in the restaurant business, we pretty much have anything you could possibly need to cook with, and generally in giant bulk containers.

Since he was from a big city, and all, I guessed Dr. Thompkins wasn't aware that in a small town, it's perfectly acceptable to ask your neighbors if you can borrow something. There was actually a lot I suspected Dr. Thompkins didn't know about our town. For instance, I suspected that Dr. Thompkins wasn't aware that even though Indiana officially sided with the North during the Civil War, there were still some people—especially in the southern half of the state, where we live—who didn't think the Confederates were so bad.

That's why the day the Thompkinses' moving truck pulled up, my mom was over there with a big dish of manicotti, welcoming them to the neighborhood, before they'd even gotten out of the car, practically. Mrs. Abramowitz, who can't cook to save her life, brought over store-bought pastries in a big white box. And the Lippmans came over with a plate of Claire's famous chocolate-chip cookies. (Her secret? They're Tollhouse Break and Bake. All Claire does is grease the cookie pan. Seriously. I am privy to secrets like this, and many other much more interesting ones, now that Claire is my brother's girlfriend.)

Just about everybody in the neighborhood, and a lot of neighborhoods farther away, showed up to welcome the Thompkinses to our town the day they moved in. I bet, coming from Chicago and all, the Thompkinses must have thought we were a true bunch of freaks, knocking on their door all day long, and even several days after they'd gotten moved in, with brownies and eggplant parmigiana and Snickerdoodles and macaroni and cheese and Jell-O salad and homemade coffee cake.

But what the Thompkins didn't know—and what we were all too aware of—was that our town, like the United States a hundred and fifty years ago, had a line running through the middle of it, dividing it into two distinct parts. There was the part Lumley Lane was on, which also held the courthouse square and most of the businesses, including the hospital and the mall and the high school and stuff. This part of the city housed what people in my school call the "Townies."

And then there was the rest of the county, outside the city limits, which consisted mostly of woods and cornfields, with the occasional trailer park and abandoned plastics factory thrown in for picturesque effect. Outside town, there were still patches of illiteracy, prejudice, and even, in the deepest backwoods, where my dad used to take us camping when we were little, moonshining. Kids at school called people who lived this far outside of town, and who had to be bused in for school, "Grits," as that is what many of them purportedly have for breakfast every morning. Grits are like oatmeal, only not as socially acceptable, and without raisins.

In my town, Grits are the ones who still sometimes drive

around with Confederate flags hanging off their pickups and stuff. Grits are the ones who still say the N word sometimes, and not because they are quoting Chris Rock or Jennifer Lopez or whoever. Although I happen to know quite a few so-called Grits who would never call someone the N word, just like I happen to know, from personal experience, a few Townies who wouldn't hesitate to call a female like myself with very short hair and a tendency to be a little quick with my fists the D word, or my friend Ruth, who happens to be Jewish, the K word that rhymes with it.

So you can see why when we saw the Thompkinses moving in, some of us thought there might be trouble from other people.

But it had been almost a month, and so far, no incidents. So maybe everything was going to be all right.

That's what I thought then. Everything's different now, of course. Still, at the time, all I did was try to put Dr. Thompkins at ease as he stood there in our foyer. Hey, I didn't know. How could I possibly have known? I may be psychic, but I'm not *that* psychic.

"Hey, *mi casa es su casa*, Dr. Thompkins," I told him, which is probably about the lamest thing on earth there is to say, but whatever. I wasn't feeling real creative, thanks to Great-aunt Rose, who is a major brain drain. Also, I am taking French, not Spanish.

Dr. Thompkins smiled, but only just. Then he uttered

the words that made it feel like it had started to snow after all. Only all the snow was pouring down the back of my sweater.

"It's just that I was wondering," he said, "if you'd seen my son."

CHAPTER 2

I backed up until my calves hit the stairs to the second floor. When they did, I had to sit down on the first landing, which was only about four steps up, because my knees didn't feel like they would hold me up anymore.

"I don't—" I said, through lips that seemed to have gone as cold as ice. "I don't do that anymore. Maybe nobody told you. But I don't do that anymore."

Dr. Thompkins looked down at me like I had said a dingo ate my baby, or something. He went, his face all perplexed, "I beg your pardon?"

Fortunately at that moment my dad came out of the dining room, his napkin still tucked into the waistband of his pants. My mom followed him, with Mike—Claire, as usual, attached to his hip—trailing behind her.

"Hey, Jerry," my dad said, to Dr. Thompkins, holding out his right hand. "How's it going?"

"Hello, Joe," Dr. Thompkins said. Then he corrected himself. "I mean, hey." He took my dad's hand and shook it. To my mom, he said, "How are you, Toni?"

"Fine, Jerry," my mom said. "And you?"

"Could be better," Dr. Thompkins said. "I'm really sorry to interrupt your meal. I was just wondering if any of you had seen my son, Nate. He went out a couple hours ago, saying he was just going to run to the store—Rowena ran out of whipped cream—but we haven't seen him since. I thought maybe he'd have stopped over here to visit with your boys, or maybe Jessica. . . ."

Over on the steps where I'd sank, I felt color start to return to my face. Sure, I was relieved—relieved that Dr. Thompkins hadn't been asking me to find his son. . . . He'd merely been asking if I'd seen him.

And I was also a little embarrassed. Because I could tell from the glances Dr. Thompkins kept throwing me that he thought I was a freak of the first order for my weird reaction to his simple question about his son. Well, and why not? He hadn't been around last summer, or even this fall. He didn't know I was the one the press had dubbed "Lightning Girl." He didn't know about my "special" gift.

MEG CABOT

But you could tell Mike, snickering behind his hand, had figured out what had happened. You know, what I thought Dr. Thompkins had been asking. And he considered the whole thing simply hilarious.

"No, we haven't seen Nate," my mom said, looking worried. She looks worried whenever she hears about any kid who has strayed away from the parental tether. That's because one of her own kids did that once, and when she'd finally found him again, it had been in a hospital emergency room.

"Oh," Dr. Thompkins said. You could tell he was way disappointed that we hadn't seen Nate. "Well, I figured it was worth a try. He probably stopped at the video arcade. . . ."

I didn't want to be the one to tell Dr. Thompkins that the video arcade was closed. Everything in our town was closed, on account of it being Thanksgiving, with the exception of the Stop and Shop, which never closed, even on Christmas.

But Claire apparently had no problem being the one to deliver the bad news.

"Oh, the arcade is closed, Dr. Thompkins," she said. "Everything's closed. Even the bowling alley. Even the movie theaters."

Dr. Thompkins looked super bummed when Claire said this. My mom even shot her a disapproving look. And in my mom's eyes, Claire Lippman can do no wrong, on account of, you know, liking my reject brother, even if it is partly because of Claire that Mike is currently attending the local community college instead of Harvard, where he was supposed to be going this year.

"Oh," Dr. Thompkins said. He managed a brave smile. "Well, I'm sure he's just run into some friends somewhere."

This was entirely possible. Nate Thompkins, a sophomore at Ernest Pyle High School, where I am a junior, hadn't had too much trouble fitting in, in spite of being the new kid—and the only African-American male—on the block. That's because handsome, athletic Nate had immediately tried out for and gotten onto the Ernie Pyle High football team. Never mind that Coach Albright had been desperate for any players, given that thanks to me, three of his best, including the quarterback, had recently taken up residency in the Indiana state men's penitentiary. Nate supposedly had real talent, and that had thrust him right into the "In Crowd" . . .

. . . unlike his older sister Tasha, a bookish senior, whom I'd spied hovering around the classroom where the yearbook committee meets every day after school. The *yearbook* committee, okay? And the girl was too shy to go in. I'd walked up to her and been like, "Look, I'll introduce you." She'd given me a smile like I'd offered to suck snake venom out of a bite on her shin.

I guess Nate's extrovertedness was not an inherited trait, since Tasha sure didn't have it.

"I'm sure he'll be home soon," Dr. Thompkins said, and, after apologizing again, he left.

"Oh, dear," my mom said, looking worried, as she closed the door. "I hope—"

But my dad broke in with, "Not now, Toni," in this warning voice.

"What?" Mike wanted to know.

"Never mind," my dad said. "Come on. We've still got four different kinds of pie to get through."

"You made *four* pies?" Claire, who, unlike me, was tall and willowy—and who must have had a hollow leg or something, because she ate more than practically any human being I knew—sounded pleased. "What kind?"

"Apple, pumpkin, pecan, and persimmon," my dad said, sounding equally pleased. Good cooks like people who appreciate their food.

No one, however, that I could tell, appreciated Great-aunt Rose.

"Joseph," she said, the minute we reappeared in the dining room. "Who was that colored man?"

It is really embarrassing having a relative like Great-aunt Rose. It isn't even like she is an alcoholic or anything so you can blame her bad behavior on outside forces. She is just plain mean. A couple of times I have considered hauling off and slugging her, but since she is about one hundred years old (okay, seventy-five, big diff) my parents would probably not take too kindly to this. On top of which I have really been trying to curtail my tendency toward violence, thanks to a lawsuit I got slapped with not too long ago for deviating a certain someone's septum.

Though I still think she deserved it.

"African-American, Rose," my mom said. "And he is our neighbor, Dr. Thompkins. Can I get anyone some more wine? Skip, more Coke?"

Skip is Ruth's twin brother. He is supposed to have a crush on me, but he always forgets about it when Claire Lippman is around. That's because all the boys—including my other brother, Douglas—love Claire. It is like she gives off a pheromone or something that girls like Ruth and I don't have. It is somewhat upsetting.

Not, of course, that I want Skip to like me. Because I don't even like Skip. I like someone else.

Someone who was expecting me for Thanksgiving dinner. Only the way things were going—

"What's wrong with saying colored?" Great-aunt Rose wanted to know. "He *is* colored, isn't he?"

"Can I get you a little more creamed spinach?" Mr. Abramowitz asked Great-aunt Rose. Being a lawyer, he is used to having to be nice to people he doesn't like.

"What'd Dr. Thompkins want?" Skip asked.

"Oh, nothing," my mother said, a little too brightly. "He was just wondering if any of us had seen Nate. Who'd like more mashed potatoes?"

"What's wrong with saying colored?" Great-aunt Rose was mad because no one was paying any attention to her. Though she probably would have changed her tune if I'd paid the kind of attention to her that I wanted to.

"I heard the only reason Dr. Thompkins took the chief surgeon job over at County Medical was because Nate was getting into trouble at their old school." Claire looked around the table as she dropped this little bombshell. Being an actress, Claire enjoys seeing what kind of reactions her little performances generate. Also, since she babysits for all the rich doctor types when she is not attending rehearsals, she knows all the gossip in town. "I heard Nate was in a *gang* up in Chicago."

"A gang!" Mrs. Lippman looked upset. "Oh, no! That nice boy?"

"Many a nice boy's fallen in with the wrong crowd," Mr. Abramowitz said mildly.

"But Nate Thompkins." Mrs. Lippman, who was big-time involved with the PTA, shook her head. "Why, he's always been so polite when I've seen him at the Stop and Shop."

"Nate may have been involved with some unsavory individuals back in Chicago," my dad said. "But everybody's entitled to a fresh new start. That's one of the ideals this country was founded on, anyway."

"He's probably out there right now," Great-aunt Rose said, with certain relish, "with his little gang friends, getting high on reefer cigarettes."

Mike, Douglas, and I all exchanged glances. It was always amusing to hear Great-aunt Rose use the word "reefer."

My mom apparently didn't find it very amusing, though, since she said, in a stern voice, "Don't be ridiculous, Rose. There are no drugs here. I mean, not in this town."

I didn't think it would be politic to point out to my mom that the weekend before, at the *Hello, Dolly!* cast party (Claire, of course, had gotten the part of Dolly), two kids (not Claire, obviously—she doesn't do drugs, as an actress's body, she informed me, is her temple) had been hauled out by EMTs after imbibing in a little too much Ecstasy. It is better in the long run that my mom be shielded from these things.

"Can I be excused?" I asked, instead. "I have to run over to Joanne's house and get those trig notes I was telling you about."

"*May* I be excused," my mom said. "And no, you may not. It's Thanksgiving, Jessica. You have three whole days off. You can pick up the notes tomorrow."

"You know somebody graffitied the overpass last week," Mrs. Lippman informed everyone. "You can't even tell what it says. I never thought of it before now, but supposing it's one of those . . . what do they call them, again? I saw it on

Sixty Minutes. Oh, yes. A gang tag. I mean, I'm sure it's not. But what if it is?"

"I can't get the notes tomorrow," I said. "Joanne's going to her grandma's tomorrow. Tonight's the only time I can get them."

"Hush," my mom said.

"Reefer today," Great-aunt Rose said, shaking her head. "Heroin tomorrow."

"You don't know anybody named Joanne," Douglas leaned over to whisper in my ear.

"Mom," I said, ignoring Douglas. Which was kind of mean, on account of it had taken a lot for him even to come down to dinner at all. Douglas is not what you'd call the most sociable guy. In fact, antisocial is more the word for it, really. But he's gotten a little better since he started a job at a local comic book store. Well, better for him, anyway.

"Come on, Mom," I said. "I'll be back in less than an hour." This was a total lie, but I was hoping that she'd be so busy with her guests and everything, she wouldn't even notice I wasn't home yet.

"Jessica," my dad said, signaling for me to help him start gathering people's plates. "You'll miss pie."

"Save a piece of each for me," I said, reaching out to grab the plates nearest me, then following him into the kitchen. "Please?"

My dad, after rolling his eyes at me a little, finally tilted his head toward the driveway. So I knew it was okay.

"Take Ruth with you," my dad said, as I was pulling my coat down from its hook by the garage door.

"Aw, Dad," I said.

"You have a learner's permit," my dad said. "Not a license. You may not get behind the wheel without a licensed driver in the passenger seat."

"Dad." I thought my head was going to explode. "It's Thanksgiving. There is no one out on the streets. Even the cops are at home."

"It's supposed to snow," he said.

"The forecast said tomorrow, not tonight." I tried to look my most dependable. "I will call you as soon as I get there, and then again, right before I leave. I swear."

"Well, Joe." Mr. Lippman walked into the kitchen. "May I extend my compliments to the chef? That was the best Thanksgiving dinner I've had in ages."

My dad looked pleased. "Really, Burt? Well, thank you. Thank you so much."

"Dad," I said, standing by the heart-shaped key peg by the garage door.

My dad barely looked at me. "Take your mother's car," he said to me. Then, to Mr. Lippman, he went, "You didn't think the mashed potatoes were a little too garlicky?"

Victorious, I snatched my mom's car keys—on a Girl Scout whistle key chain, in case she got attacked in the parking lot at Wal-Mart; no one had ever gotten attacked there before, but you never knew. Besides, everybody had gotten paranoid since Mastriani's burnt down, even though they'd caught the perps—and I bolted.

Free at last, I thought, as I climbed behind the wheel of her Volkswagen Rabbit. *Free at last. Thank God almighty, I am free at last.*

Which is an actual historical quote from a famous person, and probably didn't really apply to the current situation. But believe me, if you'd been cooped up all evening with Great-aunt Rose, you'd have thought it, too.

About the license thing. Yeah, that was kind of funny, actually. I was virtually the only junior at Ernie Pyle High who didn't have a driver's license. It wasn't because I wasn't old enough, either. I just couldn't seem to pass the exam. And not because I can't drive. It's just this whole, you know, speed limit thing. Something happens to me when I get behind the wheel of a car. I don't know what it is. I just need—I mean really *need*—to go fast. It must be like a hormonal thing, like Mike and Claire Lippman, because I fully can't help it.

So really, my parents have no business letting me use the car. I mean, if I got into a wreck, no way was their insurance going to cover the damages.

But the thing was, I wasn't going to get into a wreck. Because except for the lead foot thing, I'm a good driver. A *really* good driver.

Too bad I suck at pretty much everything else.

My mother's car is a Rabbit. It doesn't have nearly the power of my dad's Volvo, but it's got punch. Plus, with me being so short, it's a little easier to maneuver. I backed out of the driveway—piece of cake, even in the dark—and pulled out onto empty Lumley Lane. Across the street, all the lights in the Hoadley place—I mean, the Thompkins place—were blazing. I looked up, at the windows directly across the street from my bedroom dormers. Those, I knew, from having seen her in them, were Tasha Thompkins's bedroom windows. The Thompkinses, who had grandparents visiting—I knew because they'd turned down my mom and dad's invitation to Thanksgiving dinner on account of their already having their own guests—had eaten earlier than we had, if Nate had been sent out two hours ago for whipped cream. Tasha, I could see, was upstairs in her room already. I wondered what she was doing. I hoped not homework. But Tasha sort of seemed like the homework-after-Thanksgiving-dinner kind of girl.

Unlike me. I was the sneak-out-to-meet-her-boyfriend-after-Thanksgiving-dinner kind of girl.

And at that moment, I was more glad than I'd been in a long, long time to be me. I didn't wonder, not even for a second, what it might be like to be Tasha, much less her brother Nate.

Except of course if I had—if I had bothered to think, even for a minute, about Nate Thompkins—he'd probably still be alive today.

CHAPTER 3

"Gosh, Mrs. Wilkins," I said. "That was the best pumpkin pie I ever had."

Rob's mom brightened. "You really think so, Jess?"

"Yes, ma'am," I said, meaning it. "Better than my dad's, even."

"Well, I doubt that," Mrs. Wilkins said with a laugh. She looked pretty in the soft light over the kitchen sink, with all her red hair piled up on top of her head. She had on a nice dress, too, a silk one in jade green. She didn't look like a mom. She looked like she was somebody's girlfriend. Which she was, in fact. She was this guy Gary-No-Really-Just-Call-Me-Gary's girlfriend.

But she was also my boyfriend Rob's mom.

"Isn't your dad a gourmet cook?" Just-Call-Me-Gary asked, as he helped bring in the dishes from the Wilkinses' dining room table.

"Well," I said. "I don't know about gourmet. But he's a good cook. Still, his pumpkin pie can't hold a candle to yours, Mrs. Wilkins."

"Go on," Mrs. Wilkins said, flushing with pleasure. "Me? Better than a gourmet cook? I don't think so."

"Sure is good enough for me," Gary said, and he put his arms around her waist, and sort of danced her around the kitchen.

I noticed Rob, watching from the kitchen door, kind of grimace, then turn around and walk away. Maybe Rob had a right to be disgusted. He worked with Just-Call-Me-Gary at his uncle's auto repair shop. It was through Rob that Mrs. Wilkins had met Just-Call-Me-Gary in the first place.

After watching Gary and Rob's mom dance for a few seconds more—they actually looked pretty good together, since he was all lean and tall and good looking in a cowboy sort of way, and she was all pretty and plump in a dance hall girl kind of way—I followed Rob out into the living room, where he'd switched on the TV, and was watching football.

And Rob is not a huge sports fan. Like me, he prefers bikes. Motorbikes, that is.

"Hey," I said, flopping down onto the couch next to him. "Why so glum, chum?"

Which was a toolish thing to say, I know, but when confronted with six feet of hot, freshly showered male in softly faded denim, it is hard for a girl like me to think straight.

"Nothing." Rob, normally fairly uncommunicative, at least where his deepest emotions were concerned—like, for instance, the ones he felt for me—aimed the remote and changed the channel.

"Is it Gary?" I asked. "I thought you liked him."

"He's all right," Rob said. *Click. Click. Click.* He was going through channels like Claire Lippman, a champion tanner, went through bottles of sunscreen.

"Then what's the matter?"

"Nothing," Rob said. "I told you."

"Oh."

I couldn't help feeling a little disappointed. It wasn't like I'd expected him to propose to me or anything, but I had sort of thought, when he'd invited me to have Thanksgiving dinner with him and his mom, that Rob and I were making some headway, you know, in the relationship department. I thought maybe he was finally going to put aside this ridiculous prejudice he has against me, on account of my being sixteen and him being eighteen and on probation for some crime the nature of which he has yet to reveal to me.

Instead, the whole thing seemed to have been cooked up

by his mom. Not just the dinner, but the invitation, as well.

"We just don't see enough of you," Mrs. Wilkins had said, when I'd come through the door bearing flowers. (Stop and Shop, but what she didn't know wouldn't hurt her. Besides, they were pretty nice, and had cost me ten whole dollars.) "Do we, Rob?"

Rob had only glared at me. "You could have called," he said. "I'd have come and picked you up."

"Why should you have gone to all that trouble?" I'd asked, airily. "My mom was fine with me taking the car."

"Mastriani, I think you're forgetting something."

"What?"

"You don't have a license."

For a guy I'd met in detention, you would think Rob would be a lot more open-minded. But he is surprisingly old-fashioned on a large number of topics.

Such as, I was finding out, his mom and her dating habits.

"It's just," he said, when sounds of playful splashing started coming from the kitchen, "she has to work tomorrow, that's all. I mean, the whole reason we stayed here instead of going to Evansville with my uncle is that she has to work tomorrow."

"Oh," I said. What else could I say?

"I just hope he isn't planning on staying late," Rob said. *Click. Click. Click.* "Mom's got the breakfast shift."

I knew all about Mrs. Wilkins and her breakfast shift.

Before it burned down, Rob's mom had worked at Mastriani's. Since it got toasted, she's been working instead at Joe's, my mom and dad's other restaurant.

"I'm sure he's going to leave soon," I said encouragingly, even though it wasn't even ten o'clock. Rob was way over-reacting. "Hey, why don't we volunteer to do the dishes, so they can, you know, visit?"

Rob made a face, but since he is basically a guy who would do anything for his mom, on account of his dad having left them both a long time ago, he stood up.

But when we got into the kitchen, it was clear from the amount of suds being flung about that Just-Call-Me-Gary and Mrs. Wilkins were having a pretty good time doing the dishes themselves.

"Mom," Rob said, trying, I could tell, not to get mad. "Isn't that your good dress?"

"Oh." Mrs. Wilkins looked down at herself. "Yes, it is. Where is my apron? Oh, I left it in my bedroom. . . ."

"I'll get it," I volunteered, because I am nosey and I wanted to see what Mrs. Wilkins's bedroom looked like.

"Oh, aren't you sweet?" Mrs. Wilkins said. And then she aimed the dish nozzle at Just-Call-Me-Gary and got him right in the chest with a stream of hot water.

Rob looked nauseated.

Mrs. Wilkins's bedroom was on the second floor of the tiny little farmhouse she and Rob lived in. Her room was a lot like her, pink and cream and pretty. She had some baby pictures of Rob on the wall that I admired for a few seconds, after I'd found her apron on the bed. That, I thought to myself, is how my kid with Rob would look. If we ever had kids. Which would have to wait until I had a career, first. Oh, and for Rob to propose. Or take me out on a real date.

In one of the photos, Rob, who was still young enough to be in diapers, was being held by a man whom I didn't recognize. He didn't look like any of Rob's uncles, who, like Rob's mom, were all redheaded. In fact, this man looked more like Rob, with the same dark hair and smokey gray eyes.

This, I decided, had to be Rob's dad. Rob never wanted to talk about his dad, I guess because he was still mad at him for walking out on Rob and his mom. Still, I could see why Rob's mom would have gone for the guy. He was something of a hottie.

Back downstairs, I handed Mrs. Wilkins her apron. She was still giggling over something Just-Call-Me-Gary had said. Just-Call-Me-Gary looked pretty happy, too. In fact the only person who didn't look very happy was Rob.

Mrs. Wilkins must have noticed, since she went, "Rob, why don't you show Jessica the progress you've made on your bike?"

I perked up at this. Rob kept the bike he was currently working on, a totally choice but ancient Harley, in the barn. This was practically an invitation from Rob's mom to go and make out with her son. I could not believe my good fortune.

But once we got into the barn, Rob didn't look very inclined to make out. Not that he ever does. He is unfortunately very good at resisting his carnal urges. In fact, I would almost say that he doesn't have any carnal urges, except that every once in a while, and all too rarely for my tastes, I am able to wear him down with my charm and cherry ChapStick.

Or maybe he just gets so sick of me talking all the time that he kisses me in order to shut me up. Who knows?

In any case, he didn't seem particularly inclined to take advantage of my vulnerable femininity there in the barn. Maybe I should have worn a skirt, or something.

"Is this just because I drove out here?" I asked, as I watched him tinker around with the bike.

Rob, looking up at the bike, which rested on a worktable in the middle of the barn, tightened something with a wrench. "What are you talking about?"

"This," I said. "I mean, if I'd known you were going to be so crabby about it, I'd have called you to come pick me up, I swear."

"No, you wouldn't have," Rob said, doing something with the wrench that made the muscles in his upper arms bunch up beneath the gray sweater he wore. Which was way more entertaining than watching sports on TV, let me tell you.

"What are you talking about? I just said—"

"You didn't even tell your parents you were coming here, Mastriani," Rob said. "So cut the crap."

"What do you mean?" I tried to sound offended, even though of course he was telling the truth. "They know where I am."

Rob put down the wrench, folded his arms across his chest, leaned his butt against the worktable, and said, "Then why, when you called to tell them you got here, did you say you were at somebody Joanne's?"

Damn! I hadn't realized he'd been in the room when I'd made that call.

"Look, Mastriani," he said. "You know I've had my doubts from the start about this—you and me, I mean. And not just because I've graduated and you're still in the eleventh grade—not to mention the whole jailbait factor. But let's be real. You and I come from different worlds."

"That," I said, "is so not—"

"Well, different sides of the tracks, then."

"Just because I'm a Townie," I said, "and you're a—"

He held up a single hand. "Look, Mastriani. Let's face it. This isn't going to work."

I've been working really hard on my anger management issues lately. Except for that whole thing with the football players—and Karen Sue Hankey—I hadn't beat up a single person or served a day of detention the whole semester. Mr. Goodhart, my guidance counselor, said he was really proud of my progress, and was thinking about canceling my mandatory weekly meetings with him.

But when Rob held up his hand like that, and said that this, meaning us, wasn't going to work, it was about all I could do to keep from grabbing that hand and twisting Rob's arm behind his back until he said uncle. All that kept me from doing it, really, was that I have found that boys don't really like it when you do things like this to them, and I wanted Rob to like me. To more than like me.

So instead of twisting his arm behind his back, I put my hands on my hips, cocked my head, and went, "Does this have something to do with that Gary dude?"

Rob unfolded his arms and turned back to his bike. "No," he said. "This is between you and me, Mastriani."

"Because I noticed you don't seem to like him very much."

"You're sixteen years old," Rob said, to the bike. "*Sixteen!*"

"I mean, I guess I could understand why you don't like him. It must be weird to see your mom with some guy other than your dad. But that doesn't mean it's okay to take it out on me."

"Jess." It always meant trouble when Rob called me by my first name. "You've got to see that this can't go anywhere. I'm on probation, okay? I can't get caught hanging out with some *kid*—"

The kid part stung, but I graciously chose to ignore it, observing that Rob, in the words of Great-aunt Rose's hero, Oprah, was in some psychic pain.

"What I hear you saying," I said, talking the way Mr. Goodhart had advised me to talk when I was in a situation that might turn adversarial, "is that you don't want to see me anymore because you feel that our age and socioeconomic differences are too great—"

"Don't even tell me that you don't agree," Rob interrupted, in a warning tone. "Otherwise, why haven't you told your parents about me? Huh? Why am I this dark secret in your life? If you were so sure that we have something that could work, you'd have introduced me to them by now."

"What I am saying to you in response," I went on, as if he hadn't spoken, "is that I believe you are pushing me away because your father pushed you away, and you can't stand to be hurt that way again."

Rob looked at me over his shoulder. His smokey gray eyes, in the light from the single bulb hanging from the wooden beam overhead, were shadowed.

"You're nuts," was all he said. But he really seemed to mean it sincerely.

"Rob," I said, taking a step toward him. "I just want you to know, I am not like your dad. I will never leave you."

"Because you're a freaking psycho," Rob said.

"No," I said. "That's not why. It's because I lo—"

"Don't!" he said, thrusting the rag out at me like it was a weapon. There was a look of naked panic on his face. "Don't say it! Mastriani, I am warning you—"

"—ve you."

"I *told* you"—He wadded the rag up and threw it viciously into a far corner of the barn—"not to say it."

"I'm sorry," I said, gravely. "But I am afraid my unbridled passion was simply too great to hold in check a moment longer."

A second later it appeared that in actuality Rob was the one suffering from the unbridled passion, not me. At least if the way he grabbed me by the shoulders, dragged me toward him, and started kissing me was any indication.

While it was, of course, highly gratifying to be kissed by a young man who was clearly so incapable of controlling his tremendous ardor for me, it has to be remembered that we were kissing in a barn, which at the end of November is not the warmest place to be at night. Furthermore, it wasn't like there were any comfy couches or beds nearby for him to throw me down on or anything. I suppose we could have done it in the hay, but

a) eew, *and*

b) my passion for Rob is not that *unbridled.*

I mean, sex is a big enough step in any relationship without doing it in an old barn. Um, no thank you. I am willing to wait until the moment is right—such as prom night. In the unlikely event I am ever invited to prom. Which, considering that my boyfriend is already a high school graduate, seems unlikely. Unless of course I invite *him*.

But again, *eew.*

"I think I should go home now," I said, the next time we both came up for air.

"That," Rob said, resting his forehead against mine and breathing hard, "would probably be a good idea."

So I went in and said thank you to Rob's mom, who was sitting on the couch with Just-Call-Me-Gary watching TV in a snuggly sort of position that, had Rob seen it, might just have sent him over the edge. Fortunately, however, he did not see it. And I did not tell him about it, either.

"Well," I said to him, as I climbed behind the wheel of my mom's car. "Seeing as how we aren't broken up anymore, do you want to do something Saturday? Like go see a movie or whatever?"

"Gosh, I don't know," Rob said. "I thought you might be busy with your good friend Joanne."

"Look," I said. It was so cold out that my breath was coming out in little white puffs, but I didn't care. "My parents have a lot to deal with right now. I mean, there's the restaurant, and Mike dropping out of Harvard. . . ."

"You're never going to tell them about me, are you?" Rob's gray eyes bore into me.

"Just let me give them a chance to adjust to the idea," I said. "I mean, there's the whole thing with Douglas and his job, and Great-aunt Rose, and—"

"And you and the psychic thing," he reminded me, with just the faintest trace of bitterness. "Don't forget you and the psychic thing."

"Right," I said. "Me and the psychic thing." The one thing I could never forget, no matter how much I tried.

"Look, you better get going," Rob said, straightening up. "I'll follow behind, and make sure you get home okay."

"You don't have to—"

"Mastriani," he said. "Just shut up and drive."

And so I did.

Only it turned out we didn't get very far.

CHAPTER 4

Not, may I point out here and now, because of my poor driving skills. As I think I've stated before, I am an extremely good driver.

But I didn't know that at first. That I wasn't being pulled over on account of my driving ability, or lack thereof. All I knew was one minute I was cruising along the dark, empty country road that ran from Rob's house back into town, with Rob purring along behind me on his Indian. And the next, I rounded a curve to find the entire road blocked off by emergency vehicles—county sheriff's SUVs, police cruisers, highway patrol . . . even an ambulance. My face was bathed in flashing red and white. All I could think was, *Whoa! I was only going eighty, I swear!*

Of course it was a forty-mile-an-hour zone. But come on. It was Thanksgiving, for crying out loud. There hadn't been another soul on the road for the past ten miles. . . .

A skinny sheriff's deputy waved me to the shoulder. I obeyed, my palms sweaty. *My God*, was all I could think. *All this because I was driving without a license? Who knew they were so strict?*

The officer who strolled up to the car after I pulled over was one I recognized from the night Mastriani's burned down. I didn't remember his name, but I knew he was a nice guy— the kind of guy who maybe wouldn't bust my chops too badly for driving illegally. He shined a flashlight first on me, then into the backseat of my mom's car. I hoped he didn't think the stuff my mom had in the backseat—boxes of CDs by Carly Simon and Billy Joel, and some DVDs of romantic comedies she kept forgetting to return to Blockbuster—were mine. I am so not the Carly Simon, *Sleepless in Seattle* type.

"Jessica, isn't it?" the cop said, when I put the window down. "Aren't you Joe Mastriani's daughter?"

"Yes, sir," I said. I glanced in the rearview mirror and saw Rob pull up right behind me on his Indian. His long legs were stretched out so that his feet rested on the ground, keeping him and the bike upright while he waited for me to get waved through the roadblock. Rob was gazing out at the cornfield to the right of us. The brown, withered stalks were bathed in the flashing red-and-white lights from the dozen squad cars and ambulance parked alongside the road. A few yards deeper into the field, a giant floodlight had been set up on a metal pole, and was shining down on something that we couldn't see, with the tall corn in the way.

"Too bad you have to work on Thanksgiving," I said to the cop. I was trying to be way nice to him, on account of my not having a driver's license, and all. Meanwhile, my palms were now so sweaty, I could barely grip the wheel. I had no idea what happens to people caught driving without a license, but I was pretty sure it wouldn't be very nice.

"Yeah," the cop said. "Well, you know. Listen, we kinda got a situation over here. Where you coming from, anyway?"

"Oh, I was just having dinner over at my friend's house," I said, and told him the address of Rob's house. "That's him," I added, helpfully, pointing behind me.

Rob had, by this time, switched off his engine and gotten down from his bike. He strolled up to the police officer with his hands at his sides instead of in the pockets of his leather jacket, I guess to show he wasn't holding a weapon or anything. Rob is pretty leery of cops, on account of having been arrested before.

"What's going on, Officer?" Rob wanted to know, all casual-like. You could tell he, like me, was worried about the whole driving without a license thing. But what kind of police force would set up a roadblock to catch license-less drivers on Thanksgiving? I mean, that was going way above and beyond the call of duty, if you asked me.

"Oh, we got a tip a little while ago," the cop said to Rob. "Regarding some suspicious activity out here. Came out to have a look around." I noticed he hadn't taken out his little ticket book to write me up. *Maybe,* I thought. *Maybe this isn't about me.*

Especially considering the floodlight. I could see people traipsing out from and then back into the cornfield. They appeared to be carrying things, toolboxes and stuff.

"You see anything strange?" the police officer asked me. "When you were driving out here from town?"

"No," I said. "No, I didn't see anything."

It was a clear night. . . . Cold, but cloudless. Overhead was a moon, full, or nearly so. You could see pretty far, even though it was only about an hour shy of midnight, by the light of that moon.

Except that there wasn't much to see. Just the big corn-field, stretching out from the side of the road like a dark, rus-tling sea. Rising above it, off in the distance, was a hill covered thickly in trees. The backwoods. Where my dad used to take us camping, before Douglas got sick, and Mikey decided he liked computers better than baiting fishhooks, and I developed a pretty severe allergy to going to the bathroom out of doors.

People lived in the backwoods . . . if you wanted to call the conditions they endured there living. If you ask me, anything involving an outhouse is on the same par with camping.

But not everyone who got laid off when the plastics factory closed was as lucky as Rob's mom, who found another job—thanks to me—pretty quickly. Some of them, too proud to accept welfare from the state, had retreated into those woods, and were living in shacks, or worse.

And some of them, my dad once told me, weren't even living there because they didn't have the money to move somewhere with an actual toilet. Some of them lived there because they *liked* it there.

Apparently not everyone has as fond an attachment as I do to indoor plumbing.

"When you drove through, coming from town," the police officer said, "what time would that have been?"

I told him I thought it had been after eight, but well before nine. He nodded thoughtfully, and wrote down what I said, which was not much, considering I hadn't seen anything. Rob, standing by my mom's car, blew on his gloved hands. It *was* pretty cold, sitting there with the window rolled down. I felt especially bad for Rob, who was just going to have to climb back on his motorcycle when we were through being questioned and ride behind me all the way into town and then back to his house, without even a chance to get warmed up. Unless of course I invited him into my mom's car. Just for a few minutes. You know. To defrost.

Suddenly I noticed that those police officers, hurrying in and out of that cornfield? Yeah, those weren't toolboxes they were carrying. No, not at all.

Suddenly my palms were sweaty for a whole different reason than before.

Let me just say that in Indiana, they are always finding bodies in cornfields. Cornfields seem to be the preferred dumping ground for victims of foul play by Midwestern killers. That's because until the farmer who owns the field cuts down all the stalks to plant new rows, you can't really see what all is going on in there.

Well, suddenly I had a pretty good idea what was going on in this particular cornfield.

"Who is it?" I asked the policeman, in a high-pitched voice that didn't really sound like my own.

The cop was still busy writing down what I'd said about not having seen anyone. He didn't bother to pretend that he didn't know what I was talking about. Nor did he try to convince me I was wrong.

"Nobody you'd know," he said, without even looking up.

But I had a feeling I did know. Which was why I suddenly undid my seatbelt and got out of the car.

The cop looked up when I did that. He looked more than up. He looked pretty surprised. So did Rob.

"Mastriani," Rob said, in a cautious voice. "What are you doing?"

Instead of replying, I started walking toward the harsh white glow of the floodlight, out in the middle of that cornfield.

"Wait a minute." The cop put away his notebook and pen. "Miss? Um, you can't go over there."

The moon was bright enough that I could see perfectly well even without all the flashing red-and-white lights. I walked rapidly along the side of the road, past clusters of cops and sheriff's deputies. Some of them looked up at me in surprise as I breezed past. The ones who did look up seemed startled, like they'd seen something disturbing. The disturbing thing appeared to be me, striding toward the floodlight in the corn.

"Whoa, little missy." One of the cops detached himself from the group he was in, and grabbed my arm. "Where do you think you're going?"

"I'm going to look," I said. I recognized this police officer, too, only not from the fire at Mastriani's. I recognized this one from Joe Junior's, where I sometimes bussed tables on weekends. He always got a large pie, half sausage and half pepperoni.

"I don't think so," said Half-Sausage, Half-Pepperoni. "We got everything under control. Why don't you get back in your car, like a good little girl, and go on home."

"Because," I said, my breath coming out in white puffs. "I think I might know him."

"Come on now," Half-Sausage, Half-Pepperoni said, in a

kindly voice. "There's nothing to see. Nothing to see at all. You go on home like a good girl. Son?" He said this last to Rob, who'd come hurrying up behind him. "This your little girlfriend? You be a good boy, now, and take her on home."

"Yes, sir," Rob said, taking hold of my arm the same way the police officer had. "I'll do that, sir." To me, he hissed, "Are you nuts, Mastriani? Let's go, before they ask to see your license."

Only I wouldn't budge. Being only five feet tall and a hundred pounds, I am not exactly a difficult person to lift up and sling around, as Rob had illustrated a couple of times. But I had gotten pretty mad upon both those occasions, and Rob seemed to remember this, since he didn't try it now. Instead, he followed me with nothing more than a deep sigh as I barreled past the police officers, and toward that white light in the corn.

None of the emergency workers gathered around the body noticed me, at first. The ones on the outskirts of the crime scene hadn't exactly been expecting gawkers this far out from town, and on Thanksgiving night, no less. So it wasn't like they'd been looking out for rubberneckers. There wasn't even any yellow emergency tape up. I breezed past them without any problem. . . .

And then halted so suddenly that Rob, following behind, collided into me. His *oof* drew the attention of more than a few officers, who looked up from what they were doing, and went, "What the—"

"Miss," a sheriff's deputy said, getting up from the cold

hard soil upon which he'd been kneeling. "I'm sorry, miss, but you need to stand back. Marty? Marty, what are you thinking, letting people through here?"

Marty came hurrying up, looking red-faced and ashamed.

"Sorry, Earl," he said, panting. "I didn't see her, she came by so fast. Come on, miss. Let's go—"

But I didn't move. Instead, I pointed.

"I know him," I said, looking down at the body that lay, shirtless, on the frozen ground.

"Jesus." Rob's soft breath was warm on my ear.

"That's my neighbor," I said. "Nate Thompkins."

Marty and Earl exchanged glances.

"He went to get whipped cream," I said. "A couple of hours ago." When I finally tore my gaze from Nate's bruised and broken body, there were tears in my eyes. They felt warm, compared to the freezing air all around us.

I felt one of Rob's hands, heavy and reassuring, on my shoulder.

A second later, the county sheriff, a big man in a red plaid jacket with fleece lining came up to me.

"You're the Mastriani girl," he said. It wasn't really a question. His voice was deep and gruff.

When I nodded, he went, "I thought you didn't have that psychic thing anymore."

"I don't," I said, reaching up to wipe the moisture from my eyes.

"Then how'd you know"—he nodded down at Nate, who was being covered up with a piece of blue plastic—"he was here?"

"I didn't," I said. I explained how Rob and I had come to be there. Also how Dr. Thompkins had been over at my house earlier, looking for his son.

The sheriff listened patiently, then nodded.

"I see," he said. "Well, that's good to know. He wasn't carrying any ID, least that we could find. So now we have an idea who he is. Thank you. You go on home now, and we'll take it from here."

Then the sheriff turned around to supervise what was going on beneath the flood lamp.

Except that I didn't leave. I wanted to, but somehow, I couldn't. Because something was bothering me.

I looked at Marty, the sheriff's deputy, and asked, "How did he die?"

The deputy shot a glance at the sheriff, who was busy talking to somebody on the EMS team.

"Look, miss," Marty said. "You better—"

"Was it from those marks?" I had seen that there'd been some kind of symbol carved into Nate's naked chest.

"Jess." Now Rob had hold of my hand. "Come on. Let's go. These guys have work to do."

"What were those marks, anyway?" I asked Marty. "I couldn't tell."

Marty looked uncomfortable. "Really, miss," he said. "You'd better go."

But I didn't go. I couldn't go. I just stood there, wondering what Dr. Thompkins and his wife were going to do, when they found out what had happened to their son. Would they decide to move back to Chicago?

And what about Tasha? She seemed to really like Ernest Pyle High School, if her enthusiasm about the yearbook committee was any indication. But would she want to stay in a town in which her only brother had been brutally murdered?

And what was Coach Albright going to say when he learned he'd lost yet another quarterback?

"Mastriani." Rob was starting to sound desperate. "Let's go."

I didn't realize precisely why Rob was sounding so desperate until I turned around. That was when I very nearly walked into a tall, thin man wearing a long black coat and a badge that indicated that he was a member of the Federal Bureau of Investigation.

"Hello, Jessica," Cyrus Krantz said to me, with a smile that I'm sure he meant to be reassuring, but which was actually merely sickening. "Remember me?"

CHAPTER 5

It would be hard to forget Cyrus Krantz. Believe me, I've tried. He's the new agent assigned to my case. You know, on account of me being Lightning Girl and all.

Only Cyrus Krantz isn't exactly a special agent. He's apparently some kind of FBI director. Of special operations, or something. He explained the whole thing—or at least he tried to—to my parents and me. He came over to our house not long after Mastriani's burned down. He didn't bring a pie or anything with him, which I thought was kind of tacky, but whatever. At least he called first, and made an appointment.

Then he sat in our living room and explained to my parents over coffee and biscotti about this new program he's developed. It is a division of the FBI, only instead of special agents, it is manned by psychics. Seriously. Only Dr. Krantz— yeah, he's a doctor—doesn't call them psychics. He calls them "specially abled" individuals.

Which if you ask me makes it sound like they must all take the little bus to school, but whatever. Dr. Krantz was very eager for me to join his new team of "specially abled" secret agents.

Except of course I couldn't. Because I am not specially abled anymore. At least, that's what I told Dr. Krantz.

My parents backed me up, even when Dr. Krantz took out what he called "the evidence" that I was lying. He had all these records of phone calls to 1-800-WHERE-R-YOU, the missing children's organization with which I have worked in the past, that supposedly came from me. Only of course all the calls, though they were from my town, were placed through pay phones, so there was no real way to trace who'd made them. Dr. Krantz wanted to know who else in town would know the exact location of so many missing kids—a couple hundred, actually, since that day I'd been hit by lightning.

I said you never know. It could be anybody, really.

Dr. Krantz made this big appeal to my patriotism. He said I could help catch terrorists and stuff. Which I admit would be pretty cool.

But you know, I am not really sure that is something I would like to subject my family to. You know, the vengeful wrath of terrorists, peeved that I caught their leader, or whatever. I mean, Douglas gets freaked by call-waiting. How much would terrorists rock his world?

So I politely declined Dr. Krantz's invitation, all the while insisting I was about as "specially abled" as Cindy Brady.

But that didn't mean Dr. Krantz had given up. Like his protégés—Special Agents Smith and Johnson, who'd been pulled off my case and whom I sort of missed, in a weird way—Dr. Krantz wasn't about to take no for an answer. He was always, it seemed, lurking around, waiting for me to mess up so that he could prove I really did still have my psychic powers.

Which was unfortunate, because he was neither as pretty as Special Agent Smith, or as fun to tease as Special Agent Johnson. Dr. Krantz was just . . .

Scary.

Which was why when I saw him there in that cornfield, I let out a little shriek, and must have jumped about a mile and a half into the air.

"Oh," I said, when I'd pulled myself together enough to speak in a normal voice. "Oh, Dr. Krantz. It's you. Hi."

"Hello, Jessica." Dr. Krantz has kind of an egg-shaped head, totally bald on top, only you couldn't tell just then, because he was wearing a hat pulled down low over his eyes. I guess he thought this made him look like Dr. Magneto, or something. He seemed like the kind of guy who'd want to be compared to the *X-men*'s Dr. Magneto.

His gaze flicked over Rob, whom he'd met before, only not in my living room, of course.

"Mr. Wilkins," he said, with a nod. "Good evening."

"Evening," Rob said, and, letting go of my hand to grab my arm instead, he began pulling. "Sorry. But we were just leaving."

"Slow down," Dr. Krantz said, with a creaky laugh. "Slow down there, young man. I'd like a word with Miss Mastriani, if I may."

"Yeah?" Rob said. He was about as fond as scientists in the employ of the U.S. government as he was of cops. "Well, she doesn't have anything to say to you."

"He's right," I said, to Dr. Krantz. "I really don't. Bye."

"I see." Dr. Krantz looked faintly amused. "And I suppose it was only by coincidence that you stumbled across this crime scene?"

"As a matter of fact," I said, in some surprise, since for once I was telling the truth, "it was. I was just passing by on my way home from Rob's."

"And the fact that I overheard you tell those gentlemen over there that the victim happens to be your neighbor?"

I said, "Hey, you're the government operative, not me. You ought to know more about this than I do. I mean, I'd feel pretty bad if a kid got killed during my watch."

Dr. Krantz's expression did not change. It never does. So I wasn't sure whether or not my words hit home.

"Jessica," Dr. Krantz said. "I want to show you something."

We were standing a little ways away from the circle the police officers and sheriff's deputies had made around the blue tarp covering Nate's body. But the glare from the floodlight was bright enough that, even though it was nighttime, I could see the details in the photo Cyrus Krantz pulled from inside his coat with perfect clarity.

It was, I realized, the overpass Mrs. Lippman had been talking about at dinner. The one with the graffiti spray-painted onto it. The graffiti she'd assumed was a gang tag. I myself had never noticed it.

Looking at it then, in the cold white glow of the flood-light, I saw that the red squiggle—that's all it looked like to me—seemed vaguely familiar. I had seen it before. Only where? There is not a lot of graffiti in our town. Oh, sure, the occasional *Rick Loves Nancy* out by the quarry. Every once in a while someone with a little too much school spirit painted *Cougars Rule* on the side of our rival high school's gymnasium. But that was it as far as graffiti went. I couldn't think where I could possibly have seen that red squiggle before.

Then, all at once, it hit me.

On Nate Thompkins's chest.

"So it *is* gang related?" I asked, handing the photo back to Cyrus Krantz. The two Thanksgiving suppers I'd eaten weren't sitting too well in my stomach all of a sudden.

Dr. Krantz tucked the photo back where he'd found it.

"No," he said, rebuttoning his coat. Dr. Krantz was always very neat and tidy. At our house, he hadn't left a single crumb on his plate. And my mom's biscotti is pretty crumbly.

"This," he said, tapping the pocket that held the photo, "was a warning. That"—He nodded at the blue tarp—"is just the beginning."

"The beginning of what?" I asked. Mrs. Wilkins's pumpkin pie was definitely on its way back up.

"That," Cyrus Krantz said, "is what we're going to find out, I'm afraid." Then he turned around and started striding from the cornfield, back to his long, warm car.

Wait, I wanted to call after him. *What can I do? What can I do to help?*

But then I remembered that I am not supposed to have my psychic powers anymore. So I couldn't really offer him my help.

Besides, what could I do? Nobody was missing.

Not anymore.

I didn't speed the rest of the way home. Not because I was afraid of getting caught, but because I was really afraid of what I was going to find when I pulled onto Lumley Lane. Even the purr of Rob's motorcycle behind me—he followed me home—wasn't very reassuring.

When we pulled onto my street, I saw the flashing lights right away. The sheriff must have radioed in the information I'd given him, since there were already two squad cars parked outside the Thompkins house. As I pulled into our driveway, Dr. Thompkins was just opening the door to let in the officers who stood there, their hats in their hands. Neither of them turned around as Rob, with a wave to me, took off down the street, having successfully escorted me practically to my door.

My entire family had their faces pressed to the glass of the living room windows when I walked in. Well, everybody except for Douglas, who was probably hiding in his room (flashing lights are not among his favorite things: They tend to remind him of the several ambulance trips he has taken in his lifetime).

"Oh, Jess," my mom said, when she saw me. The dining room table was clear. Everyone except for Claire had left. "Thank God you're home. I was getting worried."

"I'm fine," I said.

"Where does this Joanne live, anyway?" my mom wanted to know. "You were gone for hours."

But I could tell she wasn't really interested in my answer. All of her attention was focused on the Hoadley—I mean, Thompkins—house across the street.

"Those poor people," she murmured. "I hope it isn't bad news."

"Ma," Mike said, in a sarcastic voice. "Two sheriff cars are parked in their driveway. You think they're there with good news?"

"Don't call me Ma," my mother said. Then she seemed to

realize what everybody was doing. She looked shocked. "Get away from the windows! It's shameful, spying on those poor people like this."

"We aren't spying, Antonia," Great-aunt Rose said. "We are merely looking out the window. There's no law against that."

"Mrs. Mastriani is right," Claire said primly, getting up off the couch. "It's wrong to peep through other people's windows."

Claire obviously had no clue that Mike had been spying on her through her windows with a telescope for years.

I could have told them, I guess. I mean about Nate. But the way it was, I had barely been able to make it home with my dinner intact. I wasn't all that eager to risk losing it again. Instead, I said, "I'm going to bed," and I started up the stairs to my room. Only my mother said good night, and she sounded pretty distracted.

Upstairs, I saw that Douglas's bedroom light was still on. I thumped on his door instead of just barging in, like I used to do. Douglas has gotten a lot better since starting his job in the comic book store. I figured I'd reward him by letting him have some privacy for a change. Mr. Goodhart says this is called positive reinforcement.

"Come in, Jess," Douglas said. He knew it was me by my thump. My mom taps all timidly, my dad knocks Shave-and-a-Haircut, and Mike never visits Douglas, if he can help it. So Douglas always knows when it's me.

"Hey," I said. Douglas was lying on his bed, reading, as usual.

Tonight it was the latest installment of *Superman*. "What time did everybody leave?"

"About an hour ago," he said. "Mr. and Mrs. Abramowitz had a big fight over where they're going to go for Christmas break, Aspen or Antigua."

"Must be nice," I said. The Abramowitzes are way rich.

"Yeah. Skip contributed by having an asthma attack. Between that and Aunt Rose, it was an evening to remember."

"Huh," I said. He must have seen by my face that something was wrong, since he went, "What?"

I shook my head. For a minute, I'd been picturing Nate Thompkins, as I'd last seen him, lifeless in that cornfield. "Oh," I said. "Nothing."

"Not nothing," Douglas said. "Tell me."

I told him. I didn't want to. All right, I did. But I shouldn't have. Douglas has never been what you'd call well. I mean, he was always the one the other kids picked on in school, at the park, wherever. You know the kind. The one they call Spaz and Tard and Reject. I had spent much of my young adulthood pounding on the faces of people who'd dared to make fun of my older brother for being different.

And that's all Douglas is. Not crazy. Not retarded. Just different.

When I was through, Douglas, who knows the truth about my "special ability"—but not about Rob; no one knows the truth about Rob, except for Ruth who is, after all, my best friend—let out a big gush of air.

"Whoa," he said.

"Yeah," I said.

"Those poor people," he said, meaning the Thompkinses.

"Yeah," I said.

"I've seen the daughter," he said, meaning Tasha. "At the store."

"Really?" Somehow I could not picture shy, pretty Tasha Thompkins, always so conservatively dressed, in Comix Underground, where Douglas worked.

"She's into *Witchblade*," Douglas elaborated. He seemed really concerned. I mean, for Douglas. "What did it look like, anyway?"

He had thrown me. "What did what look like?"

"The symbol," Douglas said, patiently. "The one on Nate's chest."

"Oh," I said. I went over to his desk and drew it, not very expertly, on a pad of paper I found lying there. "Like this," I said, and handed it to him.

He took the pad and studied what I had drawn. When, after a minute, he continued to squint down at it, I said, "It's supposed to be a gang symbol, or something. It only makes sense if you're in the gang."

"This isn't a gang symbol," Douglas said. "I mean, I don't think so. It looks familiar."

"Yeah," I said. "Because you've probably seen it before, driving under the overpass. Somebody spray-painted it there."

"I never go by the overpass," Douglas said. Then he did something really weird. I mean weird for Douglas.

He got out of bed and started pulling books off his shelves. Douglas has more books—and comic books—than anyone I know. Still, if you wanted to borrow one, and took it down off the shelf and forgot to mention it to him, Douglas would notice right away it was missing, even though there are maybe a thousand other ones that look exactly like it right there on the shelf beside it.

Douglas is one of those book people.

Seeing that he was going to be occupied until well into the night, I left. I doubted he even noticed. He was way too absorbed in looking things up.

In my own room, I undressed quickly, slipping into my pajamas—a pair of fleece warm-up pants and a long-sleeved tee—with lightning speed. That is because my room, which is on the third floor, is the draftiest room in the house, and from Halloween until Easter it is freezing, in spite of the space heater my dad had installed.

I don't mind the cold, however, because I have the best

view of anybody from my bedroom windows, and that's including Mike, whose view into Claire Lippman's bedroom is what caused all that trouble a few months ago, when he decided to drop out of Harvard because he and Claire were in love. My view, which is from some dormer windows high above the treetops, is of all of Lumley Lane, which in the moonlight always looks like a silver river, the sidewalks on either side of it mossy banks. In fact, when I'd been younger, I used to pretend Lumley Lane was a river, and that I was the lighthouse operator, high above it. . . .

Whatever. I'd been a weird kid.

That night, as I undid Rob's watch, which he'd given me a few months earlier, and which I wore like an ID bracelet, (much to the bewilderment of my parents, who thought it was a bit odd that I went around with this bulky man's watch weighing my hand down all the time), I didn't look down at the street. I didn't pretend Lumley Lane was a river, or that I was the lighthouse operator, guiding tempest-tossed ships safely to shore.

Instead, I looked across the street, into Tasha Thompkins's bedroom window. The lights in her room were still on. She had probably heard the news about her brother by now. I wondered if she was stretched out on her bed, crying. That's where I'd be, if I found out either of my brothers had been killed. I felt a wave of grief for Tasha, and for her parents. I didn't know anything about gangs, but I thought that whoever had killed

Nate couldn't have known him all that well, because he'd been a nice kid. Smart, too. It was a waste. A real waste.

After a while, the front door to the Hoadley—I mean, Thompkins—house opened, and Dr. Thompkins, looking much older than when I had seen him earlier that evening, came out, wearing his coat. He followed the sheriff's deputies to their squad cars, then got into one. I knew he was going to ID the body. At the front door, his wife stood watching him. I couldn't tell whether or not she was crying, but I suspected she was. Two people stood on either side of her. Nate's grandparents, I assumed.

Above them, I saw a curtain move. Tasha was standing in her window, looking down as the squad car with her father in it pulled away. I saw that Tasha's shoulders were shaking. Unlike her mother, she was definitely crying.

Poor, shy, yearbook-committee-and-*Witchblade*-loving Tasha. There was nothing I could do for her. I mean, if I had known when his father had come over that Nate was in trouble, I might have been able to find him. Maybe. But it was too late, now. Too late for me to help Nate, anyway.

But not too late, I realized, to help his sister. How I was going to do that, I hadn't the slightest idea.

All I could do was try.

Little did I know, of course, how my decision to help Tasha Thompkins was going to change my life. And the life of just about everybody in our entire town.

CHAPTER 6

The next day, when Ruth told me some kid from her synagogue was missing, I didn't make the connection. I had a lot on my mind. I mean, there was the whole thing with Nate Thompkins, of course. I hadn't forgotten about my promise to myself that I was going to try to help Tasha, if I could.

There was something else, though. Something I'd dreamed about that had been, well, pretty disturbing. Not as disturbing as having your brother left for dead in a cornfield, but still wicked strange.

"Are you listening to me, Jess?" Ruth wanted to know. She had to talk pretty loudly to be heard over the Muzak in the mall. We were hitting the post-holiday sales. Hey, it was the Friday after Thanksgiving. There was nothing else to do.

"Sure," I said, fingering a pair of hoop earrings on a nearby display rack. And I don't even have pierced ears. That's how distracted I was.

"They found his bike," Ruth said. "And that's it. Just his bike. In the parking lot. No other sign of him. Not his book bag. Not his clarinet. Nothing."

"Maybe he ran away," I said. The earrings, I thought, wouldn't make a bad Christmas present for Ruth. I mean, Hanukkah present. Because Ruth was Jewish, of course.

"No way Seth Blumenthal is going to run away before his thirteenth birthday," Ruth said. "He's supposed to be having his bar mitzvah tomorrow, Jess. That's what he was doing at the synagogue in the first place. Having his last Hebrew lesson before the big ceremony on Saturday. The kid is due to rake it in. No way would he take off beforehand. And no way would he leave his bike behind."

This finally got my attention. Twelve-year-olds do not generally abandon their bikes. Not without a fight, anyway. And Ruth was right: She'd pulled in roughly twenty thousand dollars for her bat mitzvah. No way some kid was going to run away before making that kind of dough.

"You got a picture of him?" I asked Ruth, as she worked her way through a Cinnabon she was carrying around. "Seth, I mean."

"There's one in the temple directory," she said. "I mean, it's a shot of his whole family. But I can point him out for you, if you want."

"Okay," I said. "I'll take care of it."

"Soon," Ruth said to me. "You better take care of it soon. There's no telling what might have happened to him. I mean, that gang might have gotten him."

I rolled my eyes. I actually had to keep an eye out, because I'd spotted my mother and Great-aunt Rose—horror of horrors—going into JC Penney, and I wanted to be sure to avoid running into them. I was fairly certain that if Great-aunt Rose hadn't been visiting, there'd have been no way my mom would be at the mall the day after one of her neighbors found out their kid was dead. But I suspected since the neighbor in question was the Thompkinses, my mom hadn't dared risk a sympathy visit, since Great-aunt Rose would have insisted on coming along. And knowing Rose, she'd have started in about the darkies, or something equally appalling.

She was leaving on Sunday. Which might as well have been forever, it seemed so far away.

"If I get a piece of his clothing," Ruth was asking me, "could you do that thing? You know, that thing you did with Shane? And Claire? Where you smel—"

She broke off with a cry of pain as I reached up and seized her by the back of the neck. She was so surprised, a piece of Cinnabon fell out of her mouth.

"I told you not to talk about that, remember?" I hissed at her. Over at Santa's Workshop—the day after Thanksgiving was the day Santa arrived at our local mall—a bunch of moms looked our way, disapproving . . . probably because we were still young and weren't saddled down with three whiny brats, but whatever. "The Feds are still following me around, you know. I bumped into Cyrus just last night."

"Ow," Ruth said, shrugging off my hand. "Leggo, you freak."

"I mean it," I said. "Just be cool."

"You be cool." Ruth adjusted her shirt collar. "Or try just being normal for a change. What is the matter with you, anyway? You've been acting like a freak all day."

"Gee, I don't know, Ruth," I said, in my most sarcastic tone. "Maybe it's just because last night I saw the mutilated body of the guy who used to live across the street lying mangled in a cornfield."

Ruth curled her upper lip. "God," she said. "Be a little gross, why don't you?" Then Ruth looked at me a little closer. "Wait a minute. You aren't blaming yourself over Nate's death, are you?" When I didn't reply, she went, "Oh my God. You *are*. Jess, hello? You didn't kill him, okay? His little gang-bang buddies did."

"I knew he was missing," I said. Over at Santa's Workshop some kid was screaming his head off because he was afraid of the mechanical elves building toys in the fake snow. "And I didn't try to find him."

"You knew he'd gone out for whipped cream," Ruth corrected me. "And that he didn't come back right away. You didn't know he was being murdered. You couldn't have known. Come *on*, Jess. Give yourself a break. You can't be responsible for every single person on the planet who gets himself killed."

"I guess not," I said. I turned away from the sight of the mall Santa ho-ho-hoing. "Look, Ruth, let's go home. You can show me that picture. So maybe if the bar-mitzvah boy really is missing, I can find him before he becomes crow fodder, the way Nate did."

"Eew," Ruth said. "Graphic much?" But she started heading toward the nearest exit.

Only not soon enough, unfortunately.

"Jessica!"

I turned at the sound of the familiar voice . . . then blanched. It was Mrs. Wilkins.

And Rob. Just about the last two people—with the exception of my mom and Great-aunt Rose—I'd wanted to run into. Not because I wasn't happy to see them. Let's face it, when have I ever been unhappy about seeing Rob? That would be like being unhappy about seeing the sun come out after forty days and nights of rain.

But knowing what I knew now . . . what I'd learned overnight, as I slept, without consciously meaning to, and all because of that stupid picture I'd seen on Rob's mother's bedroom wall. . . .

"Hi, you guys," I said, brightly, to cover up what I was really feeling, which was, *Oh, shit.* "Wow. Fancy meeting you here." Again, among the most toolish of things to say, but I was trying to think fast.

Rob looked about as uncomfortable as I had ever seen him. This was on account of the fact that:

a) He was in a mall.

b) He was in a mall with his mom.

c) He had run into me there.

d) I was with Ruth.

Ruth and Rob are not among one another's favorite people. In fact, I had only recently convinced Ruth to stop referring to Rob as The Jerk on account of him never calling me. Rob thought Ruth was an elitist Townie snob who looked down on non-college-bound people such as himself. Which in fact she was. But that didn't make her a bad person, necessarily.

"Isn't this funny," Mrs. Wilkins said, with a happy smile. "I've been trying to convince Rob to let me take him to get measured for a tux for my brother's wedding since . . . well, forever, it seems like. And today, when he picked me up after work, he finally agreed. So here we are. And here you are! Isn't that funny?"

"It sure is," I said, even though I didn't think it was funny at all. Especially since Rob hadn't said anything to me about having a wedding to attend. A wedding at which he might be expected to bring a date. Who by rights should be have been me. "I thought Earl was already married," I said, to cover up my inner rage over Rob having never mentioned this before.

"Oh, it's not Earl," Mrs. Wilkins said. "It's my little brother Randy. He and his fiancée are tying the knot on Christmas Eve. Have you ever heard of anything so romantic?"

Christmas Eve? A Christmas Eve wedding at which Rob would be wearing a tuxedo, and he hadn't said a word to me about it? I'd have gone with him, if he'd asked me. I'd have gone with him gladly. I'd have worn the green velvet sheath dress my mom had made me for last year's Lion's Club dinner in honor of Mike winning that scholarship. If my mom wasn't around, wearing the one she'd made herself that matched mine, it actually looked good on me.

But no. No, Rob hadn't even bothered to mention he'd been invited to this affair. Nothing. Not a word.

Suddenly I felt like blurting out what I had learned in my dreams last night about Rob's dad, right in front of everyone, just to get back at him for having purposefully left me out of this very important family event that I was now dying to go to more than I had ever wanted to go to anything before in my life.

"How nice," I said, with what I hoped was a frosty smile in Rob's direction. He was studiously avoiding my gaze. Or maybe he was just trying to avoid making eye contact with Ruth, who was pointedly returning the favor. Either way, he was a dead man.

"Oh, but, Jess!" Mrs. Wilkins's hand shot out, and she grasped my fingers, the smile wiped from her face. "Rob told me what happened to you two on your way back home last night. I'm so sorry! It must have been awful. I feel so terrible for the boy's parents. . . ."

"Yes," I said, my smile growing less frosty. "It was pretty bad."

"If there's anything I can do," Mrs. Wilkins said. "I mean, I can't imagine how I could help, but if you think those poor people could use some home cooking, or something, let me know. I do make a decent casserole. . . ."

"Sure thing, Mrs. Wilkins," I said. "I'll let you know. And thanks again for dinner last night."

"Oh, honey, it was nothing," Mrs. Wilkins said, squeezing my fingers one last time before letting them go. "I'm just so glad you could share it with us."

All that would have been bad enough. But a second later, the whole thing got about ten times worse. Just when I thought I was about to escape virtually unscathed—except for the whole not-having-been-asked-to-Rob's-uncle's-wedding thing—I heard a sound that caused the blood in my veins to curdle.

Which was Great-aunt Rose, calling my name.

"See, I told you it was Jessica," Great-aunt Rose said, hauling my mother up to us. Rose's blue eyes, which appeared rheumy, but which actually took in everything around them with uncanny clarity, crackled as she looked from Rob to me and then back again. "Who is your little friend, Jessica? Aren't you going to introduce us?"

The idea of Great-aunt Rose, a tiny shrimp of a woman, calling Rob "little" would have made me laugh at any other time. As it was, however, I merely longed for the floor of the mall to open up and swallow me as quickly and as painlessly as possible.

My mother, looking tired and distracted—and who wouldn't, having spent the day with Great-aunt Rose—put down the many bags she was holding and said, "Oh, Mary. It's you. How are you?" My mom knew Mrs. Wilkins from the restaurant, of course.

"Hi, Mrs. Mastriani," Mrs. Wilkins said with her sunny smile. "How are you today?"

"Fair," my mom said, "to middling." She looked at me and Ruth. "Hello, girls. Any luck with the sales?"

"I got a cashmere sweater at Benneton," Ruth said, holding up a bag like a triumphant hunter, "for only fifteen dollars."

"It's chartreuse," I reminded her, before she could get too cocky.

"I'm sure it's very flattering," my mother said, just to be polite, because anyone who saw Ruth's blond hair and sallow complexion would know chartreuse would not be flattering on her at all.

"And *you* are?" Great-aunt Rose asked Rob, pointedly.

Rob, God love him, carefully wiped off his hand on his jeans before extending it toward my aunt and going, in his deep voice, "Rob Wilkins, ma'am. Very nice to meet you."

Great-aunt Rose merely lifted her nose at the sight of Rob's hand. "And what are your intentions toward my niece?" she demanded.

Mrs. Wilkins looked startled. My mother looked confused. Ruth looked delighted. I am sure I looked like I had just swallowed a cactus. Only Rob remained calm, as he replied, in the same polite tone, "I have no intentions toward her at all, ma'am."

Which is exactly the problem.

I saw my mother's eyes narrow as she looked at Rob. I knew what she was going to say a second before it was out of her mouth.

"Wait a minute," she said. "I know you from somewhere, don't I?"

The sad part was, she did. But I wasn't about to let her stick around to figure out where. Because where she knew Rob from was the police station, the last time I'd been hauled in there for questioning . . . a connection I did not want my mother making just then.

"I'm sure you've just seen him around, Mom," I said, taking her by the arm and propelling her toward Santa's Workshop. "Hey, look, Santa's back! Don't you want to take my picture sitting on his lap?"

My mom looked down at me with mild amusement. "Not

exactly," she said. "Considering you're no longer five years old."

Ruth, for once in her life, did something helpful, and came up on my mom's other side, saying, "Aw, come on, Mrs. M. It would be so funny. My parents would crack up if they saw a picture of me and Jess on Santa's lap. And to get her back, I'll make Jess come to temple and sit on Hanukkah Harry's lap next week. Come on."

My mom looked helplessly at Mrs. Wilkins, who fortunately didn't seem aware that anything unusual—such as the fact that her son's supposed girlfriend was doing everything in her power to keep her mother from actually meeting him—was going on.

"Oh, go on," Mrs. Wilkins said, laughingly, to my mom. "It'll be a hoot."

My mom, shaking her head, let us steer her into the line to see Santa. It was only when I came back to say good-bye to Mrs. Wilkins—I was ignoring Rob—and to get the bags my mom had set down that I overheard Great-aunt Rose hiss at Rob, "Watch yourself, young man. I've seen your type before, and I'm warning you: Don't you even think about laying a finger on my niece. Not if you know what's good for you."

I glared at Great-aunt Rose. Just what I needed, for her to give Rob yet another excuse why he couldn't go out with me.

Rob seemed hardly to have heard her, however. Instead, he only looked at me, those smokey gray eyes unreadable. . . .

Almost. I was pretty sure I read something in the set of his square jaw. And that something said, *Thanks for nothing.*

It was only then that I realized I'd had a perfect chance finally to introduce him to my mother, and that, in my panic, I'd blown it.

But hey, who'd had the perfect chance to ask me to be his escort at his uncle Randy's Christmas Eve wedding, and blown that?

When I returned to the line to see Santa, with my mom's bags and Great-aunt Rose in tow, it was only to hear Ruth whisper in a low voice, *"You owe me."* It took me a minute to realize what Ruth meant. I heard snickering. Looking past the cottony field of fake snow that surrounded us, I saw Karen Sue Hankey and some of her cronies pointing at us and laughing their heads off.

I really don't think my mom should have gotten so mad over the gesture I made at them, despite the fact that there were small children around. They probably didn't even know what it meant. Great-aunt Rose sure didn't.

"No, Jessica," she informed me acidly, a second later. "The peace sign is with two fingers, not one. Don't they teach you children anything in school these days?"

CHAPTER 7

There were more cars than ever outside the Hoadley—I mean Thompkins—house when we got home from the mall later that afternoon.

I was surprised the Thompkinses were acquainted with that many people. For being so new in town, they were pretty popular.

"Took," Ruth said, as I got out of her car. "Coach Albright's there."

Sure enough, I recognized the coach's Dodge Plymouth. It was hard not to, as he'd had the car custom painted in the Ernie Pyle High School colors of purple and white.

"God," Ruth said, sympathetically, as I climbed out of her

car. "Poor Tasha. Can you imagine having that blowhard in your living room the day after your brother got murdered? That has to be one of those circles of hell Dante was going on about." We are doing Dante's *Inferno* in English. Well, everyone else is. I am mainly playing Tetris on my Nintendo DS in the back row with the sound off.

"Come over later with that picture," I said. "I mean, if the kid from your synagogue is still missing when you get home."

"He will be," Ruth said, bleakly. "This appears to be a day destined for human tragedy. I mean, look at my new sweater."

I slammed the car door shut and started across my yard, into the house. The snow that the Weather Channel had been talking about still hadn't appeared, but there was a thick layer of grayish-white clouds overhead. Not a hint of blue showed anywhere. And the wind was pretty nippy. My face, the only part of me exposed to the elements, practically froze during my twenty-foot walk from the driveway to our front door.

"Hey," I yelled, as I came in. "I'm home." It was safe to yell this, as Ruth and I had beaten my mom and Great-aunt Rose home from the mall. So the only people who might have heard me were people I didn't actually mind speaking to.

Only nobody answered my yell. The house appeared to be empty.

I walked over to the hall table to look at the mail. Christmas catalog, Christmas catalog, Christmas catalog. It was amazing how those Christmas catalogs piled up, starting before Halloween, even. Ours all went straight into the recycle bin.

A bill. Another bill. A letter from Harvard, addressed to my parents, no doubt begging them to reconsider letting Mikey drop out. Like they'd had any choice in the matter. Mike had purchased a one-way ticket home the minute he'd heard his lady fair had been hospitalized on account of almost being murdered, and then had refused to go back once Claire turned the full force of her baby blues on him. (It's way cooler, Claire told me, to have a boyfriend in college than one who is still in high school. I guess even if that boyfriend is a Class A-certified geek.)

There was nothing in the mail for me. There is never anything in the mail for me. All of my mail—such as it is—gets sent to me secretly from my friend Rosemary at 1-800-WHERE-R-YOU via Ruth, who then smuggles it over. But Rosemary was in Rhode Island visiting her mother for Thanksgiving, so I wasn't expecting anything from her this week. The missing kids were just going to have to wait until next week to get found.

Except for Seth Blumenthal, if he really was missing.

Sighing, I pulled off my hat and gloves, stuffed them in my coat pockets, and went to hang up my coat by the door to the garage. A perusal of the fridge revealed that no one had been by recently with any interesting offerings in the form of food solace. I nibbled on some leftover persimmon pie, but my heart wasn't in it. You would think I'd have been standing there thinking about what was going on across the street. I mean about Nate, and all. A sixteen-year-old kid, killed before he'd ever even gotten his driver's license, and for what? Wearing the wrong gang's colors?

But of course I wasn't thinking about Nate at all. I was thinking about Rob, and how hurt he'd looked when I hadn't introduced him to my mom. Well, how hurt did he think I felt when I found out about that wedding he hadn't invited me to? He couldn't have it both ways. He couldn't insist that we can't go out because of our age difference, then be hurt when I didn't introduce him to my mom.

The two of us definitely had some problems in our relationship that needed working out. Maybe we needed to go on *Oprah* and talk to that bald doctor dude she's always having on.

"Doctor, my girlfriend is ashamed of me," I could almost hear Rob saying. "She won't introduce me to her parents."

"Well, my boyfriend doesn't trust me," I would retort. "He won't tell me what he got arrested for. Or invite me to his uncle Randy's wedding."

Yeah. The two of us on *Oprah*. That was so going to happen.

It wasn't until I got upstairs that I heard the voices. I have to admit that my brother Douglas, even when he isn't having one of his episodes, has a tendency to talk to himself.

But this time, someone was talking back. I was sure of it. The door to his room was closed, as always, but I pressed my ear up to it, and there was no doubt about it: There were two voices coming from Douglas's room.

And one of them belonged to a *girl*.

I assumed it was Claire. Maybe she was consulting with Douglas over what to get Mike for a Christmas present. Or had gone to him for advice because their relationship had run into trouble. . . .

But why would she go to Douglas with something like that? Why not me? I was clearly the logical choice. I mean, I may be a freak and all, with my psychic powers, but I am way less of a freak than Douglas, much as I love him.

I couldn't help it. I knew I shouldn't, but I did it anyway. I thumped, once on the door, then threw it open.

"Hey, good lookin'," I started to say. "What's cookin'?" Only it wasn't Claire in Douglas's room. It wasn't Claire at all.

It was Tasha Thompkins.

My jaw sagged so loose at the sight of her, sitting all primly on the end of Douglas's bed, in her black turtleneck and gray wool jumper, I swear I felt my chin hit the floor.

"Oh," she said, when she saw me, her tear-filled brown eyes soft as her voice. "Hi, Jess."

"Wh . . ." I said. I couldn't think of a single thing to say. Never in a million years would I have expected to open Douglas's bedroom door and find a girl in his room. Much less one to whom he wasn't related by blood, or who was dating his younger brother. "Wh . . . wh . . . wh . . ."

"Close the barn door," Douglas said mildly to me, from where he sat in front of his desktop computer. "You're letting the flies in."

I snapped my mouth shut. But I couldn't think of anything to say. I just stared at Tasha, looking neat and pretty and strangely not out of place in Douglas's book- and comic book-filled bedroom.

"I just couldn't take it anymore," Tasha said, helping me out a little. "At our house, I mean. It's just so . . . Well, Coach Albright is there right now.'"

"I saw his car," I managed to croak.

"Yes," Tasha said. "Well. I couldn't stand it. Then I remembered that the last time I'd seen Doug, he'd said he had some really early issues of a comic book I like, and that I could come over sometime to see them." She shrugged her slender shoulders. "So I came over." When I didn't say anything, and just continued to stare at her, she said, looking vaguely troubled, "That's all right with you, isn't it, Jessica?"

I tried to say yes, but what came out was some kind of garbled noise like Helen Keller made in that movie about her life. So I just nodded instead.

"Don't worry about Jess," Douglas said. "She's just shy."

That made Tasha laugh a little. "That's not what I heard," she said. Then she looked guilty. For laughing, though, not because of what she'd said.

"I was asking Tasha about Nate," Douglas said casually, as

if he were continuing a conversation that had gotten interrupted.

I tried to make an effort to speak intelligently. "I'm sorry,"
was all I managed to get out. When Tasha just looked at me, I
went, "About your brother, I mean."

Tasha looked down at her shoes. "Thank you," she said, so
softly, I could barely hear her.

"It turns out," Douglas said, after clearing his throat, "that
Nate had a few unsavory friends."

Tasha nodded, her expression grave. "But they wouldn't
have done this," she explained. "I mean, killed him. They
were just a bunch of hopheads who thought they were all
that, you know?"

When both Douglas and I looked at Tasha blankly, she
elaborated. Apparently, it isn't just that Chicagoans say hello
instead of hey. They have a whole separate language unto
themselves.

"They were the bomb," Tasha explained. "They ruled the
school."

"Oh," I said. Douglas looked even more confused than I felt.

"It was all so lame," Tasha said, shaking her head so that the
curled ends of her hair, held back in a second clip at the nape
of her neck, swept her shoulders. "I mean, the only reason they
wanted Nate around was because of Dad. You know. Prescription pads and all. Oxy makes for a wicked weekend high."

I nodded like I knew what she was talking about.

"But Nate, he was flattered, you know? I tried to tell him those guys were just using him, but he wouldn't listen. Fortunately it wasn't long before my dad found out. Nate had always been a good student, you know? So when his grades started to slip . . . " Tasha stared at a *Lord of the Rings* poster on Douglas's wall, but it was clear she wasn't seeing it. She was seeing something else entirely.

"My dad was so mad," she went on, after a minute, "that he pulled us both out of school. He took the job down here the very next day. We moved that week."

Whoa. Talk about tough love.

But I guess I could understand Dr. Thompkins's point of view. I mean, my family's had problems for sure, but drugs have never been one of them.

"So." I didn't want to bring up what was clearly going to be a painful subject for her, but I didn't see how it could be avoided. "Is that what happened to him, then? Your brother, I mean? Those, um, hopheads got him? For not giving them any more prescription pads, or something?"

Tasha shook her head, looking troubled.

"I don't know," she said. "I mean, those guys were bad news, but they weren't killers."

I thought for a minute.

"What about that symbol?"

Douglas, over by the desk, was making a slashing motion with his hand beneath his chin. But it was too late.

Tasha looked at me blankly. "What symbol?"

I had blown it. Tasha didn't know. Tasha didn't know the details of her brother's death.

"Nothing," I said. "Just . . . um. There's been some graffiti popping up around town, and some people were speculating that it was a gang tag."

"You think my brother was in a gang?" Tasha asked, in an incredulous voice. Douglas dropped his forehead into one hand, as if he couldn't bear to watch.

"Well," I said. I couldn't tell her the truth, of course. About the symbol having been carved into her brother's chest. "That's kind of the rumor."

Tasha may not have been able to see things up close without the aid of prescription lenses, but she could see things far away without any problem. She glared at me pretty hard.

"Because he's black," she said, in a hard voice. "People assumed Nate was in a gang, and that he was the one going around tagging things, because he's black."

"Um," I said, throwing an alarmed look at Douglas. "Well, not exactly. I mean, you even said he was hanging out with, um, a bad element. . . ."

"For your information," Tasha said, standing up. Like almost everyone else in the world, she was taller than me. "That bad element happened to be, for the most part, white. We did not, as you seem to think, move here from the ghetto, you know."

"Look," I said, defensively. "I never said you did. All I said was that it's weird this symbol would start cropping up around town the same time that you happened to move here, and I was merely wondering if—"

"If we brought the criminal element down with us from the big, bad city?" Tasha reached down and grabbed her coat, which had been draped across the bed beside her. "You know, the police have been asking us the same kind of questions. They all want to believe the same thing you do, that my brother deserved to be killed because of who he associated with. Well, I've got news for the cops in this town, and for you, too, Jessica. It wasn't some evil street gang from the big city that murdered my brother. It was a homegrown killer all your own."

With that, she stomped from Douglas's room. It wasn't until we heard the front door slam shut behind her that Douglas started to applaud.

"Way to go," he said to me. "Have you ever considered a career in the diplomatic corp?"

I sank down onto the spot on Douglas's bed Tasha had vacated. "Oh, bite me."

Noting my dour expression, Douglas said, "Aw, cheer up. She'll get over it. She just lost her brother, after all."

"Yeah, and I really helped," I said. "Implying he was a gang-banger who might have had it coming."

"You didn't imply that," Douglas said. "Besides, I was basically asking her the same thing when you walked in."

"Yeah, well, I notice she didn't fly off the handle at *you*."

"Well," Douglas said. "Who could? Considering my personal charm, and all."

But I noticed a slight redness to his cheeks that hadn't been there before.

"Whoa," I said, sitting up straight. "Douglas!"

He looked at me warily. "What?"

"You like her! Admit it!"

"Of course I like her." Douglas turned back to his computer, and began to type rapidly. Douglas can out-type even Mikey, when he puts his mind to it. "She seems like a very nice person."

"No, but you *really* like her," I said. "You *like* like her."

Douglas stopped typing. Then he turned around in his computer chair and said, "Jess, if you tell anyone, I will kill you."

I rolled my eyes. "Who am I going to tell? So, why don't you ask her out?"

"Well, for one thing," Douglas said, "because thanks to you, she now hates my guts."

I took umbrage at that. "You said she'd get over it!"

"I was only saying that to make you feel better. Face it. You ruined it."

"Oh, no way." I got up off the bed. "You are not pegging her not wanting to go out with you on me. Not when you haven't even asked her yet. Why don't you ask her to go to a movie tomorrow night? One of those weird independent films comic book freaks like you are always going to."

"Um," Douglas said. "Let me see. Because her brother just got murdered?"

"Oh, yeah," I said, crestfallen. Then I brightened. "But you could ask her as a friend. I mean, she must be going crazy over there, with Coach Albright hanging around. I bet she'd say yes."

"I'll think about it," Douglas said, and turned back to his computer. "About your symbol. I've been researching it all day, but I haven't been able to come up with anything about it. Are you sure you drew it right?"

"Of course I'm sure," I said. "Douglas, I'm serious, you should totally ask her out."

"Jess," he said, to his monitor. "She's in high school."

Memories of Rob and me, in the barn the night before, came flooding back. But I shoved them firmly aside.

"So?" I said. "She's a senior, and mature for her age. You're immature for yours. It's a perfect match."

"Thanks," Douglas said, deprecatingly.

At that moment, I heard Ruth's voice calling my name. As was our custom, she had let herself into the house.

"I got that stuff," she said, appearing in the doorway a minute later, breathless and covered with flakes of snow. I guess the Weather Channel had been right after all. "On Seth

Blumenthal. You know, that kid who disappeared this morning. Oh, hey, Douglas."

"Hey," Douglas said to Ruth, not making eye contact with her, as was *his* custom.

"Was that Tasha Thompkins I just saw leaving here?" Ruth wanted to know.

"Yes," I said. "That was her all right."

"I didn't know you two were so friendly," Ruth said to me, as she began to unwind her scarf from her neck. "That was nice of you to ask her over."

"I didn't," I said.

Ruth looked confused. "Then what was she doing here?"

"Ask *him*," I said, tilting my head in Douglas's direction.

He ducked back over his computer, but I could still see the tips of his ears reddening.

"What's a guy have to do," he wanted to know, "to get some privacy around here?"

CHAPTER 8

When I woke up the next morning, I knew where Seth Blumenthal was.

And where Seth Blumenthal was wasn't good. It wasn't good at all.

Having the psychic power to find anyone, anyone at all, isn't an easy thing to live with. I mean, look at how, just by seeing his picture on the wall of Mrs. Wilkins's bedroom, I now knew this thing about Rob's dad. I would have traded anything in the world not to have been in possession of that little piece of information, let me tell you.

Just as I would have traded anything in the world not to have to do what I knew I had to next.

No big deal, right? Just pick up the phone and dial 911, right?

Not. So not.

Normally when I am contacted about a missing kid, it goes like this: I make sure, before I call anyone, that the kid really does want to be found. This is on account of how once I found a kid who was way better off missing than with his custodial parent, who was a bonafide creep. Ever since then, I have really gone out of my way to make sure the kids I find aren't better off missing.

But in Seth's case, there was no question. No question at all.

But I couldn't simply pick up the phone, dial 911, and go, "Oh, yeah, hi, by the way, you'll find Seth Blumenthal on blankity-blank street; hurry up and get him, his mom's missing him a lot," and hang up, click.

. Because ever since this whole psychic thing started, and the U.S. government began expressing its great desire to put me on the payroll, I've been having to pretend like I don't have my powers anymore. So how would it look if I called 911 from my bedroom phone and went, "Oh, yeah, Seth Blumenthal? Here's where to find him."

Not cool. Not cool at all.

So I had to get up and go find a pay phone somewhere so that at least I could give the semblance of a denial the next time Cyrus Krantz accuses me of lying about my "specially abledness."

But let me tell you, if there'd ever been a day I considered giving up on the whole subterfuge thing, it was this one. That's because when I stumbled out of my bed, heading for the space heater I always turned off before I went to sleep, only to wake with ice chips practically formed in my nostrils, I happened to look out the window, and noticed that Lumley Lane was completely carpeted in white.

That's right. It had started snowing around four in the afternoon the day before, and apparently, it had not stopped. There had to be a foot and a half at least of fluffy white stuff already on the ground, and more was falling.

"Great," I muttered, as I hastily donned an extra pair of socks and all the flannel I could find. "Just great."

With that much snow, there'd naturally be a hush over everything outside. But there seemed to be an equal silence inside the house. As I came down the stairs, I noticed that neither Douglas nor Mikey's rooms were occupied. And when I got to the kitchen, the only person sitting there, unfortunately, was Great-aunt Rose.

"I hope you don't think you're going to go out looking like that," she said, over the steaming cup of coffee she was holding. "Why, you look like you just pulled some old clothes on over your pajamas."

Since this was exactly what I had done, I was not exactly ruffled by this statement.

"I'm just going to the convenience store," I said. I went

over to the mudroom and started tugging on some boots. "I'll be right back. You want anything?"

"The convenience store?" Great-aunt Rose looked shocked. "You have a refrigerator stocked with every kind of food imaginable, and you still can't find something to eat? What could you possibly need from the convenience store?"

"Tampons," I said, to shut her up.

It didn't work, though. She just started in about toxic shock syndrome. She'd seen an episode of *Oprah* about it once.

"And by the time they got to her," Great-aunt Rose was saying, as I stomped around, looking for a pair of mittens, "her uterus had fallen out!"

I knew someone whose uterus I wished would fall out. I didn't say so, though. I pulled a ski cap over my bed-head hair and went, "I'll be right back. Where is everybody, anyway?"

"Your brother Douglas," Great-aunt Rose said, "left for that ridiculous job of his in that comic book store. What your parents can be thinking, allowing him to fritter away his time in a dead-end job like that, I can't imagine. He ought to be in school. And don't tell me he's sick. There isn't a single thing wrong with Douglas except that your parents are coddling him half to death. What that boy needs isn't pills. It's a swift kick in the patootie."

I could see why none of Great-aunt Rose's own kids ever invited her over anymore for the holidays. She was a real joy to have around.

"What about my mom and dad?" I asked. "Where are they?"

"Your father went to one of those restaurants of his," Great-aunt Rose said, in tones of great disapproval. Restauranting was probably, in her opinion, another example of time frittered away. "And your other brother went with your mom."

"Oh, yeah?" I pulled on the biggest, heaviest coat I could find. It was my dad's old ski parka. It was about ten sizes too big for me, but it was warm. Who cared if I looked like Nanook of the North? I certainly wasn't trying to impress the guys at the Stop and Shop. "Where'd they go?"

"To the fire," Great-aunt Rose said, and turned back to the newspaper that was spread out in front of her. LOCAL RESIDENT FOUND DEAD, screamed the headline, FOUL PLAY SUSPECTED. Uh, no duh.

I thought Great-aunt Rose had finally gone round the bend. You know, Alzheimer's. Because the fire that had burned down the restaurant had been nearly three months ago.

"You mean Mastriani's?" I asked. "They went to the job site?" It didn't make much sense that they'd go there, especially on a day like today. The contractors who were rebuilding the restaurant had knocked off for the winter. They said they'd finish the place in the spring, when the ground wasn't so hard.

So what were my mom and Michael doing at an empty lot?

"Not that fire," Great-aunt Rose said, disparagingly. "The new one. The one at that Jewish church."

Now Great-aunt Rose had my full attention. I stared at her dumbfounded. "There's a fire at the synagogue?"

"Synagogue," Great-aunt Rose said. "That's what they call it. Whatever. Looks like a church to me."

"There's a *fire* at the synagogue?" I repeated, more loudly.

Great-aunt Rose gave me an irritated look. "That's what I said, didn't I? And there's no need to shout, Jessica. I may be old, but I'm not—"

Deaf, is what she probably said. I wouldn't know, since I booked out of there before she could finish her sentence.

A fire at the synagogue. This was not a good thing. I mean, not that I go to temple, not being Jewish.

Still, Ruth and her family go to temple. They go to temple a lot. And if the fire was big enough that my mom and Mikey had felt compelled to go . . .

Oh, yes. The fire was big enough. I saw the dark plume of smoke in the air before I even got to the end of Lumley Lane. This was not good.

I slogged through the snow, heading for the Stop and Shop, which was fortunately in the same direction as the synagogue. They have plows in my town, but it takes forever for them to get around to the residential streets. They do all the roads around the hospital and courthouse first, then the residential areas . . . if they don't have to go back and do the important roads again, which, in a storm like this, they'd need to. They never bothered with rural routes at all. A big storm tended to guarantee that everyone who lived outside the city limits was snowed in for days. Which was good for kids—no school—but not so good for adults, who had to get to work. Lumley Lane had not been plowed. Only our driveway had been shoveled. Mr. Abramowitz, the champion shoveler in the neighborhood, had barely made a dent in his driveway. . . . Only enough had been shoveled so that he could get the car out, undoubtedly so that he and his family could head over to the synagogue and see what they could do to help, the way my mom and Mikey had. In a small town, people tend to pitch in. This can be a good thing, but it can also be a bad thing. For instance, people are also eager to pitch in with the latest gossip. Which—case in point, Nate Thompkins—was not always so helpful.

By the time I got to the Stop and Shop, which was only a few streets away from my house, I was panting from the exertion of wading through so much snow. Plus my face felt frozen on account of the wind whipping into it, despite my dad's voluminous hood.

Still, I couldn't go inside to warm up. I had a call to make on the pay phone over by the air hose.

"Yeah," I said, when the emergency operator picked up. "Can you please let the police know that the kid they've been looking for, Seth Blumenthal, is at Five-sixty Rural Route

One, in the second trailer to the right of the Mr. Shaky's sign?"

The operator, stunned, went, "What?"

"Look," I said. This was really just my luck. You know, getting a brain-dead emergency services operator, on top of a freaking snowstorm. "Get a pen and write it down." I repeated my message one more time. "Got it?"

"But—"

"Good-bye."

I hung up. All around me, the snow was swirling like millions of tiny ballerinas in fluffy white tutus. You know, like in that *Fantasia* movie. Or maybe those were milkweed pod seeds. Whatever. Any other time, it would have been pretty.

As it was, however, it was a huge pain in my ass.

I could have gone inside the Stop and Shop and warmed up, but I decided against it. It would be just my luck if Luther—Luther had worked the Saturday morning shift at the Stop and Shop since I'd been a little kid, and I had gone down there religiously every weekend to blow my allowance on licorice and Bazooka Joe—remembered I'd been there. When Cyrus came around and started asking questions, I mean, after Seth Blumenthal got found. Luther had a memory like a steel trap. He could name every race Dale Earnhardt had ever won.

The snow and wind were pretty bad, but they weren't blizzard level. You could get around, it was just really awkward. If I'd had a car, though, it probably would have been about as bad. I mean, I'd have made just about as much progress.

By the time I finally got to the synagogue, the wind had died down a little. There was still that eery silence, though, that you get when everything is carpeted in snow . . . this in spite of all the fire engines and men running with hoses. I spied my mom standing in the synagogue parking lot—all the snow there had melted on account of the flames and the water from the fire trucks—with Mikey and the Abramowitzes. I picked my way across the maze of hoses on the ground and came up to them.

"What is it with this town," I asked my mom, "and buildings going up in flames?"

"Oh, honey," my mom said, slipping an arm around me. "What are you doing here? You didn't walk all this way, did you?"

"Sure," I said, with a shrug. "Anything to get away from Aunt Rose."

My mom fingered my hood distractedly. "Why are you wearing Daddy's old coat?" she wanted to know. But I didn't have a chance to reply, because Michael punched me on the arm.

"So you finally decided to join us, huh?" he said.

"Yeah," I said. "Thanks for waking me up."

"I tried," Michael said. "You were dead to the world. Plus it looked like you were having one hell of a nightmare."

He wasn't kidding. Only it hadn't been my nightmare. It had been Seth Blumenthal's reality.

Ruth, standing there with her brother and parents, looked

miserable. Her nose was red, and tears were streaming down her face. I didn't think from the cold, either.

"Are you okay?" I asked her.

"Not really," Ruth said. "I mean, I've been better."

"Oh, Jess." Mrs. Abramowitz noticed me for the first time. "It's you." I guess she hadn't recognized me right away with my dad's ski parka on. "Isn't it awful?"

Awful wasn't the word for it. The building was almost completely destroyed. Only a couple of interior walls still stood. The rest was just charred rubble, black against the whiteness of the snow.

"They couldn't get here fast enough to save it," Mrs. Abramowitz said, wiping a tear from where it dangled off the end of her nose. "On account of the ice."

"Now, Louise," my mom said, reaching out to give Mrs. Abramowitz's shoulders a squeeze. "Remember what you told me when it was the restaurant that was burning. It's the people that matter, not the building."

"Right," Mr. Abramowitz said. He and Skip were standing there with some other men, huddled in the wind. "No one got hurt. And that's what's important."

"No," Mrs. Abramowitz said, mournfully. "But . . . but the Torah. It's just *too* awful."

I looked questioningly at Ruth.

"The Torah," she explained. "You know, the holy scrolls. They think that's what they lit on fire first."

"They?" I stared at her. "What are you talking about? Someone *set* this fire? On *purpose?*"

"Judge for yourself," Ruth said, and pointed.

Following the direction of her gloved hand, I looked. Across the street from the synagogue stood our town's only Jewish cemetery. Because there aren't a whole lot of Jews in southern Indiana—there are more churches here than there are McDonald's, for sure—the cemetery was pretty small.

So it had been pretty easy for whoever had gone to town on it to knock over every single headstone.

Oh, yes. Every single one. Except of course the mausoleums, which they couldn't knock over. But they'd satisfied themselves by spray-painting those with swastikas. Swastikas and something else. Something that looked familiar.

It took me a minute, but finally, I recognized it: the symbol I'd seen on Nate Thompkins's chest.

CHAPTER 9

"It's a gang," Claire said.

"It's not a gang, all right?" I was pacing up and down the hallway outside Michael's room. "Nate Thompkins wasn't in a gang."

"Just because his sister doesn't want to believe it," Michael pointed out, "doesn't mean it isn't true."

"She said all they wanted to do was scam prescription drugs," I said. "Does what happened over at the synagogue look like the work of people whose primary interest is in partying?"

I threw an aggravated look at the two of them, but it was no good. They refused to get as upset about it as I was. This was partly because Claire was sitting in Michael's lap. I guess it's hard to get upset about murder, arson, and bias crimes going on in your own town while you're getting cozy with that special someone.

"Grits, then," Claire said, with a shrug.

I blinked at her. "I beg your pardon?"

"Well, think about it," Claire said. "We were all so worried when the Thompkinses moved in, that the Grits were going to try something. You know, burn a cross on their lawn, or whatever. Maybe the Grits did it. Killed Nate."

Michael brightened. "Hey," he said. "Yeah. And Grits hate Jews, too."

"Oh, my God." I stared at them. "Would you two stop? Grits couldn't have done any of this."

"Why not?" Claire asked. "When we had to read *Malcolm X* in World Civ, a lot of the Grits wouldn't do it, because they said they wouldn't read a book written by a black person. Only they didn't say black," she added, meaningfully.

"And I heard a Grit," Michael said, "at the grocery store the other day, going on about how the Holocaust never happened, and was all made up by the Jews."

"Would you two cut it out?" I couldn't believe what I was hearing. "Not all Grits are like that."

"She just says that," Michael said confidently to Claire, "because she's dating one."

Claire looked at me with bright-eyed interest. "You *are?*

Oh, my God, Jess! That's so politically correct of you. But does he talk about NASCAR racing all the time? Because that would really bore me after a while."

I tried to give Michael the same kind of evil death glare Great-aunt Rose had down so perfect.

"Don't try to blame all this on the Grits," I said. "The Grits have been around a long time, and so has the synagogue, and we never had a problem like this before."

Michael looked thoughtful. "Well," he said. "That's true enough."

"Grits are, for the most part, hard-working people," I said, "who haven't had the same advantages as us. It's wrong to blame them for every bad thing that happens in this town just because they happen to have less money than we do."

Claire went, "Well, there's only one explanation, then. It has to be Nate's gang."

I rolled my eyes. I couldn't believe we were back to square one all over again.

Fortunately at that moment footsteps sounded on the stairs. We turned to see Douglas, covered from head to toe in protective outerwear, but looking chilled to the bone nonetheless, come staggering into the hallway. His face, the only part of him that wasn't covered, was flushed. There were snowflakes in his eyelashes.

"Where have *you* been?" I demanded.

"Nowhere," Douglas said, with deceptive innocence, as he

reached up to pull off his knit ski cap. His hair, beneath the cap, was sweaty looking, and stuck up at weird angles. He looked like a demented snowplow driver.

"What?" Michael said. "Did Dad corner you about the driveway?"

"Uh, yeah," Douglas said, ducking into his room. "Yeah, that's where I was."

He shut the door, so we were all looking at the DO NOT DISTURB sign he'd pinned up there.

Mike glanced at me. "Do we start worrying about him now," he wanted to know, "or later?"

The phone rang. I didn't rush to pick it up, or anything, since no one but Ruth ever calls me. And I knew Ruth wasn't home. She and her family had gone over to their rabbi's house, to try to console him over the loss of the Torah, which turned out to be a really bad thing. Like someone coming in and burning your Bible, only worse, because Torahs are harder to replace.

So you can imagine my surprise when my mom called up the stairs, "Jess, it's for you. Your friend Joanne."

Which would have been fine, of course. Except that I have no friend named Joanne.

"Hello?" I said curiously, after picking up the extension in Mike's room.

"Mastriani." It was Rob. Of course it was Rob. Who else would call me, pretending to be someone named Joanne?

"Oh," I said, watching with a fair amount of disgust as

Mikey and Claire started kissing. Right there in front of me. Granted, it was Mike's room, and I guess he could do what he wanted to in it, but excuse me, ew. "Hey."

"Listen. About tonight," Rob said, in his deep voice. I wondered how he'd managed to fool my mom into thinking he was someone named Joanne. Had he spoken in falsetto? Or had he had his mom ask for me? Surely not. I mean, then he'd have had to admit to his mom that I hadn't told my parents about him. And that was something I was pretty sure Rob wasn't going to admit to anybody.

"You still want to do something?" Rob asked.

I prickled immediately "What do you mean, do I still want to do something? Of course I still want to do something. We're going out, right? I mean, aren't we?"

Mikey and Claire, distracted by my tone of voice, which had suddenly gotten a little shrill, stopped kissing, and looked at me.

"Is that the Grit?" Claire mouthed, excitedly. I turned my back on them.

"Well," Rob said. "I don't know. I mean, yesterday at the mall, you seemed to wig out a little."

"I did not wig out," I said, appalled. "That was not wigging out. That was just . . . I mean, come on. That was weird. I mean, your mom, my mom. Whatever."

"Right," Rob said. But he didn't sound very convinced. "Whatever."

"But of course I still want to go out tonight," I said. I was clutching the phone very tightly, so tightly my knuckles were white. "I mean, if you want to. Go to dinner. Or a movie." Or to your uncle's Christmas Eve wedding. Whichever. Or both, actually.

"Well," Rob said, stretching that single syllable out unbelievably far. I hung onto the receiver in breathless anticipation. This was, I knew, ridiculous. Ruth would have killed me for it, if she'd known. Ruth has very firm rules about boys, and one of the rules is that you should never, ever chase them. Let the boys come to you.

And even though Ruth isn't what you'd call your stereotypical babe, the whole rules thing seemed to work pretty well for her.

But then again, as far as I know, Ruth isn't going out with a high school graduate who happens to have a criminal record.

Before Rob could say another word, however, the call waiting went off, as it usually did, right when I least wanted it to. I said to Rob, "Hold on. I've got another call." I tried to make it sound like this other call might conceivably be from one of the many other boys I knew who were just dying to take me out, but I don't know if I did a very convincing job. Especially since the only other boy I happen to know who wanted to take me out was Skip from next door, but Saturday nights he's always busy grand-wizarding the neighborhood

Dungeons and Dragons game, so it probably wasn't him.

So, not surprisingly, when I pressed the receiver, the voice I heard on the other line was not Skip's. But I was far from expecting to hear from the person to whom it belonged.

"Jessica," Dr. Cyrus Krantz said. He sounded agitated. "We've got a problem."

You think you've got problems? I wanted to say. *I got a guy on the other line who apparently isn't aware that I am the best thing that ever happened to him.*

Instead, I said, "Oh?" like I couldn't imagine what he was talking about. Even though I had a pretty good idea. He was calling about Nate Thompkins and the synagogue.

Only it turned out he wasn't. He was calling about something I'd almost managed to forget about . . . almost, because it was so horrible, I doubted I'd ever fully be able to forget it.

"Seth Blumenthal," he said, heavily. "We missed him, Jessica."

I felt something inside my head explode. The next thing I knew, I was screaming into the phone like a maniac.

"What do you mean, you missed him?" I shouted.

It was only when I saw the expressions on Mike's and Claire's faces that I realized what I'd just done.

Outed myself. Officially. To the head of the psychic network of the Federal Bureau of Investigation.

I felt all the blood run out of my face. Could my day, I wondered, possibly get worse?

"The officers who were dispatched to the scene," Dr. Krantz was saying, in my ear, "were unprepared for the amount of resistance they received from the—"

"Resistance?" I blurted, once again forgetting, in my indignation, that the call I'd made concerning Seth Blumenthal was supposed to have been anonymous. "What are you talking about, resistance? All they had to do was go in and get the kid and come out again. How hard is that?"

"Jessica." Dr. Krantz sounded strange. "They were fired upon."

"Well, of course they were," I practically shouted. "Because the people who took Seth Blumenthal against his will are criminals, Dr. Krantz. That's who tends to kidnap kids. Criminals. And that's what criminals do when the police show up. They try to evade capture."

"You failed to mention," Dr. Krantz said, "that Seth was being held against his will when you spoke to the nine-eleven operator, Jessica. You failed to mention—"

"That he'd been tied up and gagged and shut up in the linen closet of a double-wide? I guess I did fail to mention that, didn't I?" I could feel tears welling up beneath my eyelids. Crying. I was *crying*. "Maybe because I had to keep that call short, in the event it was traced. Something I wouldn't have to do, if you people would leave me and my family alone."

"One of the officers," Cyrus Krantz said, completely

ignoring my barb, "was critically injured in the exchange of gunfire." I realized then why it was his voice sounded strange. He was frustrated. I had never heard Cyrus Krantz sound frustrated before. I was surprised. I have to admit, I thought of him as one of those Energizer bunnies. You know, that he just kept going, and going. . . .

"The perpetrators got away," Dr. Krantz went on. "With Seth."

"Shit!" I yelled. Claire, on Michael's lap, opened her eyes very wide, but I didn't care. "Can't you people do anything right?"

"It's a little difficult, Jessica," Dr. Krantz said, "when you insist upon playing these childish games with us, claiming you no longer have your psychic powers."

"Don't you go blaming me," I yelled into the phone, "for your incompetence!"

"Jessica," Dr. Krantz said. "Calm down."

"I can't calm down," I shouted. "Not when that kid's still out there. Not when—"

My voice caught. Because, of course, it was all coming back. The fear and terror I'd felt in my dream—my dream about Seth.

Only it hadn't been a dream. Well, to me it had. But it was Seth's reality. A reality that had gone spinning out of control the minute he'd been snatched off his bike in the synagogue parking lot the day before. Who knew what all he'd endured since that moment? All I could see—all I could feel—was what Seth was seeing and experiencing at the exact moment my mind, expansive in sleep, reached out to him.

And that was the cold confinement of the closet he'd been locked into. The throbbing pain of the ropes cutting into his wrists, cruelly tied behind his back. The rough gag biting into the corners of his mouth. The muffled but still terrifying sounds he could hear outside the closet door.

That was Seth Blumenthal's reality. And my nightmare.

The fact that that nightmare was ongoing was almost more than I could bear.

"Jessica," Cyrus Krantz was saying. "I know how you feel about me, and about my organization. But I swear to you, if you would just give us another chance—one more chance for us to work together—you won't regret it. We need to find this boy, Jessica, and soon. He's in danger. Real danger. The people who have him are animals. Anyone who would torture a twelve-year-old—"

"What?" I'd been pacing up and down the hallway with the cordless phone gripped in my hand. Now I froze. "What do you mean, torture?"

"Jessica," Dr. Krantz said. "Haven't you realized by now that all of this—Nate, the synagogue, Seth—is connected?"

"Connected?" Something was buzzing inside my head. "To Seth? Connected how?"

"How do you think the people who set that fire at the synagogue knew where to find the scrolls?" Dr. Krantz asked. "Think about it, Jessica. Who would know exactly where those scrolls were kept? Someone who would have been reading from them on his birthday today."

Seth. Seth Blumenthal.

I couldn't believe it.

He didn't wait for the information to digest. Dr. Krantz said, quickly, "That's why I called. We desperately need your help, Jessica. Listen to me—"

"No, you listen to me," I said. "I tried to do things your way, and all it did was get a cop shot. We're going to do things *my* way now."

Dr. Krantz sounded more frustrated than ever. In fact, now he sounded kind of pissed off. "Oh, yes? And how, precisely, are we going to do that?"

But since of course I had no idea, I couldn't answer his question. Instead, I pressed the Talk button, ending the call.

"Whoa," Mike said, looking at me from over Claire's shoulder. She sat, seemingly frozen, in his lap. "Are you . . . are you okay?"

"No," I said. I lifted a hand to my hair, then noticed that my fingers were shaking. Slowly, I began to slide down the wall, until I was sitting in the middle of the hallway "No, I'm not all right."

That's when I heard a voice calling from the phone, "Mastriani? Mastriani!" Like someone in a dream, I brought the receiver to my ear. "Hello?"

"Mastriani, it's me." Rob's voice sounded irritated. "Remember? You put me on hold."

"Rob." I had completely forgotten about him. "Rob. Yeah. Sorry. Look, I can't go out tonight. Something came up."

"Something came up," he repeated, slowly.

"Yes," I said. I felt as if I were underwater. "I'm really sorry. It's Seth. The cops couldn't get to him, and there was a shootout, and now one of them is in critical condition, and those people still have Seth, and I've got to find him before they kill him, too."

"Whoa," Rob said. "Slow down. Who's Seth?"

"Dr. Krantz thinks there's a connection," I said. In some distant part of my brain, I realized I must have sounded to Rob like I was babbling. Maybe I *was* babbling. I just couldn't believe it. A cop. A cop had been shot. And Seth was still out there. Seth was still in danger. "A connection between Nate, Seth, and the synagogue."

"Wait a minute," Rob said. "Dr. Krantz? When did you talk to Krantz? Was that him just now?"

"I'm sorry, Rob," I said. I could see Mikey and Claire looking at me with growing concern. I knew I'd have to pull myself together soon, or Mike would go get my mother. "Look, I've got to go—"

But Rob, as usual, was already taking charge of the situation. "What's the connection?" Rob wanted to know. "What does Krantz say?"

All I wanted to do was hang up the phone, go upstairs to my room, and climb into bed. Yes, that was it. That was what I needed to do. Go back to sleep, and wake up again tomorrow, so that all of this would just seem like a bad dream.

"Mastriani!" Rob yelled in my ear. "What's the connection?"

"It's the symbol, okay?" I couldn't believe he was yelling at me. I mean, I wasn't the one who'd shot a cop, or anything. "The one that was on Nate's chest. It's the same thing that was spray-painted onto the headstones at the synagogue."

"What does it look like?" Rob wanted to know. "This symbol?"

Look, Rob is my soul mate and all, but that doesn't mean that there aren't times when I don't feel like hauling off and decking him. Now was one of those times.

"Jeez, Rob," I said. "You were there in that cornfield with me, remember?" This caused a pointed look to be exchanged between my brother and his girlfriend, but I ignored them. "Didn't you notice what Nate had on his chest?"

Rob's voice was strangely quiet. "No, not really," he said. "I didn't . . . I didn't actually look. That kind of thing . . . well, I don't really do too well, you know, at the sight of . . ."

Blood. He didn't say it, but then, he didn't have to. All my annoyance with him dissipated. Just like that.

Well, love will do that to you.

"It was this squiggly line," I explained. "With an arrow coming out of one end."

"An arrow," Rob echoed.

"Yeah," I said. "An arrow."

"An M? The squiggly line. Was it shaped like a M, only on its side?"

"I don't know," I said. "I guess so. Look, Rob, I don't feel so good. I gotta go—"

Then Rob said a strange thing. Something that got my attention right away, even though I was feeling so lousy, like I was going to pass out, practically.

He said, "It's not an arrow."

I had been about to press the Talk button and hang up the phone. When he said that, however, I stopped myself. "What do you mean, it's not an arrow?"

"Jess," he said. The fact that he used my first name made me realize the situation was far from normal. "I think I might know who these people are. The people who are doing this stuff."

I didn't even hesitate. It was like all of a sudden, the blood that had seemed frozen in my veins was flowing again.

"I'll meet you at the Stop and Shop," I said. "Come pick me up."

"Mastriani—"

"Just be there," I said, and hung up. Then I threw down the phone, got up, and started for the stairs.

"Jess, wait," Michael called. "Where are you going?"

"Out," I called back. "Tell Mom I'll be home soon."

And then, after struggling into my hat and coat, I was tearing off down the street. I couldn't help noticing as I jogged that while our own driveway was still full of snow, the Thompkinses' driveway had been shoveled so clean, you could practically have played basketball on it. All the snow that had been shoveled away was piled along the curb, as neatly as if a plow had pushed it there.

But it hadn't been the work of a plow. Oh, no. It was the work of a person. Namely, my brother Douglas.

Love. It makes people do the craziest things.

CHAPTER 10

Chick—owner and proprietor of Chick's Bar and Motorcycle Club—looked down at the drawing I had made and went, "Oh, sure. The True Americans."

I looked at the squiggle. It was kind of hard to see in the dark gloom of the bar. "Are you sure?" I asked. "I mean . . . you really know what this is?"

"Oh, yeah." Chick was eating a meatball sandwich he'd made for himself back in the kitchen. He'd offered one to each of us, as well, but we'd declined the invitation. Our loss, Chick had said.

Now a large piece of meatball escaped from between the buns Chick clutched in one of his enormous hands, and it dropped down onto the drawing I'd made. Chick brushed it away with a set of hairy knuckles.

"Yeah," he said, squinting down at the drawing in the blue-and-red neon light from the Pabst Blue Ribbon sign behind the bar. "Yeah, that's it, all right. They all got it tattooed right here." He indicated the webbing between his thumb and index finger. "Only you got it sideways, or something."

He turned the drawing so that instead of looking like 🐍 it looked like 🐍 .

"There," Chick said. There was sauce in his goatee, but he didn't seem to know it . . . or care, anyway. "Yeah. That's how it's supposed to look. See? Like a snake?"

"Don't tread on me," Rob said.

"Don't what?" I asked.

It was weird to be sitting in a bar with Rob. Well, it would have been weird to have been sitting in a bar with anyone, seeing as how I am only sixteen and not actually allowed in bars. But it was particularly weird to be in this bar, and with Rob. It was the same bar Rob had taken me to that first time he'd given me a ride home from detention, nearly a year earlier, back when he hadn't realized I was jailbait. We hadn't imbibed or anything—just burgers and Cokes—but it had been one of the best nights of my entire life.

That was because I had always wanted to go to Chick's, a biker bar I had been passing every year since I was a little kid, whenever I went with my dad to the dump to get rid of our Christmas tree. Far outside of the city limits, Chick's held mystery for a Townie like me—though Ruth, and most of the rest of the other people I knew, called it a Grit bar, filled as it was with bikers and truckers.

That night, however—even though it was a Saturday— the place was pretty much devoid of customers. That was on account of all the snow. It was no joke, trying to ride a motor-cycle through a foot and a half of fresh powder. Rob thank-fully hadn't even tried it, and had come to get me instead in his mother's pickup.

But he had been one of the few to brave the mostly unplowed back countryroads. With the exception of Rob and me, Chick's was empty, of both clientele and employees. Neither the bartender nor the fry cook had made it in. Chick hadn't been too happy about having to make his own sand-wich. But mostly, if you ask me, because he was so huge, he didn't fit too easily in the small galley kitchen out back.

"Don't tread on me," Rob repeated, for my benefit. "Remember? That was printed on one of the first American flags, along with a coiled snake." He held up my drawing, but tilted it the way Chick had. "That thing on the end isn't an arrow. It's the snake's head. See?"

All I saw was still just a squiggly line with an arrow coming out of it. But I went, "Oh, yeah," so I wouldn't seem too stupid.

"So, these True Americans," I said. "What are they? A

motorcycle gang, like the Hell's Angels, or something?"

"Hell, no!" Chick exploded, spraying bits of meatball and bread around. "Ain't a one of 'em could ride his way out of a paper bag!"

"They're a militia group, Mastriani," Rob explained, showing a bit more patience than his friend and mentor, Chick. "Run by a guy who grew up around here . . . Jim Henderson."

"Oh," I said. I was trying to appear worldly and sophisticated and all, since I was in a bar. But it was kind of hard. Especially when I didn't understand half of what anybody was saying. Finally, I gave up.

"Okay," I said, resting my elbows on the sticky, heavily graffitied bar. "What's a militia group?"

Chick rolled his surprisingly pretty blue eyes. They were hard to notice, being mostly hidden from view by a pair of straggly gray eyebrows.

"You know," he said. "One of those survivalist outfits, live way out in the backwoods. Won't pay their taxes, but that don't seem to stop 'em from feeling like they got a right to steal all the water and electricity they can."

"Why won't they pay their taxes?" I asked.

"Because Jim Henderson doesn't approve of the way the government spends his hard-earned money," Rob said. "He doesn't want his taxes going to things like education and welfare . . . unless the right people are the ones receiving the education and welfare."

"The right people?" I looked from Rob to Chick questioningly. "And who are the right people?"

Chick shrugged his broad, leather-jacketed shoulders. "You know. Your basic blond, blue-eyed, Aryan types."

"But . . ." I fingered the smooth letters of a woman's name—BETTY—that had been carved into the bar beneath my arms. "But the true Americans are the Native Americans, right? I mean, they aren't blond."

"It ain't no use," Chick said, with his mouth full, "arguin' semantics with Jim Henderson. To him, the only true Americans're the ones that climbed down offa the *Mayflower* . . . white Christians. And you ain't gonna tell 'im differently. Not if you don't want a twelve gauge up your hooha."

I raised my eyebrows at this. I wasn't sure what a *hooha* was. I was pretty sure I didn't *want* to know.

"Oh," I said. "So they killed Nate . . ."

". . . because he was black," Rob finished for me.

"And they burned down the synagogue . . ."

". . . because it's not Christian," Rob said.

"So the only true Americans, according to Jim Henderson," I said, "are people who are exactly like . . . Jim Henderson."

Chick finished up his last bite of meatball sandwich. "Give the girl a prize," he said, with a grin, revealing large chunks of meat and bread trapped between his teeth.

I slapped the bar so hard with the flat of my hand, it stung.

"I don't believe this," I yelled, while both Rob and Chick looked at me in astonishment. "Are you saying that all this time, there's been this freaky hate group running around town, and nobody's bothered to do anything about it?"

Rob regarded me calmly. "And what should someone have done, Mastriani?" he asked.

"Arrested them, already!" I yelled.

"Can't arrest a man on account of his beliefs," Chick reminded me. "A man's entitled to believe whatever he wants, no matter how back-ass-ward it might be."

"But he still has to pay his taxes," I pointed out.

"True enough," Chick said. "Only ol' Jim never had two nickels to rub together, so I doubt the county ever thought it'd be worth its while to go after him for tax evasion."

"How about," I said, coldly, "kidnapping and murder? The county might think those worth its while."

"Imagine so," Chick said, looking thoughtful. "Don't know what ol' Jim must be thinking. Isn't like 'im, really. I always thought Jimmy was, you know, all blow and no go."

"Perhaps the arrival," Rob said, "of the Thompkinses, the first African-American family to come to town, offended Mr. Henderson. Aroused in him a feeling of righteous indignation."

Chick stared at Rob, clearly impressed. "Ooh," he said. "Righteous indignation. I'm going to remember that one."

"Right," I said, slipping off my barstool. "Well, that's it, then. Let's go."

Both Chick and Rob blinked at me.

"Go?" Chick echoed. "Where?"

I couldn't believe he even had to ask. "To Jim Henderson's place," I said. "To get Seth Blumenthal."

Chick had been swallowing a sip of beer as I said this. Well, okay, not a sip, exactly. Guys like Chick don't sip, they guzzle.

In any case, when I said this, he let loose what had been in his mouth in a plume that hit Rob, me, and the jukebox.

"Oh, man," Rob said, reaching for some cocktail napkins Chick kept in a pile behind the bar.

"Yeah, Mr. Chick," I said. "Say it, don't spray it."

"Nobody," Chick said, ignoring us, "is going to Jim Henderson's place. Got it? Nobody."

I couldn't believe it.

"Why not?" I demanded. "I mean, we know they did it, right? It's not like they tried to hide it, or anything. They practically hung up a big sign that says 'We Did It.' So let's go over there and make 'em give Seth back."

Chick looked at me for a moment. Then he threw back his head and laughed. A lot.

"Give the kid back," he chortled. "Wheredja get this one, Wilkins? She's a riot."

Rob wasn't laughing. He looked at me sadly.

"What?" I said. "What's so funny?"

"We can't go to Jim Henderson's, Mastriani," Rob said.

I blinked at him. "Why not?"

"Well, for one thing, Henderson shoots at the water meter-men the county sends out," Rob said. "You think he's not going to try to take us out?"

"Um," I said. "Hello? That's why we sneak in."

"Little lady," Chick said, stubbing a finger thickly encrusted with motorcycle grease at me. I didn't mind him calling me little lady because, well, there wasn't much I could do about it, seeing as how he was about three times as big as me. Mr. Goodhart would have been proud of the progress I was making. Normally the size of my opponent was just about the last thing I considered before tackling someone. "You don't know squat. Didn't I hear you say these folks already shot up a cop earlier today, on account of not wanting to give up some kid they got hold of?"

"Yes," I said. "But the officers involved weren't prepared for what they were up against. We'll be ready."

"Mastriani," Rob said, shaking his head. "I get where you're coming from. I really do. But we aren't talking the Flintstones here. These guys have a pretty sophisticated setup."

"Yeah," Chick said, after letting out a long, aromatic belch. "You're talking some major security precautions. They got the barbed wire, guard dogs, armed sentries—"

"*What?*" I was so mad, I felt like kicking something. "Are you *kidding* me? These guys have all that? And the cops just *let* them?"

"No law against fences and guard dogs," Chick said, with a shrug. "And a man's allowed to carry a rifle on his own property—"

"But he's not allowed to shoot cops," I pointed out. "And if what you're saying about these True Americans is accurate, then somebody in that group did just that, earlier today, over at the trailer park by Mr. Shaky's. They got away—with a twelve-year-old hostage. I'm willing to bet they're holed up now with this Jim Henderson guy. And if we don't do something, and soon, that kid is going to end up in a cornfield, same as Nate Thompkins."

Rob and Chick exchanged glances. And in those glances, despite the darkness of the bar, I was able to catch a glimpse of something I didn't like. Something I didn't like at all.

And that was hopelessness.

"Look," I said, my hands going to my hips. "I don't care how secure their fortress is. Seth Blumenthal is in there, and it's up to us to get him out."

Chick shook his head. For the first time, he looked serious . . . serious and sad.

"Little lady," he said. "Jimmy's crazy as they come, but one thing he ain't is stupid. There ain't gonna be a scrap of evidence to connect him with any of this stuff, except the fact that he's head of the group that claimed responsibility. Bustin' in there—which'd be damn near impossible, seeing as how you can't even approach Jim's place by road. It's so far back into the woods, ain't no way the plows can get to it—to rescue some kid is just plain stupid. Ten to one," Chick said, "that boy is long dead."

"No," I said, quietly. "He isn't dead, actually."

Chick looked startled. "Now how in hell," he wanted to know, "could you know that?" Rob lifted his forehead from his hands, into which he'd sunk it earlier. "Because," he answered, bleakly. "She's Lightning Girl."

Chick studied me appraisingly in the neon glow. I'm sure my face, like his, must have been an unflattering shade of purple. I probably resembled Violet from that Willy Wonka movie. You know, after she ate the gum.

But Chick must have seen something there that he liked, since he didn't end the conversation then and there.

"You think we should go busting in there," he said, slowly, "and get that kid out?"

"Busting," I said, "is not the word I would use. I think we could probably come up with a more subtle form of entry. But yes. Yes, I do."

"Wait." Rob shook his head. "Wait just a minute here. Mastriani, this is insane. We can't get involved in this. This is a job for the cops—"

"—who don't know what they're up against," I said. "Forget it, Rob. One cop already got shot on account of me. I'm not going to let anyone else get hurt, if I can help it."

"Anyone else," Rob burst out. "What about yourself? Have you ever stopped to think these guys might have a bullet with your name on it next?"

"Rob." I couldn't believe how myopic he was being. "Jim Henderson isn't going to shoot me."

Rob looked shocked. *"Why not?"*

"Because I'm a girl, of course."

Rob said a very bad word in response to this. Then he pushed away from the bar and went stalking over to the juke-box . . . which he punched. Not hard enough to break it, but hard enough so that Chick looked up and went, "Hey!"

Rob didn't apologize though. Instead, he said, looking at Chick with appeal in his gray eyes, "Can you help me out here? Can you please explain to my girlfriend that she must be suffering from a chemical imbalance if she thinks I'm letting her anywhere near Jim Henderson's place?"

Which was a horribly sexist thing to say, and which I knew I should have resented, but I couldn't, since he'd called me the G word. You know. His *girlfriend*. It was the first time I'd ever heard him call me that. Within earshot of someone else, I mean.

Being his date at that Christmas Eve wedding didn't look so far out of the realm of possibility now.

But Chick, instead of doing as Rob had asked, and telling me to forget about busting in on the True Americans, stroked his goatee thoughtfully. "You know," he said. "It isn't the worst idea I ever heard."

Rob stared at him in horror.

"Hey," Chick said, defensively. "I ain't saying she should go in alone. But a kid's dead, Wilkins. And if I know Henderson, this other one hasn't got much time left."

I threw Rob a triumphant look, as if to say, *See? I'm not crazy after all.*

"And you might say," Chick went on, "this is a homegrown problem, Wilkins. I mean, Henderson's one of our own. Ain't it appropriate that we be the ones to mete out the justice? I can put in a few calls and have enough boys over here in five minutes, it'd put the National Guard to shame."

I raised my eyebrows, impressed by the *mete out the justice* line.

Rob wasn't going for it, though. "Even if we did agree this was a good idea," he said, "which I am not doing, you said yourself it's inaccessible. There's nearly two feet of snow on the ground. How are we even going to get near the place?"

Chick did a surprising thing, then. He crooked a finger at us, then started walking—though, given his girth and height, lumbering was really more the word for it—toward the back door.

I followed him, with Rob reluctantly trailing behind me. Chick went down a short hallway that opened out into a sort of a ramshackle garage. Wind whistled through the haphazardly thrown up wooden slats that made up the walls.

Flicking on the single electric bulb that served as a light, Chick strode forward until he came to something covered with a tarp. "Voilà," he said, in what I assumed was a purposefully bad European accent. Then he flung back the tarp to reveal two brand-new snowmobiles.

CHAPTER 11

Hey, I'll admit it. I wanted on that snowmobile. I wanted on it, bad.

Can you blame me? I'd never been on one before.

And for someone who likes going fast, well, what's more thrilling than going fast over snow? Oh, sure, I'd been skiing before, over at the dinky slopes of Paoli Peaks. It had been fun and all. For like an hour. I mean, let's face it, Indiana is not exactly known for its mountainous terrain, so the Peaks got old kind of fast for any thrill seeker worthy of the name.

But nothing could compare to the sensation of zipping over all that thickly packed white stuff with my arms wrapped tightly around the waist of my hot, if disapproving, boyfriend.

Oh, it was good. It was real good.

But I have to admit, the part after we'd pulled up in front of the True Americans' barbed-wire fence, and just sat there with the engine switched off, gazing at the lights of Jim Henderson's house, glimmering through the trees?

Yeah, that part wasn't so fun.

That was on account of the fact that deep in the back-woods of Indiana, on a late November evening, it is very, very cold. Bone-chillingly cold. Mind-numbingly cold. Or at least toe and finger-numbingly cold.

You would think that Rob and I could have thought up something to do, you know, to pass the time—as well as keep warm—while we waited for Chick to catch up to us with the backup he'd promised. But given the fact that Rob was still so mad we were here at all, there hadn't been much, you know, of *that* going on. In fact, none at all.

"So what are we waiting for, again?" I asked.

"Reinforcements," was Rob's terse reply.

"Yeah," I said. "I get that part. But can't we just, you know, go and wait inside?"

"And what are we going to do," Rob said, "if we find Seth?"

"Bust on out of there," I said.

"Using what as a weapon?"

I thought a minute. "Our rapier wit?"

"Like I said."

Well. So much for that.

Rob didn't seem as cold as I was. Why is that? How come boys never get as cold as girls do? And also, what's with the peeing thing? Like how come I totally had to pee, and he didn't? He'd had as many Cokes back at Chick's as I did.

And even if he had had to pee, it wouldn't have been any big deal for him. I mean, he could have just gone over to any old tree and done it.

But for me, it would have been like this major production. And a lot more of me would have been exposed to the forces of nature. Which, with it being like ten below, or something, were pretty harsh.

Whatever. Life is just unfair. That's all I have to say.

Not that I had it so bad, I guess. I mean, comparatively, I guess I've always had it pretty good. I mean, my parents are still together, and seem pretty happy to stay that way . . . except, you know, when one of us kids is causing them trouble, like hearing voices that aren't there, or dropping out of Harvard, or being struck by lightning and getting psychic powers and then causing the family restaurant to be burned down.

You know. The usual parental stresses.

At least we were pretty well off. I mean, no one was buying me my own pony—or Harley—but we weren't exactly on welfare, either. In all, the Mastriani family had it pretty good.

As opposed to, just for an example, the Wilkins family.

I mean, Rob had been working in his uncle's garage pretty much full time since he was like fourteen or something, just to help his mom make ends meet. He hadn't seen his dad since he was a little kid. He didn't even know where his dad was.

But I did. I knew where Rob's dad was.

Not that I was very grateful for the information. But there it was, embedded in my brain just like Seth Blumenthal's current location and status.

The question was, should I tell Rob, or not?

Would I want to know? I mean, if my dad had disappeared when I was a little kid. Had just walked out on Mom and Mike and Douglas and me. Would I want to know where he was now? Would I even care?

Yeah. Probably. If only so I could go pound his face in.

But would Rob want to know?

There was only one way, really, to find out. But I really, really didn't want to do it. Just come out and ask him if he wanted to know, I mean. Because I didn't want him to know I'd been snooping. I hadn't, really. His mom had needed that apron from her room. Was it my fault that while I'd been in there, I'd happened to see a picture of Rob's dad? And that afterward, as always tended to happen when I saw photos of missing people, I dreamed about his dad, and exactly where he was now? Was it my fault that, thanks to that stupid lightning, that I can't see a picture—or sometimes, even smell the sweater or pillow—of a missing person without getting a mental picture of their exact location?

"Listen," I said, pressing myself a little harder against his back. It was damned cold on the back of that snowmobile. "Rob, I—"

"Mastriani," Rob said, sounding tired. "Not now, okay?"

"What?" I asked, defensively. "I was just going to—"

"I am not going to tell you," Rob said.

"Tell me what?"

"What I'm on probation for. Okay? You can forget it. Because you're never getting it out of me. You can drag me out to the middle of nowhere," he said, "on some lunatic mission to stop a murdering white supremacist. You can make me sit for hours in sub-zero temperatures until my fingers feel like they are going to fall off. You can even tell me that you love me. But I am not going to tell you why I got arrested."

I digested this. While this was not, of course, the subject I'd meant to bring up, it was nonetheless a very interesting one. Perhaps more interesting, even, than the current location of Rob's father. To me, anyway.

"I didn't tell you that I love you," I said, after some thought, "because I wanted you to tell me what you're on probation for. Although I do want to know. I told you that I love you because—"

Rob swung around on the back of the snowmobile and threw a gloved hand over my mouth. "Don't," he said. His light-colored eyes were easy to distinguish in the moonlight. Because yeah, there was a moon. A pretty full one, too, hanging low in the cold, cloudless sky. Any other time, it might have been romantic. If, you know, it hadn't been like twenty below, and I hadn't had to pee, and my boyfriend had actually sort of liked me.

"Don't start on that again," Rob said, keeping his hand over my mouth. "Remember what happened last time."

"I liked what happened last time," I said, from behind his fingers.

"Yeah," Rob said. "Well, so did I. Too much, okay? So just keep your I love yous to yourself, all right, Mastriani?"

Sure. Like that was going to happen, after a girl hears a thing like that.

"Rob," I said, tightening my arms around his waist. "I—"

But I never got to finish. That was on account of a figure moving toward us through the trees. We heard the snow crunching beneath his feet.

Rob said a bad word and turned on the flashlight Chick had loaned us.

"Who's there?" he hissed, and shined the flashlight full on into the face of none other than Cyrus Krantz.

Now it was my turn to say a bad word.

"Shhh," Dr. Krantz said. "Jessica, please!"

"Well, whatever," I said, disgustedly. "What are you doing here?"

I couldn't believe his getup. Dr. Krantz's, I mean. He looked like somebody out of *Icestation Zebra*. He had the full-on arctic gear, complete with puffy camouflage ski pants. I had barely recognized him with all the fur trim on his hood.

"I followed you, of course," Dr. Krantz replied. "Is this where they're holding Seth, Jessica?"

"Would you get out of here?" I couldn't tell which was making me madder, the fact that he was putting our plan to rescue Seth in jeopardy, or that he'd interrupted Rob and me just when things had been starting to get interesting. "You're going to ruin everything. How did you get out here, anyway?" If he said snowmobile, I was going to seriously reconsider my refusal to work for him. Any institution that willingly supplied its employees with snowmobiles was one I could see myself getting behind.

"Never mind about that," Dr. Krantz said. "Really, Jessica, this is just too ridiculous. You shouldn't be here. You're going to get hurt."

"*I'm* going to get hurt?" I laughed bitterly—though quietly. "Sorry, Doc, but I think you got it backward. So far the only person who's gotten hurt is one of yours."

"And Nate Thompkins," Dr. Krantz reminded me softly. "Don't forget him."

As if I could. As if he wasn't half the reason I was out there, freezing my *hooha* off. I hadn't forgotten my promise to myself to try to help Tasha, if I could. And the best way to help her, I couldn't help thinking, was to bring her brother's murderers to justice.

And of course to keep them from hurting anybody else. Such as Seth Blumenthal.

"Nobody's forgetting about Nate," I whispered. "We're just going to take care of this in our own way, all right? Now get out of here, before you mess everything up."

"Jessica," Dr. Krantz said. "Rob. I really must object. If Seth Blumenthal is being harbored on this property, you are under an obligation to report it, then stand back and allow the appropriate law enforcement agents to do their—"

"Oh, bite me," I said.

I couldn't be sure, given the way the moonlight, reflecting off all the snow, made it hard to see past the thick lenses of his glasses, but I thought Dr. Krantz blinked a few times.

"I b-beg your pardon," he stammered.

"You heard me," I said. "You and the appropriate law enforcement agents don't have the slightest clue what you're dealing with here, okay?"

"Oh." Now Dr. Krantz sounded sarcastic, which was sort of amusing, considering the fact that he was such a geek. "And I suppose you do."

"Better than you," I said. "At least we've got a chance at infiltrating them from the inside, instead of going in there blasting away, and possibly getting Seth killed in the crossfire."

"Infiltration?" Dr. Krantz sounded appalled. "What are

you talking about? You can't possibly think you have a better chance at—"

"Oh, yeah?" I narrowed my eyes at him. "What number comes after nine?"

He looked at me like I was crazy. "What? What does that have to do with—"

"Just answer the question, Dr. Krantz," I said. "What number comes after nine?"

"Why, ten, of course."

"Wrong," I said. "What are Coke cans made out of?"

"Aluminum, of course. Jessica, I—"

"Wrong again," I said. "The answer to both questions, Dr. Krantz, is tin. I've just administered a Grit test, and you failed miserably. There is no way you are going to be able to pass for a local. Now get out of here, before you ruin it for the rest of us."

"This," Dr. Krantz said, looking scandalized, "is ridiculous. Rob, surely you—"

But Rob straightened on the back of the snowmobile, his head turned in the direction of the lights from Jim Henderson's house.

"Bogey," he said, "at twelve o'clock. Krantz, if you don't get the hell out of sight, you're gonna find yourself with a belly full of buckshot."

"W-what?" Dr. Krantz looked around nervously. "What are you—"

Rob was off the snowmobile and shoving Cyrus Krantz behind a tree before the good doctor knew what was happening. At the same time, I saw what Rob had seen, a light coming toward us through the thick trees on Jim Henderson's side of the barbed wire. As the light came closer, I saw that it came from one of those old-fashioned kerosene lanterns. The lantern was held by a big man in red-plaid hunting gear, a rifle in his other hand, and a dog big enough to pass for a small pony at his side.

The dog, when it noticed us, began hurtling through the snow in our direction. For a second or two, as it came careening toward us, its long tongue lolling and its eyes blazing, I thought it was one of those hell dogs. . . . You know, from that *Hound of the Baskervilles* they made us read in ninth grade?

But as it got closer, I realized it was just your run of the mill German shepherd. You know, the kind that clamp down on your throat and won't let go, even if you hit them over the head with a socket wrench.

Fortunately, just as this particular German shepherd was preparing to leap over the barbed wire between us and do just that, the guy with the rifle went, "Chigger! Down!" and the dog collapsed into the snow not two feet away from Rob and me, growling menacingly, with its gaze never wavering from us.

The man with the rifle put the lantern down, reached into his pocket, and pulled something out. *Handgun*, I thought, my heart thudding so loudly in my chest, I thought it might cause an avalanche. If there'd been any cliffs around, anyway. *The rifle's too messy. He's going to put a bullet through each of our skulls and let Chigger eat our frozen carcasses.*

Sometimes it really did seem like the whole world was conspiring against me ever seeing Rob in a tux.

"Hey," Rob said, keeping his hands in the air and his gaze on Chigger. "Hey, don't shoot. We don't mean any harm. We just want to talk to Jim."

But it turned out the thing Chigger's owner had taken out of his pocket wasn't a gun. It was a Walkie-Talkie.

"Blue Leader, this is Red Leader," Red Plaid Jacket said into the Walkie-Talkie. "We got intruders over by the south fence. Repeat. Intruders by the south fence."

"We aren't intruders," I said. Then, remembering what our cover story was supposed to be—except of course that we weren't supposed to have let ourselves get caught until *after* Chick and his friends were safely hidden in the bushes and trees around the compound, ready to bust us on out as soon as we successfully found Seth—I quickly amended that claim. "I mean, we *ain't* intruders. We want to join you. We want to be True Americans, too."

Static burst over Red Plaid Jacket's Walkie-Talkie. Apparently, someone was replying to his intruder warning. He must have been speaking in code, though, because I couldn't understand what he was saying.

"Copy that, Red Leader," the voice said. "Tag and transport. Repeat, tag and transport."

Red Plaid Jacket put his Walkie-Talkie away, then signaled for Rob and me to climb over the barbed wire. The way he signaled this was, he pointed the rifle at us, and went, "Git on over here."

Climbing over barbed wire is never a pleasant experience. But it is an even less pleasant experience when you are doing it under the watchful gaze of a massive German shepherd named Chigger. Rob went first, and didn't seem to snag anything too vital while climbing. He very politely held as much of the barbed wire down for me as he was able, so that I could arrive uninjured on the other side, as well. I didn't succeed as nimbly as he had, being about a foot shorter than he was, but all that really suffered was the inside seam of my jeans.

Once we were safely on the True Americans' side of the fence, Red Plaid Jacket went, "Git on, then," and signaled, again with the mouth of his rifle, that we should start walking toward the house.

Rob looked back at the snowmobile. "What about our ride?" he asked. "Is it safe to leave it there?"

Red Plaid Jacket let out a harsh laugh. That wasn't all he let out, either. He also let out a stream of tobacco juice from between his cheek and gum. It landed, in a steaming brown puddle, in the snow.

"Safe from what?" he wanted to know. "The coons? Or the possums?"

This was a comforting response, as it indicated that Red Plaid was as unaware of the presence of Dr. Krantz, hidden behind the thick pines, as he was of the many patrons of Chick's who had answered the call to arms by the owner of their favorite carousing spot . . . or who at least I was hoping would answer that call. And show up soon.

"Move," Red Plaid said to Rob and me.

And so we moved.

CHAPTER 12

It would be wrong to say I enjoyed our long walk toward Jim Henderson's house. I relished any time I got to spend in the presence of Rob Wilkins, as our meetings, now that he had graduated but I remained trapped behind in high school hell, had grown all too infrequent.

No matter how nice the company one might be with, however, it is never pleasant to have a rifle pointed at one's back. While I didn't think Red Plaid Jacket would fire at us in cold blood, there was always the chance that he might trip over Chigger or a stump hidden in the snow, and accidentally pull the trigger.

And though this would solve my problem of how I

was going to get Rob to invite me to a formal affair like his uncle's wedding (so I could impress him by now nice I look in a dress), it would not solve it in the right way. So it was with some trepidation that I made the long journey from the south fence to the heart of the True Americans' compound.

Once we got moving, though, I did start to feel a little less cold. Now that the blizzard had blown away, the sky was completely clear, and this far out from the lights of town, it was magically dusted with stars. I could even make out the Milky Way. It might almost have been romantic, a moonlit walk through the freshly fallen snow, the smell of wood smoke hanging tantalizingly in the air.

Except, of course, for the rifle. Oh, and the dangerous German shepherd slogging along beside us.

I am not afraid of dogs, and in general, they seem to like me. So during our walk, since we didn't dare talk to pass the time, I concentrated on trying to get Chigger to give up on the idea of tearing my throat out. I did this by thrusting my hand, whenever Red Plaid Jacket wasn't looking, and the dog came close enough, in front of Chigger's nose. Dogs operate by smell, and I figured if Chigger smelled that I really wasn't the lunchmeat type, he might hesitate about eating me.

Chigger, however, like most males I've encountered in my life, seemed remarkably uninterested in me. Maybe I should have taken Ruth's advice and invested in some perfume, instead of just splashing on some of Mike's Old English Leather now and then.

As we got closer to the buildings we were approaching, I have to admit, I wasn't too impressed. I mean, compared to Jim Henderson's place, David Koresh's compound over in Waco had looked like the freaking Taj Mahal. Henderson's entire operation seemed to consist of nothing more than a ranch-style house, a few trailers, and one rambling barn. Sure, the whole thing had that army barracks, ready-to-mobilize-at-any-minute kind of lack of permanency.

But hello, where was the bathroom? That was all I wanted to know.

To my dismay, Red Plaid Jacket, tailed by the ever faithful Chigger, led us not toward the ranch house, or either of the trailers, but directly to the barn. My chances of finding a working toilet were beginning to look dimmer than ever.

You can imagine my delight then when Red Plaid threw back the massive barn door to reveal what appeared to be the True Americans' command center, or bunker, if you will. Oh, it was no NORAD , don't get me wrong. There were no computers. There wasn't even a TV in sight.

Instead, the seat of Jim Henderson's white supremacist group resembled photos we'd seen in World Civ of Nazi headquarters, back in the forties. There were a lot of long tables, at which sat a good many fair-haired gentlemen. (Apparently, we had interrupted their supper.) And there was a giant flag hanging against the back wall. But instead of a swastika, the flag depicted the symbol that had been carved into Nate Thompkins's chest, and spray-painted onto the overpass and on the overturned headstones at the Jewish cemetery. It was the coiled snake Chick had described, with the words DON'T TREAD ON ME beneath it.

But may I just point out that there the resemblance to the Nazi war machine ended? Because the gentlemen, fair-haired as they were, gathered in the large, drafty room, were neither as tidily dressed nor as intelligent looking as your average 1940s-style Nazi, and seemed also to prefer body art to actual hygiene, a choice perhaps thrust upon them by the lack of easily available running water, if what Chick had said about Jim Henderson refusing to pay his water bill was true.

There weren't only men gathered in Henderson's barn, however. Oh, no. There were women, too, and even children. I mean, who else was going to serve the men their food? And a fine, healthy lot those women and children looked, too. The women's garb I instantly recognized as typical of a local religious sect which, besides favoring snake-handling and coming-to-the-water-to-be-born-again, also forbade its female practitioners from cutting their hair or wearing pants. This made it difficult for girls belonging to this religious group to participate in physical education classes in the public school system, as it is almost impossible to climb a rope or learn the breast stroke in a dress, so many of them opted for homeschooling.

The children were a pasty-faced, runny-nosed lot, who seemed as uninterested in a man with a rifle dragging two perfect strangers into their midst as I would have been by cooking lessons from Great-aunt Rose.

"Jimmy," Red Plaid Jacket said, to a sandy-haired man at the head of one of the long tables, who'd just been presented with a plate of what looked to me—considering that I hadn't eaten since downing a turkey sandwich around noon—like delectable fried chicken. "These're the kids we found sneakin' around by the south fence."

Kids! I resented the implication on Rob's behalf. I of course am used to being mistaken for a child, given my relatively diminutive size. But Rob stood a good twelve inches taller than me. . . .

And, I soon noticed, twelve inches taller than the leader of the True Americans, that fine, upstanding citizen who had, if we weren't mistaken, killed one kid, abducted another, attempted to murder a law enforcement officer, and burned down a synagogue.

That's right. Jim Henderson was short.

Really, really short. Like Napoleon short. Like Danny Devito short.

He also seemed kind of miffed that we had interrupted his dinner.

"What the hell you want?" Henderson inquired, showing some of those exemplary leadership qualities for which he was apparently so deeply admired by his followers.

I looked at Rob. He appeared to be at a loss for words. Either that or he was doing one of those Native American-silence things, to psych out our captors. Rob reads a lot of books that take place on Indian reservations.

I felt it was up to me to salvage the situation. I went, "Gee, Mr. Henderson, it's a real honor to meet you. Me and Hank here, well, we just been admirers of yours for so long."

Henderson sucked on his fried-chickeny fingers, his sandy-colored eyebrows raised. "That so?" he said.

"Yes," I said. "And when we saw what ya'll did to that, um, Jew church, we decided we had to come up and offer our, um, congratulations. Hank and me, we think we'd make real good True Americans, because we both hate blacks and Jews, and stuff."

There appeared to be a good deal more interest in Rob and me now that I had begun speaking. Nearly everyone in the barn was looking at us, in sort of stunned silence. Everyone except Chigger, I mean. Chigger had found a plate of chicken bones, and was consuming them with great noise and rapidity. I noticed no one leapt to stop him, which proved that the True Americans were not only despicable human beings, but also lousy pet owners, as everyone knows you should never let a dog eat chicken bones.

Henderson was looking at us with more interest than anyone. Unlike Chigger, he seemed completely oblivious to the chicken on his plate. He went, "Why?"

I'd been prepared for this question. I said, "Well, you should take us because Hank here, he is really good with his hands. He's a mechanic, you know, and he can fix just about anything. So if you ever got a tank, or whatever, and it broke down, well, Hank'd be your man. And me, well, I may not look like it, but I'm pretty swift on my feet. In a fight, you wouldn't want me on your bad side, let me tell you."

Henderson looked bored. He leaned forward to pick a piece of chicken off the bone and pop it into his little mouth. He reminded me, as he did it, of a baby bird. Except that he had a sandy-colored mustache.

"That ain't what I mean," he said. "I mean, why do you hate the blacks and Jews?"

"Oh." This was not a question I'd been prepared for. I hurried to think of a reply. "Because as everyone knows," I said, "the Jews, they made up that whole Holocaust thing, you know, so they could get their hands on Israel. And black people, well, they're taking away all our jobs."

This was not apparently the correct answer, since Jim looked away from me. Instead, he stared at Rob. He appeared to be sizing up my boyfriend. I had seen this kind of appraising look before. It was the kind of look that little guys always gave to big guys, right before they barreled their tiny heads into the bigger guy's stomach.

"What about you?" Henderson asked Rob. "Or do you let your woman do your talking for you?"

This caused a ripple of amusement amongst the men at the dinner tables. Even the women, poised at their husbands' elbows with pitchers of what looked to me like iced tea, seemed to find this hilarious, instead of the piece of sexist crap it was.

Rob, I knew, was being tested. I had not passed the test. That much was clear. It was clear by the fact that Red Plaid Jacket still had his rifle trained on us, just waiting for the order from his boss to blow our heads off. Chigger, I was certain, would gladly lick up whatever mess our scattered brains made upon the barn floor.

It was up to Rob to save us. It was up to Rob to convince Henderson that we were a pair of budding white supremacists.

And I didn't have much faith Rob was going to perform any better than I had. After all, Rob hadn't liked this idea in the first place. He had objected strenuously to it from the start. All he wanted to do, I was sure, was book on out of there, and if it was without Seth, well, that was just too bad. Just so long as we still had heads on our shoulders, I had a feeling Rob would be happy.

So you can imagine my surprise when Rob opened his mouth and this is what came out of it:

"To be born white," he said, "is an honor and a privilege. It is time that all white men and women join together to protect this bond they share by their blood and faith. The responsibility of every American is to protect the welfare of *ourselves*—not those in Mexico, Vietnam, Afghanistan, or some other third-world country. It is time to take America back from drug-addicted welfare recipients living in large urban areas. . . ."

Whoa. If Rob had my attention with this stuff, you can bet he had Jim Henderson's attention—not to mention the rest of the True Americans. You could have heard a pin drop, everybody was listening so intently.

"It's time," Rob went on, "to protect our borders from illegal aliens, and stop the insidious repeal of miscegenation laws and statutes. We need to do away with affirmative action and same-sex marriages. We need to prevent American industry and property from slipping into the hands of the Japanese, Arabs, and Jews. America should be owned by Americans—"

Applause burst from one of the tables at this. It was soon joined by standing ovations from several other tables. In the thunderous cheering that followed, I stared at my boyfriend with total disbelief. Where on earth, I wondered, had he gotten all that stuff? Was there something about Rob I didn't know? I had never heard him say any of that kind of stuff before. Was Claire right? Were all Grits the same?

The applause was cut off abruptly as Jim Henderson climbed to his feet. All eyes were on the tiny figure, really no taller than I was, as he eyed Rob, one finger thoughtfully stroking his thick mustache. Again, the room was silent, except for Chigger, who was enthusiastically licking a now empty plate.

Staring at Rob with a pair of eyes so blue, they almost seemed to blaze, Henderson finally thrust an index finger at him and commanded, "Get . . . that . . . boy . . . some . . . chicken!"

Cheers erupted as one of the women hurried forward to present Rob with a plate of fried chicken. I couldn't believe it. Chicken. They were giving Rob chicken! Easy as that, he'd been accepted into the bosom of the True Americans.

Or was it possible that they knew something I didn't? Like that Rob was maybe already a member?

Hey, I know it was a disloyal thought. And I didn't believe it. Not really. Except that . . . well, it was kind of weird that he'd known exactly the right thing to say to get these freaks to believe we were on their side. And knowing what I did about his dad, it wasn't much of a stretch to imagine there might be a few things Rob hadn't told me . . . and I didn't just mean what he was on probation for.

Rob stood there, smiling shyly as he was applauded. I couldn't help it. I *had* to know. So I asked him, out of the corner of my mouth, "Where'd you come up with that horse shit?"

Rob replied, from the corner of his own mouth, "Public access cable. Would you get this chicken away from me before I barf?"

I grabbed the plate just as Rob was engulfed in a crowd of happy white supremacists, who slapped him on the back and offered him chews from their bags of tobacco. I stood there like an idiot watching him, the plate of chicken getting cold in my hands. I couldn't believe how stupid I'd been. Of *course* Rob wasn't one of them.

But it was scary how easily I'd been swayed into thinking he might have been. Prejudice runs deep. Grits and Townies, blacks and whites . . . you grow up hearing one thing, it's hard to believe that something else might actually be true.

Hard to believe, maybe. But not impossible. I mean, look at Rob. He was nothing like your stereotypical Grit, gleefully chowing down on fried chicken while discussing the supremacy of the white race. Rob didn't even *like* fried chicken.

Who knows how long I would have stood there, admiring the genius of my boyfriend, if a voice at my elbow hadn't gone, "Well, just don't there stand there, girlie. Give that chicken to one of the men and then git on back to the kitchen fer more."

I turned and saw a doughy-faced woman with a kerchief holding back her long blond hair glaring at me.

"Go on," the woman said, giving me a push toward one of the men's tables. "Git."

I got. I put the chicken down in front of the first man I saw—a gentleman who did not appear to have as many teeth as he did tattoos—then followed Kerchief-Head out a side door. . . .

Into the cold night air.

"Come on," the woman barked at me, when I froze in my tracks, shocked by the sudden cold.

"We gotta git the mashed potatoes."

I followed her, thinking, *Well, at least this way, I'll have a chance to look for Seth.* I knew he was here on the compound somewhere. I knew that he was no longer tied up or gagged, but locked into a small, wood-paneled room. That didn't mean he wasn't still scared, though. I could feel his fear around me like a second coat.

Kerchief-Head threw open the door to the ranch house. This, apparently, was where all the cooking was done. I could tell by the intoxicating odors that hit me as I came through the door. Chicken, potatoes, bread . . . it was a dizzying set of aromas for a girl as hungry as I was.

But when we got into the kitchen—which was crowded with other doughy-faced, long-haired women—and I tried to bogart a roll, Kerchief-Head slapped my hands.

"We don't eat," she said, harshly, "until the men're done!"

Whoa, I wanted to say. *Nice operation you got going here.*

If you're a guy. What is it with women like Kerchief-Head? I mean, why are they so willing to put up with that kind of treatment? I would way rather have no guy than some guy who tried to make me wait to eat until after he was done.

But I didn't want to blow things with the True Americans, so I dropped the roll like a good white supremacist housewife and asked, "You got a bathroom around here?"

Kerchief-Head pointed down a hallway, but she didn't look too happy about it. I guess she thought I was trying to shirk kitchen duty or something.

I'll tell you something, those True Americans were pretty scary. Even their bathrooms were filled with racist propaganda. I couldn't believe it. Instead of issues of *National Geographic* or *Time* magazine, like in a normal house, there was a copy of *Mein Kampf* to peruse while you were otherwise indisposed. Like these guys had totally missed the part where Hitler turned out to be a maniac or something.

When I was through in the bathroom, I looked up and down the hall to make sure Kerchief-Head or any of her cronies weren't lurking around. Then I started testing door-knobs. I figured when I got to a locked one, that's the one I'd find Seth behind.

It didn't take me long. It wasn't like the house was so big, or anything. The room they were keeping Seth in was way at the end of the hall, past the homeschooling room—instead of the old red, white, and blue, there was another one of those

424

"Don't Tread On Me" flags hanging in there. The door was locked, but it was one of those cheap button locks you only have to turn from the right side to undo. I turned it, opened the door, and looked inside.

Seth Blumenthal, tears streaming down his face, sat up in bed, and blinked at me in the semidarkness.

"Wh-who are you?" Seth asked, hesitantly. "Wh-what do you want?"

How else was I supposed to reply? The words were out of my mouth before I could stop them. I mean, I'd only seen the movie like seventeen times.

"I'm Luke Skywalker," I said. "I'm here to rescue you."

CHAPTER 13

Seth didn't fall for the Luke Skywalker line. This was one kid you obviously couldn't pull anything over on.

"No," he said. "Who are you, really? You don't look like one of them."

I closed the door behind me, in case Kerchief-Head came looking for me. There was no light in the room, except the moonlight that came filtering in between the wooden boards that covered the windows—always a Martha Stewart "do," boarding up your windows, by the way.

"My name's Jess," I said, to Seth. "And we're going to get you out of here." But not through those windows, I now realized. "Are you hurt anywhere? Can you run?"

"I'm okay," Seth said. "Just my hand." He held out his right hand. It wasn't hard to see, even in the moonlight, what was wrong with it. Somebody had burned a shape into it, between Seth's thumb and forefinger. The burn was red and blistered. And it was in the shape of a coiled snake.

Just like the shape that had been carved into Nate Thompkins's naked chest. I knew now how they'd gotten Seth to tell them where to find the Torah.

And I wanted to kill them for it.

First things first, however.

"Six weeks hydro-therapy," I said to him, "that puppy'll be gone. Won't even leave a scar." I knew from my own third-degree burn, which had been roughly the same size, but which I'd received from a motorcycle exhaust pipe when I'd been around his own age. "Okay?"

Seth nodded. He wasn't crying anymore. "That policeman," he said. "The one they shot, back at the trailer. Is he okay?"

"He sure is," I lied. "Now listen, I've got to get back to the kitchen before they notice I'm missing. But I promise I'll be back for you just as soon as the shooting starts."

"Shooting?" Seth looked concerned. "Who's going to start shooting?"

"Friends of mine," I said. "They got the place surrounded." I hoped. "So you just hang in there, and I'll be back for you lickety-split. Got it?"

"I got it," Seth said. Then, as I started for the door, he went, "Hey, Jess?"

I turned. "Yeah?"

"What day is it?"

I told him. He nodded thoughtfully. "Today's my birthday," he said, seemingly to no one in particular. "I'm thirteen."

"Happy birthday," I said. Well, what else was I supposed to say? I was just sauntering away from the newly relocked door when Kerchief-Head appeared.

"Where do you think you're going?" she demanded. One thing I had to say for the wives of the True Americans, they weren't very polite.

"Oh," I said, giving my ditziest giggle. "I got lost."

Kerchief-Head just glared at me. Then she thrust a huge bowl of something white and glutinous in my arms. Looking down, I realized it was mashed potatoes. Only the True Americans, unlike my dad, hadn't put any garlic in them, so the aroma they gave off was somewhat nondescript.

"Take this to the men," Kerchief-Head said.

"Can do," I told her, and headed out the door.

The big question, of course, was would it work. I mean, would Chick and his friends show up in time for us to get Seth out? And what about Dr. Krantz? Let's not forget about him. The Feds had a major tendency to mess things like surprise attacks up, big time. Would Chick be able to get around whatever idiot scheme Dr. Krantz was probably, at this very moment, cooking up?

I hoped so. Not for my own sake. I didn't much care what happened to me. It was Seth I was worried about. We had to get Seth out.

Oh, yeah. And kill every True American we possibly could.

I don't normally go around wanting to kill people, but when I'd seen that burn on Seth's hand, I'd felt something I'd never felt before. I am no stranger to rage, either. I get mad fast, and I get mad often. But I could never remember feeling the way I had when I'd seen that burn.

I'd felt like killing someone. Really killing them. Not breaking someone's nose, or kicking someone in the groin. I wanted him to pay for branding that kid, and I wanted him to pay with his life.

And I had a pretty good idea who that someone was.

When I got back into the barn, everyone had calmed down from Rob's little speech, and was busy chowing down again. Being the mashed potato girl, I was pretty popular. Guys kept on raising up their plates as I passed, holding them out for me to glop mashed potatoes onto. I obliged, since what else was I supposed to do? I got through it by pretending I was a prison guard, and all these guys were demented serial killers that I was mandated by the state to keep fed.

In the back of my mind, however, this mantra was playing

over and over. It went, *Hurry up, Chick. Hurry up, Chick. Hurry up, Chick. Hurry up, Chick.*

When I reached Rob, I saw that he and Henderson were already well on their way to becoming best friends. Well, and why not? Rob would be a boon to any hate group. He was good-looking, great with his hands, and—though I hadn't been aware of this talent until very recently—he was obviously a passionate and lucid orator. I had a feeling that, given enough time, Rob would have been appointed Jim Henderson's right-hand man.

Too bad for the True Americans that it was all an act.

A good one, though. Claire Lippman would have been astounded by Rob's theatrical flair. As I leaned over his chair to lump potatoes onto his plate, he didn't even seem to notice me, he was so wound up in what he was saying . . . something about how the criminals in Washington were selling us out with something called GATT.

Wow. Rob had obviously been watching a lot more CNN than I had.

After piling some potatoes onto Jim Henderson's plate— only for a second did I fantasize about pretending to accidentally drop them into his lap—I moved on to the rest of the table, trying not to notice as I did so a disturbing thing. There were lots of disturbing things to notice in that barn, but the one that I kept coming back to was the men's hands. Each and every one of them had the same tattoo on the webbing between the thumb and forefinger of their right hand. And that was the coiled snake of the "Don't Tread On Me" flag. The same snake that had been on Nate's chest. The same snake that had been burned into Seth's hand. This was some fraternity, let me tell you.

It wasn't until my bowl was almost empty that I felt the cold, wet nudge on one hand. I looked down and saw Chigger, his big brown eyes rolling up at me appealingly. Gone was the menacing growl and raised back hairs. I had food, and Chigger wanted food. Therefore, if I gave Chigger food, I would be Chigger's friend.

I let Chigger lick what remained in the bowl.

I fully intended to go back to the ranch house kitchen and refill that bowl without rinsing it out first. In fact, I was headed toward the barn door to do just that when I noticed something that I didn't like . . . that I didn't like at all. And that was Kerchief-Head, over at Jim Henderson's table, leaning down to whisper something in his ear. As she whispered I saw Jim glance around the room, until at last his gaze found me. Those piercing blue eyes stayed on me, too, until Kerchief-Head finished whatever it was she'd had to say and straightened up.

Look, it could have been a lot of things. It could have been the thing with the roll. Heck, she could have seen me letting Chigger lick the bowl.

But I'm not stupid. I knew what it was. I knew what it

was the minute Jim Henderson's gaze landed on me.

Kerchief-Head had told him about catching me in the hallway near where they were keeping Seth. That was all.

We were dead.

It took a little while for it to happen, though. Henderson whispered something back to Kerchief-Head, and she scuttled out of there like a water bug. For a little while, I thought maybe we were all right. You know, that maybe I'd made a mistake. Rob was going on about abominations of nature and how America would never be restored to the great nation it had once been until all Christians banded together, and Henderson seemed to be listening to him pretty intently.

But then I saw something that made my heart stop.

And that was Red Plaid Jacket with the end of his rifle pointed at the back of Seth Blumenthal's neck as he forced the boy to walk across the barn floor, right up to where Jim Henderson and Rob sat.

Everyone stopped talking when they saw this, and once again, the silence in the barn was overwhelming. The only sound I could hear was the sound of Seth's sobs. He had started crying again. I saw him look frantically around the barn, and I knew he was looking for me. Fortunately, I was far enough in the shadows that he hadn't been able to see me, or without a doubt, I'd have been dead.

If I'd known, of course, what was going to happen a minute later anyway, I probably wouldn't have cared so much.

As it was, I was actually relieved Seth hadn't spotted me. I sunk my fingers into Chigger's soft fur and willed my heart to start beating again. *Hurry up, Chick. Hurry up, Chick. Hurry up, Chick!*

"Americans," Jim Henderson said to the assembled masses. I could see at once that he was every bit the orator Rob was. Everyone looked at him with that glazed expression of adoration I recognized from that movie about the Jim Jones massacre. Henderson was these people's messiah on earth.

"We've made some fine new friends tonight," Henderson went on, slapping a hand to Rob's shoulder. The only reason he'd been able to reach it was that Rob was sitting and he was standing. "And I for one am grateful. Grateful that Hank and Ginger found their way to our little flock."

Ginger? Who the hell was Ginger? Then, as a good many heads turned in my direction, I realized Rob had told them my name was Ginger.

He is such a card.

"But however impressed we may be by Hank and Ginger's professed dedication to our cause," Henderson went on, "there's really only one way to test the loyalty of a true American, isn't there?"

There was a general murmur of assent. My heart thudded more loudly than ever. I did not like the sound of this. I did not like the sound of this at all.

"Hank," Henderson said, turning to Rob. "You see before

you a boy. Seemingly innocent enough looking, I know. But innocence, as we all know, can be deceiving. The devil sometimes tries to fool us into believing in the innocence of an individual, when in fact that individual is laden with sin. In this case, this boy is soaked in sin. Because he is, in fact, a Jew."

I dug my fingers so hard into Chigger's coat, a smaller dog would have cried out. Chigger, however, only wagged his tail, still hoping for another crack at the bowl I held. Apparently, nobody had ever bothered to feed Chigger before. How else could you explain how easily I'd won over his allegiance?

"Hank," Henderson said. "Because you've already, in the short time I've known you, so thoroughly impressed me with your sincerity and commitment to the cause, I am going to allow you a great privilege I've heretofore denied both myself and my other men. Hank, I am going to let you kill a Jew."

And with that, Jim Henderson presented Rob with a knife he pulled out of his own boot.

A lot of things went through my mind then. I thought about how much I loved my mom, even though she can be such a pain in the ass sometimes, with her weird ideas about how I should dress and who I should date. I thought about how mad I was going to be if I didn't get to stick around to find out if Douglas ever did anything about his crush on Tasha Thompkins. I thought about the state orchestra championship, and how for the first time in years, I wouldn't be bringing home a blue ribbon cut in the shape of the state of Indiana.

It's strange the things you think about right before you die. I don't even know how I knew I was going to die. I just knew it, the way I knew that eventually, all that snow outside was going to melt, and it would be spring again someday. Rob and I were going to die, and the only thing we had to make sure of was that they didn't try to kill Seth along with us.

"Well," Henderson was saying to my boyfriend. "Go on. Take my knife. Really. It's okay. He's just a Jew."

Seth Blumenthal, I have to say, was being pretty brave. He was crying, but he was doing it quietly, with his head held high. I guess after what he'd been through, death didn't seem like such a bad thing. I don't know how else to explain it. I kind of felt the same way. I wasn't scared, really. Oh, I didn't want it to hurt. But I wasn't scared to die.

All I wanted was to take as many True Americans down with me as I could.

Rob reached out and took the knife from Jim Henderson.

"Thataboy," Henderson said, smiling in a sickly way beneath his mustache. "Now go ahead. Show us you are a true believer. Stick it to the pig."

So Rob did the only thing he could. The same thing I'd have done, in his situation.

He threw an arm around Jim Henderson's neck, brought the knife blade to his jugular vein, and said, "Anybody moves, and Jimbo here gets it."

CHAPTER 14

Have you ever been to a football game where the higher ranked team was so certain of winning, there wasn't even a doubt in the minds of their fans that they wouldn't? And then, through some total miscalculation on the part of the superior team, the underdog got the upper hand?

The faces of the True Americans looked like the faces of the fans of the winning team, seconds after their team mangled some play so horribly, their opponent, against all odds, scored a touchdown.

They were stunned. Just stunned.

"Thanks," I said to Red Plaid Jacket, as I relieved him of his rifle. "I'll take that."

I had never held a rifle before in my life, but I had a pretty good idea how one worked. You just pointed at the thing you wanted to hit, and pulled the trigger. No big mystery in that.

Of course, if you thought about it, there was no reason in the world for us to be so cocky. Okay, so yeah, Rob had a knife to a guy's throat, and I had a rifle. Big deal. It was still about fifty to two. Well, three, if you counted Seth. Four, if you included Chigger, who was still following me around, hoping for more mashed potatoes, even though I'd put down the bowl.

But hey, we had the upper hand for the moment, and we were going to take advantage of it while we could.

"Okay," Rob said, as the blood slowly drained from Jim Henderson's face. Not because Rob had poked a hole in him or anything. Just because the leader of the True Americans was so very, very scared.

"Okay, now. Everybody just stay very calm, and no one is going to get hurt." Hey, he had me convinced. Rob seemed totally believable, as far as knife-wielding hostage-takers went. "Me and the girl and the kid and Jimbo here are going to take a little walk. And if any of you want to see your fearless leader live through this, you're going to let us go. Okay?"

When no one objected, Rob went, "Good. Jess. Seth. Let's go."

And so started what had to have looked like one weird parade. With me leading the way, rifle in hand and dog at my heels, a dazed-looking Seth following me, and Rob, with his arm around Henderson, taking up the rear, we made our way down the length of the barn. I wouldn't want to give you the impression that Mr. Henderson was playing the silent martyr in all of this, however. Oh, no. See, people who haven't the slightest qualm about doing unspeakably horrible things to others are always the ones who act like the biggest babies of all whenever anybody in turn threatens them.

I'm not kidding. Jim Henderson was practically crying. He was wailing, in a high-pitched voice, "You may think you're gonna get away with this, but I'll tell you what. The people are gonna rise up. The people are gonna rise up and walk the path of righteousness. And traitors like you, boy— traitors to your own race—are going to burn in hellfire for all eternity—"

"Would you," Rob said, "shut up?"

Only Jim Henderson was wrong. The people weren't going to rise up. Not all at once, anyway. They were too shocked by what was happening to their leader even to think about lifting a finger to help him. Or maybe it was just that they really did believe that if they tried anything to stop us, Rob would slit their beloved Jim Henderson's throat.

In any case, the people did not rise up.

Just one person did.

Kerchief-Head, to be exact.

I should have seen it coming. I mean, it had been way, way too easy.

But I'll admit it. I got cocky. I started thinking that these people were stupid, because they had these stupid ideas about things. That was my first mistake. Because the scariest thing about the True Americans was that they weren't stupid. They were just really, really evil. As became all too clear when I heard, from behind me, the sound of breaking glass.

I realized my second mistake the second I turned around. The first had been in assuming the True Americans were stupid. The second had been in not covering Rob's back with the rifle.

Because when I spun around, what I saw was Kerchief-Head standing there with two broken pieces of my mashed potato bowl in her hands. The rest of the pieces were all over the floor . . . where Rob also lay. The bitch had snuck up behind him and cracked his skull open.

Hey, I didn't hesitate. I lifted that rifle, and I fired. I didn't even think about it, I was so mad . . . mad and scared. There was a lot of blood coming out of the gash in Rob's head. More was pouring out every second.

But I had never fired a rifle before. I didn't know how they kicked. And it is not like I am this terrifically large person or anything. I pulled the trigger, the gun exploded, and the next thing I knew, I was on the floor, with Chigger licking my face and about a million and one handguns pointed at my face.

Whatever else the True Americans might have been, lacking in firearms was not one of them.

The worst part of it was, I didn't even hit Kerchief-Head. I missed her by a mile.

I did, however, manage to do some major damage to the "Don't Tread On Me" flag.

"If you've killed my boyfriend," I snarled at Kerchief-Head, as a lot of hands started grabbing me and dragging me to my feet, "I'll make you regret the day you were ever born. Do you hear me, placenta breath?"

It was childish, I knew, to stoop to name-calling. But I'm not sure I was in my right mind. I mean, Rob was lying there, completely unconscious, with all this blood making a puddle around his head. And they wouldn't let me near him. I tried to get to him. I really did. But they wouldn't let me.

Instead, they locked me up. That's right. In that little room Seth had been locked in. They threw me right in there. Me and Seth. In the dark. In the cold. With no way of knowing whether my boyfriend was dead or alive.

I don't know how much time passed before I stopped kicking the door and screaming. All I know was that the sides of my wrists hurt from where I'd pounded them against the surprisingly sturdy wood. And Seth was staring at me like I was some kind of escapee from a lunatic asylum. Really. The kid looked scared.

He looked even more scared when I said to him, "Don't worry. I'm going to get you out of here."

Well, I guess I couldn't blame him. I probably wasn't

exactly giving off an aura of mature adulthood just then.

I crossed over to where he was sitting and sank down onto the bed beside him. Suddenly, I was really tired. It had been a long day.

Seth and I sat there in the dark, listening to the distant sounds of the women banging pots and pans around in the kitchen. I guess no matter what kind of murder and mayhem was happening over in the barn, dinner still needed serving. I mean, all those men needed to keep their strength up for making the country safe for the white man, right?

Finally, after what seemed like a million years, Seth spoke. He said, in a shy voice, "I'm sorry about your friend."

I shrugged. I didn't exactly want to think about Rob. If he was dead, that was one thing. I would deal with that when the time came, probably by throwing myself headfirst into Pike's Quarry, or whatever.

But if he was still alive, and they were doing stuff to him, the way they had to Seth. . . .

Well, let's just say that whether Rob was dead or alive, I was going to make it my sole mission in life to track down each and every one of the True Americans, and make them pay.

Preferably with a flame-thrower.

"How . . ." Seth scratched his head. He was a funny-looking kid, tall for his age, with dark hair and eyes, like me. "How did you find me, anyway?"

I looked down at my Timberlands, though I wasn't exactly

seeing them, or much else, for that matter. All I could see was Rob, lying there with his head bashed in.

"I have this thing," I said, tiredly.

"A thing?" Seth asked.

"A psychic thing," I said. Which is another thing. If Rob were dead, wouldn't I know it? I mean, wouldn't I feel it? I was pretty sure I would.

But I didn't. I didn't feel anything. Except really, really tired.

"Really?" In the moonlight, Seth's face looked way younger than his thirteen years. "Hey, that's right. You're that girl. That lightning girl. I thought I'd seen you before somewhere. You were on the news."

"That's me," I said. "Lightning Girl."

"That is so cool," Seth said, admiringly.

"It's not so cool," I told him.

"No," Seth said. "It is. It really is. It's like you've got kid Lojack, or something."

"Yeah," I said. "And look what good it's done for me. You and I are stuck in here, and my boyfriend's out there bleeding to death, and another kid is dead, and possibly a cop, too—"

I saw his face crumble, and only then realized what I had said. I had let my personal grief get the better of me, and spoken out of turn. I bit my lip.

"You said he was all right," Seth said, his dark eyes suddenly swimming in tears. "That cop. You said he was okay."

"He is okay," I said, putting my arm around the little guy. "He is, really. Sorry. I just lost it for a minute there."

"He's not okay," Seth wailed. "He's dead, isn't he? And because of me! All because of me!"

It was kind of amazing that after what this kid had been through, the only thing that really got him upset was the idea that a cop that had been trying to save him had ended up catching a bullet for his troubles. Seth Blumenthal, bar mitzvah boy, really was something else.

"No, not because of you," I assured him. "Because of those asshole True Americans. And besides, he isn't dead, all right? I mean, he's hurt bad, but he isn't dead. I swear."

But Seth clearly didn't believe me. And why should he? I hadn't exactly been the most truth-worthy person he'd ever met, had I? I'd told him I was there to rescue him, only instead of rescuing him, now I was just as much a prisoner as he was. I'll tell you what, I was starting to agree with him: As a rescuer, I pretty much sucked.

I was just thinking these pleasant thoughts as the door to the room we were locked in suddenly opened. I blinked as the light from the hallway, which seemed unnaturally bright thanks to my eyes having adjusted to the dimness of our cell, flooded the room. Then a figure in the doorway blocked out the light.

"Well, now." I recognized Jim Henderson's Southern

twang. "Ain't that cozy, now, the two of you. Like something out of a picture postcard."

I took my arm away from Seth's shoulders and stood up. With my vision having grown accustomed to the light from the hallway, I was able to see that Henderson looked slightly disconcerted as I did this, on account of him being only an inch or two taller than me.

"Where's Rob?" I demanded.

Henderson looked confused. "Rob? Who's Rob?" Then comprehension dawned. "Oh, you mean *Hank*? Your friend with the smart mouth? Oh, I'm sorry. He's dead."

My nose was practically level with his. It took everything I had in me not to head-butt the jerk.

"I don't believe you," I said.

"Well, you better start believing me, honey," Henderson said. His eyes, blue as they were, seemed to have trouble focusing, I noticed. He had what I, having been in enough fights with people who have them, call crazy eyes. His gaze was all over the place, sometimes on the boarded-up windows behind me, sometimes on Seth, sometimes on the ceiling, but rarely, rarely where it should have been: on mine.

See? Crazy eyes.

Unfortunately, I knew from experience that there was no predicting what someone with crazy eyes was going to do next. Generally, it was just about the last thing you'd expect.

I'd have taken my chances and reached out and wrapped

Jim Henderson's crazy-eyed neck into a headlock if it hadn't been for Red Plaid Jacket standing there in the hallway behind him. Red Plaid had retrieved his rifle, and had it pointed casually at me. This was discouraging, to say the least. I had a bad feeling his aim was probably better than mine.

"You know," Henderson said. "It's not just minorities like the Jews and the blacks who are ruining this country. It's people like you and your boyfriend back there. Traitors to your own race. People like you who are ashamed of the whiteness of your skin, instead of being proud—proud!—to be members of God's chosen race."

"The only time I'm ashamed to be a member of the white race," I said, "is when I'm around freaking lunatics like you."

"See," Henderson said to Kerchief-Head, who was behind Red Plaid, and was watching her leader's dealings with me with great interest. "See what happens when the liberal media gets their hands on our children? That's why I don't allow the sons and daughters of the True Americans to watch TV. No movies or radio, neither, or any of that noise people like you call music. No newspapers, no magazines. Nothing to fog the mind and cloud the judgment."

I couldn't believe he was standing there giving me a lecture. What was this, school? Hello, get on with the torture already. I swear I'd have rather been held down and branded than listen to this dude's random crap much longer.

But unfortunately, he wasn't through.

"Who sent you?" Henderson asked me. "Tell me who you work for. The CIA? FBI? Who?"

I burst out laughing, though of course there wasn't anything too funny about the situation.

"I don't work for anybody," I said. "I came here for Seth."

Henderson shook his head. "So young," he said. "Yet so full of lies. America doesn't belong to people like you, you know," he went on. "America is for pioneers like us, people willing to work the land, people who aren't afraid to get their hands dirty."

"You certainly proved that," I remarked, "when you killed Nate Thompkins. Can't get much dirtier than that."

Henderson smiled. But again, thanks to the crazy eyes, the smile didn't quite reach all the way to those baby blues of his.

"The black boy, you mean? Yes, well, it was necessary to leave a warning, in case any more people of his persuasion took it into their heads to move to this area. You see, it's important for us to keep the land pure for our children, the sons and daughters of the True Americans."

"Well, congratulations," I said. "I bet your kids are gonna be real happy about what you did to Nate, especially when they're frying your butt for murder up in Indianapolis. I know how proud I'd be to have a convicted felon for a dad."

"I don't worry about laws made by man," Mr. Crazy Eyes

informed me with a smile. "I worry only about divine law, laws handed down by God."

"Huh," I said. "Then you're gonna be in for a surprise. Because I'm pretty sure 'Thou Shalt Not Kill' came straight from the big guy himself."

But Jim just shook his head. "It's only a sin to kill those God created in his own image. In other words, white men," he explained, tiredly. "People like you will never understand." He sighed. "Living as you always have in the comforts of the city, never knowing what it is to work the soil—"

"I've got news for you," I said. "There are a lot of people I know who don't live in town and who've worked the soil plenty but who feel the same way about you freaks that I do."

He went on like he hadn't heard me. Who knew? Maybe he hadn't. Clearly Mr. Henderson was only hearing what he wanted to hear anyway.

"Americans have always dealt with adversity. From the savages they encountered upon their arrival to this great land, and then from foreign influences who threatened to destroy them. Pretty ironic, ain't it, that the greatest threat of all comes not from forces overseas, but from within the country of America itself."

"Whatever," I said. I'd had about as much as I could take. "Are you here to mess me up, or what?"

Crazy Eyes finally looked me full in the face.

"You will be disposed of," he said, in a voice as cold as the wind outside. "You, your boyfriend, and the Jew will all be disposed of, the same way we disposed of the black boy. Your bodies will be left as a warning to any who doubt that the new age has arrived, and that the battle has begun. You see, someone has got to fight for this great nation. Someone has got to keep America safe for our children, prevent it from succumbing to hate and greed. . . ."

The great Jim Henderson broke off as, from outside the ranch house, an enormous explosion—rather like the kind that might occur if someone threw a lit cigarette down a trailer's septic tank—rocked the compound.

I smiled sweetly up into Jim Henderson's crazy eyes and said, "Uh, Mr. Henderson? Yeah, I think that someone you were talking about, the one who is going to make America safe for our children? Yeah. He and his friends just arrived. And from the sound of it, you've really pissed them off."

CHAPTER 15

And then I hauled off and slugged him. Right between those crazy, shifty eyes.

It hurt like hell, because mostly what my knuckles caught was bone. But I didn't care. I'd been wanting to punch that guy for a long, long time. The pain was totally worth it, especially when, as I'd known he would, Henderson crumpled up like a doll, and fell, wailing, to the floor.

"She hit me," he cried. "She hit me! Don't just stand there, Nolan! Do something. The bitch hit me!"

Nolan—aka Red Plaid Jacket—was too busy squawking into his Walkie-Talkie however to pay attention to his fearless leader. "We got incoming! Do you copy, Blue Leader?

We are under attack. Do you copy? Do you copy?"

Red Plaid might have been more interested in what was happening to the rest of the compound, but that certainly wasn't the case with Kerchief-Head. She was pretty hacked that I'd taken a poke at her spiritual guide—hey, for all I know, Henderson might even have been her honey. She could easily have been Mrs. Henderson.

I was hopping around, waving my sore knuckles, when Kerchief-Head, with a snarl that would have put Chigger to shame, launched herself at me.

"Ain't nobody gonna do Jim like that," she declared, as her not-insignificant weight struck me full force, and sent me back against the bed, pinned beneath her.

Mrs. Henderson—if that's who she really was—was a big woman, all right, but she had the disadvantage of not having been in many fights before. That was clear from the fact that she did not go directly for my eyes, as someone better accustomed to confronting adversaries would have.

Plus, for all her doughiness, Mrs. Henderson wasn't very muscular. I easily twisted to sink a knee into her stomach, then accompanied that by a quick thrust of one elbow into the back of her neck while she was sunk over, clutching her gut. And that took care of Kerchief-Head.

Meanwhile, outside, another explosion ripped through the compound.

"Save the children," Kerchief-Head gasped. "Somebody save the children!"

Like Chick and those guys would even be targeting the kids. I am so sure.

"Who do you people think we are?" I demanded. *"You?"*

Then I reached out, grabbed Seth by the arm, and said, "Come on."

We would have gotten safely out of there, too, if I'd just hit Henderson a little harder. Unfortunately, however, he recovered all too quickly from my punch . . . or at least quickly enough to reached out and wrap a hand around my ankle, just as we were stepping over him.

"You ain't goin' nowhere," Jim Henderson breathed. I was delighted to note that blood was streaming from his nose. Not as much blood as had streamed from Rob's head, but a fairly satisfying amount, nonetheless.

"It's all over, Mr. Henderson," I said. "You better let go now, or you're going to regret it."

"You stupid bitch," Henderson wheezed. He couldn't talk too well, on account of the blood and mucous flowing into his mouth thanks to what I'd done to his nose. "You have no idea what you've done. You think you've done this country a favor, but all you've done is sign its death warrant."

"Hey, Mr. Henderson—" Seth said.

When the crazy-eyed man looked up at him, the boy

brought his foot down with all the force he had on the hand that was grasping my ankle.

"—eat my shorts."

Henderson, with another cry of pain, released me at once. And Seth and I took off down the hallway.

Red Plaid Jacket, aka Nolan, had disappeared. There were plenty of other people, however, creating chaos in the ranch house. Women and children were darting around like goldfish in a bowl, calling each other's names and falling over one another. I couldn't blame them for panicking, really. The acrid smell of smoke was already thick in the air, and it got even thicker when Seth and I finally burst outside . . .

. . . to be greeted with the welcome sight of Jim Henderson's barn and meeting house in flames.

Both trailers were on fire, as well. All around the snowy yard ran True Americans, waving rifles and looking panicked. The panic wasn't just because most of their compound was on fire. It was also because extremely large men, many of whom were wearing cowboy hats, were whipping back and forth across the yard on the backs of snowmobiles. It was a truly magnificent sight, seeing those sleek vehicles sailing over the snow in direct pursuit of an overalled True American. I saw Red Plaid Jacket try to take aim at one with his rifle. Too bad for him that the minute he did, another snowmobiler, yelling, "Yeehaw!" darted forward and knocked the gun right out of his hands.

Meanwhile, not far away, another snowmobiler had lassoed an escaping True American neatly as if he'd been a fleeing heifer, bringing him down to the snow with a satisfying thud. Elsewhere, two snowmobilers had cornered a pair of Jim Henderson's followers, and were just gliding around and around them, giving them a tiny bit of room to escape, then cutting off that escape route at just the last moment, entirely for kicks.

"Whoa," Seth said, his eyes very wide. "Who *are* these guys?"

I sighed happily, my heart filled with joy.

"Grits," I said.

And then I remembered Rob. Rob, who, last I'd seen him, had been spread-eagle on the floor of the True Americans' meeting house.

Which was now in flames.

I forgot about Seth. I forgot about Jim Henderson and Chick and the True Americans. All I thought about was getting to Rob, and as fast as humanly possible.

Unfortunately, that meant running across the snow toward a burning building while Hell's Angels and truckers on snowmobiles were ripping the place apart. It was a wonder I got as far I did. Part of it was due to the fact that Chigger appeared from out of nowhere, and, apparently thinking I still had mashed potatoes on me that he might be able to score, loped after me.

I didn't recognize him right away, however—there were

other dogs running around the place, barking their heads off thanks to all the shooting—and I thought he'd been trying to bring me down. So I kicked up my heels, let me tell you.

But when I got to the barn doors and peered inside, all I could see were flames. The tables were on fire. The rafters were on fire. Even the walls were on fire. Though I couldn't lean in very far, due to the extreme heat, I could see that no one was inside . . . not even any unconscious motorbike mechanics who happened to be on probation.

Then I was suddenly yanked off my feet. Thinking a True American had gotten hold of me, I lashed out with my feet and fists. But then a familiar voice went, "Simmer down, there, little lady! It's me, old Chick! What choo want to do, light your hair on fire? Get away from those flames, they're hot!"

"Chick!" I squirmed around in his arms until I was facing him. He was barely recognizable in his winter gear, which included a thick pair of aviation goggles. But I didn't care how he looked. I had never been so happy to see anyone in my life.

"Chick, have you seen Rob? They got him. The True Americans, I mean. They got Rob!"

Chick looked bored. "Wilkins is fine," he said, jerking a thumb at a rusted-out pickup sitting half-buried in snow about twenty yards away. "I put 'im in the back of that old Chevy. He's still out like a light, but it don't look too bad."

I clung to the front of his leather jacket, hardly daring to believe my ears. "But the blood," I said. "There was so much of it. . . ."

"Aw," Chick said, disgustedly. "Wilkins was always one to bleed like a stuck pig. Don't worry about him. He's got a head like a rock. He'll be all right, after a coupla stitches. Now what about this kid? Where's he?"

I looked around, and saw Seth still standing over by the ranch house door, shivering in the winter cold despite the heat from the many fires all around him.

"Over there," I said, pointing.

At that moment, a shot rang out. I ducked instinctively, but ended up with my face in the snow, thanks to Chick practically throwing me to the ground, then trying to shield me with his own body.

"Idiots," he muttered, not seeming the least discomfited by the fact that he was laying on top of a girl he hardly knew. "Told those boys we had to take out their muni shed first. But they said no way would the fools shoot at us with women and children around. They're true Americans, all right. True American assholes. Damn! You all right?"

I could barely breathe, he was so heavy. "Fine," I grunted. "Seth. Got to get Seth . . . out of range . . . of gunfire."

"I'm on it," Chick said. Then, mercifully, he climbed off me, and back onto his snowmobile. "You get on over to Wilkins," he said. "I'll get the kid and meet up with you, then we'll figure out a way to get the three of you outta this hellhole."

He took off with a spray of snow and gravel. I was still spitting tiny ice particles out from between my teeth when I heard a strange noise and looked down.

Chigger was still with me, and was doing the exact same thing I was—trying to get rid of all the snow and bits of dirt clinging to his hair.

I had, I realized, a new friend.

"Come on, boy," I said to him, and the two of us raced for the abandoned pickup.

They'd wrapped Rob in something yellow, then laid him out across the bed of the pickup. I scrambled up into it, Chigger following close behind. It wasn't so easy to see Rob's face in the dark, but there was still enough glow from the moon—not to mention the many fires all around us—for me to make out the fact that, as Chick had promised, he was still breathing, deeply and regularly. The wound on his head had stopped bleeding, and didn't look anywhere as serious as it had back in the barn. There it had looked like a hole. Now I could see that it was merely a gash, barely an inch wide.

Which was lucky for Mrs. Henderson. Because if she'd given my boyfriend brain damage, that would have been the end of her.

"It's okay," I said to Rob, brushing some of his dark hair from his forehead, and carefully kissing the place on his face that was the least smeared with blood. "I'm here now. Everything's going to be all right."

At least that's what I believed then. That was right before I heard the deep rumble in Chigger's throat, and looked up to see a wild man standing beside the pickup, his arms raised, and his face hidden by all his long, straggly hair.

Okay, okay. That's just what it looked like at first. I realize there's no such thing as wild men, or Sasquatch, or Bigfoot or whatever. But seriously, for a minute, that's what I thought this guy was. I mean, he was completely covered in snow, and standing there with his arms out like that, what was I supposed to think? I screamed my head off.

I think Chigger would have gone for the guy's throat if he hadn't waved the hands he had extended toward me and cried, "Jessica! It's me! Dr. Krantz." I grabbed hold of Chigger's thick leather collar at the last possible minute and kept him from leaping from the cab bed to Cyrus Krantz's neck.

"Jeez!" I said, sinking back onto my heels in relief. "Dr. Krantz, what is wrong with you? Don't you know better than to sneak up on people like that?"

Dr. Krantz flipped back his enormous, fur-trimmed hood and blinked at me through the fogged-up lenses of his glasses.

"Jessica, are you all right?" he wanted to know. "I was so worried! When these animals on the snowmobiles showed up, I thought I'd lost you for sure—"

"Take it easy, Doc," I said. "The guys on the snowmobiles are on our side. What are you doing here, anyway? I thought I told you to go home."

"Jessica," Dr. Krantz said, severely. "You can't honestly think I would leave you out here in the middle of nowhere, can you? Your welfare is extremely important to me, Jessica. To the whole Bureau, in fact."

"Uh, yeah, Dr. Krantz," I said. "And that's why you're out here on your own. Because the Bureau was so concerned for my welfare, they sent out backup right away."

Dr. Krantz pulled a cell phone from his pocket. "I tried to call for help," he explained, sheepishly, "but there must not be any relay centers this far into the woods. I can't get a signal."

"Huh," I said. "That'll make Jim Henderson happy. He's all against contact with the outside world, you know. It infects the youth with liberal ideas."

"This Henderson is an extremely unsavory character, Jessica," Dr. Krantz said. "I can't understand why you felt compelled to take him and his lot on all by yourself. You could have come to us, you know. We would gladly have helped."

"Well," I said. I didn't mention that I hadn't been too impressed by the way Dr. Krantz and his fellow law enforcement officers had handled the True Americans so far. "What's done is done. Look, Doc, I gotta get Rob to a hospital. Do you think you could help me carry him to your car? I know he's heavy, but I'm stronger than I look, and maybe between the two of us—"

But Dr. Krantz was already shaking his head.

"Oh," he said. "But I didn't drive out here, Jessica. It would be quite impossible to get an automobile way out here. The way is virtually impassable thanks to the snow, and besides, there aren't really any proper roadways to speak of. I suppose that is part of the allure of places like these for folks like Jim Henderson—"

"Wait a minute," I said. "If you didn't drive, how did you follow us out here?"

Dr. Krantz, for the first time since I'd met him, actually looked a little embarrassed.

"Well, you see, I followed you in my car as far as that extraordinary little bar you went to. Chick's, I believe it is called? And then when I saw the two of you—you and Mr. Wilkins—leave by snowmobile, why, I got my skis out of the trunk and followed your tracks."

I stared at him. "Your *what?*"

"My skis." Dr. Krantz cleared his throat. "Cross-country skiing is one of the finest forms of cardio-vascular exercise, so I always keep my skis with me in the winter months, because you never know when an opportunity might arise to—"

"You're telling me," I interrupted, "that you skied all the way here. You. Cyrus Krantz. Skied here."

"Well," Dr. Krantz said. "Yes. It wasn't far, really. Only twenty miles or so, which is nothing to a well-conditioned skier, which I happen to be. And really, I don't think it at all as extraordinary as you're making it out to be. Skiing is a perfectly viable form of exercise—"

When the shots rang out, that's what we were doing. Talking about skiing. Cross-country skiing, to be exact, and its viability as a form of cardiovascular exercise. One minute I was sitting there next to Rob, listening to Dr. Krantz, a guy that, it had to be admitted, up until then I really hadn't liked too well.

And the next, I was talking to air, because one of the bullets the True Americans sent flying in my direction pierced Dr. Krantz, and sent him flying.

CHAPTER 16

It was my fault, really. My fault because I'd known people were shooting off guns, and I hadn't mentioned anything to Dr. Krantz like, "Oh, by the way, look out for flying bullets," or, "Hadn't you better stand behind this truck instead of in front of it? It might make better cover."

Nope. I didn't say a word.

And the next thing I knew, the guy was curled up in the snow beside the pickup, screaming his head off.

Well, if you'd been shot, you'd have screamed your head off, too.

I was out of the cab bed and into the snow beside him in a split second.

"Let me see," I said. I could tell the bullet had gotten him in the leg, because he was clutching it with both hands and rocking back and forth, screaming.

Dr. Krantz didn't let me see, though. He just kept rocking and screaming. Meanwhile all these spurts of blood were coming out from between his gloved fingers, and hitting the snow all around us, making these designs that were actually kind of pretty.

But you know, I took first aid in the sixth grade, and when blood is spurting out that hard and that far, it means something is really wrong. Like maybe the bullet had hit an artery or whatever.

So I did the only thing I could do, under the circumstances. I punched Dr. Krantz in the jaw.

I felt pretty bad about it, but what else could I do? The guy was hysterical. He wouldn't let me look at the wound. He could have bled to death.

After I hit him, though, he kind of fell back in the snow, and I got a good look at the damage the bullet had done. Too good a look, if you ask me. Just as I suspected, the bullet had severed an artery—I can't remember what it's called, but it's that one in the thigh. A pretty big one, too.

Fortunately for Dr. Krantz, however, I was on the case.

"Listen," I said, to him, as he lay in the snow, moaning. "You are in luck. I did my sixth grade science fair project on tourniquets."

For some reason, this did not seem to reassure Dr. Krantz as it should have. He started moaning harder.

"No, really," I told him. I had pulled his coat up, and was undoing the belt to his pants. I was relieved to see he was wearing one. I know I sure wasn't. Though I could have used one of the laces from my Timberlands in a pinch.

"My best thing," I told him, "was tourniquets made from found objects. You know, like if you were out camping, and a big stick went through you, or whatever. You know. Maybe you wouldn't have a first aid kit with you." I ducked, and looked under the pickup. As I'd hoped, the snow wasn't so deep beneath it. I was able to find a good-sized rock . . . not too big, but not too small, either. Artery sized. I tried to get the dirt off it as best I could.

"The major thing you have to worry about," I assured Dr. Krantz—it's important that you talk to a victim of a major injury like this one, in order to keep him from slipping into shock—"isn't secondary infection so much as blood loss. So I know this rock looks dirty, but—" I jammed the rock into the wound in Dr. Krantz's leg. The blood stopped spurting almost right away. "—it's performing a vital function. You know. Keeping your blood in."

I took Dr. Krantz's belt, and looped the other end through the belt buckle, then pulled until the belt buckle wedged the rock deeper into the wound. I wasn't too thrilled about having to do this, but it didn't help that Dr. Krantz screamed so loud. I mean, I felt bad enough. Besides, all the screaming was making Chigger, still in the cab bed with Rob, whine nervously.

"There," I said to Dr. Krantz. "That will keep the rock in place. Now we just need to find a stick, so we can twist the belt, and cut off the circulation—"

"No," Dr. Krantz said, in what sounded more like his normal voice—although it was still ragged with pain. "No stick. For the love of God, no stick."

I looked critically down at my handiwork.

"I don't know," I said. "I mean, we may not be able to save the leg, Dr. Krantz. But at least you won't bleed to death."

"No stick," Dr. Krantz gasped. "I'm begging you."

I didn't like it, but I didn't see what else I could do. Fortunately at that moment, Chick sped up to us, Seth clinging tightly to his waist.

"What the hell happened?" Chick was down off his snowmobile and into the snow beside us in a flash. For a big man, he could move like the wind when he needed to. "Christ, I leave you alone for a second, and—"

"Somebody shot him," I said, looking down at Dr. Krantz's leg, which, truth be told, looked a lot like a raw hamburger. "He won't let me use a stick."

"No stick," Dr. Krantz hissed, through gritted teeth.

Chick was examining my field tourniquet with interest. "For torsion, you mean?" When I nodded, he said, "I don't think you need it. Looks like you've got the bleeding stopped for now. Listen, though, we don't have much time. You gotta get this guy out of here. Wilkins, too. And the little guy." He nodded his head at Seth, who was looking owlishly down at the crazy pattern of blood in the snow, as if it were the worst thing he had ever seen. As if what had happened to his own hand was just, you know, incidental.

"I know," I said. "But how am I going to do that? Dr. Krantz can't drive a snowmobile. Not in his condition. And Rob'd never stay on one. . . ."

"That's why—" Chick stood up, and started for the front of the pickup. "—you gotta take the truck."

I looked skeptically at the ancient vehicle. "I don't even know if it runs," I said. "And even if it does, I don't know where we'd find the keys."

"Don't need keys," Chick said, opening the driver's door, then ducking beneath the dash, "when Chick is on the case."

I looked over my shoulder. Up the hill from us, the flames from the barn now seemed to be reaching almost to the moon. Thick black smoke trailed into the sky, blocking out the cold twinkle of the Milky Way. True Americans were still running around, shooting off guns. I could dimly make out the small figure of Jim Henderson waving his arms at his brethren. He seemed to be encouraging them to fight harder.

Behind me, the pickup suddenly sputtered to life.

"There ya go," Chick said, with a chuckle. He came out

from beneath the dash and blew on his fingertips before slipping his gloves back on. "Oh, yeah," he said. "I still got the touch."

I stared at him, as wide-eyed as poor Seth.

"Wait a minute," I said. "You want me to *drive* these guys out of here?"

"That's the general idea," Chick said, not looking very perturbed.

"But there's no road!" I burst out. "You told me over and over, there's no road to this place."

"Well," Chick said, reaching up to stroke his beard. "No, you got that right. There ain't no road, exactly."

"So just how—" I realized Seth, along with Dr. Krantz, was listening to us with a great deal of interest. I reached out, grabbed Chick by the arm, and started walking him away from the truck, lowering my voice as I continued. "—am I supposed to get them back to town, if there's no road?"

It was at that exact moment that something in the barn blew up. I don't know what it was exactly, but I had a feeling it was that muni supply Chick had been talking about. Suddenly, tiny bits of metal and wood were raining down on us.

Chick let out a stream of very colorful expletives that I was just barely able to hear above all the explosions. Then he darted around to the pickup and hauled a protesting Dr. Krantz to his one good foot.

"Sorry, girlie," Chick yelled at me, as he dragged Dr. Krantz around the truck and started stuffing him into the passenger seat. "But you gotta get these folks outta here before all hell breaks loose."

"*Before?*" I couldn't believe any of this was happening. "Um, correct me if I'm wrong, but from the looks of things, I think it already has."

"What?" Chick screamed at me, as the sky was lit a brilliant orange and red.

"Hell," I yelled back. "I think we're already in it!"

"Aw, this is nothing." Chick slammed the door on Dr. Krantz, then hurried around to make sure Rob was secure in the cab bed. "Kid," he yelled at Seth. "Get in here and make sure this guy don't slide around too much. And shield him from that crap flying around, would ya?"

Seth, white-faced but resolute, did as Chick asked without a single question. He climbed into the back of the pickup and knelt down beside Rob . . . after giving Chigger a few wary looks, that is.

Then, taking me by the elbow, Chick pointed down the hill, into the thick black copse of trees that separated Jim Henderson's property from the county road far, far below.

"You just head straight down," he yelled, as, up by the ranch house, what I could have sworn was machine-gun fire broke out. "So long as you're going down, you're headed for the road. Understand?"

I nodded miserably. "But, Chick," I couldn't help adding. "The snow—"

"Right," Chick said, with a nod. "It's gonna be more of a slalom than a drive. Just remember, if you get into trouble, pump the brakes. And try not to hit anything head on."

"Oh," I said, bitterly. "Thanks for the advice. This may not be the right time to bring this up, but you know, I don't even have a driver's license."

"That guy's leg ain't gonna wait," Chick told me. "And Wilkins won't last long out here, neither." Then, perhaps noting my nauseous expression, he slapped me on the shoulder and said, "You'll be fine. Now get going."

Then he hoisted me in the air and set me down behind the wheel, beside a panting, sweating Dr. Krantz.

"Uh," I said, to Dr. Krantz. "How you doin', Doc?"

Dr. Krantz gave a queasy look.

"Oh," he said. "I'm just great."

Chick tapped on the closed window between us. With some effort, I managed to get it rolled down.

"One more thing." Chick reached under his leather jacket and drew out a stubby black object. It took me a minute to realize what it was. When I did, I nearly threw up.

"Oh, no!" I said, putting out both hands, as if to ward him off. "You get that thing away from me.

Chick merely stuck his arm through the open window and deposited the object on my lap.

"Anyone comes near you or the truck," he said, not loudly enough for Dr. K to hear, but loudly enough for me to hear him over the sound of gunfire behind us, "you shoot. Understand?"

"Chick," I said, looking down at the gun, and feeling sicker than ever. It had been one thing when I'd try to blow Kerchief-Head away That had been in the heat of the moment. But this . . .

"Hey," Chick said. "You think Henderson's the only crazy in these woods? Not by a long shot. And he's got a lot of friends. You just drive, you'll be all right. Only shoot if you have to."

I nodded. I didn't dare look at Dr. Krantz.

"Remember," Chick said through the driver's side window. "Pump the brakes."

"Sure," I said, still feeling like throwing up.

Chick smacked the rusted hood, knocking off several inches of snow, and said, "Get going, then."

Fighting back my nausea, I rolled up the window then glanced through the rear windshield and yelled to Seth, "You ready back there?"

Seth, his arms around Rob's shoulders, nodded. Beside him, Chigger sat with his tongue lolling, happy to be going for a ride.

"Ready," Seth yelled.

I looked beside me. Dr. Krantz did not look good. For

469

one thing, he was in a pretty awkward position, with one leg stretched out at an odd angle in front of him. The lenses of his glasses were completely fogged up, he was almost as pale as the snow outside his window. But he was still conscious, and I guess that's all that mattered.

"Ready, Dr. Krantz?" I asked.

He nodded tensely.

"Just do it," he rasped.

So I put my foot on the gas. . . .

CHAPTER 17

Once when we were little, Ruth had a birthday party at the Zoom Floom. The Zoom Floom was located on the same hillside as Paoli Peaks Ski Resort. It was a water slide that only operated in summertime. The way you went down it was, you laid down on this rubber mat, and an attendant pushed you off.

Then, suddenly, you were plummeting down a mountain, with about fifty billion tons of water pushing you even faster downward, and when you opened your mouth to scream, all of that water got into your mouth, and you went around these hairpin curves that seemed like they might kill you, and usually your mat slipped out from under you and you were

skidding down the slide with just your suit on. And the sur-
face of the slide was rough enough to take the skin off your
hipbones, and with every second you were certain you were
to going drown or at least crack your head open, until at last
you plunged into this four-foot-deep pool at the bottom and
came up choking and gasping for air, only to be hit in the
head by your mat a moment or two later.

And then you grabbed your mat and started up the stairs
to go again. You had to. Because it was so freaking fun.

But sliding down the wooded hill from Jim Henderson's
militia compound? Yeah, so not fun.

And if we lived through it—which I doubted we would?
Yeah, so never doing it again.

I realized pretty early on as we plunged straight at the pine
trees that formed a thick wall around the True Americans'
compound that Chick was right about one thing: The plows
certainly hadn't been near Jim Henderson's place. I found the
road pretty quickly—or what passed for a road, apparently, in
the opinion of the True Americans. It was really just a track
between the pine trees, the branches of many of which hung
so low, they brushed against the top of the cab as we went by.

But the snow that lay across the so-called road was thick,
and beneath it seemed to be a real nice layer of ice. As the
truck careened down the hillside path, branches whipping
against it, causing Seth and Chigger, in the back, to duck down
low, it took every ounce of strength I had just to control the

wheel, to keep the front tires from spinning out and sending us—oh, yes—into the deep ravine to my left. A ravine that I was quite sure in summertime made a charming fishing and swimming hole, but which now appeared to me, as I barreled alongside it, without even a token guardrail between it and me, a pit to hell.

All this, of course, was only visible to me thanks to the moonlight, which was fortunately generous. I had the truck's brights on, but in a way that only made things worse, because then I could plainly see every near-catastrophe looming before us. I probably would have been better off just closing my eyes, for all the good my jerking on the wheel and pumping the brakes, as Chick had suggested, seemed to be doing me.

None of this was helped by the fact that all the jolting seemed to have brought Dr. Krantz out from his state of semi-consciousness. He was awake, all right, and hanging on for dear life to the dashboard. There were no seatbelts in the cab—apparently, passenger safety was not of primary concern to the True Americans. Dr. Krantz was being jounced all over the place, and there wasn't a blessed thing I could do about it . . . or about Rob and Seth, in the back, who were receiving the same nice treatment.

I have to admit though that Dr. Krantz wasn't helping very much by grabbing his leg with the tourniquet on it and sucking air in between his teeth every time we passed over a particularly large rock in the road, hidden beneath all that snow. I mean, I know it must have hurt and all, but hello, I was driving. I kept glancing over to make sure the tourniquet was still tight. I had to, since he hadn't let me torque it off.

I was glancing over at Dr. Krantz's leg when I suddenly heard him suck in his breath, and not because we'd gone over a bump. I quickly glanced through the windshield, but could see nothing more horrifying that what we'd already encountered, treacherous drop-offs and looming trees. Then I heard a tap at the back window, and turned my head.

Seth, white-faced and panicked-looking, pointed behind him.

"We got company!" he yelled.

I glanced in the rearview mirror—then realized that, disobeying one of the first rules of driving, I had not thought to adjust my mirrors before I put my foot on the gas. I couldn't see squat out of them, thanks to their having been tilted for a much taller person than me.

Reaching up, I grasped the rearview mirror and tried to adjust it so that I could see what was behind us, while at the same time navigating a ten-foot dip in the road that sent all of us airborne for a second or two. . . .

And then I saw it. Two True Americans barreling after us in a four by four. A pretty new one, too, if you asked me. And these guys seemed to know what they were doing. They were gaining on us already, and I hadn't even noticed their headlights, which meant they couldn't have been behind us for all that long.

I did the only thing I could, under the circumstances. I floored it.

This strategy, apparently, was not one Dr. Krantz seemed prepared to fully embrace.

"For God's sake, Jessica," he said, speaking for the first time since being put in the cab. "You're going to kill us all."

"Yeah," I said, keeping my eyes on the road. "Well, what do you think these guys are going to do to us if they catch us?"

"There's another way," Dr. Krantz said. "Give me that gun."

I nearly cracked up laughing at that one. "No freaking way."

"Jessica." Dr. Krantz sounded mad. "There's no alternative."

"You are not," I said, "starting a shootout with those guys with my boyfriend and Seth in the back there, completely unprotected. Sorry."

Dr. Krantz shook his head. "Jessica, I assure you. I am an expert marksman."

"Yeah, but I'll bet they aren't." I nodded toward the rearview mirror. "And if they start aiming for you, chances are, they're going to hit me. Or Seth. Or Rob. So you can forget"— We hit a particularly large bump in the road and went flying for a second or two—"about it."

Dr. Krantz, it was clear, wasn't about to forget about it.

Fortunately, however, that last bump sent him into paroxysms of pain, so he was too busy to think about the gun for a little while. . . .

But not too busy to see, as I soon did, the horrifying sight that loomed before us. And that was a large portion of the road that had disappeared.

That's right, disappeared, as if it had never been there. It took me a minute or two to realize that what it was, in fact, was a small wooden bridge that, undoubtedly due to rotting wood, had collapsed under the weight of all that snow. Now there was a six-foot-wide gap between this side of the ravine and the far side . . . the side to medical care for Rob and Dr. Krantz. And to freedom.

"Slow down!" Dr. Krantz screamed. I swear, if his leg closest to me hadn't been all busted up, he would have tried to reach over with it and slam down the brakes himself. "Jessica, don't you see it?"

I saw it all right. But what I saw was our one chance to get away from these clowns.

Which was why I pressed down on that gas pedal for all I was worth.

"Hang on!" I screamed at Seth.

Dr. Krantz threw his arms out to brace himself against the roof of the cab and the dashboard, as the ravine loomed ever closer. "Jessica!" he yelled. "You are insane—"

And then the wheels of the pickup left the ground, and we were flying. Really. Just like in dreams. You know the ones, where you dream you can fly? And while you're in the air, it's totally quiet, and all you can hear is your heartbeat, and you don't even dare breathe because if you do, you might drop down to the ground again, and you don't want that to happen because what you are experiencing is a miracle, the miracle of flight, and you want to make it last as long as you possibly can. . . .

And then, with a crash, we were down again, on the far side of the ravine . . . and still going, faster than ever. Only the jolt of our landing had sent all of our bones grinding together—I know I bit my tongue—not to mention, it seemed to blow the shocks out of the truck. It certainly blew something out, since the truck shimmied all over, then made a pathetic whining sound. . . .

But it kept going. I kept my foot to that gas pedal, and that truck kept on going.

"Oh my God," Dr. Krantz kept saying. "Oh my God, oh my God, oh my God, oh my God. . . ."

Cyrus, I knew, was gone. I dared a glance over my shoulder, as the truck ground up a steep incline on the far side of the ravine we'd jumped.

"You guys okay back there?" I yelled, and was relieved to see Seth's white face, and Chigger's laughing one, right there.

"We lost 'em!" Seth yelled, triumphantly. "Look!"

I looked. And Seth was right. The four by four had tried the same jump we had, but hadn't been able to get up as much speed as we had. Now it lay with its crumpled nose in the creek bed, the two men inside struggling to get out.

Something burst from within me. Suddenly, I was yelling, "Yeehaw!" like a cowboy. I never lifted my foot off the gas, but it was all I could do to stay in my seat behind that wheel. I wanted to jump out and kiss everyone in sight. Even Dr. Krantz. Even Chigger.

And then, without warning, we were bursting through the trees, and sliding onto the main road. Just like that. The moon was shining down hard, reflecting off the snow carpeting the barren fields all around us. After being so deep in the dark woods, all that light was almost blinding . . . blinding and the most beautiful sight I'd ever seen. Even as I was slamming on the brakes and we went sliding across the icy highway, I was smiling happily. We'd made it! We'd really made it!

When the truck finally slid to a halt, I risked a glance at the wooded hill behind us. You couldn't tell, just by looking at it, that it housed a bunch of wacko survivalists. It just looked, you know, like a pretty wooded hill.

Except for the smoke pouring from the top of it out into the moonlit sky. Really. It kind of looked like pictures I'd seen of Mount St. Helens, right before it blew up. Only on a much smaller scale, of course.

I looked around. We were in the middle of nowhere. There wasn't a farmhouse, or even a trailer, to be seen. Certainly nowhere I could make a phone call.

Then I remembered Dr. Krantz's cell phone.

I glanced over at him, but the guy was out. I guess that last burst of speed did him in. I leaned over and pawed around in his coat for a minute, then finally located the phone inside a pocket that also contained a Palm Pilot, a pack of Juicy Fruit, and a lot of used-up Kleenex. I helped myself to a piece of the Juicy Fruit, then opened up the rear window and passed the pack, along with the cell phone, to Seth.

"Here," I said to him, as he took both. "Call your parents to let them know you're all right, and that they can pick you up in five minutes at County Medical. Then call the cops and tell them what's happening up at Jim Henderson's place. If the fire department's going to get up there, they'll need to bring a plow." Then I remembered the blown-out bridge. "And maybe a road crew," I added.

Seth, after stuffing the Juicy Fruit in his mouth, eagerly began to dial. I turned back to face the road. My arms ached from my battle with the steering wheel, and despite the cold, there was a ribbon of sweat running all up and down my chest. But we had made it. We had made it.

Almost.

I committed twenty-seven traffic violations getting Rob and Dr. Krantz to the hospital. I went thirty miles over the speed limit—forty outside of town—went through three stoplights, made an illegal left-hand turn, and went the wrong way down a one-way street. Not that it mattered much. There was practically no one out on the streets, thanks to all the snow. The only time I ran into traffic was outside the Chocolate Moose, where a lot of kids from Ernie Pyle High hang out. It was after eleven, so the Moose was closed, but there were still kids around, necking in their cars. When I blew past them, I laid on the horn, just for the fun of it. I saw a number of startled heads lift up as I flew by I yelled, "Yeehaw," at them, and a couple of irritated jocks yelled, "Grit!" back at me. I guess because of the truck. And maybe because of the yeehaw. And quite possibly because of Chigger.

But you know what? They couldn't have called me something that filled me with more pride.

When I swung around the entrance to the hospital, I saw that I had a choice of two entrances: the one for emergency vehicles only, and the one for general admittance.

Of course I chose the one for the emergency vehicles. I figured I'd come skidding to a halt in front of it, you know, like on *The Dukes of Hazzard*, and all these emergency room personnel would come running out, all concerned about hearing the brakes squeal.

Only it didn't happen quite like that, because I guess most emergency vehicles don't go skidding into that entrance very much, and even though it had been plowed and salted, there was still a lot of ice. So instead of skidding to a halt in front of the emergency room doors, I sort of ended up driving through them.

But hey. All the emergency room personnel *did* come running up, just like I'd thought they would.

Fortunately the emergency room doors were glass, so crashing into them really didn't cause that much damage to my passengers. I mean, once the front wheels hit the emergency room floor and got some traction, the brakes worked, so Seth and Rob were fine. And Dr. Krantz was unconscious anyway, so when his head hit the dashboard, it probably didn't even hurt that much. It was more like a little tap. I know that's how it felt when I was flung against the steering wheel. Fortunately the truck was so old, it didn't have air bags, so we didn't have to deal with *that* embarrassment.

Still, the people in the emergency bay were surprisingly unsympathetic to my predicament. I mean, you would think that after what I'd been through, they'd be a little more understanding, but no. They didn't act at all like the emergency room people on that show on TV.

"Are you crazy?" one nurse in blue scrubs was yelling, as I lifted my head from the steering wheel.

That made me mad. I mean, all I'd done is gotten a little glass on the floor. It wasn't like I'd run over anybody.

"Hey," I said. "There's a guy in the back of this truck with a head injury, and this guy next to me is about to lose a leg. Get a couple gurneys, then get off my back."

That shut her up, let me tell you. In seconds, it seemed, they'd gotten Dr. Krantz out of the cab, then helped me back the truck up so they could get outside, and help move Rob. Seth was able to climb down from the cab bed unaided, but Chigger didn't seem too pleased to see his rescuers. He did a lot of growling and snapping until I told him to knock it off. Then, ever hopeful of more mashed potatoes, he leapt from the back of the truck and followed me inside, as I trailed after the gurney Rob was on.

"Is he going to be all right?" I kept asking all the people who were working on him. But they wouldn't say. They were too busy barking off his vital signs and writing them down on charts. The weirdest part was when they unwrapped him, and I saw what the yellow thing that had been around him the whole time was.

Oh, just the "Don't Tread On Me" flag from the True Americans' meeting house.

The one with the giant hole in it, from where I'd accidentally blasted it with a shotgun.

It was as I was standing there staring at this that I heard a voice call my name. I looked around, and saw that Dr. Krantz, who was being worked on over on the next gurney, had regained consciousness. He gestured for me to come close. I edged in between all the doctors and nurses who were hovering around him and leaned down so that he could whisper to me.

"Jessica," he hissed. "Are you all right?"

"Oh, sure," I said, surprised. "I'm fine."

"And Mr. Wilkins?"

"I don't know," I said, throwing a glance over my shoulder. I couldn't see Rob, for all the doctors and nurses crowded around him. "I think he's going to be okay."

"And Seth?"

"He's fine," I said. "Really, Dr. Krantz, we're okay. You just concentrate on getting better, okay?"

But Dr. Krantz wasn't through. He had something else to say to me, something that seemed of vital importance for him to get off his chest. He reached out and grabbed the front of my coat, and pulled me closer.

"Jessica," he rasped, close to my ear. I had a feeling I knew what he was going to say, so I tried to head him off at the pass.

"Dr. Krantz," I said. "Don't worry about thanking me. Really, it's all right. I'd have done the same for anybody. I was happy to do it."

But Dr. Krantz still wouldn't let me go. If anything, his grip on the front of my coat tightened.

"Jessica," he breathed, again. I leaned even closer, since he seemed to be having trouble making himself heard.

"Yes, Dr. Krantz?" I said.

"You," he rasped, "are the worst driver I have ever seen."

CHAPTER 18

The county hospital saw a lot of action that night. And that's not even counting having a pickup ram through its ambulance-bay doors.

It also admitted forty-eight new patients, seven of them in critical condition. Fortunately none of the people listed as critical were friends of mine. No, it looked as if most of the damage that was done that night was done to the True Americans. As I sat in the waiting room—they wouldn't let me in to see Rob once he'd been admitted, because I wasn't family—I saw each person as they were wheeled in.

Of course, that didn't start happening for a while, because it took a pretty long time for the fire engines and ambulances and police to get out to Jim Henderson's place. In fact, merely my explanation of *how* to get out there took a while. The police interviewed me for about forty minutes before the first squad car even started off in the direction of the True Americans' compound.

And I'm not too sure they believed what I told them. That might be one of the reasons they didn't go tearing off right away. I mean, a militia group, under attack by a ragtag band of bikers and truck drivers? Fortunately at some point, Dr. Krantz regained consciousness, and they were able to go in and confirm everything I'd said. He must have been pretty persuasive, too, because when I saw the sheriff leaving the examination room Dr. Krantz had been shoved into while the hospital staff scrambled to find a surgeon skilled enough to sew his leg back together, he looked pretty grim.

For a short while, the only person in the emergency waiting room with me was Seth. Well, Seth and Chigger. The hospital people weren't too happy about having a dog in their waiting room, but when I explained that I couldn't leave Chigger outside in the truck, as he would freeze, seeing as how the truck had no heat—nor much of a windshield left—they relented. And really, once I'd gotten him a few packs of peanut-butter Ritz crackers from the snack machine, Chigger was fine. He curled up on two of the plastic chairs and went right to sleep, worn out from his long ride and all that barking.

Seth's reunion with his parents, which came about ten

minutes after our arrival, was touching in the extreme. The Blumenthals wept with happiness over seeing their son alive and in one piece. When they heard about my part in bringing Seth home, they pulled me into their group hug, which was fun, even though I assured them that I had, in fact, played only a very small role in the liberation of their son from the militia group that had kidnapped him.

But when Seth, while explaining precisely what the True Americans were all about, showed his parents the burn on his hand, which I had sort of forgotten about, they freaked out, and Seth got whisked off to the burn unit to have the wound treated.

So then it was just Chigger and me in the waiting room.

Finally, though, my parents, along with Douglas and Mike and Claire (because the two of them are attached at the hip) showed up, and we had our own tearful reunion. Well, at least, my mom cried. No one else did, really. And my mom only cried because she was so relieved that Great-aunt Rose had been wrong: Apparently the whole time I'd been gone, she'd been telling everyone that I had probably run off to Vegas to find work as a blackjack dealer. She had seen a show about teenage runaway blackjack dealers on *Oprah*.

Great-aunt Rose, my dad said, was leaving on the first bus out of town in the morning, whether or not she was ready to go.

It was a little while after this that Mrs. Wilkins showed

up. I had called her right after I called my parents. But Mrs. Wilkins, being family, was let into the room where they were keeping Rob, so it wasn't like we had a chance to visit or anything. She only came out once, and that was to tell me that the doctor had said Rob was going to be all right. He had a concussion, but the doctor didn't think he'd have to stay in the hospital for more than a day or two, so long as he regained consciousness by morning. My dad told Mrs. Wilkins not to worry about her shifts at the restaurant while Rob was convalescing, so that was all right.

One thing my dad didn't ask—no one in my family did— was what Rob and I had been doing, saving Seth Blumenthal and battling the True Americans together. Mike and Claire and Douglas already knew, of course, but it didn't seem to occur to my parents to ask. Thank God.

All they wanted to know was was I all right, and would I come home now.

I said I was fine. Only I couldn't come home. Not, I told them, until I'd heard that Dr. Krantz was safely out of surgery.

If they thought this was weird, they didn't say so. They just nodded and went to get coffee from the machine over by the cafeteria, which, this late at night, was unfortunately closed. I was famished on account of having had nothing to eat since lunch, so we raided the snack machines some more. I had a pretty good dinner of Hostess apple pie and Fritos, some of which Chigger helped me eat. Much to my surprise, no one in my family seemed really to like Chigger, who was quite charming to all of them, sniffing each one carefully in case he or she had food hidden somewhere. My mom looked a little taken aback when I asked if I could keep Chigger. But she softened when I explained that the police had told me any pets found on seized property would be impounded and probably put down.

Besides, no one could deny Chigger made a very good guard dog. Even the cops had given him a pretty wide berth while they were questioning me.

And then, just as I'd suspected, about an hour after this, the first of the casualties from the battle of the Grits versus the True Americans began to flood the ER. I'm not sure, but I think it was around then that my parents began to suspect that my real motivation for staying at the hospital wasn't to find out whether or not Dr. Krantz's surgery had been successful. No, it was because I wanted to be there when they brought in Jim Henderson. I wanted to be there really, really bad.

Not because I had anything to say to him. What can one say to someone like him? He is never going to realize that we were right and he was wrong. People like Jim Henderson are incapable of changing their ways. They are going to believe in their half-assed opinions until the day they die, and nothing and no one is ever going to convince them that those beliefs might be mistaken.

No, I wanted to see Jim Henderson because I wanted to

make sure they'd gotten him. That's all. I wanted to make sure that guy didn't slip away, didn't run off deeper into the hills to live in a cave, or escape to Canada. I wanted that guy in prison, where he belonged.

Or dead. Dead wouldn't have been too bad, either. Although I didn't think Jim Henderson could really ever be dead enough for me. At least in prison, I'd know he was suffering. Death seemed like too good a punishment for the likes of him.

And I wouldn't have been too sad to see Mrs. Henderson there in the morgue with him.

But though they brought in plenty of people I recognized as True Americans—all men, including the two from the four by four that had been chasing us, and Red Plaid Jacket, suffering from a bullet wound to the thigh—none of them were Jim Henderson. This was pretty disappointing, but certainly not unexpected. Of course a guy like him would run at the first sign of trouble. He wouldn't get far, though. Not with me on the case. I would make it my personal psychic business to know where he was and what he was doing at all times. That way I could alert the authorities, who would hopefully catch him when he least expected it. Like when he was sleeping, or maybe making more baby True Americans. Some time when he wasn't likely to be able to reach for a gun.

It was as I was examining the faces of the people being wheeled in, searching for Jim Henderson, that I saw one that looked more than a little familiar. I was up and out of my plastic seat in no time, and hurrying to the side of the gurney he was being wheeled in on.

"Chick," I cried, reaching for his arm, which had already been attached to an IV bottle. "Are you okay? What happened?"

Chick smiled wanly up at me.

"Hey, there, little lady," he said. "Glad to see you made it. Wilkins and the kid all right? How about the professor?"

"They're all fine," I said. "Or going to be fine, anyway. But what about you? What happened?"

"Aw." Chick looked irritably at the nurse who was trying to get a thermometer into his mouth. "Stun grenade went off early." He lifted his hands. I gasped at how raw and bloody they were.

"Chick!" I cried. "I'm so sorry!"

"Ah," he said, sheepishly. "It was my fault. I shoulda just thrown the stupid thing. But then I saw the guy had got all the women and children lined up in front of him, and I hesitated—"

"Jim Henderson, you mean?"

"Yeah," Chick said. "Bastard was using his wives and kids as the old human shield."

"Wait." I stared down at him. *"Wives?"*

"Well, sure," Chick said. "Guy like Jim Henderson's gonna keep God's chosen race going, he can't afford to be monogamous. Lady," he said, to the nurse with the thermometer,

"I ain't got no fever. What I got is burnt-up hands."

The nurse glared at both Chick and me.

"No visitors," she said, pointing imperiously at the plastic chairs, "in the ER. Get back to your seat. And keep that dog out of the trash cans!"

I looked and saw that Chigger had his head buried in the ambulance-bay trash can.

"But what about him?" I asked Chick, as the nurse, disgusted with me, began physically to push me from the crowded ER. "Jim Henderson? Did they catch him?"

"Don't know, honey," Chick called. "Place was a zoo by the time they got me out of there, cops and firemen and what all—"

"And stay out," the nurse said, as she closed the ER doors firmly on me.

I walked disconsolately over to Chigger and pulled on his leather studded collar, eventually managing to drag him away from the garbage . . . though I had to pull his nose out of a Dorito bag. "Bad dog," I said, mostly for my parents' benefit, so they could see what an excellent and responsible pet owner I was going to make.

It was as I was doing this that I heard my name called softly from behind me. I turned around, and there was Dr. Thompkins, in a blood-smeared operating gown.

"Oh," I said, holding onto Chigger's collar. The smell of the blood was making him mental. I swear, it was enough to make me think the True Americans never fed their dogs. "Hey."

My parents, seeing their neighbor from across the street, got up and came over, as well.

"I just operated," Dr. Thompkins said to me, "on the leg of a man who told me he had you to thank for keeping him from bleeding to death."

"Oh," I said, brightening. "Dr. Krantz. Is he all right?"

"He's fine," Dr. Thompkins said. "I was able to save the leg. That was certainly one of the more . . . *interesting* tourniquets I've seen applied."

"Yeah," I said, humbly. "Well, I did get an A. In sixth grade first aid."

"Yes," Dr. Thompkins said. "I imagine you did. Well, in any case, Dr. Krantz is going to be fine. He also explained to me how he happened to have been shot."

"Oh," I said, not certain where Tasha's dad was going with this part. Like if he was going to yell at me for being irresponsible or something. Had someone told him it was me who'd rammed a pickup through the ambulance-bay doors? I wasn't sure. "Well," I said, lamely. "You know."

Dr. Thompkins did a surprising thing. He stuck his right hand out toward me.

"I'd like to thank you, Jessica," he said, "for your part in attempting to bring my son's killers to justice."

"Oh." I was a little shocked. Was that what I had done? I

guess it was, sort of. Too bad I hadn't been able to catch the guy who'd been ultimately responsible. . . .

"No problem, Dr. Thompkins," I said, and slipped my hand into Nate's father's.

Just as I did so, yet another ambulance came wailing up to the doors I'd smashed. The doors to the back of the vehicle were flung open, and the paramedics wheeled out a man who had been severely injured. In fact, he was practically holding his intestines in place with one hand. He was still conscious, however. Conscious and looking all around him with wild, crazy, blue eyes.

"Dr. Thompkins," one of the paramedics cried. "This one's bad. BP a hundred over sixty, pulse—"

Jim Henderson. It was Jim Henderson on that gurney, with his guts hanging out.

So they'd got him. They'd got him after all.

"All right," Dr. Thompkins said, looking over the chart the paramedics handed to him. "Let's get him upstairs to surgery. Now."

A pair of ER nurses took over from the paramedics, and began wheeling Jim Henderson down the hall, toward the elevator. Dr. Thompkins followed them, and I followed Dr. Thompkins. Chigger followed me.

"Hey, Mr. Henderson," I said, when the nurses pulled the gurney to a halt outside the elevator doors.

Jim Henderson turned his head to look at me. For once,

his crazy-eyed gaze focused enough to recognize me. I know he did, because I saw fear . . . yes, fear . . . in those otherwise vacant orbs of blue.

"Get that dog," one of the nurses said, "away from here. He'll infect the patient."

"Jessica," Dr. Thompkins said. The elevator doors opened. "I'll finish talking to you later. But right now, I have to operate on this man."

"You hear that, Mr. Henderson?" I asked the man on the gurney. "Dr. Thompkins here is going to operate on you. Do you know who Dr. Thompkins is, Mr. Henderson?"

Henderson couldn't reply because he had an oxygen mask over his mouth. But that was okay. I didn't need an answer from him anyway.

"Dr. Thompkins," I said, "is the father of that boy you left dead in that cornfield."

Dr. Thompkins, with a startled look down at his patient, took an involuntary step backward.

"Yes," I said to Dr. Thompkins. "That's right. This is the man who killed your son. Or at least ordered someone else to do it."

Dr. Thompkins stared down at Jim Henderson, who, it had to be admitted, looked pretty pathetic, with his guts out all over the place like that.

"I can't operate on this man," Dr. Thompkins said, his horror-stricken gaze never leaving the man on the gurney.

"Dr. Thompkins?" One of the nurses slipped into the elevator and lifted a phone from a panel in there. "You want me to page Dr. Levine?"

"Not to mention," I said, "this guy's also the one who kidnapped Seth Blumenthal, burned down the synagogue, and knocked over all the headstones in the Jewish cemetery."

The nurse hesitated. Dr. Thompkins continued to stare down at Jim Henderson, disgust mingling with disbelief on his face.

"How about Dr. Takahashi?" the other ER nurse suggested. "Isn't he on duty tonight?"

"Hmmm," I said. "Mr. Henderson doesn't like immigrants very much either. Right, Mr. Henderson?" I bent down so that my face was very close to his. "Gosh, this must be very upsetting to you. Either a black guy, a Jewish guy, or an immigrant is going to end up operating on you. Better hope all those things you've been saying about them are wrong. Well, okay, buh-bye, now."

I waved as the two nurses, along with a dazed Dr. Thompkins, stepped onto the elevator with Jim Henderson. The last thing I saw of him, he was staring at me with those wide, crazy eyes. I can't be sure, but I really do think he was reevaluating his whole belief system.

CHAPTER 19

Jim Henderson didn't die. Not on the operating table, anyway.

Drs. Levine and Takahashi operated on him, in the end. Dr. Thompkins excused himself. Which was pretty noble of him, actually. I mean, if it had been me, I don't know. I think I would have gone ahead. And let the scalpel slip at a crucial moment.

But Jim Henderson lived through his surgery. He owed his life to two people who came from religious and ethnic groups he'd been teaching his followers to hate. I kind of wondered how he felt about that, but not enough actually to ask him. I had way more important things to worry about.

Primarily, Rob.

It wasn't until the next day that Rob finally woke up. I was sitting right there when he did it. I did go home right after the thing with Jim Henderson—actually, hospital security came along and threw me out, which is a terrible way, if you think about it, to treat a hero. But one of the ER nurses who'd escorted Jim Henderson to surgery apparently finked me out, saying I'd "threatened" a patient.

Which of course I had. But if you ask me, he fully deserved it.

Anyway, I went home with my parents and brothers and Claire, and got a few hours of sleep. I showered and changed and ate and walked Chigger and went a few rounds with my parents over him. They were not too thrilled to have a trained attack dog living under our roof, but after I explained to them that the cops would have sent him to the pound, and that the True Americans were not the world's best pet owners, as far as I can see, they came around. They weren't exactly thrilled with the way Chigger had chewed through an antique rug while we'd all been asleep, but after three or four bowls of Dog Chow, he was fine, so I don't see what the problem is. He was just *hungry*.

It hadn't been much of a surprise to me that on top of everything else, Jim Henderson and his followers turned out to be lousy pet owners.

Anyway, I was sitting there flipping through a copy of the local paper, which mentioned nothing about me and the important role I'd played in the capture of the dangerous and deranged leader of the largest militia group in the southern half of the state, when Rob started to come round. I put the paper down and ran for his mom, who'd also been waiting for him to wake up. She'd been down the hall getting coffee when he finally opened his eyes. She and I both hurried back to his room. . . .

But at the door, a voice from across the hall called weakly to me. When I turned, I saw Dr. Krantz lying in the bed of the room across from Rob's. Gathered around his bed were a number of people I recognized, including Special Agents Smith and Johnson, who used to be assigned to my case. Until Dr. Krantz fired them from it, that is. It was good to see they could all let bygones be bygones and get along.

"Well, well, well," I said, strolling into the crowded room. "What's this? A debriefing?" Dr. Krantz laughed. It was a startling sound. I wasn't used to hearing him laugh. "Jessica," he said. "I'm glad to see you. There are a couple of people here I want you to meet."

And then Dr. Krantz, whose leg was in a long sling, with spikes coming out of a metal thing around the patched-up wound where I'd stuffed my rock, pointed to various people crowded into the small room, and made introductions. One of the people was his wife (she looked *exactly* like him, except that she had hair). Another was a little old lady called Mrs. Pierce, whose name suited her, since she had very piercing eyes, as blue as the baby bootie she was industriously knitting. The last was a kid about my age, a boy named Malcolm. And of course I already knew Special Agents Johnson and Smith.

"That was quite the invasion of the True Americans' Compound you launched, Jessica," Special Agent Johnson said.

"Thanks," I said, modestly.

"Jessica's always impressed us," Special Agent Smith said, "with her communication skills. She seems to have a real flair for rallying people to her cause . . . whatever cause that happens to be."

"I couldn't have done it," I said, humbly, "without the help of many, many Grits."

There was an awkward silence after this, probably on account of no one in the room knowing what a Grit was, except for me.

"You'll be happy to know," Dr. Krantz said, "that Seth is going to be fine. The burn should heal without leaving a scar."

"Cool," I said. I wondered what was happening in Rob's room. He and his mom had probably had a nice little reunion by now. When was my turn?

"And the police officer," Dr. Krantz went on, "who was shot should be fine. As should all of your, um, friends. Particularly Mr. Chicken."

"Chick," I corrected him. "But that's great, too."

There was another silence. Malcolm, who was sitting over on the windowsill, playing with a Gameboy, looked up from it briefly, and said, "Jeez, go on. Ask her, already."

Dr. Krantz cleared his throat uncomfortably. Special Agents Johnson and Smith exchanged nervous glances.

"Ask me what?" I knew, though. I already knew.

"Jessica," Special Agent Smith said. "We all seem to have gotten off on the wrong foot with you. I know how you feel about coming to work for us, but I just want you to know, it won't be like it was with . . . well, the first time. Dr. Krantz has been doing groundbreaking work with . . . people like yourself. Why, Mrs. Pierce and Malcolm here are part of his team."

Mrs. Pierce smiled at me kindly above the baby bootie. "That's right, dear," she said.

"It just really seems to me," Special Agent Smith said, reaching up to fiddle with her pearl earring, "that you would enjoy the work, Jessica. Especially considering your feelings about Mr. Henderson. Those are the kind of people Dr. Krantz and his team are after, you know. People like Jim Henderson."

I glanced at Dr. Krantz. He looked a lot less intimidating in his hospital gown than he did in his usual garb, a suit and tie.

"It's true, Jessica," he said. "Someone with powers like yours could really be a boon to our team. And we wouldn't require anything from you but a few hours a week of your time."

I eyed him warily. "Really? I wouldn't have to go live in Washington, or anything?"

"Not at all," Dr. Krantz said.

"And I could keep going to school?"

"Of course," Dr. Krantz said.

"And you'd keep it out of the press?" I asked. "I mean, you'd make sure it was a secret?"

"Jessica," Dr. Krantz said. "You saved my life. I owe you that much, at least."

I looked at Malcolm. He was absorbed in his video game, but as if he sensed my gaze on him, he looked up.

"You work for him?" I asked, gruffly. "You like it?"

Malcolm shrugged. "'s okay," he said. Then he turned back to his game. But I could tell by the way color was spreading over his cheeks that working for Dr. Krantz was more than just okay. It was a chance for this otherwise average-looking kid to make a difference. He'd wanted to seem cool about it in front of the others, but you could totally tell: This kid was way psyched about his job.

"How about you?" I asked Mrs. Pierce.

"Oh, my dear," the old lady said, with a beatific smile. "Helping to put away scumbags like that jerk Henderson is what I live for."

After this surprising remark, she turned back to the baby bootie.

Well.

I looked at Dr. Krantz. "Tell you what," I said. "I'll think about it, okay?"

"Fine," Dr. Krantz said, with a smile. "You do that."

I told him I hoped he felt better soon, said good-bye to the others, and drifted back across the hall.

So? Stranger things have happened than me joining an elite team of psychic crime-fighters, you know.

And it *had* felt pretty good when I'd seen them wheeling Jim Henderson in on that gurney. . . .

Inside Rob's room, Mrs. Wilkins had been joined by her brothers and Just-Call-Me-Gary.

"Oh," Rob's mom said, as I came in. "Here she is!"

Rob, his hair looking very dark against the whiteness of the bandage around his head, and the pillows behind his back, smiled at me wanly. It was the most beautiful smile I had ever seen. Instantly, all thoughts of Dr. Krantz and the Federal Bureau of Investigation left my head.

"Hi," I said, moving toward the bed. I had, for the occasion, donned a skirt. It was no velvet evening gown, but judging by the appreciative way his gray-eyed gaze roved over me, he sure thought it was.

"Well," Rob's uncle said. "What say we check out this cafeteria I've heard so much about, eh, Mary?"

Mrs. Wilkins said, "Oh, yes, let's." Then she and her brothers and Just-Call-Me-Gary left the room.

Hey, it wasn't subtle. But it worked. Rob and I were alone. Finally.

It was a little while later that I lifted my head from his shoulder, where I'd been resting it after having become exhausted from so much passionate kissing, and said, "Rob, I have to tell you something."

"I didn't ask you," he said, "because I didn't want you getting in trouble with your parents."

I looked at him like he was nuts. For a minute, I thought maybe he was. You know, that Mrs. Henderson had scrambled his brains with that mashed-potato bowl. "What are you talking about?"

"Randy's wedding," Rob said. "It's on Christmas Eve. No way your parents are going to let you go out on Christmas Eve. So you'd just have ended up lying to them, and getting in trouble, and I don't want that."

I blinked a few times. So *that* was why he hadn't asked me? Because he'd thought my parents wouldn't have let me go in the first place?

Happiness washed over me. But still, he could have just said so, rather than let me think he had some other girl in mind he wanted to take instead. . . .

I didn't let my relief show, however.

"Rob," I said. "Get over yourself. That's not what I was going to say."

He looked surprised. "It wasn't? Then what?"

I shook my head. "Besides," I said. "My parents would so totally let me go out on Christmas Eve. We don't do anything on Christmas Eve. It's Christmas Day that we do church and present opening and a big meal and everything."

"Fine," Rob said. "But don't tell me that you'd tell them the truth. About being with me, I mean. Admit it, Mastriani. You're ashamed of me. Because I'm a Grit."

"That is *not* true," I said. "*You're* the one who's ashamed of me! Because I'm a Townie. And still in high school."

"I will admit," Rob said, "that the fact that you're still in high school kind of sucks. I mean, it *is* a little weird for a guy my age to be going out with a sixteen-year-old."

I looked down at him disgustedly. "You're only two years older than me, nimrod."

"Whatever," Rob said. "Look. Do we have to talk about this now? Because in case you didn't notice, I've suffered a head injury, and calling me a nimrod is not making me feel any better."

"Well," I said, chewing on my lower lip. "What I'm about to say probably isn't going to make you feel better."

"What?" Rob said, looking wary.

"Your dad." I figured it was better if I just blurted it all out. "I saw a picture of him in your mom's room, and I know where he is."

Rob regarded me calmly. He did not even drop his hands from my arms, which he'd reached up to massage.

"Oh," was all he said.

"I didn't mean to pry," I said, quickly. "Really. I mean, I totally didn't do it on purpose. It's just, like I said, I saw his picture, and that night I dreamed about where he is. And I will totally tell you, if you want to know. But if you don't, that's fine, too, I will never say another word about it."

"Mastriani," Rob said, with a chuckle. "I know where he is."

My mouth dropped open. "You *know*? You *know* where he is?"

"Doing ten to twenty at the Oklahoma Men's State Penitentiary for armed robbery," Rob said. "Real swell guy, huh? And I'm just a chip off the old block. I bet you're real eager to introduce me to your parents now."

"But that's not what you're on probation for," I said, quickly. "I mean, something like armed robbery. You don't get probation for stuff like that, they lock you up. So whatever you did—"

"Whatever I did," Rob said, "was a mistake and isn't going to happen again."

But to my dismay, he let go of me, and put his hands behind his head. He wasn't chuckling anymore either.

"Rob," I said. "You don't think I care, do you? I mean, about your dad? We can't help who are relatives are." I thought about Great-aunt Rose, who'd never committed armed robbery—at least so far as I knew. Still, if being unpleasant was a crime, she'd have been locked up long ago. "I mean, if I don't care that you were arrested once, why would I care about—"

"You should care," Rob said. "Okay, Mastriani? You *should* care. And you should be going out on Saturday nights to dances, like a normal girl, not sneaking into secret militia enclaves and risking your life to stop psychopathic killers. . . ."

"Yeah?" I said, starting to get pissed. "Well, guess what? I'm not a normal girl, am I? I'm about as far from normal as you can get, and you know what? I happen to *like* who I am. So if you don't, well, you can just—"

Rob took his hands out from behind his head and took hold of my arms again. "Mastriani," he said.

"I mean it, Rob," I said, trying to shake him off. "I mean it, if you don't like me, you can just go to—"

"Mastriani," he said, again. And this time, instead of letting go of me, he dragged me down until my face was just inches from his. "That's the problem. I like you too much."

He was proving just how much he liked me when the door to his room swung open, and a startled voice went, "Oh! Excuse *me!*"

We broke apart. I swung around to see my brother Douglas standing there looking very red in the face. Beside him stood, of all people, a very abashed Tasha Thompkins.

"Oh," I said, casually. "Hey, Douglas. Hey, Tasha."

"Hey," Rob said, sounding a bit weak.

"Hey," Tasha said. She looked like she would have liked to run from the room. But my brother put a hand on her slender shoulder. My brother, Douglas, touched a girl—and she seemed to regain her composure somewhat.

"Jess," she said. "I just . . . I came to apologize. For what I said the other night. My father told me what you did—you know, about catching the people who did . . . that . . . to my brother, and I just . . ."

"It's okay, Tasha," I said. "Believe me."

"Yeah," Rob said. "It was a pleasure. Well, except for the part where I got hit with a mixing bowl."

"Mashed potatoes," I said.

"Mashed-potato bowl, I mean," Rob said.

"Really," I said to Tasha, who looked faintly alarmed by our banter. "It's okay, Tasha. I hope we can be friends."

"We can," Tasha said, her eyes bright with tears. "At least, I hope we can."

I held out my arms, and she moved into them, hugging me tightly. It was only when she got close enough for me to whisper into her ear that I said, softly, "You break my brother's heart, I'll break your face, understand?"

Tasha tensed in my arms. Then she released me and straightened. She didn't look upset, though. She looked excited and happy.

"Oh," she said, sniffling a little, but still reaching for Douglas's hand. "I won't. Don't worry."

Douglas looked alarmed, but not because Tasha had taken his hand.

"You won't what?" he asked. He darted a suspicious look at me. "Jess. What'd you say to her?"

"Nothing," I said, innocently, and sat down on Rob's bed.

And then, from behind them, a familiar voice went, "Knock knock," and my mother came barreling in, with my dad, Michael, Claire, Ruth, and Skip trailing along behind her.

"Just stopped by to see if you wanted to grab a bite over at the restaurant. . . ." My mom's voice died away as soon as she saw where I was sitting. Or rather, who I was sitting so closely beside.

"Mom," I said, with a smile, not getting up. "Dad. Glad you're here. I'd like you to meet my boyfriend, Rob."

Meg Cabot (her last name rhymes with "habit"—as in, "her books are habit-forming") is the number one *New York Times* bestselling author of more than twenty-five series and books for both adults and tweens/teens, selling more than 15 million copies worldwide.

Her Princess Diaries series, which is currently being published in more than thirty-eight countries, was made into two hit movies by Disney. Meg also wrote the bestselling Mediator and Queen of Babble series, as well as the 1-800-Where-R-You series, on which the television show *Missing* was based and which is now being reissued in two volumes as Vanished.

Meg currently writes the Allie Finkle's Rules for Girls series, as well as the Heather Wells mystery series for adult readers. *Runaway*, the final installment in her Airhead series, was published in April 2010, and *Insatiable*, a new adult paranormal, in July 2010.

Meg divides her time between Key West, Indiana, and New York City with a primary cat (one-eyed Henrietta), various backup cats, and her husband.